M000035378

THE
SPECTRUM
CONSPIRACY

*Happy Birthday
Carole
I hope you enjoy
the book.*

2/29/2013

THE
SPECTRUM
CONSPIRACY

CRAIG FARIS

THE SPECTRUM CONSPIRACY
ISBN 978-1-62268-17-7

Copyright © 2013 by Craig Faris

All rights reserved, including the right to reproduce this book or portions thereof in any form whatsoever. For more information contact Bella Rosa Books, P.O. Box 4251 CRS, Rock Hill, SC 29732. Or online at www.bellarosabooks.com

This book is a work of fiction. Names, characters, places and incidents are products of the author's imagination or are used fictitiously. Any resemblance to actual events, locales, or persons, living or dead, is entirely coincidental.

First USA printing: January 2013

Library of Congress Control Number: 2012954785

Also available as e-book. eISBN: 978-1-62268-018-4

Printed in the United States of America on acid-free paper.

Cover design by Craig Faris – www.craigfaris.com

BellaRosaBooks and logo are trademarks of Bella Rosa Books.

10   9   8   7   6   5   4   3   2   1

To my wife Deena who supported and encouraged me through years of setbacks, rejection letters and countless rewrites. You are truly the best thing that has ever happened to me.

And to my children Katie and Charlie who have always given me inspiration and support.

And to my Mother, Dot Whiteside, my stepfather, John Whiteside and my mother-in-law, Frances Hester, for believing in me.

ACKNOWLEDGMENTS

This book would not have been possible without the support and assistance from the following:

To the members of my original SCWW critique group:
Gwen Hunter, who saw promise in my first novel and encouraged me to try shorter fiction. You remain my inspiration and mentor.
Dawn Cook, you were the first of us to reach the dream and boy did you ever show the way with your Kim Harrison series and nine *New York Times* Bestsellers. Thank you for the desk and your encouragement throughout the years.
Misty Massey, for your great critiques and instructions on how to "show, don't tell."
Melissa Hinnant, for providing us with those wonderful literary images I'll never forget.
Norman Froscher, for killing off my character in every one of your stories. Thanks for sharing the use of your name.
Luis Rodriguez, Charlie Burnette, Betty Beamguard, Grace Looper, Donna Wylie, and Martha Robinson, thanks for hearing the same old stories over again and your excellent critiques.

To the current members of the SCWW critique group:
Claire Iannini, Ed Green, Roxanne Hanna, Becca Dickinsion, Barbara Hooley, Carol Taggart, Kim Boykin, Laura and Andy Lawless, Pat FitzGerald, Liz Bankhead, Pete Hildebrand, Kim Hyclak, Scott McBride, Steve Denison, Susan Bosscawen, Bill Childers and all of you who took the time to read my manuscript selections, thank you for allowing me show up at random and offer those wonderful words of encouragement.

To my biggest fan, Dianne Hutchins Hall who believed that I had a future in writing before anyone.

To my editors: Lona Gilmore, Ann Cox, Susan Parado, Rod Hunter, and the late Toni Child. Thanks for fixing my horrible spelling and grammar. I couldn't have done it without you.

To Marilyn Benner Sowyak: thank you and your husband for sharing your input and all of your kind words of support. Your wealth of talent and experience in acting and writing was inspiring.

To Brenda McClain: perhaps the most gifted author I've ever met. Thanks for remaining such a supportive friend. You are the next Harper Lee.

To PJ Woodside who took my manuscript and made it come to life in your live action book trailer. I couldn't have asked for a better director.

To Mr. Richard Curtis, Sulay Hernandez and Ted Tally, for taking the time from your busy schedule to read my work and going out of your way to offer references and recommendations.

To all of you who have permitted me to bring my characters to life by allowing the use of parts of your name. You know who you are, just read the book.

To my family who continued to love me, despite the long hours, the countless disappointments and setbacks. I love you all.

THE
SPECTRUM
CONSPIRACY

PART 1

CHAPTER 1

12:25 a.m, Alexandria, VA

Beyond the iron gates that guarded the entrance to the property, beyond the manicured lawn and hedges that lined the driveway, the senator's home loomed in the darkness. Upstairs in the master bedroom, a phone warbled two sets of triplets, the pattern indicating the encrypted line.

"The President knows," the caller said.

"What?" Senator Luther mumbled, still asleep.

The message was clearer this time. "He knows about Spectrum!"

Eyes wide open, the senator lifted himself onto one elbow. "Who is this?"

"Viper," Norman Trexler replied. "He knows."

"How much?"

"All of it. He has a full report."

The senator swung his legs off the bed, fully awake. "How did it get out?"

"How the hell should I know? Someone leaked it to his Press Secretary."

"When?"

"An hour ago. I just got out of the meeting at the White House," Trexler said.

"Did you explain the implications?"

"Of course. Why do you think I'm calling? He went ballistic. He's scheduled a press conference for tomorrow at noon."

"Good Lord!"

"We'll all be indicted," Trexler choked on the last syllable.

"That idiot. Who else knows?"

"Just the Chairman of the Joint Chiefs and the Press Secretary. He wants to go public with it himself."

"The Chairman's not a problem," the senator said. "Has he contacted the FBI?"

"Hell no. Director Gregory's office leaks like a screen door. He's afraid if it gets out before tomorrow the media will accuse him of being part of it. He's beating them to the punch."

"There must be some way to reason with him."

"Believe me, I've tried. You know how righteous he is." Trexler sighed. "It's over. Spectrum is finished and so are we."

"Not necessarily." The senator glanced at his alarm clock. "Where's the press conference being held?"

"In the White House Briefing Room. Why?"

The Senator didn't answer.

"You're not serious? It can't be done!"

"I'll discuss it with Raptor."

"You've got to be crazy. It's *in* the White House!"

"Are you certain he's told no one else?"

Trexler's voice was shaky. "I can't say for sure, but I know his wife is out of town, and he wants to make damn sure the media hears it from his lips. That's all I know."

"Go home and get some rest. Call for further instructions in the morning. With any luck we'll be one step ahead of him." The senator disconnected and punched in Raptor's speed dial number.

• • •

Across the Potomac River, the Secretary of Defense, Norman Trexler, hung up his phone and steadied his trembling hand. He had never met the man they called Counselor, and had no idea to what extent he would go to protect the project. They considered themselves patriots, but selling weapons to a terrorist state was a treasonable act, and hiding their true identities was crucial. By midday the President would expose them all and his political career would end behind iron bars.

Perhaps Counselor did have the power to stop the speech. His political future might yet be saved, and if anyone could pull it off, it was the man they called Raptor.

• • •

DuPont Circle, Washington, DC

The beer cradled between his palms was warm, the foam long gone. Special Agent Devrin Crosby never liked beer, but the smell of alcohol was still tempting. FBI agents were expected to remain sober even when off duty, but Crosby was a recovering alcoholic, a disease that had nearly cost him his job. If his boss so much as smelled it on him at work, he would be cleaning out his desk the same day. The beer was a self-imposed test, a ritual he went through every Sunday evening. If he could resist the urge to taste despite its aroma and proximity, he knew he could remain sober for another week.

The glare of the bar television reflected the mirrored image of 12:34 a.m. onto his beer mug and Crosby glanced across the room at the corner of Goodtime Charlie's lounge. There, a shiny black Baldwin grand piano stood with ivory keys and a touch much finer than the electronic piano he kept in the tiny bedroom of his apartment. The lounge had a regular pianist on weekdays, but on Sundays the bench was empty. Crosby played well but his addiction had robbed his confidence, so he preferred to wait for the other patrons to leave. This evening, he had hovered over his warm mug for an hour as a young couple stubbornly remained.

The couple seemed an odd match to Crosby. The woman was blonde, well endowed and strikingly beautiful, but the man was short, bald and in a rumpled black suit. *Must be an expensive date,* he thought.

"Go ahead, Devrin," the bartender said. "They won't care."

"I'll wait. What's my latest time on the cube?"

The bartended placed a Rubik's Cube in front of Crosby and turned a few pages in his small notebook. "One minute, forty seconds. You were off pace last week."

"Depends on the starting point." Crosby studied the layout. "You ready?"

The bartender clicked a stop watch and Crosby's fingers began spinning the faces. He only glanced at what he was doing, as if each set of fingers had memorized the pattern and acted independently of each other, turning sections without even rotating the cube.

"How do you do that?" the bartender said.

Crosby shrugged, fingers flying. "It's algorithms designed to change parts of the cube without scrambling the others. Once you learn the patterns, it's simple."

"Looks impressive."

"These cubes are easy. You wouldn't believe the really complex ones. What was my best time to date?"

The bartender flipped back a few pages. "Forty-four seconds."

"Was I sober?"

"You came in looking like you had slammed a half-bottle of scotch."

"That figures. Almost there," Crosby said with a final spin. "Time?"

The completed cube sat on the bar, each color arranged perfectly. "Fifty-eight seconds," the bartender said. "Not bad."

"It's a far cry from the world record."

"You're way ahead of everyone here." The bartender closed the notebook.

Crosby glanced up at a muted news segment on the television. A reporter was standing in a park with blooming flowers behind her, and in the distant background, the White House.

She's in Lafayette Park, he thought. Images of the park flashed through his memory. The shouted warnings, the recoil of his Glock, and tiny red spots on yellow daffodils.

Even as he refocused on his beer, a smell of cordite remained. A year had passed since the incident, and there was no one to blame but himself. Well, almost no one.

•   •   •

Senator Christian Luther had no choice but to use his regular phone to make the call. He had tried Raptor's secure line, but apparently his unit was switched off. The phone rang twice before he heard a rough voice.

"What is it?" Harold Sanders said curtly.

"It's Counselor," Luther replied. "There's a storm."

Sanders waited a beat to respond. "Serious?"

"A squall line is approaching."

"Where?"

Luther hesitated, remembering his unsecure line. "Sixteenth and Pennsylvania."

Sanders remained silent for a moment. "Give me a minute. I'll call you back."

Only seconds later the senator's encrypted line rang.

"Tell me about it." Sanders voice lacked any hint of emotion.

"The President knows about Project Spectrum," Luther said. "He has a detailed report that he's going to reveal tomorrow in the Press Briefing Room. All attempts to reason with him have failed."

"You're sure?"

"Yes. Stalker is working on the confirmation."

"What time is the briefing?"

"Noon."

Sanders paused, apparently checking his watch. "Short notice."

"What choice do we have? The report is lethal to the project. He must be stopped!"

"Which plan?"

"Proceed with Operation Sweep."

"I'll need executive authorization."

"You'll have it," Luther said. "Can it be done?"

"What's the collateral damage?"

"One witness and some documentation. Stalker will handle the documents. The witness will have to look like a coincidence."

"Won't work," Sanders said. "Better to make it a consequence. Who is the witness?"

"The Press Secretary. You have someone in mind?"

"I'll see if Mig is available."

"Approved," Luther said. "The identity package is being prepared."

"What about his wife?"

"Out of town. Stalker is accessing her cell. What else do you need?"

"Stalker will have to place the propaganda material in the sponsor's home. I'll handle the camera equipment and seeding the sponsor's clothing and locker. I need access to the storage facility and the station's news van."

"Both keys will be in the package. What time?"

"By 0200," Sanders said. "See that the primary cameraman calls in sick. Give him something that's untraceable."

"I'll try not to make it too contagious."

"Whatever. Just make damn sure he doesn't show up. And one other thing."

"What's that?" Luther asked.

"Find out what time the cleaning crew vacuums the Briefing Room."

"Why?"

"Just do it."

CHAPTER 2

CROSBY

In Goodtime Charlie's lounge the couple at the bar finally got up to leave. The bartender nodded toward the piano. "Better hurry, Devrin. I'm closing at one a.m."

Crosby sat at the piano and examined his haggard face in its mirrored finish. He imagined his mother's reflection looking over his shoulder as she had during his years of piano lessons. *What would she think?* He was forty-four, but he felt ten years older. He had gained fifteen pounds since the incident in Lafayette Park, but at least his sandy blond hair hadn't grayed.

His fingers moved over the keys and the melancholy strains of a piece called, "As for Us" filled the room. He had no sheet music, just a knack for picking out tunes from memory. Above the soft melody he heard the door chime and, glancing up, saw a man rush in. The man stopped at the bar, his hair soaking wet and his suit dripping on the floor. He glanced at Crosby, ashen faced, hands trembling, and clutching a manila envelope close to his side. He said something to the bartender who poured him a shot and pointed down the street. The man downed the drink, slid money across the bar and dashed back into the storm, the envelope still at his side.

Twenty minutes later, Crosby stepped out under the awning, and the bartender switched off the neon lights behind him.

"Who was that?" Crosby asked.

"I think it was Tim Cook, the White House Press Secretary," the bartender said. "He wanted directions to the nearest mailbox."

"I thought he looked familiar."

"He left you a tip." The bartender handed him a twenty dollar bill.

Crosby smiled. "Whoa. I must have sounded okay."

"That's what I've been saying, Devrin," he said, locking the door. "See you next week."

"Thanks, Charlie," Crosby replied. It was raining hard, so he hustled down the dark familiar path toward his tiny apartment two blocks away.

* * *

Charlotte, NC

Kathryn Froscher leaned closer to the wheel trying to see through the streaks left by her windshield wipers. She was on I-77 just north of the Panthers Stadium, still in the dress she had worn to her father's wake earlier that evening. He had been terminally ill for over a year, but the news of his death had brought out far more mourners than even she anticipated. From seven until ten p.m. she had stood in the receiving line shaking hands with people she had never met and never expected to see again. Afterward, a couple of girlfriends had taken her out for a late dinner and a drink.

The dress was new, expensive and looked great with her pale skin, brown hair and green eyes. At twenty-nine she still had a great body and could have taken home any of the guys who kept eyeing her long legs under the table. *Wasn't getting laid while your father was in an open casket a sin? Surely he would know.*

A flash of lightning followed by the crack of thunder refocused her attention on the road and seemed to confirm her thoughts. *Right decision.* Her older brother, Chuck, was flying in from Oak Ridge early in the morning. There simply wasn't any time to deal with a strange guy in her bed, no matter how cute he might be.

The steering wheel began to vibrate, and she felt the rear of the car pull to one side, the unmistakable signs of tire trouble.

Oh great. The interstate was busy, the rain blinding with no emergency shoulder in sight. She spotted a bridge overpass and guided her Acura TSX to an exit ramp under the bridge hoping it might afford her some shelter from the rain.

It didn't. It was a railway bridge that let as much rain through it as around it. To make matters worse, the ramp led to another interstate and trucks were flying past her at sixty miles per hour.

She eased off the roadway as far as the guardrail would permit and turned on her emergency flashers. She found her triple-A card in her purse, but when she opened her cell phone, it beeped for a second and went dead.

"Damn it." She rifled through the glove box, failing to find the battery charger and realized that her only option was to get out and survey the damage. She glanced down at the new dress. "Just my luck."

When she cracked the door, a huge truck flew past, rocking the entire car and coating the windows in a dirty mist.

Katie slammed it shut and threw the cell phone into her purse. *Wrong decision,* she thought realizing how close she had come to having a man who could change the tire in the seat beside her. She thought about the "driving test" she would sometimes give a male passenger if he was especially cute. The Acura had a five-speed manual transmission and she would place his left hand on the stick shift and say, "Let's see if you can follow directions." She would then put her right hand down his pants, grab his joystick, and change gears by remote control.

Truck lights appeared in her rearview mirror and pulled to a stop behind her. Fear gripped her as she watched a man open his door. Ignoring the rain and oncoming traffic, he walked toward her car. He might be an off-duty policeman, or a psychopath.

He knelt down beside her flat tire for a second before approaching. She looked around the car searching for something she could use as a weapon and grabbed the heaviest thing in her purse; the useless cell phone.

The man tapped the glass, his mocha-colored face at her window. Rain had already soaked his dark curly hair, and water was dripping from his nose. She cracked her window and said, "Thanks for stopping, but I'm okay." She brandished the cell phone. "My husband should be here any second."

"You have a blowout, ma'am," the stranger said. "Do you have a spare?"

"Uh, I suppose."

"Pop the trunk and I'll check."

She hesitated, wondering if he could get into her car through the trunk. The rear seat could be folded down, but it locked from the inside.

He smiled. "It's okay, ma'am. You can trust me."

Wasn't that the psychopath's motto? He seemed nice enough and good looking, but so was Ted Bundy. If there wasn't a spare, she wouldn't have to ruin her new dress to find out. She pulled the trunk release.

Within a minute, she felt the car being jacked up and heard the squeal of loosening lug bolts. She lowered the window enough to yell, "Sir, you don't have to do that." Another truck rocked the car, showering her face with specks of mud and the smell of diesel fuel. She raised the window. *If he's crazy enough to change the damn tire, let him.*

The rain slowed and she adjusted the side mirror so she could see what he was doing. To her astonishment, the man was on all fours, his legs in the lane of traffic. Trucks were passing within inches of them, yet he seemed unconcerned. *A total stranger risking his life?*

The car was lowered and the flat placed in the trunk. Katie looked through her purse, but found only a ten-dollar bill, hardly sufficient to pay the man for his kindness. The trunk slammed shut and the stranger wiped his hands on his now filthy jeans.

"That should do it," he shouted and gave her a goodbye salute.

Lowering her window again and waving the money, she yelled, "Wait a minute."

The stranger came back to her door. He was handsome, a thirty-something version of Denzel Washington. She felt ashamed she had not lowered the window further the first time.

"Yes, ma'am?"

"How much do I owe you?"

"Nothing."

"But your jeans are soaked. At least let me pay to have them laundered."

He laughed. "I have a washer and dryer."

"You risked your life. Those trucks could have taken your legs off."

She noted that he wasn't wearing a wedding band when he turned to watch a car speed past where his legs had been.

"It's a matter of faith, ma'am," he said with a smile.

"How can I thank you?"

"You just did. Have a nice day."

Within seconds he was back in his truck and had pulled into traffic. He had been a shining example of human decency and had said more with that single act of kindness than a thousand sermons.

I didn't even get his name, she thought as she started the car.

• • •

Huge letters on each side of the van proclaimed NBC-6 to its viewers. Harold Sanders unlocked the back door and closed himself inside. With a small key he opened a storage locker containing two video cameras, one older and the other almost new. He removed the older one, opened his black bag and took out a duplicate camera, pausing to check that they were identical. He zipped the station's older camera into his bag, and placed the duplicate in the locker. To ensure that the newer camera wouldn't be chosen, he removed it from the locker, held it about three feet off the floor, and let the $55,000 camera drop. The impact did little visible damage, cracking a UV filter and denting the lens cowling. He returned the broken camera to the shelf, making certain it was turned so the damaged lens would be visible the next time the locker was opened. He checked his watch as he locked the van door. It was 2:14 a.m.

•   •   •

Gerald McMullen had stripped out of his wet clothes and taken a shower before climbing in bed. He was tired and his flight back to Washington left at six a.m. He thought about the girl's left hand. No wedding ring. *My husband should be here any second,* he recalled her saying. That was smart, given her situation. People were naturally suspicious of strangers. But when she offered him money, her smile had given him an overwhelming feeling that she wasn't married. It was only a chance encounter, but Gerald had learned to trust his feelings.

Perhaps it was hopeful thinking, or the way the light reflected off the letters as he slammed her trunk, but when he closed his eyes, a clear image of her personalized license plate remained.

•   •   •

Wesley Heights, Washington, DC

The canvas-draped Corvette was parked in front of apartment 301 in building 4174. The man, dressed in black, emerged from his truck holding a briefcase. He lifted a corner of the canvas and focused a penlight on the candy red fiberglass quarter panel. *Drives a red Corvette,* he recalled from the file. *D.C. License plate, REBA, the subject's favorite singer.* He checked the personalized license plate and spotted the NBC-6 parking sticker. He returned the penlight to his pocket and gazed at the faint light coming from a second floor window. *Nightlight in the bathroom,* the man thought.

After moving quickly to the top of the exterior staircase, he checked to make sure no one was around then unscrewed the light bulb by the door. He opened the lid of the wall-mounted mailbox and pointed the penlight at the name, Chad Stillwell. *Subject is single. One cat, no dogs,* he recalled, picturing the apartment layout he had studied. *Single bedroom, second floor apartment. Door opens into a small den. Kitchen on the left. Bedroom and bath facing the parking lot.* No direct access was available to windows from the exterior staircase. The door's threshold would have to do.

The man squatted, opened the briefcase, removed a gasmask and placed it over his head. He inserted a length of clear plastic hose connected to a metal wand into the crack under the door and attached the other end to a small yellow cylinder. He opened the valve releasing the viral agent through the tube and waited. A clear, odorless gas containing a cocktail of a genetically altered zoonotic influenza virus, THC and carbon monoxide flowed through the tube. It would give the subject a severe headache followed by flu-like symptoms. Since the bedroom was fifteen feet from the front door he had to use the entire canister to insure the desired results. The whole process took less than a minute.

• • •

By 3:45 a.m., Raptor's van was outside the gates of a storage facility located less than three miles from the sponsor's apartment. With a gloved finger, he punched the entry code on a keypad and the gate opened. The rows of cinderblock storage buildings, lit by the orange glow of sulfur-vapor street lamps, revealed the pale outlines of numbers painted on the roll-up doors. Storage locker K-11 was identical in size to the rest. Harold Sanders got out of the van, carrying a cardboard box that contained the now disassembled parts of the station's video camera. The sponsor's palm print, lifted from a microphone in the van, had been placed conspicuously on one of the camera parts.

He inserted his key into the Master lock, removed it, and lifted the door. Inside the space were stacks of cardboard boxes, flags, tent poles and what appeared to be folded white sheets. He ripped open one of the boxes, removed a handful of brochures, and pointed his penlight at the cover.

A Message of Hope and Deliverance for White Christian America, he read. *Compliments of The Imperial Knights of The Ku Klux Klan.*

Sanders put a few of the brochures into his coat pocket. He placed the camera parts on a workbench at the center of the room and relocked the door.

• • •

The White House, 5:50 a.m.

As head of the White House Secret Service detail, Harold Sanders walked the halls with total confidence. He was tall and lean with salt and pepper hair, and a ruddy face, the result of severe teenage acne. He entered the press corps offices located near the rear of the Briefing Room and nodded to the fellow agent on duty. In his hands were two cups of coffee, and under one arm, a folded newspaper. He offered the paper and a cup to the duty agent.

"Thanks," the agent said. "You're here early."

"Got a call," Sanders said. He stood opposite the duty agent and looked down the hall into the darkened and near empty Briefing Room. "Something's up."

"Haven't heard anything," the duty agent said, taking a sip. "Good coffee."

"Yeah." Sanders watched the cleaning crew running a carpet shampooer near the podium at the far end of the Briefing Room. The rest of the room was dark. "They have Danish down in the Navy Mess. Want some?"

"I'm too fat already," the agent said. He put down the coffee and opened the newspaper.

"Nothing's on the morning schedule," Sanders added, noting that the duty agent was already involved in the headlines. "Must be the President."

"Maybe he's going to address this Argentine mess," the agent said. "Ever since the coup, their self-appointed president has been making noise about leading them into the nuclear age."

"He's a mile wide and an inch thick," Sanders said. "All surface."

"I don't know. They say his father was killed in the Falklands war and he keeps talking about taking back what's theirs. I guess we'll find out soon enough," the agent replied, never looking up.

"I'm going to ask around, maybe get some Danish," Sanders said, as he stepped back into the hall that led into the Briefing Room. "Be back in a minute."

"Okay."

Sanders watched the agent from the hallway for a moment. He was still reading, oblivious to anything else. Sanders found the cord of the carpet shampooer plugged into a wall socket beside the door. It ran down the right aisle toward the front of the Briefing Room between banks of video equipment mounted on various stands. He spotted the NBC-6 video camera attached to a tripod near the aisle. It took only a second to make a loop in the cord and hook it high on one leg of the tripod.

•   •   •

7:00 a.m.

"NBC-6," the receptionist said into her headset. "How may I direct your call?"

"Gina." The voice sounded weak. "It's Chad."

"Chad? You don't sound good."

"I've come down with something," he replied coughing. "Anything on the schedule?"

"The White House called. The cleaning crew knocked over our camera. The President is scheduled to speak at noon and we need a replacement."

"Oh, great!" Chad said. "There's no way I can make it, Gina. I'm sorry. I've thrown up twice already and have a splitting headache. To top it off, my cat died."

"Miss Reba's dead?"

"Yeah. She was fifteen. Died in her sleep."

"Oh, Chad, I'm sorry."

"Call Billy for me, will you?"

"Sure," Gina said. "Can he handle setting up a replacement camera?"

"He knows the drill. There's a spare camera in the van. He'll have to fill in for me, okay?"

"I'll take care of it," she said. "You should go back to bed."

"I am. Thanks, Gina."

"You take care, Chad."

CHAPTER 3

THE FOURTH ANGEL

It was a clear Monday morning, with a slight breeze to carry the scent of the freshly mowed grass into the portico of the White House. As the April sun climbed into the sky, the moist heat rose, hinting that soon the muggy days of summer would follow. President William Joseph Barnett had begun his day like every day, by reading a passage from his Bible. He had chosen an unusual verse; Revelation 16:8. The words seemed so appropriate that he added them to the first paragraph of the speech he would deliver at his noon press conference.

President Barnett was an honest pious man and vowed that he would once again make the office of President beyond reproach. He was a born-again Christian, a former minister, and an African-American—the first direct descendent of slaves to achieve the office of President. Barnett was fifty-six, a father of three whose youngest daughter, Alma, lived with them in the White House and would soon begin her freshman year at the College of William and Mary. The First Lady, Phyllis, had taken Alma to Williamsburg for orientation, and they were scheduled to return the following evening. He had called Phyllis earlier but her cell phone signal kept fading out. At least he knew they had slept well and that Alma loved the campus.

Barnett had been up early, polishing his speech. Unlike most modern presidents, he preferred to write his own and he packed them with as many Southern clichés and jokes as he pleased. His admirers said it made him sound "down home," and his return to ordinary language caused a soar in his approval ratings after every speech. His critics rolled their eyes and sneered behind his back, but even they admitted that Barnett knew how to reach people.

He looked over the pages, committing them to memory. He moved the announcement terminating Norman Trexler to the third paragraph. He always considered his Secretary of Defense a friend, but the web of deceit Trexler had woven was inexcusable. Trexler had gone to great lengths to cover up the covert military operation called The Spectrum Project. Even when confronted with the physical proof of its existence, Trexler continued to lie. That was the one thing that Barnett never tolerated. Trexler acted as though the operation was above the law and his actions were exceeded only by his arrogance. Trexler would have to go.

The President paused at a mirror outside the Oval Office to straighten his favorite blue tie, a birthday gift from his daughter. His shirt, white with blue pinstripes, contrasted well with his navy suit and dark skin and would look great at his next portrait sitting.

•   •   •

Special Agent Devrin Crosby entered Woodbutcher's Deli a little before his lunch appointment. He wore the trademark Hoover Blues business suit of the FBI, but his tie was loosened, the top button of his shirt undone. Crosby hated ties and couldn't understand how starting the day with a noose around one's neck had ever come into fashion.

The hostess was young and in deep conversation with a waitress. She ignored Crosby.

He cleared his throat to get her attention.

She reluctantly excused herself. "How many?" she said with all the enthusiasm of a mortician.

"Two," Crosby said, nodding towards a darkened section. "We'll take that booth in the back corner."

"Sorry. That section is closed."

"Then please tell Louie that Special Agent Devrin Crosby of the FBI would prefer to have his usual table in the corner," he said in a firm tone. In any other city the title alone would be enough to warrant a degree of respect, but not in Washington. This city was crawling with "agents" of this or that, and if the title meant anything to the hostess, she wasn't showing it.

"Just a minute!" she said through clenched teeth and disappeared.

Crosby glanced around and saw a table of young women look at him and whispering something among themselves with raised eyebrows. To his left he caught a glimpse of his profile in a mirror and the slight pouch above his belt. Instinctively, he sucked it in and heard muted chuckles coming from the table.

Within moments, the owner emerged from the kitchen, took the menus from the hostess with a dismissive nod. "Agent Crosby!" he said with a Greek accent. "Your usual booth?"

Crosby nodded.

"You have a guest joining you?"

"Just one." Crosby gave the hostess a smirk as they walked into the closed section.

She marched back to her station mouthing, "Whatever!"

"College kids," Louie said, putting down the menus. "They think they own the place. I'll send a waitress when your guest arrives."

"Thanks, Louie. He has wavy black hair and looks like a model."

"My pleasure."

While Crosby waited, he looked over the laminated menu. It was clean and bore none of the tiny brown spots roaches leave when they walk across them at night. Louie ran a tidy ship. With that assurance, Crosby considered the selections against their respective calories. His stocky build had added a few pounds since he was reassigned to the Violent Criminal Apprehension Program and started spending his days in front of a computer. Surely his friend, Gerald McMullen, had put on weight as well.

They had hardly spoken at all since the incident that had landed Crosby his desk job. During the first Gulf War, Crosby's Humvee loaded with wounded prisoners had gotten lost in the darkness and wandered into a mine field. The explosion killed everyone aboard except Crosby, whose lacerations had saved his life since the Iraqi's assumed he was dead. Gerald's helicopter was one of three sent out to locate them. When met with hostile fire, the other helicopters held back, but not Gerald. His courage was the only reason Crosby was still alive.

"Devrin?" a voice said.

Crosby saw Gerald standing a few feet away. "Hi Gerry," he said getting out of the booth. The two men gave each other an awkward hug.

"You've put on a few pounds," Gerald said patting Crosby's belly.

Crosby noted that Gerald's abdomen was flat as a board. If anything, he had lost weight. Crosby had spent most of the previous afternoon at the gym at Quantico in a vain attempt to sweat off thirty pounds in three hours. He sucked in his stomach as he slid back into the booth. "It's no bigger than *normal* people in their mid forties."

"You have a girlfriend cooking for you?" Gerald said as he sat.

"I work for the Bureau, remember? The only women in my life pack a Glock and can kill you with their bare hands."

"Some women think guns are sexy."

"Yeah, but their idea of a hot date is a five-mile run to a firing range," Crosby said. "So, how's your love life?"

"Who wants a beach bum like me?"

Crosby surveyed the room, expecting a sea of waving arms from every woman in the place. "I figured you moved to the Caribbean and were feasting on turtle soup."

"Someday, buddy, I'm going to find me an island with an all-female staff and an endless supply of soup and margaritas." He took a sip of water. "Speaking of which, how long has it been?"

"I've managed to stay on the wagon for almost two months," Crosby said.

"That's good to hear."

"Are you still at the *Post*?"

"That's one of the reasons I called. I flew down to Charlotte yesterday for a job interview. The *Observer* offered me an editorial position."

"The *Observer*?" Crosby said. "I thought you loved Washington."

"I don't have a choice. Mom's cancer returned."

"Oh . . . sorry, Gerald."

"Who knows, it could be six months or six years. Ned's moved in with Mom, but with his aerial business he can't be with her all the time."

Gerald's mother was Portuguese, his late father Jamaican, and his dark wavy hair and chestnut skin was the same as theirs. Crosby had met Gerald's mother and his brother, Ned, when Gerald won the Scripps Howard Journalism Award for his story on Gulf War helicopter pilots.

"I need to spend as much time with her as I can before the end." Gerald said, a hint of sadness in his voice.

Crosby changed the subject. "Does Ned still do aerial photography?"

"No, just traffic reports. It's steady work, and he also flies air-rescue choppers when needed." Gerald leaned closer. "The thing is, as soon as all of this is over, I'm planning on coming back to the *Post*. That's where you come in, buddy."

"Me? How?"

"Are you still in that tiny apartment near DuPont Circle?"

"Of course," Crosby said. "What else could I afford?"

"How would you like to move into my condo while I'm gone?"

"Right. On my salary?"

"Here's the deal. If Mom goes into remission, I could be in

Charlotte for years. If I rent my place, who knows what will happen to it, plus I would prefer to have it available when I come back to town on assignments. It's three bedrooms and most of my furniture can go into storage. There's plenty of room for your stuff and you can use the spare bedroom for your piano."

"Sounds interesting," Crosby said, "but I can't afford it."

"If you cover the utilities, I'll lease it to you for a dollar a month."

"A dollar! What about your mortgage payment?"

"I'll be living with Mom."

"Yeah, but she's sick. You'll still have this mortgage on top of her medical bills?"

"Insurance and Medicare. She planned well. You would be doing me a big favor, Devrin. What do you say?"

"Can I pay a year in advance?" Crosby said.

Gerald laughed. "Sure. Deal?"

"Deal!" Crosby said with a handshake.

"By the way, my boss thinks I'm having lunch with my inside source at the FBI," Gerald added, "so lunch is on me."

Devrin laughed. "I've never leaked any secrets."

"They don't know that."

The waitress arrived. "What'ya havin'?"

"I'll take a Cobb Salad and bottled water," Gerald said never bothering to look at the menu.

A salad and water? Devrin thought. "What tha hell! Give me a Philly with extra cheese."

Gerald smiled. "No wonder."

•   •   •

U.S. Secret Service agent Harold Sanders examined the professional video camera carefully before placing it in front of the electronic scanner, which would X-ray it and check the lens for anything unusual. This was an old camera, not unlike thousands he had seen come through the White House security check before. A large label with the letters "NBC-6" was pasted on its side with the television station's call letters, WBC-TV. The station was a frequent visitor to the Briefing Room, but the cameraman was not their usual operator.

"Name?" Sanders asked.

"Billy Ray Anderson." He held out his press pass. Sanders examined it for authenticity.

"You have a license or other ID?"

Billy Ray handed the agent his wallet. Another Secret Service agent ran a portable metal detector over Anderson's body as Sanders typed the name into a computer. Billy Ray's name popped up on his screen. His clearance was just over three years old, but his job function listed him as a soundman.

"Remove your shoes and belt and place them on the scanner."

Billy Ray complied.

"How long have you been assigned to the press corps?"

"Three years, two months."

"You're listed here as the soundman. Where is your regular cameraman?"

"He called in sick. I'm his backup."

"I'll need his phone number," Sanders said. "Have you ever operated a camera in the Press Briefing Room before?"

"A while back, but I usually handle the sound."

"You're familiar with the protocol?"

"Yes, sir. I'm the backup."

The station's NBC correspondent, herself being scanned with the metal detector spoke up. "Sir, Billy's been with the station for twelve years."

Agent Sanders knew the correspondent's face, and her comment added the credibility he needed. "Sign here," he instructed and turned his attention to the equipment. "Why the replacement camera?"

"Don't know," Billy Ray said. "I was told to pick up another camera before coming in."

The correspondent explained. "Your cleaning crew got a power cord entangled in our tripod last night. The camera was knocked over and damaged. Your office called the station manager this morning."

Sanders already knew this, but he needed the correspondent to explain it in front of the other agents for the record.

"Write that out on this form and sign it," Sanders said, handing her a clipboard. He looked at Billy Ray. "Turn on your camera, please."

Billy Ray picked up the camera, attached a portable battery from the camera bag and switched it on. The blue-gray light glowed from the viewfinder, and he handed it to Sanders.

Sanders put his eye to the viewfinder and ran his hand in front of the lens. He noted the auto focus and the remote zoom control. Both were common options on professional cameras of this type. He tested various switches, and they all functioned as expected.

"You may proceed," Sanders said, handing the camera, belt and shoes back to Billy Ray. He slipped a camera remote into Billy's jacket pocket while he put on the belt. The camera seemed flawless and short of taking it apart, he had given it an extensive examination. Spectrum's technicians had done an excellent job.

• • •

Norman Trexler returned from his morning jog and waited to catch his breath before calling Counselor. He had put off calling but time was running short. He punched a four-digit speed dial number into his secure phone and waited through two rings.

Senator Christian Luther's voice came on the line. "Yes."

"Counselor, this is Viper. Are we scrambled?"

"Yes."

"Have you heard from Raptor?"

"We are go. You are to proceed with operation SWEEP."

"*Holy Mother.*" Trexler mumbled. Even though he knew it was coming, the confirmation sent shock waves through him. His father had been a Tennessee congressman who had lost his seat in a bribery scandal and was now serving a seven-year sentence in federal prison. He remembered his father's advice: "Your reputation's all you got," but his reputation had landed him a view of a razor-wire fence from a six by nine cell.

Today could bring Trexler a similar fate. He struggled to regain his composure. "What are my instructions?"

"The documentation has been deleted from the subject's computer and replaced with an appropriate but harmless report," Luther said. "A backup copy of the speech has been removed from the private residence safe. The subject has the final copy on his person. Your objective is to secure that copy. A replacement is already inside the podium and will be discovered afterwards. Your window of opportunity will be brief. Use it and be careful in positioning yourself. This video will be studied frame by frame."

Trexler felt sick as he hung up the phone. One screw-up and he could spend the rest of his life in a federal penitentiary. He thought about his father, his wife and their daughter. How would they ever understand? There was still time to act. He could save the President and perhaps even himself. With a little luck he might even avoid prosecution, but he knew it wasn't an option. Counselor had given him his assignment and there was no turning back now. Raptor would make damn sure of that.

• • •

Crosby took another bite of his sandwich and listened to Gerald expound about his upcoming move to Charlotte. They had both attended the University of North Carolina, but never met while there. Gerald played varsity basketball, and his one claim to fame was that he had once blocked Michael Jordan's shot in a scrimmage game.

"My boss wants to know what's up at the Bureau?" Gerald said smiling.

"Not my favorite subject," Crosby said. "Let's talk about something else."

"What's wrong, Devrin?"

Crosby shrugged. "I'm thinking about leaving."

"Leaving? The last time we talked, you said it was the greatest job in the world."

"I was reassigned. Now I sit at a computer all day profiling suspects."

"When did this happen?"

"A year ago," Crosby said, "and I fell off the wagon soon after." He again thought of the red spots on yellow daffodils.

"So that's why you stopped calling," Gerald said. "What happened?"

"I'm not supposed to talk about it."

"Come on, Devrin. I'm your best friend."

"The usual reasons. I screwed up." He pictured the slamming doors of the surveillance van; the suspect with the briefcase ignoring the shouts to stop; the White House looming two blocks away.

"That's nothing new. Anyone who falls asleep at the wheel of his Humvee during the middle of a battle should be accustomed to screwing up."

"I wish it was that simple." Crosby waited a long moment. "I blew an innocent man's face off."

Gerald's smile vanished. "*Good Lord.* Were you sober?"

"Yeah, but I had to prove it."

"That must have been rough."

"It still is," Crosby explained. "We mistook his identity and I shot the wrong guy."

"That's an accident."

Crosby shook his head. "It doesn't matter. I gave the order. After the FBI screw-up at Ruby Ridge, someone *always* takes the blame. I happened to be the most convenient."

"Can you appeal?"

Crosby resumed eating, a clear sign that his part of the conversation was finished.

•　　•　　•

Inside the super-secure domain of the Briefing Room, Agent Harold Sanders checked his mic and earphone. As chief of the White House Secret Service detail, it was his responsibility to make sure everything was ready.

"Okay, people," Sanders said, his voice almost as rough as his face. "Five minutes. Let's call them in."

"Penn Avenue entrance, clear," the agent reported. A series of responses followed as each agent reported the status of their area and ended with, "Tunnel, clear."

Sanders notified the team leader of the President's security detail. "Scout One, Briefing Room is secure. Send in the clowns."

Through his left earphone, he could monitor the President's movements.

"This is Scout Three; POTUS is in the elevator. I repeat, POTUS is in the elevator and moving. Stand by, Scout Two."

"This is Scout Two. Back hallway is clear. POTUS is now leaving the elevator. Briefing Room, he's yours in sixty seconds."

"Roger Scout Two," Sanders said. "ETA in one minute."

Everything was ready. Sanders moved his hand to his waist and unplugged one of his microphones. He then switched on a second wireless set, encrypted and programmed to an ultra-high frequency. He checked his new equipment. "Scout One, do you read? Over."

There was no response.

"Scout team? Scout team, do you read, over?" He waited ten seconds for a response. There was none. If anyone was scanning the frequencies, the only thing they might hear would be static.

"Raptor." Counselor's voice was calm through Sanders' right earphone. "Signal is scrambled. You are authorized to proceed."

•　　•　　•

The napkins lay in their plates, their drinking glasses empty. Their waitress had either forgotten them or was siding with the hostess.

"So what was that other thing you wanted to ask me earlier?"

Crosby asked.

"It's a personal favor." Gerald slid a scrap a paper across the table. "What's KT-GIRL mean?"

"It's a North Carolina license plate number. I was in a driving rainstorm in Charlotte last night and helped change this girl's flat tire. She was *something*! Only problem is I don't know her name or where she lives. All I've got is her license plate number."

"I see." Crosby smiled. "Still chasing skirts."

"I tried the DMV's website and hit a wall. I thought you might be able to suggest an agency I could contact."

"This is probably illegal." Crosby leaned forward. "But I might be able to get a name."

"I don't want to get you fired, Devrin. It's not that big a deal. For all I know she could be married."

"What the hell. I'm leaving the Bureau anyway. I'll see what I can do."

• • •

Harold Sanders spoke softly to minimize the movement of his lips. "Roger, Counselor. Switching to visual."

Sanders reached into his breast pocket and put on a pair of aviator-type sunglasses. The sunglasses were standard Secret Service gear, and since a potential assailant could not see their eyes, the agents wore them inside as well as out. To the other agents, the putting on of the sunglasses had always been their final signal to Scout One that the team was in place.

But Sanders' glasses were different, and as soon as he put them on, his visual point of view was transferred to the center of the room. A virtual image filled his lenses, shot from a news video camera twenty feet away and tapped into the signal from the video control bank located in the back. The image showed the empty podium with the White House logo in blue and white mounted on the wall behind it. Sanders took an ink pen from his pocket and casually twisted the head of it to focus the camera's lens on the logo. With the pen, he could also make the lens zoom in tighter, but it had no control over panning from side to side. A remote pan control might arouse the suspicions of his fellow agents as well as the cameraman. The job had to look like the work of one man. Additional controls were an unnecessary risk. With only a click of the pen's head, the shutter would release at exactly the right moment.

• • •

Billy Ray's hands were sweating. This was his first time as cameraman on a live presidential shoot, and he was sure that he had forgotten something vital that might ruin the broadcast. If so, it would forever kill his chances for a repeat assignment. He knew how to do this, having watched the regular cameraman, Chad, for three years. He had been a soundman for twelve years, and this was his big chance to move up.

There was something odd about this camera, though. He was sure that he had switched off the autofocus, but somehow it kept refocusing as though it had a mind of its own. This was an older model, and it was probably a faulty switch. Chad must have dropped the newer camera he found in the van, so he was forced to use this one. It was heavy as hell, and he was glad it was mounted on a tripod for the duration.

"Billy, you ready?" his NBC correspondent said.

"Yes," he replied.

"Five seconds," the director called from the control room.

Billy put his eye to the viewfinder and pressed the record switch.

• • •

At the same moment a symbol in Sanders' sunglasses notified him that the camera was recording.

"Standby Counselor," Raptor said. "We are armed and ready."

• • •

Billy Ray watched as Tim Cook, the President's Press Secretary, entered the room followed by several members of the Cabinet. The chairman of the Joint Chiefs and the Secretary of Defense took their place to the right of the podium.

"Thank you for coming," the Press Secretary said into the microphones. "I'm sure you are curious about the nature of this meeting, so without delay— The President of the United States."

The attendees erupted with applause as President William Barnett entered the room. Beside him was a surprise visitor, the Reverend Jebadiah Johnson. The President shook hands with several of the reporters, took his place at the lectern, and waited for the applause to fade.

Billy Ray zoomed in for a tight close-up, but as soon as he tried for a wider shot, the lens refused to budge.

"This sorry piece of junk!" he growled into his headset as he tried to free the lens by hand.

"What's wrong?" the NBC correspondent asked.

"The damn lens is stuck!"

•   •   •

"Raptor, you are clear to proceed," Luther's voice said.

"Affirmative," Raptor replied, "but the Sponsor is jerking the target all over the place."

"Don't take any chances," Luther said. "Make sure it's clean."

•   •   •

Billy Ray slapped the lens with his fist and it started working perfectly, just as the President began to speak. He zoomed out for the introduction.

"My fellow Americans," President Barnett began. "I have asked you here today to tell you of a matter of utmost urgency. I have spent many hours in fervent prayer as I contemplated how to proceed. I've asked a friend, whose entire life has been devoted to social change through non-violence, to join with me this morning. I'm proud to introduce the Reverend Jeb Johnson."

Reverend Johnson took the opportunity to shake the President's hand for the photographers and remained standing beside him for several seconds.

•   •   •

"Any time Raptor," Luther said.

Sanders tried to control his frustrations. "I almost had him, but the Sponsor is now focused between Barnett and Jeb."

•   •   •

Where is his speech? Secretary of Defense Norman Trexler felt a wave of panic flow over him. Barnett would often memorize his speeches, but if this one were to fall into the hands of the press, all of this would be for nothing. Raptor had told him to put on the sunglasses only if he had the speech in sight. *It must be in his jacket,* he thought and put them on anyway.

• • •

"As many of you know," the President continued, "I'm a firm believer in reading the Holy Scriptures. The Bible says that the truth shall set us free. This morning, while reading my daily passage, I came across a verse which I have deemed most appropriate for this occasion."

The President reached into his coat for his glasses. Reverend Johnson handed the President his Bible.

"I'm reading from Revelation 16:8."

• • •

The camera was back on the President, but the scene was so wide that the center of the target was on the President's neck. Instantly Raptor had an idea.

"Do it now," Luther said into Raptor's earphone. "Before he gives the whole damn thing away!"

"Just a second," Sanders growled.

• • •

Billy Ray's camera zoomed in so tight that all he could see was the President's necktie.

"Not this shit again!" The curse was just loud enough for the surrounding reporters to take notice. He tried to zoom out, but the lens wouldn't budge. His only choice was to tilt the camera up to the President's face and hope for the best.

• • •

The President read the passage with great reverence. "And the fourth angel poured out his vial upon the sun; and power was given unto him to scorch men with fire."

At that moment, Sanders placed his thumb on the head of the pen and squeezed.

• • •

Billy Ray's camera lurched and a ringing sound pierced his ears. He raised his head looking for the source, then he spotted something red sprayed across the White House logo. He put his eye to the viewfinder and repositioned the camera back to the lectern where the President's head had been. The lens was still zoomed in tight.

Blood and pieces of flesh and bone covered the formerly pristine logo behind the lectern. He tilted the camera down, the lens working perfectly as he zoomed out. A mass of humanity now surrounded the President. Secret Service agents were spread-eagled over him. Other agents brandished their automatic weapons, searching for a target.

The Reverend Johnson was once again kneeling over his martyred prince of peace, just as he had with Martin Luther King, Jr. on a motel balcony in 1968.

• • •

Harold Sanders already had his weapon drawn and pointing toward the crowd of reporters. The sunglasses and pen were safely tucked away in his pocket. The smell of gunpowder hung heavy in the room. Reporters cowered in small groups on the floor. Few of the cameramen were brave enough to still man their equipment.

"Nobody move!" Sanders ordered. "All stations, POTUS is down! I repeat, POTUS is down! Secure all sectors. No one leaves the building!"

• • •

Billy Ray kept thinking of Dallas in 1963. He had to keep his camera rolling. He thought of the Zapruder film, the only piece of evidence, which showed Kennedy's fatal head shot. His camera had been focused on the President's head moments before. It must have recorded the best possible image of the moment of impact. The tape could be worth millions and, if so, his name would soon become immortal.

Men were covering the President's body, but the images were powerful. The anguished look painted on Reverend Johnson's face; the bloody logo and the constant screaming. The Secretary of Defense, covered with blood, was holding the President's Bible over him and apparently gathering pages torn from it. The Secret Service

agents, with their automatic weapons drawn, were yelling something
and pointing their guns towards—

Billy Ray raised his head from the viewfinder . . . *They were aimed at
him!*

•   •   •

One camera swiveled towards Sanders and he brought his weapon to
bear on its operator.

"I said nobody move!" Sanders repeated.

Everyone seemed to drop closer to the floor, but the camera kept
moving, turning its lens toward the agents, its cameraman ignoring
the command in an apparent attempt to film the total mayhem. Other
agents instinctively followed that movement.

Sanders spotted the evidence he needed; the frayed, burned end of
the microphone windsock. "Gun!" he yelled. "His camera is the
gun!"

•   •   •

Devrin and Gerald stepped out of the booth and shook hands. As
they walked towards the checkout counter Gerald gave him the note
with the license plate number and a key to the condo so he could
begin moving in. Crosby heard a gasp and glanced over at the table
where the girls were whispering earlier. Most of them were visibly
upset, hands over their mouths and makeup running down their
faces. He followed their gaze to the silent television on the far wall.
Displayed was a view of the White House Briefing Room with Secret
Service agents covering someone on the floor. Other agents had their
weapons drawn and were pointing at the camera.

Gerald turned and said, "What's wrong?"

Crosby's cell phone rang. He removed it from his pocket and
noted the incoming number. It was the emergency call back number
issued from the J. Edgar Hoover Building.

He looked back at the screen, saw the red smear on the logo and
knew.

"What is it, Devrin?" Gerald asked again.

"My God, the President has been shot."

CHAPTER 4

BILLY RAY

Tuesday

Secretary of Defense Norman Trexler was an absolute wreck. Even after consuming nearly a case of beer, he had not slept a wink for fear of being arrested. His face was unshaven and he was still dressed in the rumpled, blood splattered suit he had worn to the press conference. He had not been home and was afraid to contact his family. Instead, he had spent the night in a fleabag motel scanning the television for hints of his certain arrest.

Billy Ray Anderson's face filled every television screen in America. There were childhood photos, his prom photo and pictures of a normal-looking kid on a camping trip with his parents. There were others that showed a darker side of Billy—pictures of him dressed in the white robes of the Ku Klux Klan and as a skinhead, giving the Nazi salute in front of a red swastika flag. These images were followed by the now familiar video of the President's last moments.

Trexler opened another beer, reached for the remote, and pressed the volume button. William Barnett's voice again resonated with his final words: "And the fourth angel poured out his vial upon the sun; and power was given unto him to scorch men with fire." It was followed with the sickening sound of the shot and the screams. Mercifully, the image of the President's head exploding had been replaced with a photo of the late president's portrait.

"President William Joseph Barnett was taken to Bethesda Naval Hospital, where he was pronounced dead at 12:40 p.m.," the reporter said. "His body is now lying in repose for the family in the East Room of the White House. Tomorrow the casket will be transferred to the Capitol Rotunda where it will lay in state from Wednesday until Friday. The casket then will follow the funeral route taken by the late President John F. Kennedy to his final resting place at Arlington National Cemetery."

The image switched to ABC's anchorman standing outside the J. Edgar Hoover building in Washington. He wore a grim expression. "The FBI hasn't released any official information about the weapon, but sources have confirmed that the gun was hidden inside the microphone of a professional video camera." The anchorman held up a piece of paper. "This is a copy of a letter, purportedly authored by the alleged assassin, Billy Ray Anderson. It's addressed to ABC News and was received by mail at the Washington ABC bureau office today. It contains a detailed diagram of the camera showing a gun barrel inserted inside the camera's built-in microphone boom. The original diagram and letter have been turned over to the FBI, which is checking it for authenticity. We have been told the camera was a replacement for one damaged by the cleaning crew. That camera passed through the Secret Service checkpoint only moments before the assassination. The chief of the White House Secret Service detail examined the camera and saw nothing unusual. We talked with a spokesman for the agency earlier."

"All we can say at this point," a grim-faced man said, "is that the camera looked normal and passed our most stringent security tests. Those tests will now be examined and overhauled."

"Who performed that inspection?" a reporter off camera called out.

"I cannot disclose that information, but everyone involved has been removed from active duty pending an investigation. This is standard procedure."

The report shifted to an image of Billy Ray's body slumped on the floor in a lifeless heap, his head and torso contorted by the onslaught of Secret Service bullets.

Trexler took another swallow of beer. He couldn't help but wonder what Billy Ray must have thought as the bullets ripped through his body. Did he realize the lethal shot had come from his camera? Could he have known that he was their patsy and would forever be labeled an assassin? Probably not, but as his body absorbed the bullets, he must have thought, *Why?*

• • •

Devrin Crosby inserted his FBI identification card into the lock and waited for his authorization to enter. Etched into the plaque beside the metal doors were the words "Forensic Analysis Section – Firearms and Toolmarks Unit." The morning message to meet his boss, Robert Lynch, in the forensic lab at Quantico was a welcome surprise, and perhaps a chance to see real action again. Lynch was the section chief of the Critical Incident Response Group, (CIRG) and The National Center for the Analysis of Violent Crime (NCAVE) fell under his jurisdiction.

Crosby straightened his tie to conceal his unbuttoned collar as he walked the small concrete block corridor and passed through another set of doors marked "Ballistics." The room was windowless and filled with technicians and lab tables. He spotted Lynch at the far end of the room speaking with a woman in a lab coat. Lynch looked up and motioned for Crosby to come around the barrier of tables to their side of the room. The lab table was littered with camera parts, and he assumed these were the remains of Billy Ray's weapon. Crosby found himself admiring the woman whose features became more appealing the closer he got.

"Sorry for the short notice, Crosby," Lynch said while giving Crosby's hand a quick clasp. Lynch was in his early fifties with an angular face that reminded Crosby of a cowboy.

"I'm happy for the opportunity, sir," Crosby said, thrilled at the prospect of anything other than a desk job.

"This is Dr. Marti Matthews. She is a specialist in inorganic compounds and trace evidence. The two of you will be working together on this assignment."

An assignment! Crosby thought, trying not to smile at the prospect.

Dr. Matthews wore a pair of clear-rimless glasses that added just enough contrast to her lightly freckled skin to give her the distinction that her Ph.D. deserved.

"Agent," Matthews said, extending a pale ring-less hand, the fingernails clipped short and unpolished.

Crosby shook her hand and was surprised at the forcefulness of her grip. "It's nice to meet you, Doctor." She looked to be about thirty, wore little makeup and he detected no hint of perfume. Each earlobe had a single empty pierce, and the lapel of her lab coat had a small stain, probably a drop of morning coffee.

"Dr. Matthews has been examining the weapon's design," Lynch said. "You're up to speed on the camera being a replacement, correct?"

"Yes, sir. Some type of accident by the cleaning crew?"

"Right," Lynch said.

His eyes were glazed. *He's probably been awake all night,* Crosby thought.

"Doctor, I would like to get Agent Crosby's input if you don't mind going over it again."

"Certainly," Matthews said.

"Crosby," Lynch added, "if you have questions, jump in."

Matthews picked up a short metal barrel. "The gun barrel was fitted inside the camera's microphone boom," Matthews explained. She inserted the barrel inside a twelve-inch hollow metal tube that served as the boom. "The camera's microphone isn't used in the Briefing Room, but a small working microphone was attached near the end of the barrel, so it would function if the Secret Service tested it."

Her voice was confident, her diction clear. Crosby wondered if she was an alto. Her auburn hair was in a pageboy cut and her lips were thin and smooth. He detected a slight Southern accent lingering on her words.

Matthews picked up a vial containing small lead fragments. "These were recovered from the wall behind the podium," Matthews said. "The bullet was a single, thirty caliber exploding round, which passed through the windsock as it exited the barrel."

"The frayed windsock is how the Secret Service was able to identify the camera as the weapon," Lynch said.

"Only one bullet?" Crosby asked.

"That's correct," Matthews said.

"He didn't give himself any margin for error."

"None whatsoever," Matthews replied. "Therefore, the exploding round."

"How was the gun triggered?" Crosby asked.

"The firing pin was activated electronically by simultaneously pressing the record and stop buttons."

Lynch picked up what appeared to be a small television remote. "We found this in Billy Ray's pocket," Lynch said.

"It's a remote control," Matthews explained. "It's been adapted to operate the focus, the zoom and, of course, the trigger mechanism."

Crosby frowned as he studied it. "That's odd."

"What?" Lynch said.

"If Anderson was operating the camera, why would he need a remote?"

"Good question. He wasn't the primary operator. He was the backup," Lynch explained. "Since he was the sound man, there was no guarantee the Secret Service would allow him to operate the camera. With a remote, he could still pull the trigger."

"What happened to the regular cameraman?" Crosby looked at one of the Ku Klux Klan brochures but didn't touch it.

"Called in sick." Lynch glanced at a notepad. "His name is Chad Stillwell. He claims he came down with flu-like symptoms. We're checking his story."

"So Anderson's a closet racist," Crosby said. "He sees an opportunity when the cameraman calls in sick and takes it. Correct?"

"That's how it looks," Lynch said. "What you think?"

"It's plausible," Crosby said, "but this wasn't just an opportunity. This was something he had to have planned far in advance. Not only did he have to modify the camera, he also had to find a reason to bring it into the Briefing Room. I would question the cleaning crew to see if there is any connection with Anderson."

Lynch smiled. "We have, but so far we've found none. The cleaning crew foreman insists that the cord was nowhere near the cameras and has no idea how it got entangled."

"Who else had access?"

"No one," Lynch said. "The Secret Service had someone on duty the entire time and no one except the cleaning crew entered the room."

Crosby pursed his lips. "Perhaps this was the opportunity Anderson was waiting for."

"Could be," Lynch said. "The morning papers published details about the camera and the contents of Anderson's apartment that couldn't possibly have come from us. They even reported items that we've barely had time to examine."

"What items?"

"Parts of the weapon, literature found on the perpetrator's body and in his apartment. One paper even mentioned the remote control. Any theories on how they learned that?"

Lynch loved testing his agents and Crosby suspected that this was one test he needed to pass. "Billy probably mailed the items himself. The press always assumes it's a conspiracy, and he had to know he would either be arrested or killed, so why not send out your message while you're still able to?" He pointed to the KKK brochures. "Why else would he have these?"

Lynch looked at Matthews and smiled.

She returned the grin. "He's pretty good."

Lynch gave Crosby a folded sheet of paper. "That's a reproduction of a diagram received at ABC News this morning. It shows the camera's modifications and was stapled to a letter claiming to be from Billy."

Crosby read the letter which expressed in rambling foul language that he was sick of Negros running the country. While he read, Lynch continued. "It appears to be his signature. Copies were received at three television stations and the *Washington Post* this morning. All were postmarked yesterday, all sent from a branch near Billy's apartment. Latent Prints is dusting the envelopes."

Crosby handed the copies back. "That covers the motive."

"I could use some coffee. Crosby, let's take a walk."

"Yes, sir."

Lynch turned to Matthews. "Thank you for your time, doctor. I'll let you get back to your work."

She nodded and added, "Nice meeting you, Agent Crosby."

Crosby smiled. "I'm looking forward to working with you, ma'am."

•   •   •

"Norman!" his wife screamed into the receiver. "Where the hell are you?"

"Look," he said, already regretting his decision to call. "I'm fine. I just got scared. Seeing the President shot right in front of me . . . I just freaked."

"Scared?" His wife yelled. "You're the damn Secretary of Defense! You have an army at your disposal and you're scared?"

"The President was their Commander in Chief, and he's dead."

"You disappeared without as much as a call, Norman. I should have figured you were drunk. We thought you had been kidnapped."

"I'm fine. I'm at a hotel, in town."

"You son-of-a-bitch!"

"Look, has . . . has anyone been by the house looking for me? Anyone suspicious?"

"What are you talking about? I've called the police, the FBI, even your mother. Everybody's looking for you, Norman. Come *home*."

Trexler scratched his head. "I will. I need to take a shower, then I'll catch a cab."

"Tell me where you are. I'll pick you up."

"No!"

"You have a woman there, don't you?"

"No! I'll . . . be home in a while. You and Lisa just stay there. Lock the doors. Okay?"

"Norman, the man who shot the President is dead. No one gives a rat's ass about you. Get in a cab and come home. Now!"

"I will. Listen, call the FBI. Tell them I'm fine."

"You're the damn Secretary of Defense. You tell them." She hung up.

Trexler swallowed a mouthful of beer and belched. He had seen nothing of his disappearance on the news. Perhaps his wife was right. He turned up the volume and wondered if the anchorman would report all of the information in the four envelopes he had mailed yesterday.

"Sources have indicated that the Secret Service found white supremacist literature in the pockets of the alleged assassin, Billy Ray Anderson," the anchorman explained. "A current KKK membership card was allegedly found in Anderson's locker although a spokesman for the Ku Klux Klan has denied any involvement or knowledge of the assailant."

Trexler sat back on the bed and began to relax. "It's like feeding pigeons."

The report continued with interviews of Anderson's colleagues and friends. All expressed shock and disbelief at the revelations.

"I've known Billy Ray, goin' on twenty years now," a childhood friend said. "He didn't have nutin' against duh coloreds and that's duh honest to God's truth! Someone done went and planted dat chit on dat boy."

An unnamed colleague added, "Billy Ray Anderson was always a loner. Our background checks never revealed any type of involvement in racist activities. As our Briefing Room soundman, he was near the President on many occasions. This is quite a shock."

"Rumors of a conspiracy have spread throughout the day," the reporter continued, "but investigators have refused to comment. Reporters near the gunman recall him uttering, 'Not this (expletive) again,' just prior to the assassination. An examination of Anderson's apartment led to a storage facility rented in his name, which allegedly contained a large collection of hate material geared towards African-Americans in politics as well as a collection of rifle and camera parts.

"Today President Beasley spent his first day in office announcing that he plans—"

Trexler switched off the television and grinned. Against all odds, Raptor and Counselor had pulled off the impossible crime. There would, of course, be an investigation, but Counselor's predictions were already coming true. "He who controls the media, wins the war."

•   •   •

Crosby and Lynch left the FBI lab and were headed through the maze of concrete block walls and corridors. Lynch walked at a faster pace and Crosby had to hustle to keep up.

"What did you see?" Lynch said as they rounded a corner.

"It's open and shut, sir." Crosby tried not to sound winded.

"Too much so, don't you agree?" Lynch glanced back at him. "Every time I get a case where everything falls into place, there's always one thing that doesn't quite fit."

"Loose ends?"

"Yes. The notes to the media for one. Billy had to mail those letters before he was even sure he could get the camera in the building. Plus, there's the remote. If Billy had one, why couldn't someone else? Anyone in that room could have used it."

"I agree, but your theory that the remote was for Billy's contingency plan makes perfect sense."

"Yes it does." Lynch stopped, faced him and lowered his voice. "Crosby, I just turned fifty. Mandatory retirement is six years away and this case will define my career. A swift airtight conclusion would be the icing on my retirement cake."

"I'm sure it would, sir."

"Unfortunately, it's not that simple. The Secretary of Defense, Norman Trexler, is missing. His wife says he didn't come home last night. Trexler has a drinking problem so he'll probably turn up drunk."

Crosby thought of his own addictions and nodded.

"I wish that was all. I got a call an hour ago from Director Gregory. Arlington PD found Timothy Cook at his home. He left a note. Looks like suicide."

"The Press Secretary is dead? I just saw him Sunday night."

"He and the President were close. From what I gather, the note indicated that with Barnett gone, he had nothing else to live for."

"Good Lord."

"We've managed to contain the story, but that won't last long. This changes things, and I want to know as much as I can before the media crawls all over us. That's why I called you. I want you to go over there and take a look. You won't be part of the official investigation. It's Arlington PD's case, so you're just on the sidelines."

"Why me, sir?" Crosby held open a metal door and Lynch walked through.

Lynch pursed his lips. "Your personnel file says your father was an arson investigator?"

"Yes, sir."

"Some people have a knack for it. It's the hardest kind of detective work."

"I suppose so," Crosby said with pride. "He's the reason I joined the FBI."

Lynch nodded. "I've watched your skills. You caught that slip Amil Yaspar made in his taped manifesto and you identified the sound of the fishing boat in Rod McCairn's phone calls. You inherited your father's instincts, Crosby. You see things others miss. I need someone who'll look at this crime scene and tell me what's missing. Dig through the ashes, so to speak. Do a follow-up with that sick cameraman. Interview the cleaning crew and the Secret Service agent that was on duty Sunday night. We've already secured permission."

"What about my record, sir?"

"We all make mistakes. You weren't the only one who missed the ID, and your blood tests indicated you were clean and sober. It's a damn shame you caught the blame, but I authorized your transfer to the CIRG because I wanted you out of the spotlight. You needed a rest. Well, rest time is over, Crosby. Go over to Arlington and make damn sure this was a suicide. I'll expect a report on my desk within twenty-four hours."

"Yes, sir! Thank you, sir."

"One more thing. We're on the same team here, so quit thanking me. I expect you to do your job, that's all."

• • •

Norman Trexler was just leaving the motel when the phone rang. He waited until the tenth ring before answering.

"Hello," he said disguising his voice.

"Why are you in a motel and not at home?" the voice on the line said.

He recognized it as Spectrum's chief of intelligence. The one they called Stalker. No one seemed to have a clue about his real name.

"How did you find me?" Trexler asked.

"You're an idiot. How could we *not* find you?"

"The phone call to home?"

"Maybe there's a transponder buried in your neck," Stalker said.

Trexler doubted this, but rubbed his neck anyway. "This isn't a secure line."

"Oh, I'm sure the phone lines at Motel 6 are a top priority for the FBI right now. You didn't answer my question. Why are you there?"

"I was scared, okay? The speech wasn't in any of the President's pockets. If that gets out we'll all have to go into hiding."

"Have you forgotten who we are? The speech will be found and destroyed. In the mean time, your actions are suspicious as hell and you're focusing attention on yourself."

"I was just leaving," Trexler said.

"Your cover story will be that you were in temporary shock, and needed a few hours alone. Understood?"

"Yes."

"Now go home and sober up. Counselor has called a board meeting at the mill this afternoon at 1500 hours."

"A meeting? In person?" He gasped. "I . . . I don't know. . . ."

"Shall I inform Raptor that you are *declining* the invitation?"

"No!" Trexler said quickly. "I'll be there."

"Bring a disguise, something that completely covers your face," Stalker said.

"I understand."

"Be there, or your next disappearance might be permanent."

• • •

The Arlington home of the late Press Secretary, Timothy Cook, looked no more upscale than any other on its street. It was a modest two story, brick, Georgian-style home, with the hedges and lawn kept and trimmed. Two Arlington police cars and a black van were parked out front. To Crosby's surprise, there was no yellow crime scene tape surrounding the perimeter, no reporters, and not a single news crew. Lynch was right about keeping it quiet. Crosby climbed the steps and knocked on the front door. As he waited, he noticed a small toy mouse made of a gaudy pink fur between the bushes and the brick wall. A police officer answered, and Crosby presented his FBI identification.

"Agent Crosby," the policeman said, "we've been expecting you. Director Gregory asked that we hold the body until you've had a chance to view the crime scene."

"The Director called?" Crosby said in disbelief.

The officer nodded. "Yes, sir."

Crosby's only contact with the FBI Director had been shaking his hand on the day he graduated from the Academy. If the Director was involved, he had better be extra diligent.

"CSI has finished and the coroner is inside," the policeman added. "He wants to remove the body ASAP."

A mantle of authority settled over Crosby. "I need gloves and covers."

"Just a second," the officer said and returned with a package. "I thought the FBI carried their own kits."

"I'm in a borrowed car," Crosby lied. He hadn't needed a crime scene kit in over a year. He donned the gloves, hair net and shoe covers and followed the officer inside.

The house was immaculate with no clutter whatsoever and smelled of air freshener. It looked as if it belonged in a new subdivision brochure. Dark smudges of fingerprint dust on the stair railing and door handles marked the thoroughness of the crime scene investigators. A couple of police officers were in the den. The room was decorated in shades of white with eggshell colored walls and gloss white trim on wide moldings. The carpet was an off-white Saxony, spotless except where the blood had seeped through the bottom of the couch. A white bed sheet covered the body, still sitting upright on one end of the white linen sofa. The sheet had a red stain at the left side of the victim's head.

"Why the sheet?" Crosby asked. Unless a body was in a public place it was seldom covered.

A police officer nodded to a wall of windows without curtains. "We thought the neighbors might see the police cruisers and get curious."

Through the windows was a wooded backyard. "Anyone else in the house when it happened?"

"None we are aware of," the officer answered. "The housekeeper found him two hours ago. We have her statement if you need it."

The coroner came over and removed the sheet. The whole left side of Tim Cook's head was missing; a glob of brain tissue was lying on the arm of the linen sofa to his left.

Crosby leaned closer, examined the entry wound, and separated the hairs with a pencil the officer gave him. The hole was the size of his index finger. "Single shot," he said. He found gray discoloration of the skin. "A contact wound?"

"That's how it looks," the officer said.

"I'll need a copy of all crime scene photos." Crosby looked through the hole into the cavity and lined it up with the hole in the blood splattered wall a few feet away. "The angle seems a little low," he murmured to himself. "Only a Magnum or a .45 would do this much damage."

The officer snickered. Crosby realized that they were letting him go through the motions. "Tell me what you've found so far?"

The policeman read from a sheet of paper. "Victim's name: Timothy L. Cook; Occupation: Press Secretary, United States Government; Marital status: divorced, former wife lives in Florida; Time of death: Estimated between 10:30 p.m. and 2:00 a.m. last night; Cause of death: penetrating trauma due to single gunshot wound to the right temple; Preliminary finding: self-inflected."

"Where is the gun?" Crosby asked.

"Under the coffee table," the officer said.

Crosby got on his knees and examined the weapon, an old .45 caliber pistol. Its dull rusted barrel and broken stock looked like thousands issued to GIs since World War II.

"That's pretty close to where we found it," the officer continued. "We already dusted it when we got the call from the FBI."

"How about the registration?"

"None. Numbers are filed down. It looks like a street piece. Two hundred bucks and anyone can pick up one on the corner. We figured he bought it for the occasion."

"Big gun for a street piece," Crosby said.

"It's perfect if you want to blow your brains out." The officer grinned.

On the coffee table was an empty bottle of expensive red wine and a glass with a sip remaining. Both showed evidence of dusting. Beside them was a typed suicide note, also showing smudges of fingerprint dust. Crosby leaned over the body in order to read it.

Rita,
Life sucks. Willie Barnett was my last hope, America's last hope. If you only knew what plans we had. God help us all with Beasley in office. Or rather, God help everyone else. Willie was too good for this world and I'll not watch his dreams destroyed. Like I said, life sucks. Forgive me for telling you like this. Take care of Smokey for me.
     I love ya,

Tim

The "Tim" was scrawled in ballpoint.

"Who's Rita?" Crosby asked.

"His girlfriend. She's a local schoolteacher. We're questioning her at her apartment."

"She had nothing to do with this." Crosby patted the victim's pockets.

"It's routine."

Crosby lifted the couch cushion beside the victim. The red blood had discolored the lining. The odor indicated the release of his bowels. *No saving this couch.*

"Is Smokey a cat?" Crosby said.

The officer raised an eyebrow. "A black Persian. How did you know?"

"Sounds like a cat's name. Is she kept outside?"

"We found her in the front yard. How—"

"Black cat, white sofa, white carpet," Crosby said. "Obviously, the cat isn't allowed in this part of the house." Crosby? got on his knees, lifted the couch skirt and peered underneath.

"We already looked there."

He ignored them. *The toy mouse was outside,* he thought. *An outside cat. If the cat was free to roam the neighborhood, only Tim would know about it, unless it was inside at the time.* "If the note was forged how would the perp know the cat's name?" Crosby murmured.

"What was that?"

"Just thinking aloud. Did the cat have a name tag on its collar?"

The officer nodded. "Yeah. Smokey."

Crosby got up. "Did you find the pen?"

"What pen?"

"He signed his name on the note with an ink pen. Where is it?"

"There wasn't a pen in here."

"Maybe the guy who dusted forgot to put it back."

"We all dusted. The only pens we found were in a cup beside his computer."

"Where's the computer?"

"In his office. I'll show you."

Crosby saw the coroner and told him he was free to move the body, then followed the officer into an adjoining office. The desktop computer was still on, its screensaver repeating a bubble pattern. Beside the monitor was a cup filled with various ballpoint pens. "Can

I move these?"

"Yes. We're finished in here."

Crosby picked up the cup with his gloved hand and gave it to the policeman. "Bag these and have the lab check the inks for a match on the note, and be sure each was printed." *Like they haven't dusted every square inch of this house already.* He sat down in front of the computer. Black fingerprint powder clung to the keys. It was already imbedded into the fingertips of his latex gloves.

"Have you checked the hard drive for the suicide note?"

The officer studied his notepad. "The computer tech found it under the documents folder. The time stamp indicates it was printed at 10:53 p.m. That coincides with the coroner's estimated time of death."

"Was there anything in the recycle bin?"

"Nope. It's empty."

"How about e-mail?" Crosby moved the mouse to clear the screensaver and navigated to an e-mail program.

"The tech found no entries in his Outlook folder."

"Did he check to see if he used another e-mail program?"

"Uh, can't say. The computer tech left earlier."

Crosby clicked on the program files and found an older copy of Netscape. He pulled up a folder but there were no current entries in the sent box. He opened the inbox and found a few pieces of junk mail but nothing unusual. "Did your guy look for deleted e-mails?"

"Don't know." The officer once again checked his notepad. "It says the recycle bin was empty."

"E-mails have their own trash folder," Crosby clicked on the icon. It was empty as well. The fact that the folders were empty was odd in itself. Hardly anyone kept their files this clean. "Did the tech try to recover deleted folders?"

"It says he ran a utility program, but didn't find any files. He felt there was no reason to go further than that."

"That's odd." Crosby said. "This computer is several years old and it had no deleted files whatsoever?"

The officer shrugged. "So what. Look at his house. This guy wasn't exactly a pack rat. He was downright anal."

The second officer made a snide grin. "You can say that again. We found a copy of a gay magazine hidden under his bathroom sink."

"Did you dust it?" Crosby asked.

"Yeah, and checked it for semen residue," the officer said.

"And?"

"Nothing. It must be new. Not a single print."

"No prints at all?" Crosby said.

"Nope."

"Then how did he get it home?"

The officer shrugged. "We found a large manila envelope in the outside trash bin. Maybe it came in that."

"Do you have it?"

"It went to the lab for print fuming."

"I'd like a list of everything you found." Crosby started to get up. "Did the tech log on to Cook's e-mail server to check for new messages?"

"Server?" The officer looked confused. "You mean his—"

"His Internet mail provider. Perhaps he received some messages between eleven last night and now."

"Don't know." The officer studied the notes. "Wait, it says here he tried to log on but he didn't know Mr. Cook's password. He's requested a court order to retrieve those records."

Crosby opened the browser and clicked on "Get Messages."

"You're wasting your time," the officer said. "Our guy's an expert."

A window popped up showing Tim's user name but no password. Crosby typed in "Tim," that was rejected. He tried "Rita" with the same result.

"He tried those," the officer said. "Also tried his birth date and Social Security number. It could be anything. The tech should have the password within a day or so."

"They might be gone by then," Crosby mumbled. He thought of the toy mouse and typed in "Smokey." The server responded with a message: Downloading 1 of 2 messages.

"I guess your expert missed that one."

The officer frowned. "Lucky guess."

The first message was from a political blog site. Crosby clicked the second one. "Bingo!" he said scanning the document. "That's interesting."

"What?" the officer said.

"An airline confirmation." Crosby dialed Robert Lynch's cell.

"What does the evidence say Crosby?" Lynch said.

"Suicide. But why do you suppose Mr. Cook would make an airline reservation to Rio de Janeiro and then shoot himself?"

• • •

A chain-link fence surrounded the abandoned textile mill in the town of Clinton, Maryland, thirteen miles south of Washington. The fence was rusty and the padlock securing the gate had a bullet hole through it. Norman Trexler's rented car was parked inside the warehouse. The meeting was held in what used to be the corporate offices. A portable generator was humming out back, providing enough power for the lights.

Senator Christian Luther, disguised in the role of Counselor, sat at the head of a new conference room table purchased for these occasions. Four other members of the Spectrum team sat in matching chairs. The room was old and dusty, the floor littered with debris. Counselor's black cape and fencing mask gave him the look of the Grim-Reaper presiding over the damned; exactly the look that the senator wanted to portray. Trexler sat at the opposite end from Counselor. Each wore a wig or a hood covering their heads. Their faces were hidden behind various types of masks that to an outsider would appear as an absurd attempt at a costume ball. The masks, along with the code names, were to insure each member's anonymity. They couldn't testify against each other if they weren't aware of their true identities. Stalker, of course, had a file on all of them, but other than him, only Counselor knew their real names.

Counselor had used an emissary to recruit Trexler because of his friendship with President Barnett and the Senator was able to convince the President that Trexler could handle the position of Secretary of Defense. Trexler was promised what he craved most, power and position. As long as he cooperated and kept their secrets, other rewards would soon follow. Perhaps someday even the Presidency. The members had given Trexler the code name Viper, which seemed appropriate considering the way he had just betrayed his Commander in Chief.

The chair to the right of Counselor was usually occupied by Raptor, but during the Secret Service investigation, his seat would remain empty. The chair to his left belonged to Stalker, the group's chief of intelligence. Stalker was a round, heavyset man with thin pale hands and a high-pitched voice. He wore a Jabba-the-hut mask, but he looked more like Humpty Dumpty with a chair growing out of his butt. Despite his appearance, Trexler feared him almost as much as Raptor. He knew every detail about each of them. Rumor was if you crossed Stalker, your children could end up as Happy Meals at McDonalds. Of the two remaining members, one was a man that

Trexler knew nothing about named Warrior, and the other a scientist who wore an Albert Einstein mask and went by the name of Scholar.

Counselor began. "Thank you for coming, especially those of you who had to travel."

"I wanted to personally voice my objection to the fact that we were not informed of this plot until after the fact," Scholar said.

"It was unavoidable," Counselor explained. "Had we not acted, all of us would now be in federal holding cells."

"We didn't sign on for this."

"Your objection is noted, but we are patriots. Patriotism has always required sacrifice."

"Not murder."

"Really? Shall we examine *your* record on that subject?"

Scholar didn't answer.

"I thought so." Counselor held up several newspapers and began reading the headlines. "Assassin Allegedly in KKK," he read from the *Sentinel.* From the *Washington Post,* "Assassin a White Supremacist." And this from the *New York Times,* "Racist Assassinates President." Counselor put down the papers. "The outcome is clear. The media has swallowed our bait and run with it."

"That means nothing if they find the President's speech," Trexler warned.

Counselor turned to Stalker. "The private residence was searched?"

Stalker nodded. "The President's computer indicates that he printed two copies of the final draft. One was found in his personal safe. The other one, who knows? It's not at Tim Cook's or Reverend Johnson's apartment."

"Did Raptor check the Oval Office?" Trexler asked.

"Of course. It's clean. The Secret Service found the replacement we planted on the podium. It matches the document we placed on Barnett's hard drive."

"Should we start a rumor about a fake document?" Warrior asked from behind his Colin Powell mask. They were the first words Trexler had ever heard him speak.

"No," Counselor said. "A rumor would only cause more scrutiny of the replacement speech."

"How much did he tell Reverend Johnson?" Trexler asked.

"Very little," Stalker said. "We arranged a traffic delay at the gate, so Johnson arrived only minutes before the briefing. If he knows anything, he hasn't told anyone. Not even his wife."

Trexler cringed at the thought that his own bedroom might be under Stalker's surveillance. "That leaves only the Chairman of the Joint Chiefs and the Press Secretary," Trexler said.

"Just the Press Secretary," Warrior said.

"I'm afraid that Mr. Cook is no longer with us," Counselor announced. "It appears that he committed suicide last evening."

One of the members chuckled from behind his mask.

"Suicide?" Trexler said.

"Raptor couldn't have handled it," Scholar said. "You said he's under investigation."

"It wasn't him. We used someone on the outside."

"With whose authorization?" Warrior asked.

"Mine," Counselor said. "It was someone we've used before; a Cuban contract agent. He's proficient, and never fails."

"But it's too soon." Trexler said. "The public will never buy it."

"That's precisely why they will," Stalker said. "Tim Cook and the President were friends. Good friends. Tim was distraught. They'll buy it alright, especially when they find the copy of *Sweetboy* we planted under his bathroom sink."

Warrior laughed.

"My biggest concern is securing the leak," Counselor said. "Whoever gave that report to the President is still out there."

"It couldn't have been any of my people," Scholar said. "I handpicked each one."

"Of course it was one of yours," Stalker said. "No one else knows how to build the damn device."

"Whoever it was prepared a detailed report," Counselor explained. "No one could have pulled that off without accessing our files. We'll start with the computer technicians and work our way through Scholar's team. This bastard has enough information to build one. I don't have to tell you what that could mean."

"Suppose he gives the report to the FBI or the media?" Trexler said.

"We have taken steps in that regard," Stalker said. "We'll find him."

"How long before the device is operational?" Warrior asked.

"The molecular production is on schedule," Scholar said. "All totaled, within twenty-four months we should have nearly a gram. At that point we can extract enough for the test device."

"At what yield?" Warrior said.

"A quarter gram might yield five kilotons."

"Is it enough?" Counselor asked.

"Adequate," Warrior said, "but that's one fourth of our total production."

"Correct, but stability is still our key problem and one that must be solved before we compile any of it for mass production," Scholar said. "This isn't something you want laying around in large quantities."

"What about transportation?" Trexler said.

"I have my top men at Oak Ridge working on a containment that we believe can withstand the vibration as well as the desert heat," Scholar said. "Once our client takes delivery, we estimate it will take three days to reach their research facility."

"A lot can happen in three days." Trexler said.

"We'll track it with GPS," Counselor said.

"The heat is our main problem," Scholar said. "We're working on a self-contained power source to keep it cold, but I believe seventy-two hours is doable."

"For now it looks as if the project has weathered this storm," Counselor said. "Gentlemen, open your packets. Memorize your instructions and leave everything on the table when you leave."

•   •   •

The sky was overcast and threatening in Denton, North Carolina, but it wasn't raining. Katie Froscher, again in the black dress, kept an eye on the clouds as she stood by the grave of her father and listened to a bagpiper play "Amazing Grace." As she listened, she thought about the stranger who changed her tire. *It's a matter of faith*, he had said. She was facing the worse experience a child ever has to go through, yet those words gave her comfort. There were still good people who would risk everything by faith alone. She wished she were one of them.

Katie kept her arm around her mother, who was crying. Ruth Froscher was twenty years younger than her husband when they married, his first wife having died childless. Katie watched her older brother, Chuck, ever stoic as her father had been. Relatives, as well as the last remaining members of Colonel Charles Froscher World War II company, the 509th, joined them.

Their numbers had dwindled. They were old and tired, but still they came to pay their respects to one of their crewmembers. Over sixty years had passed since their bombardier had looked through the bombsight of a borrowed B-29 Superfortress named *Bockscar* and released "Fat Man" onto the unsuspecting victims of Nagasaki. With a single squeeze of his fingers, they had won the war.

The bagpipes ended, the guests shook hands, offered their condolences and drifted away. Relatives led their mother to the car, leaving Katie alone at the grave with her brother, Chuck. They stood close, but did not embrace.

"Why here?" Chuck growled.

"What do you mean?"

"Why not Arlington? You know he wanted to be buried with the rest of his crew."

"It was Mom's decision. She wanted him here. Besides with the President's murder it would have been a nightmare to arrange."

Chuck looked up, tears in his eyes. "I don't care. It's what he wanted. You know how close he was to the 509th."

"Only a couple of his crewmates are buried at Arlington," Katie pointed out. "General Tibbets isn't even there. They scattered his ashes over the English Channel."

"But Dad wanted to be there."

"Mom spoke with the lawyer. There's no mention of Arlington in his will. If Daddy had wanted it that bad he would have written it down. You know he loved us more than them."

"I suppose," Chuck sighed. "Everything is so screwed up." He kicked at a clod of red clay that had escaped from under the green Astroturf. "What about you? How's grad school?"

"Exams don't start until next month, thank goodness."

"Take my advice, Sis. Stay the hell away from the military. The world has become an ugly place."

"Is that your professional opinion?" she teased.

"Yeah. Amateurs built the ark, but professionals built the *Titanic*."

She took his hand and squeezed. "No need to worry. Unlike Daddy I have absolutely no interest in joining in the defense of our country. One of the banks in Charlotte is offering info-tech students forty grand to start, and I know someone in their personnel office."

"I wish I had majored in anything other than physics."

"Daddy was really proud of you."

A tear rolled down his cheek. "Well, I'm not." He faced her. "Katie, if I gave you something would you promise *not* to look at it?"

She frowned. "What is it?"

"Just a document, but I need you to hide it for me. It needs to be someplace completely safe where no one can find it, not even me."

"Not even you?" Her face filled with concern. "Why?"

"It's only for a little while, and I'll leave instructions inside, just in case."

"In case of what?"

"I just can't know where it is. A guy named Ryan Papineau might call. You can give it to him, but *only* if he gives you this exact phrase: *Little boy is safe.*"

"Who's the little boy?"

"No one. It's just to indicate that he's ready."

"Okay." She bit her lip. "What exactly do you do at Oak Ridge?"

Chuck stared at the grave. "It's classified. But believe me, you *never* want to know."

• • •

"United Flight 1170, service from Reagan National to Chicago O'Hare will now begin boarding first class ticket holders," the gate attendant announced.

Passengers gathered their bags and made their way towards the gate entrance. Across the terminal a man raised himself from his chair and picked up his briefcase. Inside was the Albert Einstein mask he had worn at the old mill. The meeting had shaken him. He wasn't sure, but he had a good idea who leaked the information. Security wasn't his responsibility. He was a physicist, not a politician or the academic professor his Scholar code name implied. Still, it didn't take a genius to realize that Spectrum's leaders had lost their minds. Their path was suicidal. No one had ever gotten away with killing a President, and despite Raptor's amazing performance, it was only a matter of time.

He had to find a way out, but to do so would leave his life's work in the hands of madmen. The smarter course might be to delay the project. His facilities already had well over a gram spread out in remote locations; more than enough for Warrior's needs. The lie about production levels might buy him a few months, but he couldn't hide it forever. The biggest problem would be disposing of the material. That might prove even more difficult than its creation and if Counselor found out, his own demise would be far easier to conceal than that of the President's.

Scholar handed his pass to the gate attendant and made his way toward the plane. He thought of the containment trap Chuck Froscher's boys in Oak Ridge were working on. *With enough traps, and in small enough quantities, we could annihilate most of it harmlessly*, he thought. *A little here, a little there.* It might work, but doing so would subject Froscher and the citizens of Oak Ridge to more peril than they could possibly imagine.

•   •   •

The package arrived in the mailroom of the *Washington Post* on Tuesday afternoon, about the time the rain began. A clerk delivered it to the desk of Gerald McMullen and placed it on a pile of unread mail. Gerald had planned on announcing his move to Charlotte Tuesday morning, but like the morning of 9-11, the world had suddenly changed. His mother and the new job in Charlotte would have to wait until things calmed down. The stresses of the last twenty-four hours had taken its toll and Gerald was exhausted when he returned to his cubicle at eleven p.m.

He had known Tim Cook personally and was determined to cover every aspect of the assassination and Cook's supposed suicide. He and Tim had briefly shared an apartment his first year at the *Post* and there wasn't a gay bone in his body. His bones were filled with booze and surrounded with women. He was a neatness freak who later traded in the alcohol for a brief marriage and political commentary. Once Tim was appointed Press Secretary for Barnett's administration, he counted on Gerald for fair and unbiased reporting at the *Post*. Tim's loss made the assassination personal.

Gerald faced the pile of mail with dread. He flipped through the letters, dropping the important ones in his briefcase. He paused at a manila envelope and studied it. The return address, 604 H Street NW, Washington, seemed oddly familiar. *That's Chinatown.* He tossed the envelope in with the others, closed the briefcase and headed home.

•   •   •

Christian Luther was in his car when he received the call. Stalker's voice squeaked with excitement. "I just heard from one of my contacts in the White House. Barnett gave Tim Cook the second copy of the speech."

"Why wasn't it at his home?" Luther asked.

"He mailed it before he got there," Stalker said.

"Where?"

"Don't know. One of the White House pastry chefs said the Press Secretary came down to the kitchen around midnight with a manila envelope and asked if he would drop it in the nearest mail box. He said Tim seemed very nervous and kept stressing how important it was to get it in the mail *that* evening. The chef agreed to take it, but explained that he wouldn't get off work until eight a.m., Tim said never mind and left with it."

"A pastry chef. He didn't trust the Secret Service?"

"Hell no. He knew the names in that report. He must have figured we had others in the agency."

"Did the chef see the address?"

"No, but as Tim left, the chef remembered him mumbling something about an editor believing it."

"Bastard mailed it to the *Post*?" Luther said.

"I doubt it was the *Post*. I checked their mainframe to see if there were any conspiracy stories in the queue. Nothing but funeral crap."

"Then where?"

"I'm working on it. Do you want Raptor to stimulate the pastry chef's memory?"

"No. Raptor needs to lay low for now. See if it turns up in the queue at any other papers. If so, you know what to do. Is the worm ready?"

"Yes. It can wipe a mainframe in fifteen seconds. If we're too late the arson team will take care of the rest."

• • •

Norman Trexler was in his study, his wife and kids locked in their rooms upstairs, livid and refusing to acknowledge that he was even home. He settled on the couch with a pillow and blanket. When he switched on the news he saw the report on Spectrum's latest victim. CNN was already referring to Tim Cook's death as a suicide. The report stated that the gun was a street piece, probably purchased by Cook sometime Monday evening. There was no mention of the gay magazine even though he knew that Stalker had leaked that information. The report then flashed his own photo and noted that he had earlier been reported missing by his family, had turned up distraught by the death of his friend, but otherwise safe and sound.

Once again Trexler checked each door and made sure the security alarm was armed. He knew that Stalker wouldn't hesitate to take him out if he pulled another stunt like the Motel 6 incident. Christian

Luther wasn't taking any chances, and Trexler knew far more about Spectrum than Tim Cook ever could.

•   •   •

The rain was heavy and traffic was hell to be so late, but Gerald McMullen made it to his town house at 11:40 p.m. He sat his briefcase on his chair, opened it and placed the stack of mail on the pile already covering his desk. The manila envelope lay on top, but Gerald was exhausted.

He closed the briefcase, sat down to remove his wet shoes and noted the red flashing light of his voice mail machine on the credenza behind him. He spun his chair around to press the play button. When he did, the backrest of his chair bumped against his desk just enough for the manila envelope to slide off the pile and wedge itself unseen between the rear of the desk and the wall.

The message was a hang-up, so McMullen shut off the desk lamp and went to bed.

CHAPTER 5

BLACK JACK

Wednesday

Devrin Crosby and Dr. Marti Matthews signed in at NBC-6 at 8:30 a.m. The receptionist was talking into her headset and motioned that she would be with them momentarily. "NBC-6," she repeated again. "How may I direct your call?"

Crosby had suggested to his boss, Robert Lynch, that Dr. Matthews accompany him. Her familiarity with the disassembled camera used in the assassination would be invaluable in the interview, so Lynch agreed. Crosby knew her expertise was best utilized in the lab, but in truth he just wanted to get to know her better.

"How may I help you?" the receptionist said.

Crosby showed her his badge as he noted her name tag. "Gina, I'm Special Agent Crosby and this is Agent Matthews of the FBI. Is Chad Stillwell working today?"

"Yes, sir," Gina said. "But he's not feeling well and he's scheduled to shoot a segment in about twenty minutes."

"This won't take long," Crosby said.

"Just a second." She punched a few keys. "Chad, there's some agents here from the FBI. They need to speak with you." She paused and listened. "Yes, I know. They said it would only take a few minutes. Okay. Sure, I'll tell them." She looked up at Crosby. "He can give you five minutes before he has to set up the shoot. Down the hall to the left; third office."

"Thanks," Crosby said.

Dr. Matthews and Crosby saw a tall, lanky young man in his late twenties step out into the hall. He sneezed violently into a tissue as they neared.

"Mr. Stillwell. I'm Special Agent Devrin Crosby and this is Dr. Marti Matthews of the FBI."

Chad nodded. His forehead was sweaty and pale, obvious signs that he was indeed sick. He sneezed again.

"Bless you," Dr. Matthews said.

"Thanks," Chad said. "I've already spoken to the FBI. What's this about?"

"We have a few follow-up questions," Crosby said. "It will only take a minute."

Chad directed them to two chairs in his office. It was a workroom lined with shelves and counters. Tripods, cameras, and wires occupied every square inch. Chad leaned against the counter.

"How are you feeling?" Matthews asked.

"Lousy. Must be the flu. I came in for a shoot. We're short handed now that Billy Ray is gone."

"How long did you know Mr. Anderson?" Crosby said.

"I've been here seven years. Billy Ray was here before I was hired."

"How long did you work together?"

"The entire time. We started shooting the press releases at the White House three years ago. I ran the camera and Billy Ray handled the sound."

"Did he ever say anything that might indicate—"

"*No*. Nothing. That's what I told the other agents."

"Which agents?"

"I don't know." Frustration laced his words. "The FBI, the Secret Service. They went through my apartment twice. Real *jerks*. I hope they all come down with the flu or whatever I've got."

"When did you get sick?" Dr. Matthews said.

"I woke up feeling miserable Monday morning. I felt fine when I went to bed. It just came over me. It might have been what killed Miss Reba."

Crosby and Matthews glanced at each other. "Who's Miss Reba?"

"My cat. She was like fifteen and died in her sleep."

"Did the other agents take her to the lab for a post-mortem?" Matthews asked.

"No. I threw her in the dumpster."

Dr. Matthews raised her eyebrows. "What? You threw your pet into a dumpster?"

"Look, I awoke with a splitting headache and throwing up my guts. I had a dead cat, a smelly litter box, and I wasn't exactly feeling up to taking her to Feline Memorial Gardens, or wherever the hell you take dead cats. The dumpster was there, and I used it. So, sue me."

Matthews just shook her head.

"Which dumpster?" Crosby said. "We need to examine the cat."

"Don't bother. They come around on Tuesdays to pick up the garbage. By now she's at the landfill."

"So much for that idea," Matthews mumbled. "Have you been around anyone sick lately that might have given you the flu?"

"Not that I recall and I was alone all weekend. If that's all—"

"What about the camera?" Crosby said. "Did Billy Ray repair them?"

"We both did minor repairs. Billy mostly handled the microphones and sound equipment. We sent the cameras out for electronic problems."

"How long has it been since this camera was repaired?"

"I don't know. More than a year." Chad wiped his forehead with a tissue. "Your agents already confiscated our records."

"Did Billy have twenty-four hour access to the cameras and equipment?"

"He had a key to the lab and the van. Sometimes he would take the van home if we had an early shoot, but no way Billy built that camera."

"Why?"

"Because it would have taken him months to make those modifications; the ones they listed in the papers. These cameras are workhorses. We use them every day. Besides, Billy wasn't a racist. I went to lunch with this guy for seven years. If he hated blacks, I would have heard something."

"He never mentioned the KKK?"

"*Hell no.* I told him once that I didn't agree with mixed-race dating, but he acted like he didn't give a damn. That topic is like a flame thrower to a racist."

Crosby jotted notes.

"Did you normally leave a camera in the Briefing Room?" Dr. Matthews said.

"Whenever we could. There's a briefing almost every day and the security check is a real hassle with a camera."

"Who authorized the replacement for the one damaged by the cleaning crew?"

"I suppose I did. I learned about the accident when I called in sick. I told the receptionist to call Billy Ray and have him use one of the cameras in the van."

"So you believe that's the one he picked up?"

"Of course," Chad said. "We had two, but he must have dropped the other one," Chad pointed to the damaged camera on the table. "I found it this morning with a dent and cracked lens. That's not like Billy. He was very careful."

"What about the remote?" Matthews asked.

"What remote?"

"A remote control was found in Billy Ray's pocket that controlled the focus, the zoom and operated the trigger for the gun."

"Some of the cameras have remotes, but we never used them."

"Never?"

"Rarely, except if you're alone on a shoot." Chad pulled a small cardboard box from under the counter and handed it to Matthews.

The box contained various parts and three remotes just like the one found on Billy's remains. "I'll need to take one of these to examine." Matthews said, securing a stray strand of hair behind one ear.

"Sure," Chad shrugged. He glanced at his watch. "I need to start setting up that shoot now."

"Just one more thing." Dr. Matthews removed a test tube from her bag with a cotton swab in it. "We need to take a throat culture."

"Why?" Chad's anger was rising. "I didn't have anything to do with this."

"We're not saying you did," Crosby explained. "But you obviously came down with something and this will prove that you *were* sick if you ever had to testify."

Chad opened his mouth.

●   ●   ●

A cold misty rain fell on Washington as Crosby dropped Dr. Matthews off at the J. Edgar Hoover building. Crosby was rusty at dating and he couldn't seem to get up the courage to ask her out. The conversation always seemed to come back to the case. He offered to buy her a cup of coffee, but she wanted to get Chad's throat culture to the lab.

He called his office and was told that Mr. Lynch had arranged a meeting for him with the cleaning crew at the White House in one hour. It took Crosby nearly a half hour to pick his way around the blocked off streets. The President's body was lying in repose for dignitaries in the East Room of the White House and thousands lined the streets to get a glimpse of the casket when it would later be transferred to the Capitol. It took another fifteen minutes to get through the increased White House security.

A Secret Service agent escorted Crosby up the stairs and across the West Colonnade. They passed the door to the Press Briefing Room still sealed with yellow crime scene tape. The meeting was set up in the press kitchen break area on the first floor of the West Wing. The room had a laminated counter and barstools with vending machines lining the walls. The agent left Crosby in the room and returned with Emelo Hernandez, the cleaning crew manager.

"Mr. Hernandez, please have a seat," Crosby said, motioning to a stool. "This will only take a few minutes."

"Gracias," he replied. "I have told what happened to the secret police, already."

"How many times has the Secret Service questioned you?"

"Tres times," he said, holding up three fingers. "I tell them same thing each time. They give me lie detector test. I still say same thing."

"Then this should be easy. Have you ever met Billy Ray Anderson?"

Hernandez shook his head. "No. Never see him."

"You don't remember him ever working in the Briefing Room?"

"No one here but secret police when we work."

"Have you ever been a member of the Klu Klux Klan or the Skinheads?"

Mr. Hernandez laughed. "This group you speak of, they hate Blacks, Jews, and Hispanics, any minority. How could I be member of this group? It is they who put blame on us. Sí?"

Stupid question, Crosby thought. "You were operating a carpet shampooer at the time of the accident. Is that correct?"

"Sí."

"The power cord became entangled in one of the legs of the camera's tripod. Is that correct?"

"That what secret police say. We clean this room same way, each day. Never before any problem. We shampoo floor each week, Sí? The cord plenty long. I give it a pull, next thing I know, big crash. Police comes in room. Camera parts all over floor."

"After it fell, did you see the cord wrapped around any of the legs of the tripod?"

"No. The cord just lying under camera," Hernandez replied.

"Why did you have the cord plugged in at the back of the room? Why not in the front where you were working?"

Mr. Hernandez motioned with his hands. "Plug not fit other sockets."

"You mean the shampooer had a special socket for its voltage?"

"Sí. Not fit anywhere else."

"Do you believe the cord rubbing against the tripod caused it to fall?"

Mr. Hernandez shrugged. "Never before, but possible." He shook his head. "I think someone plan this. Maybe they push camera over on purpose then blame me."

"But you saw no one else in the room."

"No, señor. Terrible thing what happened Mr. Barnett. He was good man. Good man."

"Thank you, Mr. Hernandez. That will be all."

• • •

Crosby spent another hour taking statements from the rest of the cleaning crew. None of them were near the camera when it fell and all seemed to wonder why they were being questioned.

At 10:30 a.m., staff members came into the room and switched on the wall-mounted television. CNN showed the long line of mourners standing in the misty rain along both sides of Pennsylvania Avenue. At one p.m., the late President's body would be transferred from the White House to the Capitol Rotunda, where it would lay in state until Friday.

While he waited for his 10:45 appointment, Crosby opened his briefcase, took out his laptop and logged on using the Wi-Fi connection in his phone. Most of the e-mails were hotline posting, or junk that had slipped through his spam filter and he almost deleted an e-mail from Gerald McMullen. The message was short and simple:

Devrin,
Enjoyed lunch despite the terrible turn of events that followed. I wanted to let you know that it will be several weeks before I make the move to Charlotte. Tim Cook was a friend and I'm apparently the only one at the Post who isn't buying that cock-in-bull story about him being gay. If you want to go ahead and move in that's fine. I won't be able to help much though. Just let me know and here is my cell number if you need me.
      Take care buddy and I'll talk with you soon.
      Gerry
      "Life's a beach!"

Crosby smiled at Gerald's postscript. He found the note with the North Carolina tag KT-GIRL still tucked in his wallet. His friend was too honorable to ask for anything more than the name of an agency that could help, even though he knew the FBI could access most any database. Crosby typed a quick e-mail to Lauren Hyatt at NCAVE and asked her to pull anything she could find on the license plate. A copy of the girl's driver's license would also be helpful.

Crosby was alone in the room when his next appointment arrived. David Farley was the Secret Service agent who was on duty outside the Briefing Room the morning of the assassination. The White House was cooperating with Lynch's request, as long as the agent interviews could be arranged near their assigned stations and during their break times. Crosby introduced himself and Agent Farley sat down.

"Agent Farley, were you the only person on duty at the press room during the early hours of Monday morning?"

"Yes, sir," Farley said. He had close-cropped hair and looked like a professional wrestler.

"What time did you come on duty?"

"I worked from midnight to 0800."

"Did you ever take a break?"

"Yes. I ate breakfast at 0400 in the Secret Service office on the ground floor," Farley said.

"How long did you stay?"

"I ate a sandwich and a candy bar. I was there fifteen minutes, max."

Crosby glanced at the vending machines and felt a craving when he spotted the orange wrapper of a Reese's Cup. "Was anyone watching the Briefing Room while you were away?"

"No, sir. The room was empty and dark the entire time. It's not a secure area."

"While you were at lunch, could someone have entered the Briefing Room?"

"It wasn't locked."

"After you returned, did anyone enter the Briefing Room?"

"The cleaning crew. They came in at 0500."

"This was the crew headed by Mr. Hernandez?"

"Yes, sir."

"Did anyone else go into the Briefing Room?"

Farley scratched his head. "I don't believe so. Agent Sanders stopped by the press room sometime around 0600, but only stayed a minute and left."

"Agent Sanders?"

"Yes, sir. Harold Sanders is our chief agent in charge of the White House detail."

"Where is Agent Sanders today?"

"He's on administrative leave pending the investigation."

"Why?"

"He fired at the assassin. It's normal procedure. All of the agents who discharged their weapons are put on administrative leave."

"We have the same policy," Crosby said. "You stated that Sanders only stayed a minute. Why did he stop by?"

"He brought me a cup of coffee and the newspaper. I'd appreciate it if you kept the newspaper out of your report. We're not supposed to read while on duty."

Crosby nodded. "Where did he go?"

"He mentioned there was Danish in the Navy Mess room. He also said he was going to ask around. He had gotten a call to come in early. Something was up."

"Sanders was in charge, but still didn't know why he was called in?"

"Right, but that's not unusual. Anytime the President speaks, the whole security detail is called in by dispatch. They aren't told why. We weren't briefed about the news conference until 0800."

"Sanders never entered the Briefing Room?"

Farley thought for a moment. "Now that you mention it, I'm not sure if he went out through the Briefing Room or down the stairs."

"Why would he leave though the Briefing Room?"

"It's a few steps shorter to cut through it. It was unlocked so I suppose he could have left that way."

"But you don't remember for sure?"

"No, sir."

•   •   •

Twenty minutes later, Crosby was back in his car, an empty Reese's Cup wrapper crumpled on the seat beside him. He was on his cell phone with Bob Lynch.

"Yes, sir," Crosby said. "The duty agent isn't sure if Sanders exited through the Briefing Room or not. I would like to talk with Sanders if you believe it's worth pursuing."

"Probably isn't," Lynch said. "We can get a copy of his statement from the Secret Service. Agent Sanders is catching flack for letting the camera in the building. Even if he went by the book, he'll still have to step down as chief of the White House security detail. He was just in the wrong place at the wrong time."

"I know the feeling, sir."

"Crosby, I hate to do this, but we're going to have to wrap this up earlier than I anticipated. President Beasley is calling for a special prosecutor to handle the assassination case. That means he'll hand-pick his own investigative team. The Office of Homeland Security might be put in charge of the inquiry."

"This isn't a terrorist act, it's a criminal investigation."

"I know," Lynch said, "but it's not up to me. Unless we can come up with something concrete to give to Director Gregory, we'll end up on the sidelines. Do you have anything new?"

"Only Tim Cook's e-mail with the flight confirmation."

"That's not much. Anything on the remote?"

"The sick cameraman, Chad Stillwell, says that the remotes were seldom used. He doesn't believe Billy Ray had the technical skills to modify the camera, nor the motive. They were good friends and he's sure he would have known if he was a racist."

"If they were such good friends maybe he's covering for him," Lynch said. "They found Billy Ray's fingerprints on some camera parts in his storage building. There were also manuals and weapons magazines buried in the KKK literature. There's little doubt he had a part in this."

"I see. We took a throat culture, but Chad looked sick to me. I believe he's telling the truth."

"Wait for the results and add it to the report," Lynch said.

"The cleaning crew supervisor, Mr. Hernandez, had no motive and the Secret Service duty agent says Agent Sanders was the only person who could have entered the Briefing Room."

"Yeah we knew that."

Crosby closed his notepad. "Has the lab found anything on the letters mailed to the media?"

"They were all photocopies, not originals."

"So Billy's signature could have been lifted from another document?"

"It's not enough, Crosby. If that's all you've got, we need to wrap it up."

"You gave me twenty-four hours, Mr. Lynch. Let me speak with Agent Sanders."

"The Secret Service has cooperated so far, but they'll balk on a second interview with Sanders. Remember these people are willing to take a bullet to protect the President, so they're not accustomed to being questioned about their motives. Let's look over his previous statement first. If we find something odd, I'll let you pursue it."

"Yes, sir," Crosby said. "I have a couple of things to follow up and then I'll issue my report."

"Good."

Crosby hung up the phone and felt the energy drain from him. *So much for his return to active duty.* He was sure that by the end of the week he would be back in front of his computer again. He reached in his coat pocket and retrieved a second candy bar.

●   ●   ●

It took Crosby over an hour to make the thirty-six-mile trip from Pennsylvania Avenue to Quantico, Virginia. He entered the lobby of the Behavioral Science Building and punched the elevator button. The doors opened and he squeezed into an already packed car. It was almost one p.m. and the lunch crowd was returning to their offices.

"Hey, Crosby," he heard a familiar voice behind him say. It was Kelly Rankin, a fellow agent. They had once been friends, but ever since the incident at Lafayette Park, Kelly seemed to relish rubbing salt into Crosby's open wounds.

"I heard a rumor that you took a vacation from data entry to scope out the White House Briefing Room. Any truth to that?"

Crosby responded without turning, "You know I can't discuss the case, Kelly."

"He doesn't deny it," Rankin said to someone else. "I was just wondering if they thought the ghost of Amil might have pushed that camera over."

Crosby glanced over his shoulder at Rankin and gave him a "go-to-hell" look. Rankin's nose had once been broken and his cheeks and lips still bore the scars of a near fatal car wreck from twenty years earlier. Despite the scars, or perhaps because of them, Kelly's rugged features landed him dates with an amazing number of single women in the Bureau. He wondered if Rankin kept a checklist.

"Hey, Crosby, if Amil Yaspar was neck deep in concrete, what would you have?"

Crosby raised an eyebrow, but said nothing.

"Not enough *concrete*." Rankin gave him his best Cheshire cat grin.

The other agents laughed as the bell dinged and the doors opened.

Crosby ignored the joke and went to his office.

He sat at a gray metal desk older than he was and flipped through his mail. An oversized envelope with the word "Evidence" stamped across it in red was opened first. It contained a set of the crime scene photographs he had requested from the Arlington police. There was also a photocopied list of items bagged and removed from the late Tim Cook's home. Two of the items caught his attention. The first he already knew about: the pristine copy of *Sweetboy* magazine that held not the slightest trace of fingerprints. Only a mention had been made of the second item, a used, empty, bubble-mailer envelope, measuring nine inches by twelve inches and addressed to Tim Cook at his home. There was no return address and the notation said it had two sets of known fingerprints, Tim's and those of the local postal carrier. A third thumbprint on the postage stamp had yet to be identified. The postmark indicated it had been mailed the previous Thursday at a post office in Knoxville, Tennessee. He continued to scan the list.

"Mr. Crosby?" a voice behind him said.

He turned to find Lauren Hyatt, a college intern that Crosby recruited regularly because of her ability to type over one hundred words a minute. Even though she was half his age, Crosby found himself instinctively holding in his stomach. "Yes."

She handed him a folder. "This is the information on the North Carolina license plate."

He took the folder. "That was quick."

"There wasn't much to it," she said. "It's registered to a Kathryn Froscher in Denton, North Carolina. I pulled a copy of her latest driver's license. No arrests, no citations, no parking tickets. It's all there."

"Thanks, Lauren," Crosby said.

She smiled, and gave him a wink as she left. "Any time."

Crosby shook his head and thought, *Not a good idea.*

He took out his laptop, clicked his e-mail icon and entered Gerald's e-mail address. He opened the folder Lauren gave him and examined the color photocopy of the driver's license. The girl was indeed pretty, about average height and weight with dark hair. He flipped to the next page for the information Gerald wanted. The car title indicated that a Charles Froscher, Sr. had purchased the Acura TSX for his daughter, since she was listed as the primary driver on the insurance. When the title was transferred into her name, twelve months ago, it had been recorded as Kathryn R. Froscher. Nothing indicated her marital status, but since she was still using her maiden name, Crosby reasoned that there was a good chance she was single.

• • •

Gerald McMullen stood in a cold rain that fell on the handful of mourners who were huddled around the green funeral tent covering the grave of his friend Tim Cook. The vicious rumor, suggesting that Tim was gay, had kept away most of his political friends and apparently his personal ones as well. Tim's final resting place was in the Mount Olivet Cemetery two and a half miles northeast of the Capitol Rotunda. There, lines of mourners had surrounded the Capitol building and extended down Pennsylvania Avenue, all waiting to walk past the closed casket of their slain President.

Because of a racist madman, William Barnett was gone and now his friend and former roommate had ended up dead as well. It made no sense. All of Gerald's research into Billy Ray's past had shown no history of involvement in the Klan, no pattern of hate crimes and no indication whatsoever that he was planning to kill the President. Yet, there was the storage locker rented in his name and his fingerprints on the camera parts found within. The evidence against Billy was too obvious to ignore.

Gerald wiped tears from his cheek, as Tim's casket was lowered. The truth usually made sense, but this didn't. Looking down at the vault of his friend, he made a silent vow that he would do whatever it took to find the truth.

• • •

Devrin Crosby was home by five p.m. He wanted to get an early start on typing his report and he hadn't eaten anything but two candy bars all day. He browned some ground beef, added a can of spaghetti sauce and dropped a half-box of angel-hair pasta into water to boil. He poured a glass of sweet iced tea and was taking a sip when his doorbell rang. Opening the door, he was surprised to see Dr. Marti Matthews, holding an umbrella too small to shield her from the rain.

"Hi," she said. "Sorry to bother you."

"Uh, no bother at all. Come in, please," he said, sounding too enthusiastic.

She stepped inside and he took her umbrella. "Thanks." Her

overcoat was dripping on his carpet. "Sorry. This will only take a minute."

"How did you know where I lived?"

"I got your address from Lynch's secretary." She sniffed. "Am I disturbing your dinner?"

"No, I was just making spaghetti. Would you care to join me?"

"No," she said, embarrassed. "I didn't mean to impose. I should have called first."

"Look, I have plenty. I always make way too much and end up having to throw half of it in the garbage," he lied. In reality, he seldom had any leftovers; a prime reason for his weight gain.

"It smells wonderful. Are you sure you wouldn't mind?"

"Let me take your coat," Crosby said. He hung it in the hall closet. "The bathroom is right down the hall if you need to freshen up."

"Thank you. That would be great." She walked down the hall then turned at the bathroom door. "This is a real treat. It's been a long time since someone's fixed me a home-cooked meal."

Crosby smiled and, the moment the door closed, he bolted into the kitchen to bury the spaghetti sauce can deep in the garbage pail. He glanced around, searching for spices, an onion, or anything to help mask the taste of the store-bought sauce. There were no spices except pepper and oregano. He found an onion in the bottom of the refrigerator sprouting stalks six inches long. He quickly chopped the onion and the stalks to give the sauce some greenery. There were two wine glasses in the back of the cabinet and an unopened bottle of red Zinfandel in the refrigerator left over from his melt-down. He poured his tea into one of them. Maybe she wouldn't notice that it was darker than the wine.

"I found something interesting," he heard Matthews say from behind him. He turned to see her standing in the doorway. *What had he left in the bathroom?* "I hope it wasn't my dirty underwear."

She laughed. "No, nothing bad. I got the results of Chad Stillwell's throat culture."

"Oh?" Crosby stirred the onions into the sauce, added some oregano, and tasted it, as though he had made it from scratch. "What did you find?"

"The result was positive. He has a virus with the classic symptoms of influenza, but this is different. So different we've sent a sample to the Center for Disease Control in Atlanta."

"Really?"

She walked closer and stood at the counter. "Flu viruses appear each year in different strains, sometimes mild, sometimes worse. On occasions they can be epidemic, like the 1918 Spanish strain."

"I saw something about that on The History Channel."

"It killed twenty-one million worldwide. That strain was especially lethal because the victims would wake up healthy and be dead within twelve hours. They didn't even have time to see a doctor."

"But Chad's getting better." Crosby drained the noodles in a colander.

"He's lucky. There are five variations of the influenza virus: human, swine, avian, equine, and canine. The last two only affect horses and dogs, but this one looks like a mutation that has a very short infectious period."

"You mean it dies?"

"No. The virus is still there, but now it's non-infectious, at least to humans. From Chad's description, he went from zero symptoms to being extremely sick within four to five hours. Yet, when his apartment was searched twelve hours later, not one of the investigators came down with it."

"Not yet, you mean."

"True." She rolled a stray dry spaghetti noodle between her fingers. "Influenza has a one- to four-day incubation period, so he probably picked it up earlier. But I think it might have been a mutant zoonotic swine virus that's made the jump from animal to human."

"A what?"

"When viruses are transmitted to another species it's called zoonotic. Cats don't catch the flu, yet his cat died. The cat might have been the carrier. If we had the cat, we'd know."

"Is that rare?"

"About sixty percent are zoonotic. This virus may have mutated into one infectious to both cats and humans, then became non-infectious, probably after being exposed to sunlight."

"Have you ever seen a virus do that?"

"Never for cats, nor that quickly. It's almost as though it had a built in alarm clock; like it was . . . engineered to change."

"Engineered?"

"Sounds incredible," Matthews said, "but it's as if it was genetically altered."

•   •   •

Twenty minutes later Marti Matthews was dabbing her lips with her napkin and leaning back in her chair. "That was wonderful."

Crosby admired the shape of her body. It had been ages since he had someone over. "Sorry I didn't have parmesan cheese."

"No, grated cheddar was fine. It reminds me of home. When I was growing up we never had that 'fancy cheese,' as Daddy called it."

"Where was home?"

"Virginia." She poured the last of the wine into her glass. "Did you want some?"

"I'm fine."

"We had a farm outside of Petersburg. When we were kids, my older brothers and I played in the trench-works used by the Confederates during the Civil War. We were always getting in trouble with the park rangers for digging up buttons and belt buckles. It's hard to believe we were playing where so many men died. I guess that's what got me interested in forensics." She took a sip from her glass.

Crosby looked into her brown eyes. She was beautiful, intelligent and best of all, he felt comfortable with her; something he had not felt with a woman in years. All he needed was enough courage to ask her out.

"How about you? Where's your home?"

"North Carolina. A little town called Harrisburg, northeast of Charlotte. My father was an arson investigator. One day after a fire, he stepped through a floor and fell into a basement. The fall killed him."

"Sorry."

"He always wanted to find the cause; to search for the truth. He's why I joined the FBI."

"You're doing that in this case."

"Nothing I can prove. My report is pretty thin."

"You've found reasonable doubt. People have been freed on less."

"There's no supporting evidence. Besides, it won't matter. From what I hear, the President is going to appoint a special investigator to handle the case."

She frowned. "That's what Kelly told me."

"Kelly?" Crosby felt a tingle of jealousy. "You mean Agent Rankin?"

"Yeah. He mentioned you two were friends. Isn't he a hoot? We've been dating two months and he still cracks me up every time we go out."

Crosby closed his eyes, too dumbfounded to respond.

"Hey, maybe we should invite him over," she added with a grin. "He could bring us another bottle."

All Crosby could do was mumble, "A real hoot."

"Devrin?" Matthews said. "Are you okay?"

• • •

Friday morning found Crosby with a backlog of profiles to enter into the National Center for the Analysis of Violent Crime's computer system. The rain had given way to a clear blue sky and the sun was burning the last puddles off the streets. At precisely eight a.m. on Thursday, he had hand delivered his finished report to Morgan Carver, Robert Lynch's assistant. Miss Carver had failed to apply her makeup that morning and was bent over her desk, peering into a tiny mirror with an eyelash curler clamped to one eyelid. With her free hand, she had taken the report and announced that Mr. Lynch was out. He had left no messages or further instructions for Crosby. All that day and into the night Crosby had checked his voice and e-mail messages. There was no response. With no further instructions, he had returned to his desk at Quantico, his short stint as an investigator over.

Very little actual work was taking place, as every available television at the FBI Academy was tuned to the funeral parade that accompanied the late President's body on its trek to Arlington National Cemetery.

In the Critical Incident Response department, usually filled with the sound of clicks and taps, not a single keystroke could be heard as Barnett's flag-draped casket was carried from the black-shrouded rotunda of the Capitol. An honor guard of soldiers from each branch of the military loaded the casket aboard a 1918 artillery caisson that had borne the body of President John F. Kennedy. Six horses, all saddled, but three without riders, pulled the caisson through the streets of Washington. Behind them, a horse named Sergeant York walked with empty boots reversed in the stirrups, a tradition affording the dead Commander in Chief a last look at his troops.

A long-retired anchorman was offering commentary on how in 1963 President Kennedy's horse, Black Jack, had been so spooked by the crowd that he had nearly bolted.

Chopin's funeral march accompanied the procession in a steady beat over the Potomac and up the hill into Arlington National Cemetery. There, William Joseph Barnett joined William H. Taft and

John F. Kennedy as the third President to be buried at Arlington.

The call came at 1:40 that afternoon. It was Miss Carver and her message was as brief as her morning makeup. "Agent Crosby, Mr. Lynch wishes to see you in his office," she said, then added, "now."

Crosby bounded up the stairs, two at a time. He was at Lynch's desk within three minutes where his boss was studying a report. Lynch looked over his reading glasses and saw that he was out of breath.

"Good Lord, Crosby, it's only three floors. Do I need to send you back to the academy for physical training before I put you back in the field?"

Crosby took a breath. "No, sir."

"Have a seat."

Crosby sat in a gray metal chair several decades newer than his own. "Did you say I was going back in the field?"

"That's right. The Director read your report. Good job."

Crosby laid his head back and mouthed a silent, *Yes!*

"Director Gregory was impressed. Those were some interesting leads. The original investigative team is eating crow and taking a closer look."

"Do I have permission to talk with Agent Sanders now?"

"I spoke with Sanders myself. No reflection on you. The Director just thought it would go better with the Secret Service if it came from me."

"I understand, sir."

"Sanders did look in the Briefing Room, saw the cleaning crew but no one else. He doesn't remember seeing an extension cord. He may have left before they began shampooing the floor. It also looks like he documented every procedure when checking in the camera. We've reviewed the surveillance video and he went right by the book."

Crosby nodded.

"At any rate, it's now official. The President has appointed a special investigator in the assassination case. He's asked Senator Christian Luther to head up the Office of Homeland Security. Luther's poll numbers have fallen in his home state, so it's doubtful he would have won reelection. The Secretary of Defense will step in as the new Vice President."

"Trexler's the new VP.?"

"Right. The Attorney General has asked for our continued assistance, but Homeland Security will pick the top people with the most experience in violent crime. Unfortunately, because of the

Lafayette Park incident, you probably won't be included. Tough break, Crosby."

Crosby hid his disappointment.

"However, an amendment has been added to your official record expunging you from any blame in the Lafayette Park identification. We can't remove the shooting incident from the record, but Director Gregory is aware of your contribution and we will call on you if needed."

"Thank you, sir."

"I've already put in your transfer from NCAVE. Report to firearms at 1500 to pick up your piece and kit." Lynch opened a folder. "I'm partnering you with Special Agent Kelly Rankin. I believe you two know each other."

Crosby's face betrayed his shock.

"I see you prefer someone else. Kelly can be difficult sometimes, but he's good at what he does. He was a street cop. Still thinks like one. You won't have to worry about your back with Rankin."

"Yes, sir. Agent Rankin has excellent skills, but I should inform you up front that we don't get along."

"I'm fully aware of that," Lynch said. "You want to know why I put you two together? My uncle once had two hunting dogs that always fought with each other and he showed me an excellent way of curing that problem. He'd shut them both up in an old abandoned car with a bowl of water and leave them for twenty-four hours. I was always amazed at how quickly they became best of friends when confronted with the problem of escape. The best way to gain someone's respect, Crosby, is to make him dependent on you."

"I see what you mean, sir."

"Unfortunately, it's only temporary. Rankin has put in for a transfer to the Office of Homeland Security."

"Sir, he'll take every piece of evidence we've gathered and claim credit for it."

Lynch frowned and Crosby immediately regretted the statement.

"I don't care how the case gets solved, Crosby. I care about catching these bastards. This isn't about taking credit. If Agent Rankin solves this case, then I'll be just as proud of him as I would if he had never left. You've done your part."

"Sorry, sir. I misspoke."

"Your report is part of the official record now. Nobody's taking that from you." Lynch stood and extended his hand. "Congratulations, Devrin. Welcome back."

• • •

That evening Crosby stopped by Goodtime Charlie's Lounge on the way home.

"I really need a drink," he said to the bartender.

"Beer or Coke?" Charlie said from behind the bar.

"Make it my usual."

Charlie poured him a draft beer. "Want to try the cube?"

"Not tonight. I have a lot on my mind." On the one hand, he was elated to be back on active duty and away from his boring desk job. But on the other hand, he now had a partner he couldn't stand, who was dating the only woman he was interested in.

He took the beer and touched it to his lips, then thought of Marti. "What a hoot," he said, then put it back on the bar and headed toward the piano.

PART 2

CHAPTER 6

DILLON

Thirty-Eight Months Later

Leslie Pryce parked her car at the crest of a hill located behind the branch of OleWest National Bank in the Rocky Mountain community of Dillon, Colorado. With an elevation of 9,017 feet, the snow-capped mountains surrounding the town hid the sunrise until late morning. In the valley below, an earthen dam held back the crystal clear waters of Dillon Reservoir. A plaque across the parking lot announced that the town was founded in 1873. Leslie had never stopped to read the fine print, but had heard that the town had been moved several times and that the original site was now buried some two hundred fifty feet below the surface of the lake. She imagined an old city still resting there like the lost city of Atlantis, awaiting discovery by future generations.

Leslie took in a deep breath of the cool mountain air and unlocked the bank's door. The building had a rugged wooden exterior and landscaping of tumbleweed and cactus. At nineteen, she was OleWest's youngest employee, but for her this was only a temporary position. Her goal was to save enough money to attend the University of Colorado and major in business.

One of her morning tasks was to switch off the alarm and check the bank's security cameras, which provided a real time streaming video link to OleWest's corporate headquarters located in Denver, some seventy miles east. She punched in her security code and received confirmation that nothing unusual had taken place during the past forty-eight hours. She wiped down each teller window with a dust cloth and adjusted the calendars to Friday, November 23, allowing for the previous holiday. At 8:45 the timer on the vault clicked, indicating that Denver had just released the vault's security system. Other employees drifted in, still bloated from their Thanksgiving feast and cranky at having to work while the rest of

America shopped. Most of Dillon's residents were either at sales at Denver's numerous malls or enjoying the first major snowfall of the season at the nearby ski slopes.

The morning hours passed and by 12:30 p.m. the tellers were discussing whether to have lunch at the café across the street or go into Silverthorne for pizza. Leslie noticed a man who entered the bank at 12:50 and sat outside the branch manager's office, a briefcase by his chair. He was well dressed with short black hair and a moustache and appeared to be waiting for her boss, David Anthony. Perhaps they had a lunch appointment. Several customers were already in line when a second man entered five minutes later. He wore a dull olive green suit and appeared to be in his early thirties. He was about five nine, thin framed, with combed-back sandy hair and a wispy mustache and goatee. In his right hand was a brown leather briefcase.

"Next," Leslie said, smiling at her last customer before lunch. The man in the green suit approached.

"I would like to make a withdrawal, please," the man said in a soft, pleasant voice.

"Do you have your account number?"

"Yes." The man smiled with a hint of a wink. He placed his briefcase on her counter and opened it. "I need my checkbook." He took out a small radio and placed it on the counter as he removed papers. "Sorry, I should have found this earlier."

Leslie smiled and waited. One of the tellers stood by the outside door to lock it as customers left while the others totaled the morning receipts.

"Here it is." The man opened his checkbook and handed her a bank deposit ticket. A note was typed across its face.

As Leslie read, the color drained from her. She looked at the man and then at Mr. Anthony, who was shaking hands with the man outside his office. Her hands trembled as she reread the note:

Stay calm and remain quiet. The radio is a bomb. The remote is in my hand. If you activate the alarms, we *all* will die. The bomb is capable of leveling the building. Act normal and fill the briefcase with large bills. DO NOT attempt to sabotage the money. Once I'm safely away, I'll send a signal disarming the bomb. REMEMBER; <u>Do Not Touch The Radio</u>! Follow these instructions, and you'll live.

Leslie was so scared she couldn't talk, only nod.

The man smiled again and patted the radio. "Cooperate and you'll be laughing about this later."

Leslie remembered her training and glanced up at the security camera. A robber would usually follow a teller's eyes, giving the camera a clear view of his face, but the man didn't fall for the trick.

"Nice try," he whispered. "I know where the alarm buttons and cameras are located. Is this money worth your life?"

She slowly shook her head. *To hell with the money, it wasn't hers.* She removed all of the hundreds from her drawer and placed them on the counter.

"Use your calculator, as you normally would," the robber whispered.

Leslie punched in three stacks, each worth $10,000.

"We're a small branch," she whispered nervously. "We don't have many large bills."

"Take your bag and go to the vault. I'll wait."

A loud voice arose from within Mr. Anthony's office. "What was that look?" a man was saying in a foreign accent. "If I were not Muslim, you would never treat me with such *contempt.*"

Leslie did as she was told. The confrontation had produced the desired effect. None of the tellers noticed Leslie going into the vault. The vault held an unusually large amount of cash since this was the busiest shopping day of the year. The man had done his homework. Leslie loaded a tray with hundreds and fifties. Someone would notice. As she turned to leave, she spotted the computer panel on the wall inside the vault. With one button she could alert Denver, and no one here would ever know. She reached for the panel, but stopped herself. *What would they do? They'll call the Dillon police! The note said the bomb was capable of leveling the building.* Her heart pounded.

Was he lying? He was so calm and confident. That could only mean that the bomb was all too real. To alert Denver was the same thing as screaming at the top of her lungs. She wanted to go to college and she wasn't getting killed over a damn stack of paper.

She found a canvas bag and stuffed the bills inside. There would be no alarms, not if she could help it. When she returned to the window, she smiled at the man. "I put those bonds in this bag for you, Mr. Jones." She handed it over. "You can drop off the bag the next time you're in. Okay?"

"Yes, thank you." The man smiled back, checked the bag for dye canisters and placed it in his briefcase. "Very good," he whispered.

"Remember, no alarms and no touching until I send the signal." He extended the radio's antenna and pushed one of the buttons. Its red light glowed brightly. Leslie couldn't take her eyes off of it.

The man calmly thanked the teller at the door as she unlatched it. Leslie tried to see which direction the robber was walking, but he immediately disappeared behind the insurance building next door. Within seconds the dark-haired man emerged from Mr. Anthony's office, shook his hand as if everything was resolved, and left the building.

"I wonder what that was about?" one of the tellers asked.

"Who cares, I'm hungry," another teller said. "Leslie, are you ready?"

"What?" Leslie murmured.

The teller chuckled. "Are you ready to go to lunch?"

"Lunch? No." She remained frozen, staring at the glowing red light.

"Leslie? Are you all right?"

She shook her head. "No. That man who just left, he said there's a bomb in the radio."

"A *bomb*. Why didn't you press the alarm?"

"*No!*" Leslie screamed. "Don't touch anything. Please, just get Mr. Anthony."

• • •

The car was parked outside the bowling alley on Main Street. When the Iranian reached it, the robber had already removed his green suit and was lying on the floor of the back seat. The Iranian got into the driver's seat and started the engine.

"What's happening?" he asked with a Middle Eastern accent.

"She's scared," the robber said from behind the seat. He kept his head down, but listened carefully to his earphones. The transmitter, located inside the radio had a range of three miles.

The Iranian turned left onto Fiedler Avenue and calmly drove right past the front entrance of the bank. "No activity on the outside," he said as he turned right onto LaBonte Street and headed west.

"Hurry, she just told the other tellers it's a bomb. She's getting the branch manager."

"I can't. The police department is across the street and the speed limit is twenty miles per hour."

They drove past the café and stopped at the intersection of LaBonte and Dillon Dam Road.

"Any alarms?" the Iranian asked.

"Not yet, but I hear yelling in the background."

They were one minute and fifty-two seconds away when they began crossing the dam. Suddenly the robber could hear the branch manager's voice clearly.

"You are a *fool!*" the manager yelled.

"But Mr. Anthony," Leslie's voice pleaded. "He said it's a bomb. He's going to send a signal to disarm it as soon as he's safely away."

"*Idiot!* You were robbed with a radio." There was a sound of static as the radio was snatched from the counter. "See, it's nothing but a *damn radio.*" In the same moment he heard the bank's alarm signal and the sound of the recording starting.

The robber sat up in the back seat snatching the earphones from his head. "Floor it. That idiot manager just armed it."

"But we're three kilometers away," the Iranian said.

"Just *do it!*"

• • •

Leslie had both hands clutching her head in terror. As the recording played, a familiar voice came from the radio's speaker:

"My fellow Americans," William Barnett's voice began. "I have asked you to gather here today to tell you of a matter of utmost urgency."

Everyone stared at the radio in terror. "That's President Barnett's speech," one of the tellers said. "Right before he was . . ."

"My *God.*" Leslie covered her open mouth. At that moment, she saw the briefcase the first man had left on the floor by his chair, a tiny antenna extending from it.

• • •

They were almost up to eighty when they passed a Summit County Sheriff's car headed in the opposite direction. The cruiser's emergency lights came on but it had trouble turning around on the narrow dam road.

The Iranian cursed in Farsi. "*Zarba!* He's coming after us."

"Won't matter. It's too late."

"How long?"

The robber climbed into the front passenger seat. "If we're not in the shadow of that mountain in fifteen seconds, we're fried."

The Iranian glanced at his host and pushed the accelerator to the floorboard.

* * *

The late President's voice continued from the radio. "I'm reading from Revelation 16:8."

Everyone was backing away from David Anthony, who was still clutching the radio. "What the hell is wrong with you people? It's just a *recording*." He held it out toward them. "*A speech!*"

Leslie couldn't take it anymore and ran toward the locked doors and fumbled with her keys.

The President's voice slowed as he read the passage. "And the fourth angel poured out his vial upon the sun; and power was given unto him to scorch men with fire—"

* * *

A flash, brighter than the spectrum of the sun made everything go white. Even in the shadow of the mountain, now between them and Dillon, the two robbers were temporarily blinded. The car's engine and electrical system immediately failed and they coasted to a stop. A shock wave roared past them across Dillon Lake, sending huge boulders crashing around them and into the reservoir. The temperature, where the bank had stood, rose to ten million degrees. In an instant, the iron ore deposits in the rocks melted and turned the silica in the ground into molten glass. As the shock wave spread towards Frisco and Breckenridge, the intense heat first scorched the forests and laid them flat like broken toothpicks. The sides of the mountains began giving way in massive landslides as tons of snow melted. The clear waters of Dillon Lake were slammed with thousands of tree trunks and reduced to a steaming cauldron of debris. The town of Silverthorne, lying in the valley below the earthen dam, was initially protected from the heat of the blast, but huge boulders, swept from the crest of the hill, showered down upon it. The waters in the lake rose five feet in the first minutes as pulverized trees and debris began filling the spillway.

They remained in their car, unable to see anything but white ash covering the windows. Eventually they climbed out, coughing in the thick smoke. The clear morning sky had been replaced by dark clouds and dust. Clumps of hot ash rained down around them as a gray snowfall. When the smoke cleared, they began to see behind them. The sheriff's patrol car had not made it past the edge of the mountain. Its windows were gone; the paint sandblasted from it and black smoke poured from the charred remains of its driver. The smell of burning hair and flesh filled the air. They walked back past the ghastly remains of the deputy and watched hundreds of fish jumping from the scalding gray waters of Dillon Lake only to fall onto its steaming shore. They rounded the edge of the mountain and stood in awe at what they saw. The town had vaporized and the entire valley looked like the surface of the moon.

"Allah Hu Akbar!" the Iranian said. "What explosive that small could do this?"

The robber peeled off a latex nose mask and fake goatee then removed a short wig. Her blonde hair fell almost to her shoulders. "And that's only the trigger, Amil," Lucy Harris said. "Bidding starts at twenty million. Still interested?"

CHAPTER 7

LITTLE BOY

Devrin Crosby stepped off a small jet, chartered by the FBI, at 6:30 Friday afternoon at Denver International Airport. He had been in the Atlanta field office when he got the call from Robert Lynch's office to meet the jet at Atlanta's Hartsfield Jackson International. All he was told was that there had been an explosion in the Rocky Mountains near Denver. He assumed it was a military site, but he had no access to television or radio reports on the plane. To complicate matters, his cell battery had died and the spare was in his luggage, therefore he had remained in the dark for four hours.

During the long flight, Crosby wished he had remembered to bring Gerald's recently published book, *The Conspirator's Angels.* Gerald McMullen had given him an autographed copy the last time he had visited Washington, but despite his best intentions, Crosby had not read much more than the dust jacket. Gerald always felt that President Barnett's assassination and the death of his Press Secretary, Tim Cook, were elaborate conspiracies, not the work of a lone racist. Like Crosby's own report, issued three years earlier and set aside for lack of evidence, the most any of these conspiracy books offered were theories. He wondered if Gerald had uncovered any new evidence to support his claims. *Probably not.* He would have mentioned anything that might reopen the case.

Crosby was greeted on the tarmac in Denver by Special Agent David Smith of the Denver FBI office and General Edward J. Glasscock of the U.S. Army Criminal Investigation Command. All three were ushered aboard a waiting Sikorsky S-76 Eagle helicopter that lifted off and headed toward a distant plume of smoke highlighted over the Rocky Mountains in the red glow of the afternoon sun.

Crosby settled in, put the spare battery in his cell to use it as a voice recorder and began. "Okay, what have we got?"

"This wasn't an accident," General Glasscock said.

"That's what we're assuming," Agent Smith corrected.

"The hell it isn't. We've checked with the Air Force and all of the special service branches. No one has reported missing ordnance and we also have no missing aircraft or missiles in this area."

"So you believe it's a terrorist attack?" Crosby asked.

Agent Smith nodded. "Based on what we currently have, yes."

"What are we talking about as far as damage; Beirut, Oklahoma City, or ground zero?" Crosby asked.

Agent Smith looked dumbfounded. "You haven't seen the news?"

"I've been on a private jet for four hours."

"This certainly wasn't any airplane or truck bomb," the general said.

"What was it?"

"*Hiroshima,*" Agent Smith said.

Crosby's jaw dropped. "Nuclear?"

"*Absolutely,*" the general said.

"We don't know for sure, but it was huge."

Crosby closed his eyes. Their worst terrorist nightmare had finally come true. "How big?"

"Rough estimates range from ten to fifteen kilotons," the general said. "In the nominal A-bomb range."

Crosby took a deep breath. "Good Lord. They said a terrorist bombing. I had no idea it was nuclear."

"Initially, we thought it was one of ours," the General said. "An accident."

"There's a no fly zone around the area and we're refusing comment for now," Agent Smith said. "The media is relying on eye-witness accounts and amateur videos of the mushroom cloud."

Crosby recalled Lynch saying the investigators wouldn't find much. Now he understood why. "How many casualties?"

"Unknown," the general said. "Thank God most of the population wasn't home at the time."

We have perhaps 300 burned victims in the surrounding hospitals. Most of those won't make it."

"What about fallout?"

"We're monitoring the situation. A robot is on the way, but strangely enough, the gamma levels are mild. They're elevated, but nothing close to the levels typical from this size explosion. The winds may be affecting our readings. Once the robot arrives we should be able to get an accurate fallout reading and identify where the plutonium was manufactured."

"Any idea on motive?" Crosby asked.

Agent Smith shrugged. "There's nothing there. A town, lake, condos. Beats the hell out of me."

"What about the location?" Crosby said.

The agent pulled a crumpled ski resort brochure from his pocket. "This is all I've got. Dillon provided lodging for local ski resorts. Population 2300. Founded in 1873. The entire town was moved twice in 1882 to be near two railways. In 1961, they built Dillon Reservoir, which forced the town to move again, this time to a hill overlooking the lake. That's where it stood until this afternoon."

"Now it's been removed," Crosby mumbled.

"This town's had a hard life."

"General, are there any secret military facilities in this area?"

"None that the Army is aware of. NORAD is eighty-seven miles south. The Air Force maintains a recreational facility nearby, but that's *all* it is."

"Why Dillon?" Crosby asked.

"You tell us," Agent Smith said.

• • •

The Sikorsky climbed over the twelve thousand-foot Loveland Pass and Interstate 70 disappeared into the Eisenhower Tunnel below it. All traffic on I-70 was being detoured north at Idaho Springs around the blast sight. A four mile section of I-70, five miles west of the Eisenhower Tunnel to Frisco, had ceased to exist. There, the mountains were shrouded in a plume of smoke and the few trees that were still standing were scorched black.

"Right over Tenderfoot Mountain is where it happened," General Glasscock said.

As they reached the top, everything except the lake was a gray moonscape.

"That dark red spot on the east side of the lake," Agent Smith said, "that's where Dillon was. The blast sheered off a portion of the earthen dam, and debris filled the spillway. Ironically it's the crater that saved Silverthorne and all of the cities downstream on the Blue River. The water from the sudden snowmelt filled the crater and spared the valley downstream. A team of engineers has volunteered to clear the spillway if the lake gets any higher."

"Why does the water look red?" Crosby hesitated. "It's not—"

Glasscock shook his head. "Not blood. It's from the sulfur and iron pulverized in the lake water. The smell is like dead fish mixed with rotten eggs. You'll need to get into one of these suits." He held up a bag containing a yellow radiation suit. "We'll set down on the western side of the lake. The wind will be at our backs and these badges will monitor your radiation exposure. Once either of you reach your limit, we're out of here. Understood?"

Crosby nodded. "Any chance of finding forensic evidence of the bomb?"

The general shook his head. "We can't even find evidence of the *town*."

"Jeez! What the hell does Lynch expect me to find?" Crosby's cell phone vibrated and he pressed it to his ear.

"Crosby, this is Lynch. Where are you?"

"We're hovering over the blast site at Dillon and about to set down."

"Never mind that. Hightail it back to Denver ASAP. I'm on the Lear with Dr. Matthews and Agent Rankin. I'll meet you on the tarmac in an hour. I think we might have a photograph of our terrorist."

"How?"

"Believe it or not, the bastard used the bomb to rob a bank in Dillon. We have the whole thing on a streaming video that was sent to Denver."

"On our way, sir." Crosby punched the end key. "We're headed back to Denver. They believe the motive was a bank robbery."

Smith frowned. "Hell of a way to cover your tracks."

The general shook his head. "Who the hell uses an A-bomb to rob a bank?"

"Someone with more money than sense," Crosby said.

• • •

Stalker had studied the message for hours before calling Counselor with the news. "We might have a problem."

"What is it?" Christian Luther said.

"Dillon. Your department is investigating, right?"

"Looks like an accident. What have you learned?"

"I found this in the personals section of yesterday's *New York Times*. It might have been addressed to some of our clients." Stalker began reading. "Little Boy seeks successful demonstration at 1:00 p.m. Proceeding with Fat Man. Call 1-439-3765 23-106-0265."

"What the hell is that supposed to mean?"

"Check the prefix. Those are not phone numbers. I believe they're map coordinates. N is the fourteenth letter in the alphabet and W is the twenty-third letter. North 39 37.65, West 106 02.65 is smack in the center of Dillon, Colorado."

"Stalker, haven't you got anything better to do? Those numbers could be anything."

"The Dillon blast was at 1:05 p.m. Colorado time and 'Little Boy' was the nickname given to the first atomic bomb dropped on Hiroshima."

"So?"

"Scholar's prototype design was nicknamed 'Little Boy' by his team members."

Luther took a moment to consider this. "Dillon is one of ours?"

"I don't know, but it's possible. We never accounted for the particle material that was missing from Fermilab after the episode with Chuck Froscher."

"Froscher's dead. Besides no one could stockpile core particles. It's been over three years. The particles would have annihilated within months."

"I found a memo from one of Scholar's Los Alamos physicists. He claims to have developed a 'Liquid helium thermos,' based on Froscher's concept of taking the particles down to absolute zero."

"Impossible. Scholar said we can't reach absolute zero. That's why the government killed the project."

"But you can get pretty damn close. He suggested that it might be enough for extended storage."

"That's a long shot," Luther said.

"Maybe, but I have a bad feeling about this. The newspaper ad said, 'Proceeding with Fat Man.' Fat Man was the bomb used on Nagasaki, and it was bigger. Froscher may have given a copy of his plans to someone other than the President. What if our clients have obtained the missing particle material and built their own device?"

"Stay on it and keep me informed."

• • •

Gerald McMullen stared at the crumpled piece of paper in his hand. He had taken a few hours off from writing and had spent the afternoon cleaning his mother's home while she was at the doctor's office with his brother Ned. The piece of paper had been found wedged in a crevice of their sofa while vacuuming. The page was a printed copy of an e-mail from Devrin Crosby, dated three years earlier. Gerald had long since forgotten the girl's name. He had tried calling her once, but he couldn't think of anything to say, and had hung up when she answered. Sometime after moving from Washington to Charlotte, he had lost the page and then he met Renee.

His relationship with Renee was rocky. They had planned to take a cruise the following week, even purchased tickets, but after their last fight, she had walked out and wouldn't be back. His vacation would be spent alone.

He sat down and read the name, Kathryn Froscher. The face of the pretty brunette, her car disabled by the side of a busy interstate in a pouring rainstorm, was etched in his mind. Crosby had underlined the fact that the car title had been issued to a Kathryn Froscher. The same last name as her father. She was probably single; at least she was three years ago.

Gerald sighed, crumpled the paper into a ball and almost tossed it, but hesitated. Finding it after all this time, he was overcome with intuition that a greater power had caused him to pull over that night. Her plate number had been etched in his memory. How could he just toss it? He thought about sitting on the beach alone. What did he have to lose by calling?

He punched the numbers into his cell.

•   •   •

The meeting was held on the forty-second floor of the OleWest National Bank building in downtown Denver. The conference room had a large table and a flat screen, high-definition television mounted on the far wall. OleWest's president, Harry Foy, was short and bald with fringed white hair.

Section Chief Robert Lynch sat at the center of the table across from Foy. To his right were Agent Crosby, Agent David Smith and General Glasscock. To his left were Dr. Marti Matthews and Kelly Rankin, serving now as the FBI liaison from Homeland Security. Rankin was brash, yet he had the type personality that most people envied. If Kelly were ever brought before the Director for a reprimand, within minutes he would have his feet up on the desk, telling the joke-of-the-day. He was that kind of guy. Rankin's precarious relationship with Dr. Matthews was a sore spot with

Crosby who had given up the possibility of a relationship with her. Despite this, he and Rankin managed to keep their rivalry on a professional, if not friendly, basis. Lynch's two-dogs-trapped-in-a-car technique had served its purpose well.

Foy pressed a remote key and an image of the OleWest bank building in Dillon appeared on the screen. He outlined a history of the branch and listed the names of employees believed to be on duty at the time of the incident. "The Dillon Branch," he began, "was equipped with four security cameras. Each transmitted a streaming video feed, via cable, to our security center in the basement of this building. Normally, the disks are archived there for three months and then recycled. It wasn't until we reviewed the disks that we realized we had experienced a robbery just prior to the explosion. We have four angles, but this is the only one that shows the culprit's face." Foy punched the remote. He stopped the video at 12:53:26.

"He enters the branch at this point," Foy explained while pointing to a figure dressed in an ill-fitting olive green suit. "He waited to enter just prior to their lunch closing, so he could be the last in line, and kept his head down." Foy let the video move slowly forward.

They watched as the teller greeted the man.

"Who's the girl?" Agent Rankin asked.

"Her name is Leslie Pryce." Foy corrected himself. "I mean *was*. Sweet girl. I saw her just last week at our annual Thanksgiving luncheon. She was only nineteen."

"*Bastard.*" Rankin muttered.

Crosby thought the remark typical for Rankin, not so much that she was cut down in her prime, but that her beauty was wasted before he had the chance to get her into bed.

"Our cameras were equipped with microphones," Foy said, "but the robber spoke so softly we can only guess at what he's saying."

"There's a specialist in lip reading at the academy in Quantico," Dr. Matthews offered.

"Excellent suggestion," Lynch said. "I want the video analyzed as soon as we return."

The image inched forward and the group watched the robber remove the radio from his briefcase and place it on the counter.

"That's your bomb, gentlemen."

General Glasscock leaned closer to the screen and shook his head. They watched as Leslie retreated into the vault only to return moments later with a bulky bag.

"Any idea on how much cash she gave him?" Lynch asked.

Foy paused the video. "Who knows? We lost everything. We have the wire deposits from six p.m. on Wednesday, but we have no idea how many deposits were made over the holiday or how much cash was given out during the morning hours."

"A branch that small wouldn't have that much cash, would it?" Lynch asked.

Foy shook his head. "Maybe a hundred thousand. It was the busiest shopping day of the year, so there was more than normal."

"Of all banks, he picks a tiny one in the middle of nowhere," Rankin said. "It doesn't make sense."

"Do all the tellers have access to the vault?" Crosby asked.

"Normally no, but they have a tendency to bend the rules when they were busy."

"Wouldn't the other tellers notice her going into the vault?" Rankin asked.

Foy frowned. "They should have, but they might have been busy counting receipts."

Crosby looked at Lynch. "Or a diversion?"

Lynch nodded. "Have you reviewed the other angles? Perhaps he had an accomplice."

"I was about to mention that there was a brief argument in Mr. Anthony's office. I'll have someone check the time stamp to see exactly when it occurred."

"We'll take care of that," Lynch assured. "We'll need to examine all the disks."

Foy nodded and the video continued. They watched the culprit wait for the door to be unlocked and leave.

"Look, the teller is just standing there," Rankin said. "Why the hell isn't she pressing the alarm?"

"There was also a computer panel in the vault that she could have pressed to alert us, but for some reason she didn't."

"Could she have been in on it?" Rankin asked.

"No," Dr. Matthews said. "Look at her. The poor girl is scared to death."

"She's right," Crosby said. "If he told her it's a bomb, then I bet he had a remote in his hand. She wouldn't dare set off an alarm knowing that."

They watched as the second man came into view and waited for the door to be unlocked. For just a second he glanced back towards the teller window and the camera caught his face. Crosby gasped, and uttered, "Wait." He glanced at Lynch who shook his head and nodded back toward the screen.

Foy looked at Crosby. "Did you say something?"

"Never mind," Lynch said. Crosby knew the nod indicated he had seen it too and they would discuss it later.

"Here it comes, gentlemen," Foy said.

Suddenly they could hear the bank manager swearing at the teller. They watched as David Anthony picked up the radio.

Crosby heard faint voices. "Can you turn that up?"

Foy pressed the volume to maximum. They could barely make out the voice of the late President.

"That's President Barnett's last speech," Dr. Matthews said.

"It's coming from the radio," Crosby added.

". . . and power was given unto him to scorch men wi . . . zzzzzzz" The image turned to static.

"*Good Lord,*" Rankin murmured.

Lynch stood. "We'll need to take charge of all of the masters," he said turning to shake Foy's hand. Everyone followed by getting up and gathering their coats.

"Don't you want to see the other angles?" Foy asked with a confused look.

"We have plenty of time to study them. You've been a great help, Mr. Foy."

"I'll need copies for our insurance company," Foy added.

"You'll have them by tomorrow."

• • •

Ruth Froscher was in the kitchen putting away the dishes when the phone rang. She had never heard the man's voice before and almost hung up thinking he was a salesman.

"Ma'am my name is Gerry McMullen and I was trying to reach a Miss Kathryn Froscher."

She tried to remember if Katie had even mentioned anyone named Gerry. It sounded like an old college or high school acquaintance.

"I was given this number," he continued.

"My daughter's name is Kathryn. How may I help you?"

"I met your daughter a while back, and I was wondering if she was still in town?"

"Oh, so you're an old friend?"

"Well," Gerald hesitated, "we only met briefly and frankly, I misplaced her number." He laughed. "I recently found it buried in my sofa."

"I see." *So, she gave him her number. Perhaps this was more than just a casual acquaintance.* "I'm sorry but Katie doesn't live here any more," Ruth said cautiously. "She works in Charlotte."

"Yes ma'am. Would she still be listed under her maiden name?"

"It's unlisted."

"Okay," Gerald conceded. "Sorry, ma'am, for the bother."

"But she's still single, if that's what you're asking?"

Gerald laughed. "Yes ma'am. I'm afraid you've caught me. I don't want to invade her privacy, but I would like to get in touch. Does she have a number at work or a cell phone where I could reach her?"

"Well, I don't believe she would mind if I gave you her work number. Hold on a second." Ruth retrieved Katie's business card from under a refrigerator magnet and read the number to him. "But I'm afraid you'll have to wait until Monday to catch her. She spent Thanksgiving with some friends, and she's away for the weekend."

"Thank you, Mrs. Froscher. I'll leave her a message at work."

Ruth hung up the receiver and wondered if she had done the right thing. He seemed genuine enough and what was the harm in giving him Katie's work number? She would give her a call and tell her to expect. . . . *What did he say his name was?*

• • •

As soon as the elevator doors closed at OleWest's headquarters, Lynch started issuing orders. "Dr. Matthews, I want you to accompany General Glasscock and Agent Smith back to the blast site. We have lead-lined radiation suits available. Take whatever samples you need and brief the Nuclear Incident Response team. I want to know exactly what type bomb that was."

"There's no way the radio was the bomb," the general said. "Not at ten kilotons."

"Probably a transmitter," Crosby said.

Matthews nodded. "Then the bomb must have been located elsewhere."

"If it was an old W-84 warhead it would weigh nearly four hundred pounds," the general said. "He probably had it in the back of a rental truck parked outside, like in Oklahoma City."

Lynch glanced at Matthews. "Any chance of finding an axle?"

Matthews shook her head. "The heat from a nuclear blast is

twenty-thousand times hotter than the surface of the sun. If we find anything at all we'll be lucky."

"Any debris is on the bottom of the lake," Crosby said.

"Along with a million trees," Agent Smith added.

"Too risky for divers. We'll have to drain the lake," Lynch said.

Agent Rankin turned to Lynch. "Sir, since this appears to be a terrorist action, the Office of Homeland Security will want to assume command."

"I'll deal with that when we get back to Washington. Either way, it's still a bank robbery and therefore a criminal investigation. It looks as if we're all working this one, Kelly. Right now, I need your help before the trail gets cold. Can we count on your cooperation?"

"That's why I'm here."

"Good. I'm assigning twenty agents to help you cover the car rental agencies. Check everywhere within a hundred mile radius, especially truck rentals. Start with the major airports."

"He may have rented in Salt Lake and driven east," Crosby added.

Rankin nodded. "I'll need blowups or composites of the unsub."

"Done," Lynch said. "Ride with us. The regional office should be able to reproduce the pictures within the hour."

"Crosby, you're with me," Lynch said. "General, we appreciate everything you've done."

"You'll let me know what you find?" the general said, shaking their hands.

"We'll keep you posted," Lynch said. Crosby knew full well that General Glasscock's part in the investigation had just ended. It was now a criminal matter.

Agent Crosby, Rankin and Lynch entered the van that would take them to the FBI's regional office blocks away. Crosby took the seat beside Lynch. Rankin was in the seat behind them. Tires squealed as the van lurched into motion.

"Kelly," Lynch said, "what did you see?"

"One unknown suspect, possibly two," Rankin said. "Both male. One thin, blonde hair and mustache about five foot nine by the door tape. Green ill-fitting suit, carrying a brown leather briefcase. The other unsub had black hair and mustache, dark skinned, possibly Middle Eastern or Indian decent. He's about five eight or nine."

"Sounds like your man, Crosby."

"You saw him too, sir?" Crosby said.

Lynch nodded. "You should know. You've studied his face long enough."

Kelly interrupted. "Excuse me. Am I missing something?" Rankin had never quite made the transition to the politically correct demeanor of the typical FBI agent. Now that he was with the Office of Homeland Security, he spoke his mind.

Lynch glanced back over his shoulder. "Agent Crosby thinks he recognized the accomplice."

"Well? Are you going to tell me or am I supposed to absorb it by osmosis?"

"Amil Yaspar." Crosby knew how Rankin would react.

"Amil? *Ha!*" Rankin hooted. "Here we go again. Hell, Crosby, you blew his damn head off once and he *still* managed to take out an entire town with a transistor radio."

"Go to hell, Rankin," Crosby said.

"Jeez, Crosby, when did you become such a tight ass?"

"That's enough, Kelly," Lynch warned. "If Agent Crosby thinks it was Amil, then we follow the lead."

"Look, boss." Rankin's tone was more conciliatory, "I don't want us to make the same mistakes we made the last time, especially if we're working the case together."

"Then go *home*," Crosby said. "We'll do fine without you."

"No one is going anywhere," Lynch said. "You two will either work together or I'll make damn sure you're both off the case. Understood?"

"Yes, sir," they simultaneously said. Even though Rankin was no longer under Lynch's direct supervision, there was little doubt that he had enough influence in Washington to have Rankin removed from the investigation.

"I know his face," Crosby said. "It was Amil, all right, and he used a bank just like he did in Madrid. But why pick a place like Dillon? It's not his style."

"Okay," Rankin said, "let's suppose it was him. An A-bomb would have costs millions, so why waste it?"

"Maybe there was another reason," Crosby said. "Something we missed."

"If that bomb was in a briefcase or even the radio, then we've just witnessed a whole new level of terrorism in this country," Lynch said, "and that scares the hell out of me."

• • •

They said their goodbyes in the parking lot outside Fillmore

Municipal Airport in Utah. Amil Yaspar had chartered a twin engine Beechcraft that would take him two hundred fifty miles south to Las Vegas. He had gotten the idea of using private planes from a best-selling novel and found them to be his safest mode of travel. Despite the increased security after the 9-11 attacks, private airports like Fillmore lacked any of the security features found in major airports. There were no X-ray machines. At most, he might be asked to open his bag by the attendant.

Using the name on her current Colorado Driver's License, Lucy Harris would drive on to Salt Lake International. There, she would lose the car in long-term parking and board the red-eye to Atlanta, assuming it hadn't been canceled. This car was their second; the first one having succumbed to the effects of the blast. After they abandoned the stolen getaway car, they had to walk a mile to the First Baptist Church in Frisco, where the second car was parked. The tan Honda had been rented a week earlier under the name Vanessa Harrison from the airport in Denver. She had paid cash for a two-week agreement, so it wouldn't show up as missing for another week. A suitcase containing disguises and various wigs was in the trunk. The only item she and Amil had taken from the car disabled by the blast, was the briefcase containing the money.

"Do you want any of this?" Lucy nodded at the dust covered briefcase in the rear seat.

"No," Amil said, his English excellent. "You have done well. The demonstration was both effective and thrilling. We are prepared to close the deal. You have expenses; the car and transportation."

"Your deposit covered those. I don't want to leave this in the car and a briefcase full of money will pose a problem for me at the airport."

"Why not put it a cardboard box and mail it to a friend? Our anthrax letters were never traced through your postal system."

"An excellent idea."

"When can we expect delivery?"

"Once we have confirmation that the money is in our account, I'll contact you with the instructions," Lucy said. "The device will already be in place. It will be up to you to set it off." Lucy handed him a small brass key.

"What if it fails?"

"Start cutting wires. Eventually you'll hit the right one."

"How do I know you can be trusted once you have our money?"

"You're the terrorist, Amil. How do we know we can trust you?"

Amil smiled. "Now so are you, comrade. Remember we share the same fate." He handed her a slip of paper containing a series of numbers. "This is how you can reach me. I suggest you memorize it."

Amil got out of the car and walked toward the small metal hanger. He never looked back.

•   •   •

Saturday

Crosby was tired. He and Lynch had left Denver at nine p.m. and the four-hour flight to Ronald Reagan Washington National Airport was exhausting. He was still at his desk, staring blankly at computerized images of passengers who had arrived at Denver International that morning. So far, none of them fit Amil's profile. He had just nodded off when the phone rang.

He picked up the receiver and heard the alert voice of Dr. Matthews. "Devrin, bad news," she said.

Crosby tried to clear his head. "What have you got?" He looked at his watch. It was nearly three a.m. in Washington, midnight at the Dillon site where Matthews was calling from.

"I'm with the Nuclear Incident Response team from Los Alamos. We just got the data in from the robot rover. We've sent it all around the crater, but we're getting nothing. Slightly elevated levels of gamma radiation, but that's it. No trace elements whatsoever."

"What does that mean?"

"There's no trace of the plutonium or uranium used in the bomb. This wasn't *nuclear*."

"What? How could that be?"

"There's a room full of scientists here all asking the same question."

"Then what was it?"

"We're not sure." Her voice lowered a bit. "Or they're not saying."

"What about something conventional like TNT or fertilizer?" Crosby heard her repeat the question to the scientists on her end. It was several seconds before she was back on the line.

"They say no way. It would take fifteen thousand tons of TNT to equal this blast. The biggest that's ever been tested at Los Alamos was only one hundred tons and that stack was as big as a house. Fifteen thousand tons would be a stack a hundred and fifty times that size."

"Something caused it," Crosby said.

"We're going back to square one. One of the scientists even suggested that it might have been a meteorite."

"No, Amil was there."

"Who?"

"Never mind."

"Go home, Devrin," she said. "We're all tired."

CHAPTER 8

FAT MAN

Katie Froscher awoke Saturday morning, made herself a cup of coffee, and walked onto the balcony of her Fort Lauderdale hotel room to watch the sun rise. It was beautiful clear day, the temperature approaching seventy. A work crew in orange vests were gathering seaweed on the beach that had washed ashore. The vests reminded her of prison garb and she pictured herself wearing an orange suit as the doors to her cell slammed shut.

She shuddered at the thought and went back to the television set. It displayed yesterday's pictures of the mushroom cloud rising forty thousand feet, far above the snow-covered mountains west of Denver. She had not been surprised to see it, but the news that a town had been vaporized was shocking. The media was now reporting it as a deliberate terrorist attack; the motive unknown. Someone had sneaked a camera into the restricted zone and the images of burned-out cars and the gray moonscape were unbelievable.

She had heard nothing from Lucy. Something must have gone terribly wrong.

Katie surveyed the packages strewn across her bed, the results of a shopping spree the previous day. In light of Dillon, she wondered if her plans had changed. *Was it all for nothing?*

In her open suitcase, two cruise ship tickets beckoned her to either continue or go home. As she reached for her's, the hotel phone rang.

"Katie," the voice said. "It's me."

"Lucy? Are you okay?"

"Yes. I'm in Atlanta. My flight was delayed."

"What happened?"

"I'll tell you later. My plane leaves in fifteen minutes. Do you have my passport?"

"Yes, and your ticket, driver's license and credit card. I used it extensively yesterday. Are we safe?"

"Yes." Lucy paused. "I sent you a package. Just ask for it at the Carnival Customer Service Desk. I'll see you in paradise."

•   •   •

Crosby knocked on Robert Lynch's open office door before crossing the threshold. Lynch was pouring himself a cup of coffee.

"Good morning, Crosby," Lynch said. "Care for some?"

"Yes, sir. I was up until three. The transcript of the Dillon recording arrived."

Lynch took the papers.

The lip reader was good, but she didn't have a clear view of the unsub's mouth the whole time."

Lynch flipped through the pages. "Where are the disks now?"

"They're in the lab. We're running the faces through the NGI Biometric facial recognition database."

"Are you still convinced it's Amil?"

"More than ever. He entered the bank five minutes prior to the other suspect, but didn't ask to speak to the branch manager until the unsub arrived. It seems the commotion happened seconds before the teller entered the vault."

"So it was a diversion. They must have had a signal."

"Or an ear piece. Amil never looked toward the teller window, not once. The transcript of the argument video is on page eight."

Lynch turned to the page. "Who's David Anthony?"

"He was the Dillon branch manager."

Lynch skimmed the page:

David Anthony: Of course you will have to personally guarantee the note.
Bank Suspect: What was that look? If I were not Muslim, you would never treat me with such contempt.
David Anthony: It has nothing to do with race. That's our standard policy on all personal loans, sir.

Lynch put down the transcript. "Clever how Amil's 'look' comment could have been used at any point in their conversation."

"Perfect for a diversion. The lab is trying to lift a voice print from the disk. They should be able to match it with earlier tapes of Amil."

"Make damn sure it's him. The press will eat us alive if we blow the identification again. Any word from Agent Rankin?"

"He emailed his report. The forensic team found an abandoned rental car at the perimeter of the area of total destruction. It could be the getaway car. The electrical system failed due to electromagnetic pulse. It was rented in Denver by a Ms. Delia Shultz on Wednesday. She reported the car stolen from her hotel in Breckenridge that evening. She was checking in when the theft occurred and the keys were still in the ignition."

"Anything on her?"

Crosby shook his head. "She's a single mother on a ski vacation with her daughter. She didn't see anything."

"Where's the car?"

"It's at the forensic lab in Denver."

"Any footprints around the car?"

"Nothing useful. The car's location was protected from the blast by the mountain and by the time Kelly's team arrived hundreds of spectators had walked by and put their hands all over it. Forensics will have a time with that one."

"What did Dr. Matthews say about the bomb?"

"The type of weapon is unknown. They've ruled out uranium and plutonium as the fissionable materials. The robot rover found no trace elements whatsoever. The yield was about twelve kilotons, slightly smaller than Hiroshima." He checked his notes. "We have 154 confirmed casualties, 326 hospitalized with cuts and burns and approximately 250 unaccounted for."

"*Good Lord.*"

Crosby nodded. "All of the evidence, thus far, puts the source of ignition at the bank building."

"You mean the bomb was inside the bank?"

"Given the location of the crater, the evidence seems to point there."

"The briefcase on the counter?"

"The unsub took the briefcase. It had the money in it."

"Did Amil leave anything?"

"It's possible. We're going though the video frame by frame. So far it seems the only thing left in the bank was the radio."

"How could a bomb the size of a radio do this?"

"The Nuclear Incident Response team says no way. Dr. Matthews thinks the radio was a transmitter and the explosive was located outside the building. Without knowing the bomb type we can't determine its size by the crater."

"What do you think?"

"A truck parked outside the building would be logical, if it was nuclear."

"But Matthews says it wasn't," Lynch said. "What else could cause this type of explosion?"

"I don't know, sir. It wasn't conventional and NORAD had nothing on radar, so that rules out a meteorite or comet."

Lynch stood and faced his bulletin board, now covered with pictures of Dillon before and after. In the center of the board was a photo of the nineteen-year-old teller, Leslie Pryce. Lynch crossed his arms. "The only mistake this girl made yesterday was to go to work. That's all any of them did." He pulled Leslie's photo from the board and handed it to Crosby. "She was trying to earn enough money to go to college, her whole life in front of her. I've got a daughter her age." He closed his eyes as if trying to fight back a tear. "We know who did this, Crosby. Find the bastard before he does it again."

• • •

Gerald McMullen listened to the phone ring five times before Kathryn Froscher's voice mail kicked in. Her voice was pleasant, yet professional, the message evidently recorded earlier in the week:

"This is Katie Froscher. I'll be away from my desk from Thursday, November 22 until Monday, December 3. If you would prefer to leave a message or need to reach me during this time, please contact my executive assistant, Mandy Davis, at extension 239. Happy Thanksgiving."

"December *third.*" Gerald said exasperated. *So much for the beach idea.* He was supposed to file several columns for the *Charlotte Observer* by then. He decided to leave a message with her assistant. Perhaps she wouldn't be so shy about giving out Katie's cell phone number. He punched in the three digits and waited for the voice mail. Instead he got a real voice."

"Hello?" the lady said.

"Yes ma'am, is this Ms. Davis?"

"Yes, it is."

"My name is Gerald McMullen. I didn't expect the office to be open today. I was trying to get in touch with Katie Froscher."

"Oh," Mandy said. "I took Friday off, so my office calls are forwarded to this number."

"I'm sorry to disturb you on a Saturday, Ms. Davis."

"No bother, but I'm afraid that Ms. Froscher will be away from her desk for about a week. She's on vacation."

"Do you happen to have a number where I could reach her?"

"I do, but it wouldn't do you any good. She'll be on a cruise ship next week."

A cruise. Gerald had just canceled the cruise he and Renee had planned to take. *If I could get on board Katie's cruise ship, it would be the perfect place to meet her again.* He had to think quickly.

"I'll be glad to take a message and have her return your call when she gets back."

"I was afraid of that." Gerald faked disappointment in his voice. "It's probably too late to catch her. I just got off the phone with her mother. She can't remember the name of the ship either."

"I thought Katie was traveling alone?" Mandy said.

"She was. I didn't think I could get away, but my plans changed. Now I can, but Katie didn't leave me her cell number and I can't remember the name of the cruise ship."

"You spoke with her mother?"

"Yeah, I called Ruth last night. I'll give you her number if you want to confirm that."

"That's not necessary. You said your name was McMullen?"

"Gerald McMullen."

"Have you and Katie known each other long?"

"Only briefly, but this cruise might have changed that." He sighed. "Just my luck."

"I'm sure she'll be disappointed that she missed you. I would offer to call her for you, but she's shopping in Miami today and rarely turns on her cell while on vacation. Her ship doesn't leave until tomorrow afternoon, so you could try contacting Carnival to leave her a message when she checks in."

Carnival. Almost there.

"If she calls in before then, I'll be glad to tell her you called. She has your number?"

"She better," he lied. "I was hoping to fly down and surprise her. With my luck, I'll probably end up on the wrong ship."

"Well, let me think," Mandy said. "Katie showed me a brochure. It had something to do with 'winning,' because I thought of a football game when I saw the ship's name. Sorry, that's all I remember."

"That's more than I had," he said. "I'll call the cruise line. Carnival can't have that many ships leaving on Sunday."

"Good luck, Mr. McMullen. I hope everything works out."

"Thanks again, Ms. Davis. I owe you." Gerald hung up the phone and smiled at the prospect of spending a week snorkeling and lying on warm white sandy beaches. But first there were arrangements he had to make and very little time.

• • •

The girl at the wheel of the boat was beautiful with long brunette hair and her black string bikini left little to the imagination. Captain Barney couldn't take his eyes off of her as she piloted the forty-three-foot *Island Breeze* around Key West Harbor with expert precision. When asked about her experience, she explained that she had grown up aboard her father's thirty-six-footer in the Mediterranean. Satisfied with her expertise, they returned to the dock where she filled out the rental agreement. She seemed capable of handling the boat, so the captain agreed to rent the *Island Breeze* for two days, without an attending first mate, for twelve hundred dollars per day.

Her companion, a dark-skinned man who seemed oblivious to English, loaded fishing gear aboard, and Captain Barney helped him with an oversized ice chest.

Captain Barney looked over the forms. "Okay, Miss Harrison, all I need is your driver's license and a credit card and you're on your way."

"A credit card?" Lucy Harris said with a frown. She gave him her fake Vanessa Harrison driver's license. "All I have is cash. My credit cards are packed." She nodded toward the pile of bags being loaded. "You're not going to make me go through those are you?"

"Sorry, but I can't rent her without two forms of ID."

"Hmm," she moved closer and rubbed the tip of her finger across his chest. "Could you identify me from this?" She pressed her lips to his.

To the captain the kiss seemed to last forever and it didn't help that she was pressing the rest of her body against him as well. When she released him, Captain Barney was too stunned to respond.

"Or will you need a little more?"

The captain chuckled. "What do you have in mind?"

Lucy pulled a roll of hundred dollar bills from the pocket of her cut-offs. "Oh, I was wondering if Mr. Franklin's ID might suffice."

As the boat pulled away, Captain Barney counted his money. Five thousand wasn't bad, considering this was the off season, but he did wonder why she was hesitant to produce a credit card. Perhaps she wasn't planning on fishing at all. Considering her companion's looks and his business-like attitude, she might be headed on a one-way trip to Cuba. He peeled off five hundreds to buy additional boat insurance. The *Island Breeze* was getting old, and the sleek new fifty-footer he had his eye on would make a nice addition to his fleet.

He smiled and stuffed the rest into his pocket. The girl turned, blew him a kiss and a wave. Somehow he had a premonition that he would never see the boat again.

•   •   •

By eleven a.m., Crosby was in his Washington condo packing his overnight bag for a return trip to Denver. Just off the bedroom was an office that Gerald had left furnished with a desk, a television and old computer. Crosby regularly used it to check his e-mail and log onto the Internet. CNN was on the television and he kept an eye on the news while he packed.

He placed the Dillon file in his laptop case. Attached to the cover was a photo of the young teller, Leslie Pryce. Since the getaway car had survived the initial blast, there was now hard evidence that might place Amil Yaspar at the scene and someone might have seen the unsubs fleeing the disabled car on foot. The culprits may have been taken to a hospital, or stolen another car.

Crosby turned up the TV volume to hear the latest updates on Dillon.

"We have just received a statement from OleWest's corporate headquarters in Denver that a bank robbery took place at the Dillon branch moments before the explosion," the reporter said. "The Summit County Sheriff's Department in Breckenridge has confirmed reports that one of their officers, a Ms. Campbell, radioed that she was en route to Dillon a few minutes prior to the blast. The spokesman said she was responding to an alarm at the OleWest National Bank in Dillon. We have not been able to ascertain whether this development has anything to do with the explosion itself. Unfortunately, it appears that Officer Campbell was a victim of this terrible tragedy. Her remains were found in her cruiser and she may have been in pursuit. The FBI removed the cruiser and another car from the site last night. The FBI has not confirmed this."

"Thank you," the anchor said. "Meanwhile, President Beasley has instructed the Attorney General to reset the national threat level from red to orange. A White House spokesman stated that the threat level would remain orange pending an investigative report. The FBI and the Office of Homeland Security have refused comment, but sources have said there is some question as to whether this was a nuclear device or some other type of explosive. It has been suggested that perhaps a truckload of fertilizer traveling through Dillon on Interstate—"

Crosby muted the television and called Kelly Rankin's cell number.

"Hey Crosby," Rankin answered. "What lies on the bottom of the ocean and twitches?"

"Not now, Kelly."

"A nervous wreck," Rankin said with a laugh.

"Have you watched the latest on CNN?"

"Of course I watch CNN. That's where I get all my leads."

"The news seems to have better information than we do."

"That's because *they* stay at the scene. We've known about the missing sheriff's deputy since yesterday."

"That wasn't in your e-mail summary. Why do I have to get the news from CNN, Kelly?"

"I gave you the latest. The deputy spotted the unsubs fleeing the scene, turned around and followed them. That's how we knew the Chevy Lumina was the getaway car. It's all in my report, but you requested *just* a summary, and that's what I sent."

"Fine. Anything new?"

"In fact, there is. One of the agents spoke with a minister of Fresco Baptist church, four miles from the site. He said there was a tan Honda parked in their lot for two days. When he checked the church for damage Friday afternoon, the car was gone. I figure our unsubs might have stolen it, or left it there to switch vehicles."

"Did he give the year and model?"

"Four door, late-model Accord. He didn't get the tag."

"So we're looking for the most common car in America."

"I figure they headed west since the interstate to Denver was closed and any fallout was blowing east. We're checking the lots at the airports, but that's a long shot."

"Can you have someone pick me up at the airport in Denver? I'm coming back this afternoon."

"I'm headed in the opposite direction," Rankin said, "but Marti's already in Denver for some appointment with a retired scientist. You have her number?"

"Of course."

"One other thing, just so you'll know that I'm not keeping anything from you . . ." Rankin paused long enough to irritate Crosby. "We found your boy's prints in the car. Looks like it was Amil after all."

• • •

They arrived at the western-most islands of the Marquesas Keys in the late afternoon. The uninhabited ring of islands was perfect, lying thirty miles west of the Keys, fifty miles east of the Dry Tortugas, and ninety miles due north of Havana. They anchored the *Island Breeze* a hundred feet from shore and enjoyed a nice dinner under the canvas awning. After the meal, they relaxed in lounge chairs and poured the wine. The sun had set on the western horizon when the conversation turned to the business at hand.

"Why do you betray your country?" Carlos asked, his Spanish accent thick.

"I have my reasons," Lucy said. "It's personal."

"They will find you. Your FBI is good."

"I have an advantage."

"What advantage?"

"I know what's coming. They don't." Lucy took another sip of wine. "You owe me $5,900 dollars for the boat rental and supplies, Carlos."

He shrugged. "If your demonstration is as impressive as you say, mi guapa, our government will owe you far more than that."

"I'm serious, Carlos. The fifty-nine hundred is in addition to your deposit. When I place my call to Grand Cayman in the morning, it better be there."

He rested his foot on the cooler. "I could save my government a tremendous amount of money by killing you and taking this bomb. We could, como se dice? backwards engineer."

Lucy's wine had made her tipsy. "That's a hell of an idea, Carlos. Why don't you do that?"

His voice turned serious. "You laugh, but perhaps it is worth considering, no?" He removed a .38 caliber pistol from his waistband and placed it on the table. "But sheer beauty such as yours should never go to waste."

"What? You want to rape me, Carlos?" She spread her arms.

"Have at it."

"Senorita, you mistake me."

She pulled her bikini top over her head and tossed it to the floor. "Go ahead, Carlos. That way we can *both* go out with a bang!"

Her attitude and indifference to his threat took him aback. "What are you saying?"

"It's simple, Carlos. You want this body, take *it*." She stood, unzipped her shorts, pushed the bikini bottoms over her hips and let them fall to her ankles. She stepped out of them and into the light. "As you see, I'm unarmed. You want to use your *gun* on me, Carlos? Go ahead. You want to take that bomb? Be my *guest*."

"You're *loco!*"

"What do you expect, Carlos? I just wiped out fifteen hundred men, women and children without any warning. I maimed and disfigured many more. There is nothing you could do to me that I wouldn't deserve. The heat from that blast is like a cool morning breeze compared to where I'm headed."

He could sense her pain and felt embarrassed by her nakedness.

"I'm not stupid, Carlos. If you don't believe me, look in the cooler."

Carlos laid the pistol on the table and slowly unlatched the lid of the cooler. Inside, a second metal cooler was frozen solid and surrounded by dry ice and wires. Frozen gases overflowed its sides. He fanned at the fog then noticed the glowing LED numbers of a timer, counting down hours and minutes. His eyes widened and he slammed the lid. "*Santa Maria!* It is armed?"

Lucy nodded, now pointing the pistol at Carlos. "Armed and ready; has been since we left." She aimed at his crotch. "Now, it's your turn to strip."

"What?"

"Strip. Take your clothes off and put them on the table. I want to be certain that this was your only weapon."

Carlos removed his shirt and shorts. They both faced each other in the twilight with nothing to hide.

"You see, in less than thirty hours the temperature on that island will rise to twenty-three million degrees." She wrapped the gun in his clothes and tossed them overboard. Carlos started to protest, but Lucy moved closer and placed her fingers on his lips. "Shhh. I need you for my escape, Carlos, and since I am the only person who can disarm this bomb, I strongly suggest we keep *each other* alive."

•   •   •

Crosby didn't see her until he reached the security checkpoint in the grand hall at Denver International. Dr. Marti Matthews was in her street clothes, not in her lab coat, and her hair was different. She approached him as if she were going to give him a hug. Instead, she stood there and smiled. She was wearing makeup and looked different.

"Hi," she said. "Do you have any luggage?"

Crosby nodded at his overnight bag. "Just this."

"Good, I have a meeting and if we don't hurry I'm going to be late. Sorry, I don't have time to drop you anywhere."

"That's okay. I'm just glad I'm riding with you instead of Kelly."

"You make him sound like an ogre and you're not giving him a chance, Devrin."

"He had his chance. Who's the meeting with?"

"His name is Dr. Gebo. Careful how you pronounce it. It's Jêe-bow. I hear he's sensitive about that. He's a retired weapons designer from Los Alamos."

"Any new developments?"

"Kelly left for Utah two hours ago. A general aviation pilot is missing from Las Vegas. He flew a private charter from Fillmore Municipal, in Utah on Friday evening. The description of the passenger matches Amil."

•   •   •

Gerald McMullen peered out of the jet's window at the cruise ships lined up at the Port of Miami. Somewhere, down there in a hotel room, not far from the port, was Katie Froscher. He doubted if she would remember him and that was good. If she recognized him, or learned that he had tracked her through her mother and her assistant, he would come across looking like a stalker. That was the last thing he wanted.

The Fasten Seat Belt sign dinged and he tightened his. This was an expensive gamble; one that might lead nowhere or the start of the best week of his life. He remembered Katie's eyes peering through the crack of her window and the smile she had given him. What was said that night applied now more than ever. It was a matter of faith.

•   •   •

The meeting was in the lounge at the Denver Sheraton. The lighting was low and a musician was playing "Blue Moon" on a piano across the room. Doctor Urban L. Gebo, Ph.D. was in his mid eighties by Marti's estimate. The black leather chair seemed to swallow his elderly body, but his mind was as sharp as a twenty-year-old. Matthews and Crosby sat across from him, their matching leather chairs pulled close. On the coffee table between them were drinks; a brandy and water for Dr. Gebo, a Diet Coke for Matthews and a Hazelnut Latte for Crosby. In Marti's lap was a thick manila folder containing photos and technical data reports on the blast findings. Since this was her interview, Crosby sat back and watched.

"Thank you for agreeing to see us, Doctor," Matthews said. "I hope you didn't have to travel out of your way?"

"Not at all. I have a daughter who lives south of here in Englewood," Gebo said, his voice scratchy but his diction clear. "My wife and I spent the Thanksgiving holidays with her family. We saw the mushroom cloud from her home. That's when I called."

"How long did you work at Los Alamos?" Matthews opened her notepad.

"First, let's establish the ground rules, shall we? When I retired from the military, I signed an oath not to divulge secrets about the operations I took part in. I take that oath seriously. I'll answer general questions, without going into specifics on classified projects."

"That's understood, sir. We are trying to find out how our unknown suspects were able to acquire this bomb."

"I will help however I can, but I would appreciate something in return. A favor."

"What kind of favor?"

"I want to see the case file. I have spent most of my life designing weapons and I don't have very many years left. I need to know if my research was responsible for this weapon."

Matthews and Crosby exchanged glances. "We'll see if that can be arranged," Matthews said, "but we can't promise anything."

"In answer to your question, I worked at the Los Alamos facility for forty years. I was a physicist assigned to the Trinity test bomb, part of the Manhattan Project. I retired in the late eighties, but was asked to come back as a consultant. I missed the work, so I agreed."

"Was the consulting work at Los Alamos?"

"No. It was at Oak Ridge, Tennessee, and Batavia, Illinois."

"Can you tell us what you did there?" Matthews asked.

"I'm afraid that's still classified. In the interest of time, why don't you tell me what you've learned so far at the Dillon site?"

Matthews opened the file and handed the photos to Dr. Gebo. "The yield was about twelve kilotons. The hypocenter was located at a bank near the center of town. The Los Alamos team found no radioactive trace elements and they've ruled out uranium and plutonium as the fissionable materials."

Gebo nodded as he flipped through the photos. "What was the size of the package?"

"The package?" Crosby asked. "You mean the bomb or its container?"

"The bomb. How big was it?"

"We're not sure," Matthews said. "It may have been as small as a radio, but we think the radio was actually a transmitter linked to a truck bomb parked outside."

"A radio? That's interesting." Gebo studied one of the aerial photos for a moment and placed it on the table. "Tell me, Dr. Matthews, the men who came to you from Los Alamos, have any of them suggested that this was a truck bomb?"

Matthews considered this. "No, they haven't."

Gebo seemed to be expecting that reply. "Do they shake their heads, stand around and look at each other?"

"As a matter of fact, they do."

"And they offer few suggestions, correct?"

"That's right."

"They know what it is, don't they?" Crosby said.

"No." Gebo swirled his drink in the snifter. "But they know what it isn't. That's half the solution."

"Do you know?" Matthews said.

"Perhaps."

A noisy group of tall girls entered the lounge and sat at the bar. They appeared to be part of a college basketball team that had slipped past their coach for a nightcap.

Dr. Gebo eyed their long legs with a grin before continuing. "Did these men happen to mention anything about cold fusion?"

Matthews straighten in her chair. "Yes, they did."

Gebo smiled, sipped his drink and rubbed the moisture from his lips with a napkin. "What *exactly* did they tell you?"

"That a cold fusion device has never been tested, but it would account for the lack of radioactive fallout. They also said that science has been unable to isolate a reliable cold fusion process."

"That's correct." Gebo put down his drink. "They never will. It's *bullshit!* Something we dreamed up to scare the Russians. We became quite creative for the CIA and other counter-intelligence agencies. Majestic-12 was such a project. It was classified as Ultra Black, and they leaked just enough to make Stalin believe we had captured an alien spacecraft. Brilliant scheme. It worked so well we even convinced Eisenhower. He poured so much funding into the project that we continued the ruse for over forty years."

"What's Ultra Black mean?" Crosby asked.

"Ultra-secret. Things I doubt even the Presidents knew. I find it interesting how secrets we once swore to protect with our lives, are now considered entertainment on the Sci-Fi Channel. My grandkids are into that sort of thing. Have you watched the *Star Trek* series by any chance?"

Crosby grew frustrated by the digression. "I liked the original series and the *Next Generation.*"

"So did we." Gebo took a long sip of brandy and returned the snifter to its coaster. "It's interesting how its creator, Mr. Roddenberry, based his theories on *real* science. I recall one particular episode where Kirk and Scotty had to destroy a giant amoeba with a magnetic bottle. It's amazing how creative the writing was for its time. Very little bullshit went into the making of that show."

"What are you getting at, Doctor?" Matthews said.

"Just think about it." He smiled and looked at his watch. "Well, it's getting late."

Crosby gave Marti a concerned look.

"My wife and daughter are meeting me downstairs for dinner. I believe we're staying here tonight. Could we speak again in the morning? I could join you in the restaurant for coffee at ten."

"That would be fine, Doctor."

"Good. I'll see you then. Now if you'll excuse me, I'm going to indulge these old eyes on those young legs as I make my exit."

Crosby helped the doctor to his feet and Gebo slowly walked a few steps before looking back. "I believe this hotel has Internet access. Perhaps later I'll try to look up the name of that *Star Trek* episode. A search on the subject, positrons, will be an excellent place to start."

"Goodnight, Doctor," Crosby and Matthews said in unison.

As soon as Dr. Gebo was out of earshot Crosby turned to Matthews. "Positrons? What's that?"

Matthews shrugged. "Who knows?"

"He's either senile or has watched way too much *Star Trek*."

"I not sure, but I think he just told us what they were working on at Oak Ridge, without really telling us."

CHAPTER 9

MARQUESAS

Sunday

"El hombre gordo desea una exposición en 11:25," Stalker read aloud into the receiver. "Llamada de—"

"In English please," Christian Luther said.

Stalker translated. "The Fat Man desires an exhibition at 11:25. Voyeurs call, 1-424-3314, 2-382-0991."

"He's used the same code."

"Probably didn't expect us to stumble across it so quickly."

"Where did you find it?"

"The personals section of this morning's *El Nuevo Herald*. It's the Spanish language edition of the *Miami Herald*. The same ad was in the Miami edition of *Craig's List*."

"You're reading the personal columns of every newspaper in the world?"

"A child could find something that obvious," Stalker said.

"So much for our team of experts. Where is the location?"

"The Marquesas Keys, thirty miles west of Key West. The ad might be directed at our Cuban clients since the Marquesas are less than ninety miles from Havana."

"Is there an airport?"

"The closest one is in Key West. The Marquesas are an uninhabited game reserve."

"That location is as vague as Dillon. I'm sending Raptor."

"That would be risky," Stalker said.

"Why?"

"It's too late. He's long gone by now and the bomb could be anywhere on those islands. Today is November 25th so the 11:25 is probably the date *and* time. It might detonate at 11:25 this morning or tonight. Who knows? It could even be this afternoon at 1:04 p.m."

"Why then?"

"It's when he took out Dillon. Maybe it's significant."

"What do you suggest?"

"Have Raptor wait until after two p.m. That will give him nine hours to search the area."

"The earliest Raptor could get there would be five or six p.m."

"Then forget it. That's too late. I've ordered a set of satellite photos covering the past forty-eight hours. The only way on or off that island is by helicopter or boat. If it's a boat, he had to take it somewhere."

"Good idea. Why didn't you do that at Dillon?"

"The only satellite shot of Dillon that day was taken after the blast."

"If the perp knew that, then why pick an island covered by dozens of satellites?"

"Maybe this time he wants to show off."

• • •

Crosby awoke to knocking at 7:30 a.m. and realized that he was in his hotel room at the Sheraton. The knocking was coming from the door to the adjoining room where Dr. Matthews was staying.

"Crosby, are you decent?"

He slipped on his trousers, before unlocking the door. "Come in," he said. "What's up?"

She was dressed in jeans and a sweatshirt. "I just heard from Kelly. He wants you to meet him at the downtown private aircraft terminal at 10:30 this morning. I'm having coffee in the restaurant with Dr. Gebo at ten. I don't know how long he'll talk, so here are the car keys."

"What's up with Kelly?"

"He's wants to go over what they found on Amil."

"He could do that over the phone."

"He said the forensics team found something in the getaway car that you guys need to look at."

"What is it?"

"I don't know, but it must be important. Don't forget to come back for me, okay? Oh, one more thing. I did a web search last night on that *Star Trek* episode. It was entitled "The Immunity Syndrome" and the magnetic bottle Doctor Gebo referred to contained anti-matter."

Crosby laughed. "It's science fiction, Marti."

"Not anymore. I looked up positrons and found what Dr. Gebo was implying. A positron is an antiparticle. It's the mirror image of an electron. In 1994, Swiss scientists were able to capture enough antiparticles to create a molecule; antihydrogen. They've since created hundreds of those."

"Why is it important?"

"When a particle of matter comes in contact with a particle of antimatter, they annihilate each other with one hundred percent efficiency. The energy released is far greater than what we get from splitting atoms."

"You're kidding? They were building an antiparticle bomb?"

"Apparently. It would require a magnetic containment trap, just as he said. That might be what Dr. Gebo's team was working on at Oak Ridge."

"Rankin will never buy it. He already thinks I'm crazy."

"Don't mention it until I've had a chance to do more research. I'll print out the articles as proof."

"Marti, do you believe it's possible?"

She nodded. "I do. This isn't bull, Devrin. It's *real* science. The article said the energy released from a teaspoon of antimatter could vaporize a city the size of Los Angeles."

•   •   •

Doctor Matthews and Doctor Gebo sat in the corner of the restaurant alone, their breakfast plates and coffee cups in front of them. Gebo's wife, knowing they had business to discuss, had retreated to her room to pack.

"You seem disturbed," Gebo said. "You must have found our *Star Trek* episode."

"Yes. Scary stuff. How long has the government had this weapon?"

"They don't." Gebo took a sip of coffee. "It was President's Reagan's dream to build a satellite defense system; Star Wars, as it became known. But he also wanted to make nuclear weapons obsolete. I was involved in the search to find a replacement. However, the project was abandoned."

"Why?"

"Let's just say that our research indicated a problem with stockpiling."

"So you couldn't store it." Matthews pulled the puzzle together in her mind. "Was it unstable?"

Gebo gave a slight nod. "The Super-conducting Super Collider was killed by Congress in 1993; the project heads disbanded, and all our research destroyed . . . supposedly."

"So, 'supposedly' must mean that some of it escaped the shredder. Do you believe our terrorist stole it?"

"Something big took out Dillon," he said. "It wasn't a meteorite. It wasn't nuclear fission and it certainly wasn't conventional. You tell me."

"An antiparticle bomb?"

He shrugged. "I couldn't say."

"Okay, let's assume that a terrorist was able to build such a weapon. How big would it be?"

"We're speaking hypothetically?"

"Sure."

"I imagine the actual device would be about the size of a thermos."

"Like a coffee thermos?"

"Yes," he said. "About sixty milligrams of the material would be sufficient."

"Jeeze, that's like the size of a grain of sand."

"It's one of the advantages." Gebo lowered his voice. "This isn't bullshit, Doctor. One gram of antimatter contains about the same amount of energy as twenty-three space shuttle fuel tanks."

"*Great God!* Why was it abandoned?"

"The container would have to be kept extremely cold," he said.

"How cold?"

"Minus four hundred fifty-two degrees Fahrenheit. Liquid helium would serve as a suitable refrigerant."

"That's almost absolute zero," she said grasping the conception. "At that temperature, molecules don't move around."

"You certainly wouldn't want antimolecules to come anywhere near their counterparts."

"Is there anyone in your former team who had the capability of building such a device?"

"That question is not hypothetical, Doctor."

"We're trying to catch a killer. If what you're saying is true, Dillon may have only been a dry run for something bigger."

Gebo scratched his chin. "At one time, there were two. Very talented. Together, they pioneered the electromagnetic thermos concept. They were perfecting its refrigeration system when the project was terminated."

"How can I contact them?"

"They're both deceased."

"How?"

"One was murdered by someone attempting to burglarize his apartment. The other was killed when his car skidded on ice and plunged off a bridge into a frozen river. They were both brilliant young men; a terrible tragedy."

"I need their names, Doctor."

"I'm sorry that's confidential, but I'm sure the FBI has access to death certificates and CSI reports from around three years ago."

Matthews smiled. "Doctor, one of the websites stated that a teaspoon of antimatter could wipe out an entire city. Is that true?"

"A teaspoon? Gebo shook his head. "No."

Matthews relaxed. "Well, I didn't think—"

"I believe it would be far worse than that."

"What could be worse?"

Gebo took a moment to think. "It might come close to Mount Mazama, which exploded seven thousand years ago."

"I've never heard of it."

"Today it's called Crater Lake in Oregon. The explosion vaporized twelve cubic miles of an eleven thousand-foot mountain, leaving a crater, two thousand feet deep."

Matthews was too stunned to reply.

"Mt. Saint Helens, by comparison, blew only a half a cubic mile from its summit," Gebo added. "So you see it would only take *one* mistake."

•   •   •

Agent Kelly Rankin arrived at eleven a.m. aboard a single engine Piper Cub at the downtown Denver airport. Crosby was waiting in Matthews' rented sedan beside a chain-link gate outside the old terminal building. The air had turned bitter cold and the overcast sky spit a snow flurry here and there. The temperature in Washington had been seventy-eight when he left and in his haste to pack, Crosby had neglected to bring his down parka. The freezing air cut through his Hoover Blues like a knife.

"You're late," Crosby said the moment Rankin climbed in the passenger seat.

"It's a private plane," Rankin said. "They don't follow strict schedules. Hell, Devrin, you got it hot enough in here?"

"Would you rather walk?"

"No, but that reminds me of what the snail said when he crawled onto a turtle's back."

"I'm not in the mood for jokes, Kelly."

Rankin grinned and said, "Wheeee!"

Crosby shook his head. "What have you found on Amil?"

"This is how he's moving around." Rankin nodded at the private plane. "I tried it and the security is almost nonexistent. The pilot, Troy Dills, left Fillmore Airport around five p.m. on Friday and filed a flight plan to Las Vegas. Filmore is right off Interstate 15, about thirty miles north of where it intersects with I-70. The flight arrived in Vegas at seven p.m. and both men drove away in Dills' car. He lives in Vegas and owns a single engine Cessna, which he keeps at a grass strip near his house. Both Dills and his plane are missing."

"Any chance Dills and the bomber are the same person?"

"No. He flew up from Vegas on Friday to pick up the fare. We got Amil's alias off the rental manifest at Fillmore Municipal Airport. Amil claimed to be Yousif al-Saad, a diplomat, and he had credentials to prove it."

"A diplomat? So customs couldn't check his diplomatic pouch."

"Right. Perfect way to get a bomb into the country. We ran the alias through the computer and got a hit. Yousif al-Saad is listed as a diplomatic clerk assigned to the Iranian embassy in Mexico City. I figure Amil was headed there and made Dills an offer to fly him across the Mexican border."

"Probably an offer he couldn't refuse," Crosby said.

"He'll turn up dead. I filed a formal request to meet with the Iranian Ambassador in Mexico, but it will never happen."

"Anything on the car?"

"No tan Hondas at Fillmore or Provo Municipal. Amil and the unsub must have split up. We have a list of cars coming in from the airports, bus and train stations within three hundred miles west of Denver. Going through each one will be tedious."

"We should check homicides near Fillmore, Salt Lake and the Las Vegas area," Crosby said. "Amil's bank robber may have exhausted his usefulness."

• • •

The taxi pulled up outside the Carnival terminal at the port of Miami a little before three p.m. Passengers were pouring out of tour buses and placing their luggage on carts color-coded for each ship. Several huge cruise ships lined the dock as if contending for size and status. Two of these sported the red-winged funnels of the Carnival line.

Gerald McMullen paid the taxi driver, unloaded his lime green luggage, and carried it inside. Everything, right down to his underwear and socks, was new. He had spent the morning in Miami buying shorts, shirts, swimsuits, snorkels, flippers, suntan oils and evening attire. If he was going to meet this girl, he wanted to look his best.

He had been assured that there were plenty of staterooms available on both of the Carnival ships. One would leave at four p.m. for the western Caribbean, the other at five p.m. for the eastern route, but he still wasn't sure which ship Katie Froscher was aboard. Armed with the information Katie's assistant had given him, he approached the ticket desk. The majority of the passengers already held tickets and he was surprised to find the line short.

"Welcome to Carnival, the most popular cruise line in the world," the ticket agent said to Gerald. "My name is Desha. How may I help you?"

"I'd like to book one of today's cruises."

"Which tour?"

"I don't know. I'm supposed to meet my girlfriend aboard, but I'm not sure which cruise she booked. She said the ship's name sounded like 'winning a game.'"

"Winning?" Desha frowned. "Well, we have the *Victory*, leaving for the western Caribbean at four, or we have the *Triumph*, leaving for the eastern Caribbean at five. Which of those best fits your winning description?"

Oh that's great. "Could you perhaps look up her name for me? It's Kathryn Froscher."

"I'm sorry, sir. We're not allowed to give out that information. Once you're aboard you could ask at the Purser's office, but you'll have to buy a ticket first."

"What if I'm on the wrong ship?"

"I suppose you could come back and we could switch you to the other ship, but the biggest problem is your luggage. Once it's tagged, it's going on whichever ship you choose first."

"That's a serious problem." Gerald gave her his best beaten-puppy-dog frown. "Look, if I get on the wrong ship I could easily miss the opportunity of a lifetime. Is there anything you can do to help me, *please*."

The agent glanced around. "Was her ticket pre-purchased?"

"Yes."

She nodded across the room. "Then you could use that phone to call Guest Services. They might be able to tell you which ship she's on, but you'll need to hurry. The *Victory* is leaving in about forty minutes."

• • •

"Katie?" Ruth Froscher said. "Where are you?"

"Hi, Mom," Katie said into her cell phone. "What's up?"

"Well, I've been trying to reach you for three days, honey. I called your apartment and left a dozen messages. I was getting worried. I wish you would tell me when you're going off for the weekend."

"I'm fine, Mom. I'm also *thirty-two*."

"Someone called last Friday and was trying to get in touch with you."

"Male or female?"

"Male. He said he was an old friend and sounded nice, but I can't remember his name. I didn't give him your address, just your work number."

Katie was concerned, but it was probably one of her old boyfriends she had dumped in high school. "Okay, I'll check my voice mail at work. I bet it's Kevin from Denton High."

"Wasn't he the football player? You always dated such sweet boys."

Sweet? A groping pervert. If Mom only knew what half those guys were like, she would have locked me in my room.

"Where are you, dear?"

Katie looked out across the wake of the cruise ship. The skyscrapers of Miami were disappearing on the horizon. "Oh, I'm near the beach." Not exactly a lie. "I just needed to get away for awhile."

"I was scared to death that you had gone skiing in Colorado. Did you hear about all of those poor people in that town?"

"Just what I've read in the newspapers," Katie said. "Have the police learned anything?"

"The morning news said it might be a terrorist attack. Can you imagine? They used an atomic bomb. I just don't know what the world is coming to."

"You said 'they?' Was there more than one?"

"I assumed so. Don't terrorists work in groups?"

"I wouldn't know. Do they have any suspects?"

"It didn't say, but the headlines have dubbed the terrorist *The Fourth Angel.*"

"Did they say why?"

"No. Isn't that a strange name?"

Katie thought for a moment. *What in the world had Lucy done?*

"The other reason I called, was I need you to come by when you get back in town. Your dad's estate lawyer called this morning. He was moving files when a note, in your dad's handwriting, fell out of his will. He claims he missed it because it was at the bottom of the envelope."

"What does it say?"

"There's a line saying how much he loved us—m" Ruth sniffled. "—and he requested that his remains be buried at Arlington National Cemetery alongside his crew members. There is even a receipt for the burial plot. I called the Arlington director this morning and he's confirmed everything. Your father made the arrangements before he got sick."

"But you wanted us all together, Mom. Chuck is buried in Denton. Where would we bury you and me?"

"I've thought about it. Your dad and brother have been here almost three years and it doesn't make things any easier. Dad gave us the best years of his life. I feel we should honor his last request."

"Are you sure, Mom?"

"Yes, but I couldn't bear to watch them dig up his casket."

"I'll take care of everything. Don't worry about it."

"Since it was the lawyer's mistake, I think he should pick up the cost of the exhumation, don't you?"

"*Right.* That's a snowball's chance in hell."

"I know. Well, I'll cash in a bond to take care of it and the transportation costs."

"No, Mom. Let me take care of it. I want to do this for Daddy."

"But it's lots of money, dear. Are you sure you can afford it?"

"Mom, it's okay," she reassured. "I'll handle it."

• • •

It was late afternoon by the time the *Island Breeze* reached a spot of ocean ten miles southwest of the Marquesas. Lucy cut the engine and yelled for Carlos to come up on deck.

Carlos emerged, bare-chested with a pair of swimming trunks hanging on his waist. "Señorita, why have we stopped?"

"This is as far as we go."

Carlos glanced back toward the ring of islands still visible in the distance. "Here? But we still see the islands, no? You say explosion would be huge. You play me for a joke, right?"

She dropped down the ladder. "It's no joke, Carlos." She handed him a piece of paper and went inside the cabin.

"What is this?" He looked at the note.

Lucy emerged from below wearing men's shorts and the same short blonde wig she had used while on the beach. "Our coordinates. The water is plenty deep here. Get on your radio and make the call." Lucy moved to the back of the boat.

"But we are still within U.S. territory. International waters are a few miles south. Why are we stopping here?"

"Covering our tracks." Lucy tried to lift the section of fiberglass deck covering the engine compartment. "Carlos, give me a hand with this."

Carlos helped her lift the heavy cover. They stood it up and let it fall over upside-down onto the deck. She positioned it partially over the opening.

"Why you do this?"

"What does it look like, Carlos? I'm creating an oil slick."

"Why?"

"Because it will look like engine trouble."

"Engine trouble," he looked at the islands. "How you say? Sons of bitch!"

Lucy smiled. "Relax, Carlos. The engine is fine." Lucy got down on her stomach and leaned over into the compartment. Carlos watched as she dipped a plastic pitcher into the oily bilge water. She stood and poured it over the side of the boat, the oil forming a thin colored sheen on the ocean's surface.

"Why you do that?"

"It's for them." Lucy pointed skyward. "What does it look like we're doing, Carlos?"

"*Ah!*" His eyes lit up. "*Bese mi asno.* We're *working* on the boat."

"*Exactly!*"

"That's why you left the seaweed on the beach. You one smart hembra."

Lucy smiled. "How about scattering some tools around the opening, okay? I need to start blowing up the dolls."

"Dolls?"

"Yeah, the inflatable sex dolls."

He gave her a strange look. "To aspire mi dick?"

"*No*," she said in disgust. "*Men*. Only one train of thought." She shook her head. "They are life size, Carlos. We dress them in our clothes and leave them on the boat. Comprendo?"

"*¡Oh!*"

• • •

Gerald McMullen sat on the edge of his tiny bed, in his tiny cabin on the Riviera Deck and stared out his tiny porthole at the ocean. At least he had a porthole. Two sets of tickets lay beside him. One set for the *Triumph* and one for the *Victory* and each had cost him $749.00 plus a surcharge of half that amount for having the cabin to himself. He had taken Desha's advice to call Guest Services, but had twice been placed on eternal hold. With time running out, he purchased tickets for both ships with the assurance that he might be able to get a credit, or at least some of his money refunded, on whichever cruise he didn't take. At the last minute, he had called Mandy Davis, Katie's executive assistant, and given her the names of the two ships. She was pretty sure the 'winning name' had been *Victory* and not *Triumph*. Thus, he sat aboard the *Victory*, with a $2250 hole in his credit card. What irked him was that he could have taken the cancelled cruise with Renee, and had one of the finest suites aboard for the same amount.

There was a knock at the door. His room steward was standing in the hall with Gerald's lime green luggage. At least he had gotten on the right ship.

• • •

They picked up Dr. Matthews at the hotel and headed toward the FBI lab in Denver. None of them had eaten lunch and since Crosby also skipped breakfast, he was especially hungry. Their meeting was scheduled for noon, and while they drove, Matthews briefed them on what she had learned from Dr. Gebo, careful not to mention antimatter in front of Rankin.

"Why couldn't Dr. Gebo just tell you the names?" Crosby said.

"He felt bound by his security oath."

"Forget the death certificates," Rankin said. "They'll give you the cause of death and nothing on the circumstances surrounding it. Start with the police and sheriffs departments in Oak Ridge and Chicago. Have them check the accident reports for cars plunging into frozen rivers. It couldn't be that many. The burglary-murder will be tougher to track down."

"There are no frozen rivers in Tennessee," Crosby said. "I'd put my money on Oak Ridge for the burglary."

When they arrived, the lab was actually a converted garage with a roll-up door. The car sitting in the middle of the lab was a late model Chevy Lumina, gray ash obscuring much of the brown paint. Handprints in the ash were all over the sides and windows, where spectators at the site had peered inside to see if the passengers had made it out alive. The windows were cracked and the plastic lens covering the headlights and turn signals were sagging where they had melted in the intense heat of the flash. All four doors were now open and a team of forensic experts with hoods were going over every inch of it.

A man in a white lab coat approached and introduced himself to Rankin and Crosby as Professor Brandon Auten. "A real nightmare," he said, as though the conversation started on the second page of his thoughts. "So far we've recovered nearly two hundred samples." He led the three of them over to a microscope and invited Matthews to have a look.

"Looks human," she said peering into the sample, "very dry; brittle; about two inches in length. Probably was bleached with cut marks at one end. A broken loop on the other end." She looked over the scope. "This hair was knotted. A wig?"

"Looks that way," Auten said. "Question is; did it come from your perp?"

"Why not?" Rankin asked.

"The car is a rental, so we've got multiple fingerprints all over the inside, fibers, mud, even dog hair. The rental company didn't spend much time cleaning their cars between fares. We've identified only the prints from the terrorist, Amil Yaspar. We're running the rest of the prints through the index."

"Any way to narrow it down?" Crosby asked.

"I need negative comparison hair samples and fingerprints from Ms. Shultz, her daughter and from the employees at the rental company. Given this much evidence, it's going to be impossible to identify everything. The bank video helped. We found some olive green polyester fibers that are consistent with the unknown suspect's

suit. Also strands of wig hair in the floor of the rear seat, and this—"
He held up an evidence bag containing a single hair. "Blonde.
Human. No root. Nine inches in length."

"A woman's?" Crosby said.

"Could be," Auten said, "but no telling how long it's been there.
If Shultz's daughter was playing in the back seat, if may have come
from her."

"Is she blonde?" Crosby asked Rankin.

"Who knows?"

•   •   •

"Raptor, where are you," Stalker said, using the scrambled line.

"En route to Miami," Harold Sanders said. "We're securing the
VP's location."

"I thought our Iranian clients accepted the terms of your black-
market negotiator."

"They did." Sanders was strapped in his seat aboard a commercial
jet. He made sure no other passengers were within earshot. "We have
their deposit and Scholar has scheduled delivery as soon as the device
is ready."

"Then why am I looking at a photograph of Amil Yaspar standing
in a bank in Dillon, Colorado?"

"When was it taken?"

"Friday, about ten minutes before the town vaporized."

"Where did you get the photo?"

"Our mole at the FBI. The bank's security video was transmitted
to the main branch just prior to the blast. His image was lifted from
it."

Why would Amil be in a bank in Colorado?

"The explosion was triggered by a radio transmitter in a briefcase.
He used it to rob the bank. Sound familiar?"

The sun was streaming in through the jet's windows, illuminating
the cabin with a yellow glow. Sanders recalled the file they had
recovered from the President's safe. Chuck Froscher's design had
described the device as being smaller than a shoebox, triggered by a
radio transmitter.

"Amil had someone else with him. Not our negotiator and he
looked somewhat like one of our former designers. You're sure
Froscher is dead?"

"I was there, remember?" Sanders thought back to the man he

had left on the floor in an apartment in Oak Ridge, Tennessee. His own family had identified the body. "He's dead. Run the photo against our facial recognition program?"

"Too grainy. We're trying to enhance the image."

"But you're sure the other one was Amil?"

"Yes."

Sanders thought for a moment. "So the bank was a demonstration."

"Just as he did in Madrid. Rob a bank. Wait for the alarm to attract a big crowd and boom. Surprise, surprise, surprise, as Gomer Pyle would say. Only this time the boom was a hell of a lot bigger than Madrid."

"So that's why he chose Dillon. The mountains were the only way they could get away in time."

"Precisely," Stalker said, "and at this moment, they are standing on the back of a fishing boat, ten miles south of the Marquesas Keys."

"You're sure?"

"No. The satellite is directly overhead, so all I see are tops of heads. But there are two of them, at the coordinates posted in the ad, and this morning they had a rather large cooler aboard. Now it's missing."

"Give me the coordinates. I can be in Key West in three hours."

"No need," Stalker said. "They're not going anywhere."

"Why?"

"There's an oil slick. It appears that their boat is having some engine trouble."

•   •   •

Dr. Matthews and Crosby spent the afternoon working the phones in a borrowed office at the FBI regional headquarters in Denver, their gray metal desks facing each other.

"Yes, sir. It's a Cessna 152," Crosby said into the receiver. "Serial number N1978R. I need to find out how far it can fly before refueling." He looked across at Dr. Matthews who also had a receiver to her ear. As she listened, she took a bite of her salad and licked the Ranch dressing from her lips. *Such beauty wasted on someone like Kelly Rankin.* Crosby's lunch, a half-eaten Big Mac, was in his right hand. He glanced down at his belly, thought about the 570 calories and tossed the burger in the wastebasket. "What's the difference between long range and regular tanks? I see. I don't know which kind it had. Give me both. Yes, I'll hold."

"Any luck?" Matthews said, giving her phone a rest.

"He's checking on the Cessna's range. I'm hoping they refueled somewhere between Vegas and Mexico."

"Why Mexico?"

"Just a hunch. Any luck on your end?"

"The police department in Oak Ridge was cooperative. They're pulling any burglaries with a homicide within the past three years and faxing them. I can't seem to get in touch with the right person in Chicago. Maybe Kelly can work his cop charms on them."

"Where's Kelly?"

"He's at Hair and Fiber, running down those negative comparisons."

"Yes, I'm still here," Crosby said into the phone. "Only twenty-six gallons? Is that all?" Crosby jotted down the figures. "So, 315 nautical miles on a standard tank at 8000 feet, 540 nautical miles on the long range tank. Yes, I've got it. Do range and flight time vary depending on altitude? I see. Thank you. He hung up the phone and used a dividing compass to measure out three hundred miles on the map's scale.

Matthews punched figures into her calculator. "Wait a minute, Devrin. You didn't convert the nautical miles into statute." She held up the calculator's results. "It's 362 statute miles. Assuming he wouldn't run on an empty tank, you need to figure on about 350 miles, not 300."

Crosby rubbed his face and sighed, "Of course. Too many figures in my head at once." He drew a circle around Las Vegas at 350 miles and another at 525 miles. It was a tremendous area encompassing both San Francisco and Los Angeles to the west, San Diego and Phoenix to the south and Santa Fe to the east.

Even Dr. Matthews was surprised. "That's one hell of a haystack to poke around in."

Crosby nodded. "Especially when the needle can move."

• • •

Harold Sanders' flight didn't arrive in Key West until eight p.m. and it took another hour before he found what he needed. The helicopter was an old Bell 47-B Sioux with pontoons, the type used by the MASH units during the Korean War, but the only thing that Sanders cared about was the searchlight mounted under it. The house had a faded sign in the front yard that read, "Island Helicopter Tours."

"Sorry, señor," the Hispanic pilot replied. "She has no navigational computer and the sun, it has gone down, no? Come back in the morning."

"I need it tonight." Sanders flashed his Secret Service badge. "It's a matter of national security."

The pilot studied the badge. "Secret Service? Qué es ésto?"

"It's about a boatload of counterfeit money. Either rent me the chopper, or I'll have Homeland Security commandeer it."

"Sí, no problem. But navigation? It is a big ocean with no landmarks at night."

"My phone has GPS."

The pilot considered this. "There are still many risks and expenses to consider, señor. Maintenance and fuel is expensive, no?"

"I'll give you five hundred dollars per hour."

"Cash?"

"Sí," Sanders said.

"Hell *sí!* Let's go."

●   ●   ●

Matthews and Crosby returned from dinner to find Kelly Rankin looking over the circles and pins on the map that Devrin placed on the bulletin board. They had spent the afternoon calling the airports, each marked with a pin, to see if Troy Dills' Cessna had refueled there Friday evening. So far they had found nothing.

"Where have you been?" Matthews asked Rankin.

"I drove up to Breckenridge to track down Ms. Schultz and her daughter. I found them in the ski lodge and got hair and fiber samples from the clothing they wore on Wednesday. I also got samples from the Denver rental agency personnel."

"You've been busy," Matthews said.

"Was the Schultz girl blonde?" Crosby said.

"She had blonde highlights. It's probably hers." He continued to examine the map. "You skipped over LA and San Diego. Why?"

"He probably stuck with the small airports to avoid the security. We'll run those if nothing turns up."

"Why two circles?"

"We don't know if Troy Dills' plane had long range tanks or standard."

"Why not ask someone who's serviced Dills' plane."

"He kept it at his private airstrip," Matthews said. "Where do you take an airplane for an oil change?"

"The airport that does his charters. While you're at it, see what type of navigation equipment the plane had."

"I should have thought of that," Crosby said.

"Why?" Matthews said.

"If he had only basic navigation," Crosby explained, "Dills would have followed the interstate highways."

"Good idea, Kelly," Matthews said.

•   •   •

The Global Positioning System application built into Harold Sanders' cell phone converted SV signals into position, velocity, and time from a constellation of satellites located in six inclined orbital planes above the equator. As the helicopter raced toward the last known coordinates of the *Island Breeze*, the GPS program told them precisely where to go. When they arrived at an empty spot of ocean, Sanders called Stalker. "The boat's gone," he said.

"You're in the Keys? Are you out of your mind?" Stalker blasted. "The message said 11:25."

"That gives me over an hour to find them."

"If Amil's boat is anywhere near there, he's as good as dead."

"I want to ask him why he's backing out of our contract. Then I'll *convince* him to show me where the bomb is located."

"You'll never disarm it."

"I don't intend to try. I just want to look at it."

"You're *crazy*."

"Tell me which way the boat was drifting."

"At six p.m. she was drifting northwest at three knots, but listen Raptor, Scholar said the blast radius of that device could be three miles. That means you need to be at least twenty-two miles away when it goes off. You need to get the hell away from there. *Now*."

•   •   •

"Yes, a Cessna 152, serial number N1978R. You have the receipt?" Crosby was on the phone and whispered across the desk at Matthews, "It refueled Friday evening."

"Where?" Matthews had a red pushpin ready in front of the map.

"Yes, sir. Casa Grande Municipal, south of Tempe, Arizona, on Interstate 10. Right, I've got it. Who has the fuel manifest? What's an FBO attendant? I see. Could you put him on the line? Thanks, I'll hold."

"That's two hundred ninety-four miles," Matthews said, punching her calculator. "Dills must have standard tanks."

Crosby nodded. "Yes, you're the fixed based operator? How many gallons? Nineteen paid in cash. Can you give me a description of the pilot? And his passenger?"

Matthews had a pencil and ruler and was drawing a line on the map from Vegas to Casa Grande.

"Are you sure? Someone from the Tempe field office will pick those up. Thank you very much." Crosby hung up.

"What's wrong, Crosby?"

"There was only one person aboard the plane."

"Was it Amil or Dills?"

"Sounded like Amil."

•   •   •

Katie Froscher sat at the Normandy Bar at the aft end of Carnival's cruise ship *Victory* sipping her margarita and typing on her laptop computer. The open sky dome above her gave her computer a clear connection through her sat-phone to the satellite above. The website she entered required 128-bit encryption and four passwords. The homepage contained no fancy graphics, only instructions on how to bid and a brief description of each device for sale.

She clicked on the icon entitled Little Boy. There were many bids ranging from five figures to eight. The "shoebox" design was most popular with the countries that sponsored terrorism. The Iranians and North Koreans led the bidding with the Syrians a close third.

The second icon, Fat Man, had two pending bids, one from Cuba and the other from Argentina. At this point, neither was over six figures, but that would soon change.

The third icon had no bids as of yet. It was titled The Monster.

Each bid required a twenty-five thousand-dollar nonrefundable deposit through wire transfer to a numbered account in a bank in Grand Cayman. There was already a small fortune in deposits and it would be very tempting to take the money and run, but Katie Froscher knew better. There were bigger fish in the sea and she would gladly fry each one of them.

•   •   •

It took twenty minutes, but they finally found the *Island Breeze*. It had drifted back to within five miles of the Marquesas Keys and all of its lights were out. When the helicopter approached, one of the inflated dolls blew out, carrying the lounge chair with it. As Sanders suspected, the disabled boat was a ruse to cover their true getaway. The pilot bathed the boat in water spray from its rotors as the searchlight explored for evidence of life.

"Can you get me close enough to jump aboard?" Sanders asked.

"Sí señor, but too many antennas to get close enough to pick you up."

"When I'm ready to leave, I'll try to lower the antennas on the bridge. If that doesn't work, I'll jump overboard and swim far enough away for you to extract me."

"Sí señor. Be careful, compadre."

Sanders stood on the right pontoon and lowered himself until he was hanging above the upper bridge. Without hesitation he dropped the six feet to its roof and waved the helicopter clear.

Sanders knew where to look. A trashcan could provide more information than a FBI investigation. From what was missing, he established there had been two of them. There were no tampons, tissues with lipstick smears, or spent condoms and they had eaten three meals while aboard. The empty wine bottle was a cheap brand and they had used paper cups instead of plastic wineglasses. One look at the commode confirmed his suspicions; the lid was up. *Two males.* The rubber dinghy was also missing and the open engine compartment looked staged.

He moved to the bridge and turned the key. The engine cranked immediately. Satisfied that he had found everything, he climbed to the upper bridge and began lowering the antennas. As he did, he noticed an empty trashcan at his feet. Behind it, he found a crumpled piece of paper.

Idiots, he thought. He dropped it into a plastic evidence bag and examined it through the plastic. Scribbled in ballpoint on a napkin, was a rough diagram of the thermos particle trap.

•   •   •

Katie Froscher, sitting at a table near the Sirens' Pool at the very rear of the ship, checked her watch and glanced around to see if anyone was watching. She closed her laptop and took a pair of very dark sunglasses out of her purse. She turned towards the large Lido Deck windows overlooking the rear of the ship, put on the glasses and waited.

• • •

Four decks below, Gerald McMullen was strolling along the promenade of the Lobby Deck, watching the white foam drift by on the black water of the Gulf of Mexico. The promenade was empty with twelve lifeboats hung over the deck, ready for the next encounter with an iceberg. *No chance of that here.* The air was warm, the seas calm and the only breeze was that generated by their speed through the night air. All he needed was a companion.

He leaned on the railing. He had tried to locate Katie in both dining rooms with no luck. Perhaps she had put on a couple hundred pounds since their first encounter, or dyed her hair. Dinner was available twenty-four hours a day, so she might have chosen to eat in her room, or at one of buffets scattered throughout the ship. Tomorrow he would hang out at the main pool on the Lido Deck. He might spot her there, but with three thousand passengers aboard, this wasn't going to be as easy as he thought. If all else failed, he could check with the Purser's Office. He had gone there earlier, but was once again confronted with the prospect of what to say. He imagined knocking on her door, trying to explain how he had once changed her tire, waited three years, and was now chasing her around the Caribbean. Having a door slammed in his face was not the scenario he had hoped for. A better approach would be to find a seat beside her at the pool or a bar, strike up a conversation, and let it build from there. Whatever he did, eventually he would have to reveal the truth. He hoped he would have the chance to do so before she talked with Mandy Davis or her mother.

• • •

Fifty miles to the northeast, Carlos and the woman who had called herself Lucy Harris, stood on the deck of a former Soviet Kilo class submarine that had been acquired by the Argentinean government. Lucy was dressed in jeans and a halter top. Carlos stood beside her. In his hands were two glasses and a bottle of champagne.

"Care for a toast, Señorita?" Carlos said, offering her a glass. Lucy took it. "That depends on your bid."

"That's in the hands of our government, no? Salud, to Fat Man."

"Salud." Lucy clinked their glasses together.

Several high-ranking representatives of their current military regime were also present to witness the event. A white linen tablecloth waved in the breeze as the delegation helped themselves to cocktail shrimp, finger food and glasses of champagne. At the very end of the reception table, beside the dessert tray, were twelve sets of welding goggles.

Carlos refilled their glasses and Lucy offered her own toast. "To *The Fourth Angel*. May her bids be high and her pathway clear."

"*Al Quarto Ángel.*"

• • •

Sanders spotted the rubber dinghy with the searchlight as they flew over the first of the Marquesas Keys islands. The pilot set down the helicopter on the beach near it and kept the throttle up. Raptor checked his watch; 11:10 p.m.; plenty of time. He removed his service revolver from its holster before stepping onto the wet sand. The wash from the rotors whipped at his hair and twisted his coat up around his shoulders. He gave the dinghy a cursory search and felt the engine for signs of warmth. *Cool.* On a hunch, he walked to the edge of a tiny patch of palm trees and aimed his flashlight into the underbrush. The wind blowing through the palm fronds gave the area an eerie feeling of desolation. A glint of metal caught his eye and he made his way towards the reflection. It was a gold coin embossed with the figure of liberty. When he picked up the coin, he realized it was cold and lying on something that had been buried in the sand. Brushing away the sand, he discovered a large cooler covered in frost. Sanders got down on his knees and examined the lid for booby traps. Finding none, he opened it. Inside was a smaller cooler frozen solid and surrounded by dry ice and wires. The liquid helium inside turned the air around him into a frosty mist. Within the tangle of wires he spotted the faint glow of LED timer numbers and wiped the frost from them.

Sanders emerged from the woods in a full gallop. He leapt into the helicopter. "Go, go, go, *go!*"

The pilot pulled back on the stick, lifting the chopper into the air, unaware of the impending danger. "Which way, compadre?"

"Anywhere, just *go*." Sanders sucked in gasps of air, trying to catch up with his pounding heart. He arched his neck looking back at the island, beads of sweat on his forehead.

The pilot glanced at Sanders' anxious face. "Relax, amigo. Whatever happened, you're safe now."

"How fast can she go?" Sanders panted, still out of breath.

"One hundred and twenty knots."

"Can it go any faster?"

"No, this is top speed, señor."

It took Sanders only a few seconds to do the math. Sixteen miles, it wasn't enough. In less than eight minutes the shock wave would blast them from the skies.

CHAPTER 10

LUCY

"Uno minuto. Por favor, ponga encendido sus anteojos," the captain of the Argentinean submarine announced from the conning tower.

Carlos put down his plate of shrimp and translated. "Time to put on the goggles, señorita. One minute to go."

"Don't look at the flash, Carlos," Lucy warned. "It will spoil your night vision and you'll need that for the most beautiful part."

"Sí, señorita. Whatever you say." The two of them put on their goggles and turned facing away from everyone else.

• • •

Harold Sanders looked at his watch. One minute to go and at best they were only fourteen miles from ground zero. He cursed to himself and kicked at an old wadded lunch bag. The floor of the helicopter was a mess. A toolbox lay at his feet and strewn all around it were some used brown paper bags and plastic zip lunch bags. The plastic bags gave him an idea.

"How far is the nearest island?" Sanders asked.

"We passed Barracouta Key," the pilot replied, and pointed forward. "Joe Ingram Key is over there."

"Perfect. Set us down on the beach on the far side."

"But why? There is nothing but palms and sand, no?"

"Just land," he yelled, then softened it with an explanation. "I need to pee."

"Oh sí, señor! El pis!" The pilot chuckled, and descended toward the island.

Sanders retrieved the evidence bag containing the napkin from his pocket. He opened it and dropped in his cell phone. He then placed that bag inside one of the discarded baggies from the floor. Tiny bits of green mold clung to crumbs of old bread, but he didn't care. He grabbed a couple more of the bags, blew air into them and stuffed them into his pockets.

"What are you doing?" the pilot asked as the pontoons touched down on the wet sand.

"Stay here. I'll be right back." Through the plastic Sanders could see the GPS coordinates on his phone. He memorized them and jumped out.

•   •   •

The confused pilot watched as Sanders grabbed the toolbox, dropped it onto the wet sand, blew air into a couple more bags, and stuffed them inside his coat. He ran up the beach about thirty yards then waded out waist deep into the surf carrying the heavy toolbox with him.

"¿Está loco?" the pilot yelled at the man. Only his head was still visible in the surf. With the roll of cash the man had given him, he could afford new tools. He checked his throttle and stretched his legs between the pedals. He was facing north and over his right shoulder he could barely make out the glow of Key West in the east. It had been a long day and he rubbed his eyes with his left hand.

In that moment, the night sky turned as brilliant as the gates of Heaven. The flash was so bright that even through closed eyelids, he could see the bones in his hand. Instinctively he crouched and put his head in the crook of his arm. A moment later the intensity faded. When he opened his eyes, midnight had turned to noon and white billowy clouds could be seen against a purple sky. Towards the Marquesas Key a huge glowing red ball expanded on the horizon, engulfing islands in its path. The pilot spotted a shock wave coming across the surface of the water towards him and knew why the man had taken the bags. He pushed the throttle forward and glanced at where he had last seen his betrayer. "Bastardo!" he yelled, but as expected, the man was gone.

The fireball expanded to three and a half miles across and sent its mushroom shaped cloud into the stratosphere. The helicopter lifted off moments before the heat scorched every tree on the tiny island and ignited the vegetation. It flipped the chopper on its side, rotors sheering off as pieces struck the sand and pierced the fuel tanks. The shock wave followed, bending over every tree and stripping the island of everything except the blackened tree trunks. The chopper's leaking fuel exploded, its wreckage swept out to sea along with the sand, trees and the charred remains of its pilot.

• • •

Ninety miles to the south, an old man wearing green military fatigues puffed on a Cuban cigar and watched from the door of his mansion as the tip of Florida was bathed in light. His older brother's dream was finally within reach. He turned to his secretary. "Hacer la oferta," he said. "Con el nuevo proveedor. Make the bid with the new supplier."

• • •

Even at thirty-five miles distant, Carlos could feel the heat. "Santa Maria, Madre del Dios! Es enorme!"

"Sí," Lucy Harris replied. "Look how it creates layer upon layer of clouds as it rises. Isn't it beautiful?" She looked at the vista as a painter might look upon a favorite landscape.

"Espantosamente. How big?"

"Perhaps ten megatons or more."

Carlos whistled. "All from uno ice chest?"

"The coolers were only to keep it cold. The device itself is no bigger than a two-liter Coke bottle, and the total amount of positron material within is smaller than a gain of sand."

"Gran Día!"

"It's lightweight, portable and inconspicuous with plenty of bang for your buck."

"Sí, but the quantity of bucks, that is the real question, no?"

"Yes. If not you, then someone else. Show's over, Carlos. It's time for you to put your money where your mouth is."

• • •

Gerald McMullen was entering the Seven Seas lobby when the windows facing the outside deck lit up like it was high noon. There was no sound except the collective gasp of thousands of passengers. They had all heard about Dillon, but to see the mushroom cloud in person was terrifying. Most people refused to believe Dillon had been deliberate, preferring to believe it was some horrible accident. Now, as they gathered around Gerald, he heard one of them say, "That's in the direction of Miami."

Dillon was no accident. Finding Katie now seemed unimportant.

•   •   •

Sixteen miles from ground zero, a hand emerged from the sea, feeling the air temperature. Harold Sanders had sat submerged in six feet of water, the toolbox across his lap, sucking breaths of air from his makeshift plastic scuba tanks. The baggies of air had given him seven minutes of precious time and saved his life. When he stumbled onto the scorched beach, both his ears were ringing but he could still hear. The cell phone with its GPS coordinates had remained dry in his pocket, sealed from the seawater by a lazy pilot's refuse. All that remained was for Raptor to regain his composure, wait for the ringing in his ears to subside and phone Stalker with his location.

•   •   •

Dr. Matthews had gone to her room and Crosby was tired as well. He was using the hotel's printer and fax machine to send a report of the day's findings to Lynch's office, when Kelly Rankin came through the lobby.

"Hey, Crosby," Rankin said. He motioned his head toward the bar. "I'm buying."

"It's late, Kelly. I'm turning in."

"One beer isn't going to kill you."

"I quit drinking, Kelly. It's been a rough day."

"Rough? Try flying through the mountains in a single engine plane, then drive two hours up to Breckenridge and back. All you did was work the phones all day, buddy. Come on, I hate drinking alone."

"Fine. I'll sit with you and drink a Coke, but that's all."

Walking toward the bar, Rankin told his latest joke-of-the-day. "Did you hear about the cannibal that *passed* his brother in the woods?"

Crosby shook his head in disgust. "You're really sick, Kelly. You know that?"

"You once had a sense of humor, Crosby. What happened?" He caught the bartender's attention. "Scotch on the rocks."

Crosby sat on one of the barstools. "Getting screwed took all the humor out of me."

"What are you having?"

"A Coke."

"Bring him a bourbon and coke," Rankin told the bartender. "He needs it."

Crosby shook his head at the bartender then thought about Goodtime Charlie's lounge, "Just bring me a draft beer."

"Regular or lite?"

"Doesn't matter."

Rankin raised an eyebrow. "Yeah, what the hell. It's only a beer, right?"

Crosby didn't respond. He took the beer, held it in his palms and smelled it like so many times before. The only thing missing was the piano and a Rubik's Cube.

"I hear you got a lead on Amil's plane." Rankin stirred his drink and Crosby took a few minutes to fill him in.

"So, Amil can fly a Cessna?"

"I should have known. He was part of the initial training group for 9-11, but his notoriety kept him from participating. The pilot's body is probably in the desert somewhere between Las Vegas and Casa Grande Airport."

"Don't beat yourself up. It doesn't change anything."

Crosby huffed. "You're one to talk." A whiff of the beer reminded him of that terrible year after the shooting incident.

"Okay, maybe I came down too hard on Lafayette Park," Rankin confessed, "but you have to admit that conspiracy theory was a bit much."

"Lynch didn't think so."

"Where's your proof? Billy Ray was a closet racist. Open and shut."

"That's the problem with American justice. We always want to blame the madman. The evidence was right there, but no one was willing to look at it. They have their tidy assassination all sewn up and anyone who gives it a second thought is labeled a nut."

"Because you can't convict on conjecture and theory."

Crosby rolled his eyes. "Can we please change the subject?"

"Sure," Rankin motioned for a refill from the bartender. "We struck out in the lab. The blonde hair doesn't match the Shultz girl's."

"Our unsub might still be a female."

"True, but I doubt it. A woman doesn't fit this profile."

"Why not? Five nine isn't unusual and the weight ratio works."

"Less than three percent of bank robbers are women and they hardly ever choose explosives as their weapons. They prefer guns or poisons."

"Until a few years ago, women suicide bombers were unheard of. Now they're common."

"Good point," Rankin said. "I'm not suggesting you forget it, but a long hair can also come from a male. Don't go off on some wild goose chase. Okay?"

"I never do."

Rankin reached for his wallet, took out a couple of bucks and stuck them in the tip jar. "I'm running a little short on cash. How about covering this and I'll find an ATM and catch up with you tomorrow." He downed his drink and headed toward the lobby.

Crosby shook his head. "I should have known," he said, handing his debit card to the bartender.

The bartender gave Crosby the receipt to sign. "I haven't seen that guy pay a tab since he arrived."

"He never does." Crosby signed the ticket and left.

• • •

Monday

"Mr. President?" the national security advisor called, knocking on the bedroom door.

"What is it?" President Lawrence Beasley rubbed his eyes and looked around his bedroom at Camp David. It was 12:04 a.m. He had returned from a flyover of the Dillon site and had gone to bed early.

The advisor opened the door. "We've had another explosion, sir."

The President sat up. "Where?"

"Near Key West, Florida."

"Key West? *Damn it!* Didn't we cancel a golf tournament there this week?"

"Yes, sir but it wasn't scheduled until Wednesday. The explosion wasn't actually in Key West. It was off shore, out in the Gulf."

"What the hell is there?"

"Nothing. Some uninhabited islands."

"Thank *God*. Anyone hurt?"

"It's a tentative report, but there's no mention of causalities."

"Good!" The President rubbed his eyes. "Was this thing as big as Dillon?"

"I'm afraid so, sir. Actually, bigger."

"By how much?"

"Seismic figures indicate in the range of ten to fifteen megatons."

"Hell, Dillon was twelve. That's not much bigger."

"No, sir. Dillon was twelve kilotons; this was *megatons!* That's fourteen hundred times stronger than the Dillon device."

"Good *Lord.* Did this have anything to do with our golf tournament?"

"It's too early to tell, sir."

"I suppose we need a press conference. Where's Norman?"

"Vice President Trexler is still in Miami, sir."

"*Miami.* This is the biggest crisis since 9-11 and he's in Florida?"

"It's not a vacation, sir. The Secret Service has shuttled him around on Air Force One for security. He's in Miami over the weekend with his staff."

"*Right.* How many interns did he take with him this time?"

"Ugh—I wouldn't know, sir."

"Never mind. If that miscreant wants to stay on my ticket in two years, he better start looking presidential. Tell him to get sobered up and do a flyover tomorrow if possible. I want to see his face on the six o'clock news and he better have a damn good statement on how we are going to fight these bastards! You got me?"

"I'll pass that along, sir."

"Contact Christian Luther at Homeland Security. We're back to threat level red."

• • •

Crosby had fallen asleep when he heard pounding on the adjoining door to Marti's room. "Devrin, wake up," he heard her say from behind it. "It's important."

He sat up with a start and pulled on a pair of boxer shorts. He didn't bother to find a shirt before unlatching the door. "What's wrong?"

"Turn on CNN," she said, ignoring his half naked body. "There's been another explosion."

"Where?"

"In the Florida Keys."

• • •

Harold Sanders stepped into the rescue basket and was soon hoisted aboard a Coast Guard helicopter. The crew was amazed, not only by the fact that he was alive, but also by the manner in which he was dressed. His crumpled business suit was covered in wet sand and both feet were bare.

A crewman gave him a blanket and asked, "How in the hell did you live through that?"

"You'll have to speak up," Sanders yelled, his ears still ringing.

The man repeated the question only inches from his ear.

"I saw it coming," he yelled. "I was lucky to be near the water."

"You've got that right."

A medic examined Sanders' ears. "His eardrums are okay, but he has tinnitus, and we need to have him examined for internal injuries at Key West Memorial."

Sanders removed his cell phone from the plastic bag and punched in Stalker's code. "I'm en route to Key West Memorial," he said. "I can't hear, so don't bother replying. The package is our design, no question." He heard only the ringing in his ears. "Also, find out who owns a boat called the *Island Breeze*."

"I'm on it," Stalker said.

•   •   •

Lucy Harris closed her tablet computer case and settled back onto the thin mattress. The bidding on Fat Man would last throughout the night as it had with Little Boy. Already the demonstration was pulling in eight-figure bids. If it kept up at this pace, the deposits alone would be more than enough.

The dive alarm sounded and she could sense the sub sinking into the abyss out of the range of satellites and radar. Carlos was already asleep in the bunk across from her; a faint snore coming from his parted lips.

She pulled the blanket up around her, reached into her bag and removed a small package painstakingly wrapped in linen cloth. She untied a ribbon securing the cover and removed a tattered hard-bound book entitled, *Dawn's Last Gleaming, The Diary of a Nisei Survivor.* Taped inside the cover, in yellowed cellophane still bearing her grandmothers fingerprints, was a twenty dollar gold piece. She opened the book to a well-worn page; its corners turned down into makeshift bookmarks, and began reading the familiar passage.

August 6, 1945:

I awoke from a strange dream this morning. Father was

standing by my bed kissing me on the forehead, as he had that day on the docks when I was only three. He kept whispering in my ear, "Don't look at the light, sweetheart. Turn away from the edge of darkness and come with me." Then I saw my mother. She was telling me to go with him. She reassured me that it was only for a while, but when I looked back, I knew I would never see her again. The familiar scent of steaming rice and my mother's voice was what awakened me from the dream.

"Kato," mother said in her broken English. "Time to get up now. Come eat your breakfast."

The images had been so hauntingly real. Mother was at her place in the kitchen, preparing the food and humming the tune to "Sakura." I wiped the sleep from my eyes and kissed the photo of my father. He looked so brave in his American pilot's uniform. Soon the war would be over and he would come to take us home. Our home in America was a vague memory. I remembered my room; the swing set in the backyard, but little else. I was only three when we left and our visit to my grandparents had lasted four years longer than expected.

"Kato," mother repeated, this time in her native Japanese, "come, we don't have much time." Mother insisted on speaking English, lest I forget it, so this slip into Japanese meant she was serious.

"I'm getting dressed, Mother," I replied.

I was still very tired since we had spent most of the night at the air-raid shelter. Once again our town had been spared from the bombing. How I wished the war would end. Mother told me that if we prayed hard enough, Jesus would answer my prayer. I had prayed every day. I even prayed in the Buddhist temple while my grandparents lit their prayer candles, but it wasn't directed at their God. Their God, with his fat belly and bronze smile seemed like a storybook character when compared to the thin, suffering Jesus. Of course, I never said these things in front of my grandparents, as it would be considered disrespectful. I had been named Kato to honor their family name and disrespect was never accepted from a child.

I opened the drawer to Mother's dresser, and slipped on my favorite smock. The gold coin Father had given Mother on their wedding day lay on top of the dresser, its weight surprising. One side was engraved with a beautiful woman holding a torch in one hand and an olive branch in the other. The rays of the sun rose behind her as if she were walking in the dawn of the day. The date reflected the year they were married, 1932, only months before President Roosevelt removed the country from the gold standard and had all the 1933 coins destroyed.

"Kato!" Mother repeated, now at the door to our room.

"Coming, Mama-san," I said.

"No, Kato. Call me Mother."

"Yes, Mother."

I slipped on my wooden sandals, grabbed the tattered American doll and without thinking, dropped the gold coin into the pocket of my smock. I followed Mother's voice into the kitchen.

"Where are Sato-san and Mito-san?" I asked, looking for my grandparents.

"They got up early to gather firewood in the Mitaki Hills. It's a beautiful day."

The morning air blowing though the open windows was cool and the sky was clear. I could see why they had gone for a walk.

"Why didn't they wake me? I love to gather firewood."

"You know the rules, Kato. We must clear the streets."

Although our city had never been attacked, we were told it was only a matter of time. We were on the western side of Japan and we hoped this might spare us, but since the defeat at Okinawa, the American firebombing raids were closer. The Army ordered everyone to help demolish old buildings to create fire prevention lanes. Since we lived only two kilometers from the center of town, we had to do our part.

A little after eight a.m., Mother and I went into the garden to gather vegetables for lunch. As she picked from the vines, I looked up at the deep blue sky, where I heard the distant sounds of a plane and spotted its reflection very high towards the north of the city. Mother was picking peas and I asked her if it was an American plane; the type my father flew. She looked up, but since the plane was alone, she said it wasn't.

I could see the sun reflecting off of its shiny surface, and somehow I knew my father was aboard. I saw a shiny object falling from it, and a parachute open. I pulled on Mother's skirt and pointed upward, "Papa-san! Papa-san!"

"Kato," Mother said, "it's Papa, not Papa-san!"

"But Mother look. Papa has jumped from the plane. He's coming for us."

I pulled harder on Mother's skirt and implored her to look, please look. In that moment I had convinced myself that it was indeed my American father who was parachuting into the city. Our prayers had been answered. The war was over and Father was coming to tell us. Mother gave in, gazed up at the tiny object, and blocked my view for only a second.

Lucy closed the book, shutting her grandmother's memories like the lid of her casket. She wrapped the memoir in its linen shroud and returned it to her bag. She always stopped at this point, preferring to freeze the hands of time at precisely 8:15 a.m. She pictured her grandmother as a child; still gazing at the sky with the faint flicker of answered prayer. The Americans had come. It was the moment her grandmother, Kato Nagai Stevens, had always remembered; that fleeting second of innocence, preserved like a marble plaque, for all of the burned children of Hiroshima.

CHAPTER 11

ISLAND BREEZE

"Are you Captain Barney Taylor?" the man standing on the marina dock asked.

Captain Barney looked up from the engine compartment of a thirty-five-foot fishing boat at the man silhouetted against the morning sun. He shielded his eyes from the light, but he still couldn't see the stranger's face. "Who wants to know?"

The man dressed in the business suit reached into his inside breast pocket and removed a wallet-sized leather booklet. "United States Secret Service."

Barney thought it was a badge, but it was only a notebook that the man started writing in. Barney wiped some grease from his hands with a shop rag. "That's my name, but most folks call me Capt'n Barney. What can I do for the Secret Service?"

"Do you own a boat called the *Island Breeze?*"

Captain Barney continued to rub his hands. This either had to do with the previous night's explosion or the suspicious girl. Perhaps both, but he wasn't going to mention her to a perfect stranger. "Is this about the explosion? The morning news said a nuclear sub might have blown."

"Is the *Island Breeze* your boat? Yes or no?"

"She's one of my rentals. It was due back this morning at seven, but I haven't seen any sign of her. After last night, I wonder if I'll ever see them or the *Breeze* again."

"Them?"

"Yeah, two guys," Barney lied. "One said he was taking her out to the Marquesas Keys to do some fishing. Paid in cash. He had one hell of an ice chest."

"Can you describe them?"

"Don't rightly remember their faces, but the one doing the talking was blond, light skin with a slight build."

"And the other one?"

"Dark hair, dark skinned. Why is the Secret Service interested? You don't think *they* had anything to do with the explosion, do you?"

The agent stepped closer and the captain saw why his silhouette looked weird. He had white bandages covering both ears. "What the hell happened to you?"

The agent ignored the question. He put one foot on the edge of the rail and leaned his weight on one knee. "You keep rental records?"

"Of course."

"Did you get a name?"

"Yeah. But I can't say whether it's real or not."

"Where do you keep the records?"

"In a file cabinet in the back office."

"Is anyone one else working today?"

"I have a boy who comes around to help wash the boats. No need for anyone else." The question was strange and Barney began to wonder if this guy was really Secret Service.

The agent reached under his coat and replaced the notebook.

"I'll show you the file," Barney said, trying to climb up out of the engine compartment. "I'm going to have to pull a copy anyway for the insur—" His words froze when he realized he was staring down the barrel of a pistol. "Now wait a minute, mister. There's no need for that. I'll tell you everything you want to know."

Raptor smiled. "I'm sure you will."

•   •   •

Section Chief Robert Lynch stepped aboard the FBI Learjet with a handful of reports. The Lear 45, which and had been seized by drug enforcement a few years earlier from a Texas millionaire, could hold nine passengers. Lynch had five agents with him and the Lear beat the hell out of the old prop planes they had been using.

Lynch took a seat near the cockpit and punched on an overhead lamp. He buckled his lap belt and began to scan the reports. Agent Michael James, who specialized in electronics, was in the seat beside him with an open laptop on the drop-down table in front of him. "How long before you establish the connection?" Lynch asked.

"Logging on now, sir. I should have the uplink by the time we're at cruising altitude."

Another agent took the seat directly behind Lynch and handed him his cell phone. "Agent Crosby is on the line, sir."

"Crosby, where are you?"

"Somewhere over Oklahoma on Delta flight 320 to Atlanta. Half the flights in and out of Denver were canceled. If we can get on the flight to Miami, my ETA should be around 2:50 p.m."

The Learjet's engines began their high-pitched whine as it started down the runway. Lynch spoke louder. "All right, we're going to meet you in Atlanta. All commercial flights into Key West have been canceled. Where's Agent Rankin and Dr. Matthews?"

"Rankin is coordinating the transfer to Key West. They're flying out of Denver later this morning on United Flight 458, if it's not canceled. It's a direct flight into Miami. The Nuclear Incident Response team is flying down to survey the site. Their ETA will be around four p.m. I guess they will have to rent a car in Miami and drive down.

"No good," Lynch said. "Fallout rumors have the Keys in a panic. Both lanes of U.S. 1 are packed with cars headed toward the mainland. There is no way into Key West except by boat or aircraft. I'll send the Lear back to Miami to pick them up. We've arranged for a command center at Boca Chica Field. It's thirty-five miles downwind, but Gamma emissions are within safe levels."

"Yes, sir," Crosby said. "We should arrive in Atlanta at 11:50 a.m."

"I'll phone ahead and get the gate number," Lynch said. The small jet climbed into the blue sky and the whine of the engines softened. "Meet us on the tarmac beside the plane."

"Yes sir. What have you learned?" Crosby asked.

"We've established a live data link with Key West PD. It's coming through now." Lynch read from the laptop's screen. "The U.S. Coast Guard has a reconnaissance helicopter near the site. The hypocenter was at the far western edge of a group of islands called the Marquesas Keys. It appears that the blast was about ten megatons. No significant tidal surge, so it wasn't submerged. Damage to Key West was minimal."

"Any causalities?"

"None reported as of 0500 hours this morning. The islands were an uninhabited game reserve."

"That's a contrast from Dillon. Anything left?"

"Not much. The hypocenter is a dark blue crater."

"We need to get on the surrounding islands as soon as possible," Crosby said. "The Nuclear team is bringing their robot to determine the bomb type."

"Good. Boca Chica is gathering data on the contamination levels. So far it's 'clean,' but they're not taking any chances. They've advised everyone to either stay indoors or evacuate to the mainland."

"Any idea on how the bomb was delivered?"

"Key West air traffic control is checking their radar records over the site and cartography is investigating the reconnaissance satellites for surface activity near the islands prior to detonation. That's all I've got. What about on your end?"

"We've found nothing on Amil since he left Casa Grande." For a moment Crosby's signal turned to static. ". . . ought his plane was headed south toward the Mexican bor. . . ."

"Crosby? You're breaking up."

"Yes, sir . . . I'm on an air-phone . . . you're clear."

"Are these islands within the plane's range?"

"No. They would have to refuel several times. I've expanded our search area along the gulf coast. We're . . ." The signal again faded. "There are hundreds of the small airports . . ." *static* ". . . he may have switched to a float plane with longer range."

"Crosby, my signal is breaking up, so just listen. We need full co-operation with Rankin on this. So far we've been equal partners with Homeland Security, but in Dillon we had the felony bank robbery and interstate flight, so they had no choice. If we can't establish a tie between the Dillon unsubs and this one, Homeland Security is going to take charge of the case. We need probable cause that Amil was involved. Did you get that?"

"Most of it, sir," Crosby said. "I understand. We'll discuss it on the plane. See you in Atlanta."

Lynch returned the phone to the agent, and handed him a note to give to the pilot. He sat back and began reading his reports.

• • •

Katie Froscher approached the information desk on deck three and asked to speak with the ship's purser. She was dressed in a bikini top and had a towel wrapped around her waist. Her blonde wig was wet and droplets of water dripped from them and rolled across the olive skin of her cleavage. The purser, a frumpy woman in her late thirties emerged from her office.

"How may I help you?" the purser said in a British accent.

"Yes ma'am, I seem to have misplaced my cardkey."

"Your cabin number?"

"It's room 9203."

The purser typed the information into the computer. "Yes, and your name?"

"Froscher. Katie Froscher."

"Right, Ms. Froscher. I'll print you out a new card and cancel your sign and sail on the old one. It won't take a moment."

"Could I get a new photo? I hated the last one."

"I suppose. Step inside that door and I'll snap one."

Within minutes the purser gave her the new card. Katie's name and her new portrait with the Carnival *Victory* graced its surface. Except for her hair color, it was identical to the one that was hidden in the waistband of her bikini bottoms.

"Will the old one still work?"

"Not for tour charges or drinks, but it will open your cabin. I shouldn't worry about that. Cabin numbers are not printed on the cards."

Katie allowed herself a smile. "Thank you."

"Good day," the purser said.

•   •   •

"That sorry-ass lying *bastard*." Harold Sanders yelled into his phone.

"Are you sure you checked the right file drawer?" Stalker asked.

"I checked *every* drawer. It's not here. All of the other records are right where he said, but not that one. You can't trust *anybody* these days. That sorry—"

"Raptor, just go back and ask him?"

He huffed a laugh. "Like that's an option."

"Oh. Then quit wasting your time. It's Amil."

"Amil already had his demonstration. This is the other guy from the bank."

"Chuck Froscher leaked the material. He had to have planned this."

"It's not Froscher. The shot took out half his brains. Not even Houdini could have pulled that off. It's someone he knew. You track down every classmate, roommate and fraternity brother that he ever breathed on. I want to know about his family, his friends, his co-workers. Did he have any girlfriends? Hell, maybe he had a *boyfriend*. I don't care what it takes, you *find* him. I'm getting sick and tired of this piss-ant and I am through being mister nice guy." Raptor slammed his cell on the table, pulled out his pistol and shot two holes in the file cabinet.

· · ·

He had been trying all morning, but all Gerald McMullen was getting on his cell phone was the no service symbol. He was certain that Crosby had heard about the explosion, but felt that he should tell him what he had seen. Gerald shut off the phone, put it back in his pocket and walked inside the grand lobby. The purser's desk was to his right and for once there was no line. He was tired of hanging around pools, camping out at the entrance to the dining rooms and looking over his shoulder at every brunette that happened by. Certainly the purser could tell him if she was aboard.

"How may I help you, sir?" the purser said.

"Yes, I was supposed to meet a friend aboard, but I can't seem to find her," Gerald said.

"Right. The name?"

"Katie Froscher."

The woman looked at him suspiciously, wrinkled her brow and typed the name into the computer. She spelled it out for clarification. "F, R, O, S, C, H, E, R?" A few moments passed. "We have a Kathryn."

Gerald beamed. "That's her."

"Does she perchance have a medium build with shoulder length blonde hair?" the Purser asked, her British accent heavy.

Blonde? Maybe the sun bleached it. "So, she's aboard?"

"You just missed her. She was here about ten minutes ago," she nodded at his feet, "dripping on the carpet there."

"*Great!* What's her room number?"

"I'm sorry, sir. We're not allowed to give out that information."

"Could you give me her phone number?"

Again she shook her head. "I could ring her for you, sir."

Gerald bit his lower lip. *What to say?* "You said she was dripping? Was she in her bathing suit?"

"She was wrapped in a towel as I recall. I suppose it covered a swimsuit."

"Which way did she go?"

The purser pointed up at the great sliding board, eleven stories above them. "Pools are on the Lido deck, sir."

Gerald bolted toward the elevators yelling, "*Thanks.*"

•   •   •

The FBI Learjet pulled alongside United flight 320 at 11:45 a.m. Crosby had been escorted onto the tarmac by a security guard and soon he was aboard the Lear. The small cramped cabin of the plane was filled with agents and technical personnel. Agent Michael James, who had established the data link, gave up his seat, so Crosby could sit beside Lynch. Ten minutes later they were back in the air and headed to Boca Chica Field in Key West.

Crosby unbuckled himself and breathed a sigh of relief. His face was unshaven, his suit crumpled and stained. The rings under his eyes told of his fatigue.

"You look horrible," Lynch said. "Did you get any sleep on the plane?"

"Some kid kept kicking the back of my seat, but I'm all right. I'll sleep later."

"Get plenty of rest tonight. I need you sharp on this one. I got your report from last night. Anything new on the bomb type?"

"There's nothing but theories."

"What do you think?"

"Dr. Matthews seems convinced. My gut tells me she right."

"Anything on the unsub?"

"Rankin's team has been searching for tan Accords at every airport, bus and train station between Dillon and Salt Lake. Rental companies too. Nothing yet. The lab has enhanced the Dillon video, but the unsub hasn't produced any hits on our NGI Biometric facial recognition database. Forensics in Denver found evidence of a wig hair in the car and some green fibers that may have come from the unsub's suit. They also found a long blonde hair. It may have been in the rental for months or it could have come from the unsub. We've expanded the profile to include females."

"Can they do a DNA analysis on the hair?" Lynch said.

"I don't think so. There's no root."

"Any ideas on motive?"

"I believe Dillon was a dress rehearsal. In Madrid, Amil robbed the bank and then blew it up after a crowd gathered, but his bomb was too small. In Dillon he got everyone in town."

"Why didn't he claim responsibility?"

"He has. The bank was his signature and he didn't try to get rid of his fingerprints in the car knowing we would find them."

"Who else has profiled the case?"

Crosby opened the file. "Jordan Massey."

"Good man. What's his view on the female aspect?"

"He doesn't think it fits. Neither does Rankin."

"What about you?"

"Amil is Arabic, so it's unlikely he would work with a woman unless she was vital to the plan. So, maybe she was."

"Why would Amil waste bombs this powerful on a tiny town and an uninhabited island instead of a major city?"

"I don't know, and Jordan's profile doesn't offer a clue."

"Then speculate. You know Amil better than anyone."

Crosby thought for a long moment. "He's a terrorist, so his method of operation is to be seen inflicting terror. He left his fingerprints and looked directly at the cameras, so there would be no doubt that he was the one responsible."

"He could have done that by standing outside one of the network studios in Times Square. Why Dillon?"

"Maybe he isn't ready to martyr himself yet. Dillon was survivable only because of its location in the mountains. Even then he barely escaped."

"There are a lot bigger mountain cities," Lynch said.

"Yes, but the threat of terror is far more powerful than the actual act. Dillon got the world's attention and showed how he's working with a new weapon. But a town that size didn't incite the type of crackdown that 9-11 did. It took us awhile to figure out it wasn't an accident, and that gave him the window he needed to get away."

"Interesting theory."

"I believe the Marquesas bomb was intended to raise the level of terror, and it has given him the power to scare the hell out of us."

"He's certainly has our attention," Lynch said.

"The next time, it's going to be something very important, and there won't be a damn thing we can do to prevent it."

"No," Lynch said. "There won't be a next time, Crosby. We're going to find this *bastard.*"

•   •   •

"Mr. Vice President," the aide said as she knocked on the door to his Miami hotel suite, "Agent Sanders has arrived."

"Yes. Send him in please. And hold all my calls," the Vice President, Norman Trexler, said.

Agent Sanders entered the room but left the door half-open

behind him. Trexler noticed the bandages covering his ears. "What the hell happened to you?"

"It's tinnitus. Ringing in the ears," Sanders said. "The bandages help with loud noises."

"What the hell—"

"I took a ride out to the Marquesas Keys last evening."

"You did? Why?"

"I was checking out the fishing site that you wanted to try today. Remember?"

"What fish—?"

Sanders put a finger to his lips and winked. "You know, where today's *fishing* expedition was supposed to take place. The game preserve at the Marquesas Keys."

Trexler looked confused. "We weren't—"

Sanders held up a hand, exaggerated the wink again and motioned in the direction of the half-opened door.

"Oh, *right*." Trexler said, realizing that aides were within earshot in the adjoining hotel suite. "That *fishing* trip. The one we were going to take today. I suppose we can write off that one, can't we?"

"Unless you're interested in glowing fish."

Trexler laughed a little too loudly. "What were you doing there?" he said in a whisper.

Sanders rolled his eyes and spoke louder than normal. "I barely made it out of the area alive."

Trexler didn't know whether to whisper or yell. "What happened?"

"I rented a chopper from one of the locals," Sanders said at the appropriate volume and gave the Vice President the "okay" symbol. "We flew out to the Marquesas Keys. The area looked secure, so we headed back. We were about fifteen miles out when the blast overtook us."

"Overtook you? How did you survive?"

"I had to relieve myself."

"What?"

"I had to *pee*. The pilot sat the chopper down on the beach of one of the islands. When I saw the blast, I dove underwater. I guess you could say it was blind luck."

"*Jeez.* What happened to the pilot?"

"I don't know. When I reemerged, the chopper and all of the vegetation on the island was gone."

"*Holy Mother.* How did you get off the island?"

"A Coast Guard helicopter picked me up early this morning." Raptor lowered his voice to a whisper. "Now, that's the official story on why I was out there. You got it?"

Trexler nodded and mouthed, "Is it true?"

Raptor smiled. "Of course."

• • •

Crosby was still aboard the Lear and looking over the Marquesas reports when his cell phone vibrated. He didn't recognize the incoming number. "This is Agent Crosby."

"Devrin. It's Gerald."

Crosby glanced at Lynch, who was deep in thought. "Mr. McMullen," he said sounding professional, "I'm tied up right now. Can I call you back?"

"Probably not. Just listen for a minute. I saw the explosion last night. It couldn't have been a hundred miles from us."

"Where are you?"

"I'm on a cruise ship that left Miami yesterday. We're on the way to Cozumel. But never mind that, what the hell happened?"

"We don't know yet. I'm en route."

"They're saying it's a terrorist. Is that true?"

"We have no information on that," Crosby said carefully.

"You have someone with you?"

"Yes."

"Save my new cell number. I won't be back until next Sunday, but if you can get through, give me a call when you can."

Crosby jotted down the number. "Why are you headed to Mexico?"

"You know me, always chasing a skirt."

"Well, be careful."

"I'm always careless," Gerald said.

Crosby put away the phone and Lynch glanced at him over his reading glasses. "Do we have an agent named McMullen on this case?"

"No, sir. He's a friend aboard a cruise ship headed to Mexico. He saw the explosion last night and wanted to report it."

"I see. We are allowed to have friends, Crosby. Why didn't you talk to him?"

"I didn't feel it was appropriate at this time, sir."

"Don't let your friendship keep you from seeing the whole

picture. He witnessed the blast. We never know where the clues might fall, Crosby. We have to gather up everything we've got and hope that the one that will make a difference is within the basket.

•   •   •

The FBI command center was setup in an aircraft hangar located at the Naval Air Station at Boca Chica Key. The Section Chief and the agents aboard the Learjet had gotten a brief view of the blast area before they landed. A helicopter flyover was planned for the next morning so Agent Rankin and Dr. Matthews would have a chance to examine the site firsthand. Computer equipment, linked via satellite to FBI headquarters in Washington, was set up along with a make-shift conference table. Glass partitions provided temporary office space for Lynch and his team. Shortly after arriving they received the expected information from Key West air traffic control. There were several anomalies, which were forwarded to the FBI lab in Wash-ington for further analysis. The reconnaissance satellite photographs of the blast site arrived via e-mail from Washington and enlarge-ments were requested of specific targets. Crosby had stopped counting the cups of coffee he drank to stay awake, but as each enlarged image arrived they seemed to deplete his strength. At least he still had a role in the investigation.

Across the hangar, several agents had gathered around the makeshift conference table and Lynch motioned for Crosby to join them. Agent Michael James, their electronics expert, had established a video link with Dr. Matthews' tablet computer. She, Agent Rankin, and the Nuclear Incident Response team were on a direct flight to Miami. Matthews had just received some important information.

Crosby took a seat behind Lynch and tried not to fall asleep.

"Dr. Matthews," Agent James said, while adjusting the video camera. "We have Section Chief Lynch here with us."

Lynch leaned into the camera's range. "Hi, Marti."

She smiled. "Good afternoon, sir. Can you hear us?"

"Yes, fine. We're sending the Lear back to Miami to pick up you and the team. It will be there at 1630 hours."

"Thank you, sir."

"You have some new information?"

"Yes, sir. I assume Agent Crosby has filled you in on the wig and the blonde hair we found?"

Crosby's eyes opened at the mention of his name. He had almost dozed off.

"Yes," Lynch said. "What else have you got?"

"We cross-referenced the information provided by Dr. Gebo with military service records and the accident reports in Oak Ridge, and got a hit that looks very promising. The computer identified him as Charles 'Chuck' Froscher, Jr., a former weapons designer assigned to the Oak Ridge Weapons Research Facility in Tennessee."

"A weapons designer?" Lynch said. "That's our man."

"He died three years ago."

"Are you sure?"

"Yes. I have the police report. Dr. Gebo said he had the technical capability to construct a bomb, but Froscher was the victim of a botched burglary and was shot in the head. Both the police and the family made a positive ID. Fingerprints and dental records have confirmed the death."

"Anything on the other one?" Crosby asked.

"Not yet, but Kelly's working with Chicago PD to find his records." Matthews shuffled through some papers, held up a page, and read from it. "One interesting footnote about Froscher. According to Tennessee motor vehicle records, he was five foot ten and weighed one hundred sixty pounds. This photo was taken right before his death." She held up Froscher's driver's license photo in front of the camera. The photo showed a man with sandy blonde hair and a thin moustache.

Crosby blinked his eyes clear and leaned closer to the screen. "I'll be damned," he murmured. "He looks just like our unsub."

• • •

The boy was in his mid teens and had worked for Captain Barney Taylor for three years. After the previous night's explosion, he and his parents had tried to flee to the mainland like everyone else, but the roads were impassable. The boy had come to the docks on the chance that Captain Barney might take his family to the mainland. With the rental office locked, he walked down to the docks where the *Island Paradise* was tied up. He found the engine hatch open and tools scattered around the deck.

"Capt'n," he called out and jumped aboard. Captain Barney never left his tools out in the open. He pushed open the door to the lower deck. "Capt'n, are you—" The last word stuck in his throat. At the base of the steps a sea of blood sloshed from side to side with the tide; the captain's body slowly rolling in it. The boy ran from the boat, choking back bile, too shocked to scream.

• • •

It was late evening when Agent Rankin and Doctor Matthews arrived at the Boca Chica field office. Lynch had ordered Crosby to get some sleep, but an hour on the hard cot in the break area had produced little rest. He awoke at their arrival and fixed himself another cup of coffee as they brought him up to speed. Matthews excused herself, saying she was tired, hungry and needed a few minutes alone.

A photo technician came over and handed Crosby two enlarged aerial photographs. Both had arrived via e-mail from Washington. One showed a group of islands in a semicircle; the Marquesas Keys prior to the explosion. The other shot was an enlargement of the westernmost island. It showed the beached rubber dinghy and the fishing boat anchored a hundred yards off. Crosby and Rankin studied the photos for a while, argued over what they were seeing and wanted Lynch's opinion. He was in his temporary office.

"I thought you were asleep?" Lynch said.

"I was. New development, sir." Crosby handed the photos to Lynch.

"What's this?"

"These were taken by our GEOS weather satellite yesterday afternoon. They're pretty grainy."

Lynch used a magnifying glass to examine each picture.

"The suspects used a rubber dinghy from this fishing boat to place what appears to be a large rectangular box on the island," Crosby's words were slow, his eyes heavy. "Judging from its size and shape, it's an ice chest and a white gas seems to be venting from the box. That could be dry ice."

"Which proves it's nothing but a case of beer," Rankin said. "Why would a nuclear bomb need to be kept cold?"

Lynch frowned at Crosby. "You haven't told him about your conversation with Dr. Gebo?"

"What conversation?" Rankin asked.

"Sir, until we have conclusive evidence that this device is even possible, it would be premature to share—"

Lynch cut him off. "Don't give me that. We're partners in this. We share any and all information we get with Homeland Security. No matter how strange it sounds. Understand?"

Crosby lowered his head. "Yes, sir."

"Gebo? That was the guy Marti got those names from," Rankin asked. "What device?"

"Dr. Matthews got more out of the interview than a couple of names," Crosby said. "Gebo is a retired Los Alamos physicist who suggested, rather convincingly, that these bombs might not be nuclear."

"Of course they're nuclear. What the hell else could they be?"

"Something new," Lynch said, looking at Crosby. "Tell him and leave nothing out."

"Yeah, Crosby. *Tell me.*"

"Dr. Gebo told us about a project the government was working on in the early nineties. It was a research project to develop a new type of weapon of mass destruction, but it was too unstable to stockpile, so the project was abandoned before a prototype was ever built. At first I was skeptical, but we've found evidence on the Internet that supports what he's saying. Research into this area has been going on for quite some time. The thing that convinced me was the size; no bigger than a coffee thermos, and it would have to be kept extremely cold."

"Gee thanks, Crosby. That would have been nice to know."

"We didn't think you would believe us before Marti confirmed our findings."

"Believe what? What's this bomb made of?"

"Positrons. It's a form of antimatter."

"Antimatter?" Rankin scoffed with a laugh. "Next we'll be issued phaser weapons."

"Dr. Gebo's an expert in his field," Crosby tossed him the photo. "Look for yourself."

"Maybe the cooler was full of beer that got shook up too much."

Lynch stopped the banter. "This isn't fiction, Rankin. We're seriously pursuing it. Crosby, was the cooler on this boat big enough to hold a conventional nuclear device?"

"Dr. Matthews believes so, but not one large enough to have a yield of ten megatons."

Agent Michael James tapped on the glass partition with a pink slip in his hand.

"Then the bomb was either planted on the island earlier than these photos indicate, or this thing was incredibly small," Lynch said. He motioned for James to enter.

"The director is on line two, sir," Agent James said.

"Antimatter?" Rankin said. "You're actually considering this? This was a ten *megaton* blast for heaven's sake."

"Rankin, we're looking at this from every angle. I'm sure that the first airplane or microwave oven seemed impossible to most people at the time."

"With all due respect, sir, it seems that we are assuming a lot already. All we have is a couple of grainy photos and a cooler." Rankin stood. "Marti and I are going to take a ride out to the Marquesas site first thing in the morning and take a look at *real* evidence. If anyone wants to tag along, we can all catch up on our gamma tan."

"I saw it when we flew in," Crosby said. "But you go right ahead and if you find any evidence of fissionable materials, I'll eat these photos."

"I'd rather you buy me a drink," Rankin said.

"You still owe me for the one yesterday."

"Then we'll be even." Rankin walked past him and turned. "Watch out for that beer, Crosby. It packs one hell of a punch."

Lynch held up a hand before Crosby could respond. "He has a point, you know. Those islands were a prime fishing area. This could have been a couple of fishermen in the wrong place at the wrong time with a cooler of beer."

Lynch picked up the receiver and punched line two. "Robert Lynch. Yes, sir."

As Lynch talked, a photo technician delivered more of the enlargements Crosby had requested. When Crosby examined them his frown changed into a smile.

Lynch hung up. "The Vice President is in Miami. He's doing a flyover of the site in the morning. Believe it or not, he was scheduled to take a fishing trip out to the Marquesas Keys today."

"Are you thinking the same thing I am?"

"You're assuming, Crosby. That's what got us into trouble the last time, so before you mention anything about assassinations, we need solid evidence."

"At least we now have evidence that the crimes are connected." Crosby dropped the enlargement onto the desk. "Amil left his calling card."

Lynch took the photo. On the beach, spelled out in seaweed and palm fronds, was the number four followed by the outline of a snow angel in the sand.

• • •

The call arrived late and Stalker's caller ID traced it to his FBI mole in Boca Chica Key. "What have you learned?" he said.

"They found a blonde hair in the car and evidence of a wig. Amil is using private planes to move about and they believe the second suspect may have had connections to a dead weapons designer named Chuck Froscher."

"Anything else?"

"Yeah. It's weird, but they think this bomb has something to do with antimatter."

CHAPTER 12

COZUMEL

Tuesday

The bright morning sun was just peeking above the horizon as the huge Carnival cruise ship inched itself up to the long concrete pier of Cozumel, Mexico. The seas surrounding the island were the clearest that Katie Froscher had ever seen. Even in forty feet of water, every detail of the bottom was visible. She took a boat ride up the coast, rented snorkel gear and stayed longer than expected snorkeling around submerged eleventh-century Mayan ruins. Hanging from her neck was a small waterproof case containing her cardkey along with several hundred dollar bills. The cardkey was her ticket to get back aboard the cruise ship. She stretched out on her towel and let the sun dry her damp skin. She imagined how easy it would be to forget it all and disappear into the Mexican frontier.

A half-hour later, she lifted her sunglasses, looked out across the coarse white sands and knew this was where she belonged. Maybe not this beach, or in this country, but she vowed someday to live out her days among the islands of the Caribbean Sea.

* * *

Crosby awoke at seven a.m. with a crick in his neck. He couldn't believe that anybody actually got any sleep on these cots. A pile of rocks would be more comfortable. He had tossed and turned all night trying to develop assassination scenarios. None made sense, and each ended with the same question. Why would Amil attempt to kill the Vice President when he could have used the bomb in Washington? Trexler had no real power and an attempt on his life would only cause the President to "go to ground," making him even harder to locate. There was also the question of how Amil could have learned Trexler's schedule. The only way to find that out was through the

Secret Service. Trouble was, if the FBI started treating this as an assassination attempt, the Secret Service would swarm over the investigation in minutes. With no solid proof to back up this theory, Crosby would once again be hung out to dry.

He sat up and swung his legs off the cot. The file folder was sitting on the floor beside his feet. Paper-clipped to the outside was the photo of Leslie Pryce, the bank teller in Dillon. *"The only mistake she made that day was going to work,"* Lynch had said. If this was only a plot to kill Trexler, then what was the point of Dillon? Crosby lay back on the cot and thought about it for a long time.

•   •   •

Dr. Marti Matthews checked the helicopter's Geiger counter, as it hovered over one of the remaining Marquesas Islands. The clouds of white powdered sand stirred by the rotors swirled around them and the needle indicated three rads per hour. She motioned to the pilot that he could land and shut down the engine.

"Is three rads safe?" Kelly Rankin said.

"If we don't stay very long," Matthews said.

"So it was nuclear?"

"Not likely. You get this much gamma radiation from just the flash of the explosion."

They donned their yellow radiation suits, waited for the rotors to slow and the cloud of dust to settle before opening the chopper door and climbing out. What had first appeared to be white sand turned out to be white ash, several inches deep. They were a little over a mile from ground zero, which appeared as a dark blue patch of ocean on the horizon. The remains of the easternmost islands were completely devoid of any signs of plant life. Matthews reached down and picked up a piece of coral in her gloved hand. It immediately crumbled into a white powder. She ran her portable Geiger counter over the ashen remains.

"What are we looking for?" Rankin's headgear made his voice resonate.

"Fallout. I need to take a few samples."

"Take your time." It was hot in the suit and he wondered how long he would last if he removed it.

Matthews began picking up samples and putting them into evidence bags. "In 1956, there was a series of thermonuclear tests on the Bikini Islands," she said.

Rankin rolled his eyes. *Another one of her history lessons.* Marti loved history and would go on for hours about the most boring subjects imaginable. The only history he cared about was printed on the back of baseball cards.

"The blast pulverized tons of coral and lifted it into the stratosphere where it rained down highly radioactive particles on a group of Japanese fishermen. They all got radiation sickness."

"So our terrorist wanted the fallout to cover Key West or Miami?"

Matthews dropped the ash and brushed off her gloves. "If he was hoping for fallout, he didn't get much." She unzipped her hood and took it off. "We found the same low levels of radiation in Dillon. These bombs are surprisingly clean. Exactly as Dr. Gebo predicted."

Rankin removed his hood as well, and they walked down the beach together.

"You don't believe a positron bomb is possible?"

"Last night was the first I've heard of it. I haven't seen any convincing proof."

"Look around," she said. "If this was a hydrogen bomb, even with these suits we'd be dead by now."

"All that proves is it wasn't a hydrogen bomb."

"Why do you give Devrin such a hard time, Kelly?"

"Who says I give him a hard time?"

Matthews furrowed her brow. "Me for one. You seem to love getting on his case."

"I used to be a cop. I give everyone a hard time."

"Not me."

"That depends on your definition." He leered.

"I'm serious, Kelly."

"You see, that's the problem I had with the FBI. Everybody's too serious. The only guys worse than the FBI are the Secret Service. Now, there's a group that *can't* take a joke."

"It's a serious business, Kelly. What is it between you two?"

"I think we have the same taste in women."

She grabbed his shoulder, turning him toward her. "What are you saying?"

He shrugged. "It's a gut feeling."

"You think Devrin is interested in me?"

"I believe you're interested in him."

"Wait . . ." she said. "You're jealous?"

"No, but he is."

"Romantically?"

"Oh yeah. I can see it in the way he looks at you."

"Really?"

"See, you do care about him, don't you?"

"Well, sure. He's a wonderful colleague. He's smart and—"

Rankin interrupted. "And given the right circumstances you wouldn't mind getting to know him a little better. Am I right, or what?"

"I never gave it much thought."

"Well," Rankin said with a sigh, "since we're no longer an item, maybe you should."

"You're serious? You wouldn't mind?"

"You're avoiding him because of me, and I'm just saying, it's not necessary."

Matthews gave him a hug. "You know, beneath all of that bravado, you're really a sweet guy."

"Careful, you'll tarnish my image."

She checked her watch. "If we don't leave soon it won't matter, we'll be stuck with each other."

"Why?"

"Because we'll both be bald, sterile and covered with lesions."

• • •

368 miles due south, a former Soviet Kilo class submarine hovered at a depth of three hundred feet. It was located in the Cayman Trench less than five miles off the coast of Grand Cayman. Aboard, Lucy Harris studied her face in a mirror and applied a last bit of makeup. An empty bottle of hair color lay in the sink and her brunette hair was now back to blonde. Now to wait for the cover of darkness to descend over the ocean above and the sub to surface.

Everything was ready. She opened her purse, removed a birth certificate and driver's license and examined them closely. The name printed on both was Kathryn Froscher.

• • •

About the time Katie Froscher was climbing out of the water to lay on the beach, Gerald McMullen was donning his snorkel and mask to go in. Less than five hundred yards of sand separated them, but because they had signed up for different tours, they were dispatched to separate beaches.

Gerald loved to swim along the surface of the clear, salty warm water until he spotted something on the bottom, then dive down to investigate. He thought of Renee and how their cruise would have taken them to these same waters. She may have bronzed her long limbs on the beach, but would never have followed him into the water. "There are things out there that can eat you," she often said, and there was no convincing her otherwise.

He wondered if Katie had similar fears. She might still be aboard the ship, taking advantage of the lack of passengers around the pool, or perhaps she was a history buff and had taken the tour of the Mayan ruins. Whatever the case, so far she had managed to evade detection. He had grown weary of scanning the pools and the seats in the huge onboard theater. He thought he had spotted her once, only later to see two children and a husband run up to greet the woman. He knew Katie was aboard. He had to run into her at some point.

In the meantime another mistress was tugging at his emotions. He had once again fallen in love with the Caribbean and was determined that at their next port of call, either Grand Cayman or Jamaica, he would locate a real estate agent. Gerald wasn't getting any younger and a house on the beach was almost within his financial grasp.

•   •   •

When Dr. Matthews and Agent Rankin returned from the blast site, Lynch announced a meeting with his investigators at eleven o'clock. Lynch asked Crosby into his makeshift office to discuss how to approach the subject of the possible assassination attempt.

"You know how Kelly's going to react," Lynch said.

"Yes, sir. But the more I think about it, the less I'm convinced the bombing had anything to do with the Vice President."

"What changed your mind?"

"Why would Amil kill Trexler when he could have used this bomb in Washington and gotten the President, the VP and all of Congress in one swoop?"

"Good point."

"Plus the Secret Service knew Trexler's plans, so why aren't they treating this as an attempt?"

"Have you asked?"

"I thought we should discuss it first."

Lynch looked at his watch. "All right, here's how we'll handle it. I'll mention the Vice President's flyover and ask Kelly to contact the

Secret Service to find out why Trexler was in Miami. That way we keep Homeland Security informed, and they can decide if the blast was connected with an assassination attempt."

"Sounds good. The morning news said that the Vice President has scheduled a press conference downtown after his flyover. Perhaps Kelly and I should drive over there and see what he has to say."

"Good idea," Lynch said.

A minute later they entered the makeshift conference room. "We have some new information," Lynch announced. He held up a stack of photos. "Our terrorists have given themselves a name. Meet *The Fourth Angel.*"

Crosby handed out reproductions of the photo of the drawing in the sand to each of them. "Amil knew we had satellites over the Marquesas Keys, so he left us his calling card."

"The arrogant bastard was showing off." Rankin tossed the photo on the table.

"Like he did in Dillon," Lynch said. "We believe that's why he looked directly at the bank's camera."

"So what's his motive?" Agent James asked.

"A terrorist doesn't need one," Crosby said. "He wants attention and he's taken extraordinary measures to make certain we knew he was responsible. We believe these two bombs were intended to raise the level of terror. They're a prelude to something."

"To what?" Rankin said.

"Something bigger," Lynch said.

"The two targets are total opposites," Rankin said. "Amil is a millionaire, so why the bank?"

"The bank had video cameras to prove he did it," Agent James said.

"Not if you blow up the cameras along with it," Rankin said.

Everyone was silent for a moment. "He *knew* about the streaming video to Denver," Crosby said. "The unsub *had* to have worked at the Dillon branch."

"There's the missing piece," Lynch said.

"The Denver Bureau ran the employee records against photos of the accomplice and came up empty," Rankin said.

"How about security guards?" Matthews said.

"Or simply someone who could read a wiring diagram," Crosby added, "like the system's maintenance guy."

"I want the records from every employee and every security guard who's worked for OleWest during the last five years," Lynch said.

"Have them cross-reference for any ties to the Florida Keys and be sure the profile includes anyone of Middle Eastern descent."

"I'm on it," James said, feverishly typing into his laptop.

"Anyone have anything else to add?"

"Check Key West's local law enforcement for traffic violations along the Highway 1 escape route," Rankin said. "Both Tim McVey and Ted Bundy were captured because of traffic tickets."

Crosby rubbed his temples. "Be sure to include any women around five nine and have them check for Internet searches for *The Fourth Angel*. It was on the Dillon recording and now here. It may give us a lead."

"James, make sure that Quantico gets these on the hotline ASAP," Lynch said. "The Vice President is doing a flyover of the blast site as we speak. He's holding a press conference at Fort Taylor at two p.m., and Crosby, I want you and Rankin to attend. The base commander has allowed us the use of their motor pool. Drive over and see if you can speak with some of Trexler's Secret Service personnel. Maybe they can explain why the VP was staying in Miami on Monday."

"I know why," Rankin said. "Whenever there is a crisis, either the President or the Vice President is kept in the air or at a separate location. Trexler plays golf, and since Wednesday's golf tournament was canceled, he decided to park his butt in Miami where he could squeeze in some practice rounds. So why . . ." He paused. "Wait a minute. You think this was an attempt on Trexler?"

Crosby shook his head. "No."

"You do, don't you? Another assassination theory—"

"We're not ruling out anything, Kelly," Lynch said, "especially what may have been a botched attempt on the Vice President. The bomb may have exploded prematurely."

"Yes, sir. But might I also point out that the Secret Service isn't treating this as an assassination attempt. They must have a good reason."

"That's why I'm asking you to find out so we're not jumping to conclusions. *Any* opinions will be treated with respect or I'll find someone who is respectful. Do I make myself clear?"

"Perfectly, sir," Rankin said. "I apologize."

"That's the last apology I'm accepting from you. Now carry on."

•   •   •

Vice President Norman Trexler was upset as he stepped from the helicopter and walked to the podium where the microphones had been set up. The wind off the ocean ruffled his hair and he held it as he walked. He hated press conferences, especially fielding questions, but President Beasley had given him little choice. Beasley loved to toss him hot potatoes and watch him fumble. He vowed that this time he would toss it right back.

Surrounding Trexler was his entourage of Secret Service agents. Agent Sanders was near the back; white bandages still over both ears.

Trexler put his mouth too close to the microphones and sent a screech of feedback through the crowd. He adjusted and began. "My fellow Americans, I have just returned from an air reconnaissance flight over the site of Sunday night's massive explosion. First and foremost, I want to reassure the residents of the Florida Keys, that there is no need to evacuate. I have the personal assurance from the Emergency Management Director for Key West that radiation readings have dissipated to acceptable levels. Secondly, the FBI and Homeland Security have made the search for the perpetrators its number one priority. I spoke with the Directors of both agencies and they assure me that every available agent is working this case. I will now take a few questions."

"Mr. Vice President," a CNN reporter, blurted out, "Can you tell us if this is the work of an organized terrorist group or an in-dividual?"

"I can't comment on that while the investigation is underway."

The reporter persisted. "The media is calling the terrorist *The Fourth Angel.* Is it true that a recording of President Barnett's infa-mous fourth angel speech was playing prior to the Dillon ex-plosion?"

Trexler was taken aback. "Well, I can't imagine how any recording could have possibly survived the Dillon explosion." He then ignored her, desperately wanting to change the subject. A reporter for the *Washington Post* that Trexler recognized as a regular at the White House briefings raised his hand. President Barnett's "real" speech had never surfaced, and as long as that smoking gun was unac-counted for, there was always the danger that the next question could be loaded. He took the question anyway.

"Mr. Vice President, you say that the radiation is within safe levels. Can you tell us exactly what is considered safe?"

"Rich, nice to see you outside of Washington for once. I take it they're safe enough for you."

The crowd laughed right on cue.

"I have been informed that the radiation levels have steadily decreased to a current reading that is considered not harmful. As a matter of fact," Trexler swallowed, "to prove that it is now safe enough for residents to return, I'm staying to play a round of golf tomorrow."

• • •

At 1600 Pennsylvania Avenue in Washington, President Lawrence Beasley stood up from his chair and yelled, "*What!*" at the television screen. "That stupid *son-of-a-bitch.*" He kicked at his trashcan, missed and caught the corner of his desk with his little toe. He screamed a torrent of curses.

The President's secretary rushed in to see the President hopping around the Oval Office on one foot.

"Sir, are you all right?"

Beasley looked up. "Get that idiot on the phone. We're under attack by terrorists and he's playing *golf.*"

"Who?"

Beasley pointed at the television. "*Trexler!*"

• • •

Trexler took several more questions then closed. "Now if you ladies and gentlemen will excuse me, I must get back to the business at hand. Thank you for your time."

Crosby and Rankin stood near the rear of the spectators and watched Trexler leave. Most of the reporters seemed anxious to leave despite the Vice President's assurance that radiation levels were safe. During Rankin's two years with Homeland Security, he had gotten to know some of the Secret Service agents well. He spotted a familiar face among them and walked over to ask a few questions.

The ocean breeze reminded Crosby of the smells of beach vacations his family took when he was only a boy. He longed to return to those simple days. A seagull hovered in the air a few feet away before landing on the lawn to search for food. Looking up, he noticed a tall Secret Service agent staring at him from behind the lectern. He had white bandages on his head and appeared to be talking into his concealed microphone.

Rankin finished with the other agent and rejoined him. "That was Agent Zack Blew. He's a pretty straight up guy but no sense of humor. Must be a prerequisite for joining the Secret Service."

"Who's that?" Crosby nodded toward the bandaged man.

Rankin studied him for a moment. "Well, that's Agent Harold Sanders."

"I thought so."

"I wonder why the bandages?"

"I've never met him," Crosby said, "only seen his photo in the news."

"I'd try to stay clear of him if I were you. He's probably not your biggest big fan since your report booted him down to Vice Presidential duty."

"The man allowed a gun into the White House Briefing Room, Kelly. It wasn't me that got him booted."

"Try explaining that one to him. The other agents call him Hawk."

"Why?"

"He sees everything like a bird of prey."

"He didn't that day, did he? What did you find out from Agent Blew?"

"Basically what I told you. Norman can't play worth a damn, so he spends every chance he gets on the golf course—" Rankin lowered his voice. "—among other things."

The gull spread his wings and lifted off with something in his beak, squawking as he disappeared.

"What other things?" Crosby said.

"He likes deep sea fishing and enjoys a little horizontal refreshment when he can escape from the reporters."

"Horizontal?"

Rankin grinned.

"*Oh.*" Crosby nodded.

"You should give that a try. It may put a smile back on that mug of yours."

"I've had my fill of fishing, thank you. Did you ask Agent Blew why they aren't treating this as an attempt on the VP?"

"They are. That's why they have so many agents here."

"You could have fooled me."

"Trexler has the looks and talks the talk," Rankin said, "but they all think he's an idiot. I don't see them taking *any* threat on his life seriously."

• • •

"What did they say?" Stalker asked.

"Nothing," Sanders replied. "They were discussing Trexler's golfing habits. He was about to tell him something else but a damn bird flew off with the bug before I could get any more. The damn seagulls must think they're oysters."

"Rats with wings."

"How much has our FBI snitch learned?"

"They believe Amil and the bomber were aboard the boat, but they haven't located it yet."

"Nor will they. It couldn't have been more than three miles from the hypocenter," Sanders said. "Any clue on how the crew escaped?"

"I'm working on a couple of ideas. Our Cuban clients have taken an interest. They've put our negotiations on hold and apparently are talking with the perpetrators."

"Good. They'll lead us right to them. Have you gathered my list of Froscher's connections?"

"It should arrive at your hotel this evening. A waste of time if you ask me. Whoever did this has done one helluva job at covering his tracks."

"Nobody's that good." Sanders examined the plastic bag containing the coin. "I found a gold coin sitting on top of the Marquesas bomb."

"What's on it?"

"There's an engraved image of Liberty holding a torch and an olive branch. She's standing in front of a rising sun with a flowing cloth around her shoulders. It makes her look like an angel."

"What's the date?"

"1932, but I think it's a reproduction."

•   •   •

At five minutes till five, Kelly Rankin pulled into a parking lot on Duval Street. The building was covered in multi-colored wooden planks and old license plates from every state imaginable. The name on the outside sign read: RockaCharlies, Sports and Entertainment Bar.

"What's this," Crosby asked.

"Sports bar," Rankin said. "You said you were hungry. Don't you like hot wings?"

"I was thinking about seafood."

Rankin was already getting out of the car. "This is better for your waistline."

Crosby followed Rankin inside. The music was loud and the walls were covered with antique sporting equipment. Television screens were visible from every angle. Several locals were sitting at the bar and a few others were crowded around an empty stage with mirrors on the ceiling and a pair of chrome dancing poles mounted in the floor. Rankin took a seat at the bar and ordered a beer. With the music blaring, a long-legged girl dressed only in a trench coat and dental floss underwear emerged from the backstage curtains and began dancing to the cheers of the few patrons.

"Kelly. This isn't a restaurant."

"Sure it is." He handed Crosby a four-item menu of buffalo wings, hot wings, barbeque wings and spicy chicken strips. "Don't you like chicken?"

"I would prefer to eat in a restaurant, not a topless bar."

"This isn't topless. It's a sports bar."

Crosby nodded at the stage. "What do you call that?"

"Enticing entertainment, but not topless. She'll dance around awhile, maybe drop the coat and strip down to her bra and a G-string, but that's all."

"How do you know?"

"Did you pay a cover charge?" Rankin's beer arrived and he took a sip.

"No."

"You only get what you pay for around here, buddy. See those four guys over there?"

"Yeah."

"Weren't there six when we came in?"

Crosby noted the diminished number.

"Now if you step behind those curtains, there's a cover charge, but that's a whole different establishment." Rankin smiled. "We're in the sports bar. Get it?"

"I see."

"You want a beer?"

"I quit drinking and we're still on duty, Kelly."

"You might be on duty, but Homeland Security got off work about . . ." he examined his watch, "three minutes ago. How about a beer and some hot wings?"

"No and you're buying your own. You still owe me for the bar tab in Denver. Remember?"

"I thought I paid that." He grinned.

Crosby shook his head. "You stiffed me, as usual, and I'm not paying again."

"You're so uptight, Crosby. What state are you from?"

"North Carolina."

"That's where they invented the toothbrush, right?"

"I wouldn't know."

"I think it was," Rankin said. "Otherwise it would have been called the *teethbrush*."

"Okay, that does it. I'll wait in the car."

Crosby started to get up, but Rankin extended a hand to stop him. "This isn't the reason we're here. Watch the door for a couple of minutes." Rankin nodded at the mirror in front of them.

Crosby noted the reflection of two men standing at the door. Both of them wore dark suits and sunglasses. One had white bandages on his ears.

"Sanders? What's he doing here?"

"Protecting the Vice President." Rankin kept his eyes on the mirror. "Agent Zack Blew mentioned that Trexler sneaks in here when he's in town to help him unwind after a hard day of golf."

They watched as the Vice President, disguised in a flowery print shirt, floppy straw hat and dark sunglasses entered. He immediately headed toward the stage, paused long enough to ogle at the dancer, and disappeared behind the curtain. Two of the agents remained outside the curtain to stand guard.

"See we missed our chance," Rankin said. "We'll never get inside now."

"Too bad, but why are we here? Trexler goes to strip bars, so what?"

"One thing I've learned about the boys in the Secret Service," Rankin said, "if you need a favor from them, you better have something to bargain with."

"Now I suppose we turn around, and let his two goons get a good look at us?"

Rankin picked up his beer. "Good idea." He motioned for the bartender. "Bring me one for my buddy, and while you're at it, send a couple of beers to those guys over against the curtains." He motioned over his shoulder with his thumb.

"Sure thing," the bartender said. "Add it to your tab?"

"Right." They waited on their barstools and watched the agents in the mirror. The moment the cocktail waitress approached them with the beers, Rankin and Crosby turned around and tipped their glasses in their direction. The two agents refused the offer, but the message had been delivered.

The cold beer in Crosby's hand brought back a flood of pleasant memories, the aroma, the taste and the beat of the music while sitting around a bar with college friends. He missed those days and he wanted to taste it so bad. Only one taste, surely he could handle that. A dancer was gyrating around the metal poles and Crosby's attention drifted towards her. The thong and tiny bra on the girl left little to the imagination. Her legs were long, but it wasn't until the dancer wrapped her bare legs around the pole that he realized why. It spawned an idea that took root just like Jack's magic beans. "Son of a *bitch*." Crosby took a twenty out of his wallet and threw it on the bar. He grabbed Rankin's sleeve and pulled. "Let's *go*."

"You're buying? What's the hurry?"

"Look at her shoes."

Rankin apparently had to pull his eyes away from the girl's breasts long enough to notice her feet. "So?"

"She's wearing six-inch stiletto heels, Kelly. I just realized why we're batting zero with the bank employees in Dillon. Our unsub wasn't *five nine*."

• • •

The last rays of sun dropped beyond the horizon at 5:47 p.m. An hour later, Lucy Harris grabbed her overnight bag and followed Carlos through the maze of passageways leading up to the sub's conning tower. The blue and white stripes of the Argentine flag contrasted against the purple starlit sky as she emerged on deck. She shook the Captain's hand and thanked him in Spanish. Carlos backed down the steps first and helped her into the rubber dinghy. She sat facing towards him. He pressed a piece of paper into her palm, cranked the engine and headed for the lights of Georgetown, Grand Cayman.

"What's this?" she asked over the din of the outboard.

"A number where you can reach me," Carlos said.

She tossed the paper overboard. "You can place a bid at our ISBN number until Tuesday."

"But I don't know your real name and you may need my help, no? Your government will never stop searching."

"Better that you don't. I'll either end up dead or somewhere else."

"I will miss you terribly, señorita. If you make your escape, someday you must promise to contact me."

"You once tried to rob and rape me at gunpoint, Carlos. Do you think I've forgotten that?"

"But señorita, that was only business."

"If I hadn't convinced you that the bomb was armed, I might be floating face down now."

"We have since become quite close, no? Our lovemaking was muy bueno."

"Ah, but as you say, that was business," she said. "You are an exceptional lover, Carlos and the photos turned out far clearer than even I expected."

"What photos?"

"A little insurance I uploaded to the web. My phone has a video camera and I had to be sure I could trust you."

Carlos chuckled. "Video of me. Who would care?"

"No one, except certain members of Spectrum, the CIA, or perhaps your wife. Since Margarite is Catholic, I think she would care."

His smile vanished. "What wife?"

"Carlos, you have three kids, who live with Margarite in Mar del Plata. Do I have to give you the street address as well?"

"How do you know this?"

"Does it matter? All I want is your country's bid, then your silence. Don't come looking for me, Carlos, and I won't come looking for you. As long as you keep your end of the bargain, neither of us has anything to fear."

He thought about it for a minute before a small hint of a smile returned.

"Agreed?"

He nodded. "Was I really an exceptional lover?"

She leaned forward and kissed him on the lips. "The *best.*"

"As I said before, señorita, you are one *smart* hembra."

•   •   •

Harold Sanders tossed the envelope on the bed of his hotel room and noticed the light on his phone was blinking. He picked up the receiver and punched in his room number. The first message began to play. It was Vice President Trexler's voice. "Agent Sanders, I just got off the phone with Washington. POTUS is moving to Bethesda; something about a broken toe. We'll only have time for one round before we head back to DC. See if the blonde from RockaCharlies knows how to drive a golf cart."

The message beeped and the second message played. This time it was Stalker's voice. "Raptor. When you get the package, call me."

The third message was from the Vice President again and this time he sounded nervous. "We may have a problem. Some members of the FBI may have been at the sports bar this evening. If it gets out that I was there it could result in an unfortunate scene for the administration."

Should have thought about that before you had the private lap dance.

"See if you can find out who these guys were," the Vice President continued. "Maybe they could use a pair of Super Bowl tickets to help them forget. Keep me posted on the results, okay?"

Sanders could only shake his head. He had recognized one of the men at the bar as Kelly Rankin, an agent at Homeland Security. He knew that Rankin was a player and the least likely person to spread Trexler's secrets. He suspected the other was FBI agent Crosby, but he was a burned-out alcoholic who had lost the last vestiges of his creditability three years earlier with his crazy conspiracy theories. Neither of them was worth a bullet, much less Super Bowl tickets.

•   •   •

Kelly Rankin and Devrin Crosby were arguing when they came through the hangar doors at the airbase.

"Where the hell have you two been?" Dr. Matthews asked. "Lynch was about to put out an all points bulletin."

"Earth shattering news," Rankin said. "Crosby had a *thought*."

"Have you been drinking?"

Rankin winked. "Just shadowing the Vice Pres, my dear. All in the line of duty."

She grabbed him by the arm. "Go gargle and brush your teeth. Lynch has been waiting on you for over two hours and he's not in the mood for jokes."

"Hey, I'm off duty."

"You're *never* off duty on this case." She turned towards Crosby. "Have you been drinking, too?"

"No, I was just with him."

"You were gone for three hours. Where have you been?"

"Discovering that Trexler is not the greatest pillar of our community."

"When you see Lynch, I'd come up with a better answer than that.

Come on, he's waiting."

Matthews and Crosby entered the makeshift conference area and found the Section Chief on the phone. "Yes, sir," he said into the receiver, "we're doing everything we can to locate them." He shot Crosby a cold glance. "I have my best men on it, sir. I will. Thank you." He hung up. "Where's Rankin?"

"He's using the restroom, sir," Matthews said.

Lynch looked at Crosby. "Well?"

"Officially the Secret Service is considering this an aborted attempt on the VP, but according to Agent Rankin's contact, they aren't taking the threat seriously."

"Then his contact is mistaken. I talked with Director Gregory. The President has raised the threat level to red and cleared his calendar. What else?"

"Agent Sanders was there. He had bandages over both ears."

"Tell me something important."

"Vice President Trexler frequents strip bars in disguise."

"It took three hours to find that out? We've known that since he was appointed. Anything else?"

Crosby took a breath. "I'm now convinced that the unsub is a woman, and—"

"We've been over this, Crosby." Lynch threw an enlarged satellite photo of the boat on the table. "We're not even sure this is Amil anymore."

"Why?"

Matthews explained. "All we have is their shadows to go by, but these height ratios are shorter than our suspects."

"I know that. We've been looking for Dillon employees that were five nine, but if she wore platform shoes under her suit she could have been any height."

"Why are you convinced?" Matthews said.

"Other than the manager, less than a handful of male employees worked at the Dillon branch over the last five years. None fit the profile. Who's left?"

"Women," Rankin said. He was leaning against the doorframe, his tie askew and his hair uncombed. "Aren't angels usually portrayed as women?"

Matthews seemed astonished that Rankin was acting so nonchalantly after her previous warning.

"The angels in the Bible all have masculine names." Lynch motioned Rankin towards a chair. "At least you two agree on something."

Matthews held an aerial shot of Dillon. "You really believe a woman did this?"

"Yes. I want a closer look at a profile shot of the unsub. If I'm right, we eliminate a third of the employee files."

"Do we have a good profile?" Lynch asked.

"Not from the bank video, but there is a photo of them with the ice chest," Matthews said. "It's from overhead, but it's pretty clear." She found the satellite enlargement in the stack and pulled it from its folder. They all took turns looking through a micro viewer.

All Lynch could see was the tops of their heads and shoulders. "Is this the best enlargement we can get?"

"I'm afraid so," Matthews said. "These were taken by a GEO's weather satellite. They're designed to photograph cloud formations not spy on boats."

"Is there another source?"

"There's the Office of National Reconnaissance," Rankin said. "They operate the government's spy satellites for NORAD. In their photos you can see what brand of cigar Castro's brother is puffing in Havana."

Lynch dropped the photos to the table. "Will someone please tell me why we are screwing around with weather satellites when those are available?"

"They're not available. It takes special permission from the Pentagon."

Lynch stood. "I can't believe what I'm hearing. Does the Office of Homeland Security not feel a ten-megaton blast warrants *special permission?*"

"No one has asked me until now," Rankin said.

Lynch turned to Crosby and Matthews. "Did you know about this?"

They both shook their heads.

"I should replace all of you. Don't go anywhere." Lynch stormed out of the room and silence filled his wake.

"That went well," Rankin said.

"Sometimes, I think you want to get kicked off this case," Matthews said.

"You could have mentioned those earlier," Crosby said.

"How was I to know what kind of satellite you were using?"

"We can't worry about it now," Matthews said, returning to the micro-viewer. "This guy has Amil's hair color. The other suspect has a small frame. Could that be the curve of a breast to the right of her chin?"

Rankin took the viewer. "Looks like boobs to me."

"This isn't funny, Kelly," Crosby said.

"By binding her breasts and using a short wig and moustache, she could fool a bank teller." Matthews said.

"But it wouldn't fool Amil," Rankin said. "He's Muslim, so no way he would work with a woman."

"Unless she knew something important," Crosby said. "Maybe he had no choice."

"Or he isn't through with her," Rankin said. "Why keep her disguise while on the boat in the Keys?"

Lynch returned, his anger subdued. "The CIA says that the Mexican police found wreckage of Troy Dills' plane at Agua Prieta, six miles south of the border near Douglas, Arizona. Dills is dead and there is no sign of Amil. Looks like there was a small explosion in the luggage compartment after takeoff."

Another trail had come to an end, and another folder would have to be added to Amil's file of victims. With nearly three hundred names attributed to him already it would soon outgrow its file cabinet.

"So assuming that is Amil on the boat, then he either had to fly out of Mexico to Key West, or travel across Mexico to the Brownsville area and rent the boat somewhere along the western gulf coast." Rankin said.

Dr. Matthews looked up from her smart phone. "Either way, that's eighteen hundred miles and I don't see how he could have made the nine hundred mile trek across the gulf by boat in less than two days."

"Don't assume anything," Lynch said. I just left a message for Director Gregory, but don't wait on his permission. Rankin, contact NORAD, and tell them I want a set of enlargements of this area sent here *immediately*."

"Yes, sir." Rankin said.

"Also order a set from the day before and the day after. I want to know where that boat came from, and more importantly, where the hell it *went*."

•　　•　　•

Stalker's envelope was under Sanders' door when he returned to his hotel. He ripped open the package and scanned the contents. He activated his Bluetooth headpiece and punched a four-digit code into his cell.

"Yes," Stalker replied in his high-pitched voice.

"I have the package," Sanders said.

"Item one. Ruth Froscher, the mother."

Sanders looked at the eight by ten photo of a gray-haired woman entering a law office.

"Don't waste my time," Sanders growled, tossing it on the bed. "Next!"

"Katie Froscher, the sister. She's a systems analyst for First Nations Bank in Charlotte, North Carolina."

The photo was black and white and looked as if it had been lifted from a college annual. "Is this a current shot?"

"We couldn't find one. She's on vacation in the Caribbean."

"Where?"

"Don't get excited, I'm way ahead of you. I tracked her credit card receipts. She was in Charlotte the whole week of the Dillon blast and already aboard the cruise ship when the Marquesas Keys blew up."

"Where did the ship depart?"

"Miami."

"Did it stop in Key West?"

"No."

"Anywhere else?"

"In Cozumel. It should be headed to Grand Cayman now."

"Did she have time to arrange it before the cruise?"

"No way. She spent the previous day shopping all over Fort Lauderdale. Left a trail of paper a blind man could follow."

"What else?"

"She supposedly won the cruise last summer in a promotion sponsored by a car dealership. Besides, she's a bank systems analyst. She couldn't build a bomb if her life depended on it."

"Neither could her mother. It's *your* list." Sanders tossed the photo and rubbed his temples. "Next."

"Beth Morrison. Dated Chuck Froscher during his junior and senior years in high school. Attended the prom together and broke up in 1989. She—"

"What the hell is this?" Sanders flipped through the photos. "All of these are at least twenty years old. I asked for current information, not ancient *history*."

"That's it," Stalker said. "Other than an occasional one night stand, I can't find a single relationship Chuck Froscher had during the last ten years of his life."

"Was he a monk?"

"He was a weapons engineer. Apparently, they don't get out much."

"What about his drinking buddies?"

"They all worked for us, and we've been through them with a nit comb."

"Then go though them *again*. Someone is sending us on a wild goose chase by pinning this on Froscher. There's a connection somewhere. *Find it!*"

• • •

It had been a long day and everyone at the FBI field office was tired and hungry. For Devrin Crosby, even a snack was impossible, as he had blown his last twenty in his rush to leave RockaCharlies. The smell of hot wings loomed in his memory, aggravating the fact that once again Kelly had gotten free drinks at his expense.

Rankin was supposed to be across the giant hangar, typing in his daily report to Homeland Security, but Crosby had little doubt that he managed to sneak out for a nice dinner and probably another round at RockaCharlies. At least Dr. Matthews was still here to keep him company. She was on the phone trying to convince the Agua Prieta policía department to fax a coroner's report on Troy Dills to her attention, with little luck.

Crosby had poured over hundreds of the weather satellite photos for two days. More were en route, but those weren't the ones Lynch wanted. With little else to do, he grabbed a stack of OleWest employee records and headed back to Lynch's office. This time he was determined to ask for a much needed dinner break.

"According to our records, Amil is five foot eight," Lynch was saying to Agent James as Crosby entered. "And you're saying that the lab calculates this shadow at five foot four inches?"

"Give or take a half-inch," James said. "Shadows can be distorted, but that's what they're saying."

Lynch looked up. "Crosby. How can platform shoes make someone shorter?" He didn't wait for an answer and nodded at the package in Crosby's hand. "Are those the NORAD photos?"

"No, sir. They may not arrive until tomorrow morning. These are Dillon employee records that were rejected because of their height.

I'm about to go back through them, but I was—"

"Good. Have a seat, and get started."

This was obviously not the time to ask for a dinner break. Crosby sat and opened the package.

"Where the hell is Rankin?"

"He's writing his report to Homeland Security." Crosby knew it was probably a lie and wondered why he was covering for him. He was sure Rankin would never return the favor.

Lynch resumed with Agent James. "What about the other guy? How does he compare with our unsub in Dillon?"

"This one's shadow is about five foot six."

"So, the height is a good three inches shorter than our terrorist."

"Yes, sir," James said.

"They could have been barefoot onboard," Crosby interjected.

"Good point, Devrin. Is there any other way to ID that boat?"

"Not from this angle," James said. "Once we have a full series from NORAD, we should be able to trace it back to its home port."

"We could have had those two days ago."

Crosby started with the most recent employment records, the top folder belonging to Leslie Pryce. A copy of her application, written in the printed hand of a teenager, lay just inside. The rest of the file contained a drug screening form, criminal background check, a six-month evaluation where she had scored excellent, but little else. Crosby moved on to the next folder. It belonged to the branch bank manager, David Anthony. He was about to open it when Dr. Matthews rushed into the room.

"The NORAD photos have arrived." She handed her tablet computer to Crosby. "You need to look at these *now.*"

Crosby clicked on the first photo, taken during daylight, and immediately noticed a sheen of oil around the boat. He handed the tablet to Lynch while Matthews transferred a flash card of the files to the big flat screen.

"What's this?" Lynch pointed to the sheen on the water.

"An oil slick," Matthews said. "We may have seen the last of our terrorist."

"Why?"

"This photo indicates that their boat broke down less than eight miles south of the islands," Matthews explained. "It looks like they tried to fix it, but all the while the current was carrying them back towards ground zero."

Matthews opened the second photo, snapped during the explosion. "I'll be *damned*," Lynch mumbled. Bathed in the light of the blast, was a shock wave only seconds from sending the *Island Breeze* into oblivion.

CHAPTER 13

CAYMAN

Wednesday

The Carnival *Victory* arrived in Georgetown Bay at eight a.m. For all of its wealth, Grand Cayman had never built a deep-water dock, so the passengers relied on tenders to ferry them to shore. Twenty minutes later, Katie Froscher, wearing dark sunglasses, stepped off the tender onto British territory. Her long brown hair was pulled tightly into a ponytail, extending out the back of a baseball cap. She made her way across the wharf and out onto the streets of Georgetown. Lucy Harris fell into step beside Katie and kept walking. Lucy was also wearing dark glasses and in her hand was an electronic bug detector.

"Are we okay?" Katie asked without looking toward Lucy.

"Just background frequencies. If someone's listening, it's with a parabolic dish." Lucy put away the device.

"I'm surprised you made it."

Lucy shook her head. "Not here. Let's walk for a few blocks first. The hotel is about half a mile up the beach."

The crowds around them dispersed until they were walking alone. Katie handed Lucy a sign and sail card and a duplicate of her own driver's license, but with Lucy's photo. "You'll need these to board the ship. Our cabin number is 9203. Your sign and sail card will open the door, but we will have to use my card to order drinks and room service.

"Do I have a room?"

"Yes, but it's the size of a closet and has no porthole. Ours is much nicer. Be careful of the room steward. He thinks I'm alone."

Lucy looked at her sign and sail card. "This card has your name on it and your photo in a blonde wig?"

"So you can reboard the ship," Katie said. "Mine is identical except for the hair. We're using real names to provide an alibi and I think it's best if you can prove you stayed aboard the ship at Grand Cayman."

"Good idea. But how will you get aboard?"

"With my cards. I'll explain how later."

"So this is all we'll need?"

"Just that and my fake driver's license. Security's not bad until we get off in Miami. There, you can use your real driver's license and passport to re-enter the country. The moment it's scanned your alibi is airtight."

Lucy smiled and slipped the card into her purse. "Did you get the new documents?"

"I picked them up in Miami. His work is flawless. I opened the account using your Annie Kagle identification. Is she real?"

"One of Trexler's former aides," Lucy said. "She accused him of sexual harassment about two years ago and dropped the charges after he paid her off."

"Nice touch."

"A little insurance. Everything ties back to Trexler, in one way or another. Where are the documents?"

"They're in here." Katie opened her bag and handed Lucy an envelope. Your passport, your real driver's license and credit card along with the fake North Carolina driver's license, birth certificate and credit card. The name on the Florida license was Gwendolyn Fisher. "Who's Gwen?"

"She's an exotic dancer I once worked with in Alexandra. Another one of the Norman conquests."

Katie gave her a sideways glance. "You'll have to brush up on your pole dance."

"Let's stick to practicing our names. Did you get my package in the mail?"

Katie nodded slowly. "It was at the Carnival desk when I checked in. Thank goodness I waited until I was in my cabin before opening it."

"How much?"

"I stopped counting at one hundred and fifty thousand. I can't believe you mailed that. What the hell are we supposed to do with it?"

Lucy shrugged. "I don't care. Buy a beach house."

"I should buy a yacht in Jamaica and disappear."

"Go ahead, as long as you give me the worm first."

"You'll get it soon enough. How did it go in the Keys?"

"No problem. Carlos was interesting. Did you receive the photos?"

"Nice ass. Do you think we'll need them?"

Lucy shook her head. "He's harmless."

"As long as he doesn't have a bomb. He was cute. You get all the cute men, don't you?"

"*Right*. You get to kick back on a cruise ship for three days, while I'm stuck inside a cramped submarine as the personal toy of an oversexed Argentinean."

"You could have said no."

"It was part of the sales pitch," Lucy said. "Besides, what else was there to do aboard a sub?"

Katie smiled. "I think you're confusing who was whose sex toy."

•　•　•

Gerald McMullen waited anxiously at the gangplank for the second tender to tie up alongside. He had seen her, not ten minutes earlier, from the back of the line. She had gotten aboard the first tender wearing a baseball cap and carrying an oversized black bag. This time, he was certain it was Katie Froscher.

•　•　•

"*Crosby,*" Kelly Rankin yelled. "Are you going to sleep all day?" Rankin was standing at the barracks door. Light flooded the room where Crosby was sleeping.

Crosby squinted. "What time is it?"

"Get up. It's nearly eight. Lynch wants us to oversee the search for the fishing boat."

Crosby's mouth felt sticky. "What fishing boat?" He had tossed and turned since three a.m. on the hard cot.

"The one in the photos."

"Give me a *break*." Crosby turned over. "That boat's history."

"It may have sunk, but it's still on the bottom. Lynch wants it found."

Crosby turned and opened one eye. "Are you serious?"

"There might be bodies aboard."

"After two days in the Caribbean? They would have been scavenged within hours. You're joking, right?"

"Not this time. Lynch has a whole team of divers lined up. The

Navy has loaned us a magnetometer and the use of a side-scan sonar unit."

"That's fabulous," Crosby mumbled, swinging one foot to the floor.

"How do you take your coffee?"

"Cream and sugar."

"Sounds good." Rankin grinned. "Bring me a cup when you get yours, okay?"

· · ·

They walked north toward seven-mile beach and practiced their aliases. Lucy explained how she came ashore under the cover of darkness and showed Katie the beach resort where she was staying. They ordered room service and ate breakfast on their private verandah overlooking the wide white sands with turquoise waters as far as they could see.

"I could get accustomed this," Lucy said.

"I already have. If we survive this, I'm moving here."

"I'm sure it beats the hell out of prison."

"Speaking of which—" Katie's expression turned serious. "—what the hell happened in Dillon?"

Lucy shifted in her chair. "Amil insisted on a real demonstration."

"You offered him that. A remote valley in the mountains, where he could witness it, yet still be protected from the blast. You said no one would die."

"I told you my disguise wouldn't work. Amil said the only way he would trust a woman was if I got my hands dirty."

"You mean bloody?"

"He had a gun pointed at my head, Katie. He wanted a bank job, just like he did in Madrid, with or without me. I had no choice."

"Why Dillon?"

"It was the smallest town I could think of," Lucy said. "I figured on the day after Thanksgiving most of the inhabitants would be shopping at the malls in Denver. Amil insisted on Denver, but I convinced him that with city traffic, there was no way to get away in time."

"Why does he choose banks?"

"Banks are full of alarms. He likes a crowd." Lucy could tell that Katie was starting to see her side of the story. "If that stupid bank manager had just followed procedure, they would have evacuated and no one would have died. What idiot picks up a bomb?"

"That's a lame excuse, Lucy. It's like blaming a baby for pulling the pin on a hand grenade."

Lucy shook her head. "This guy wasn't ignorant. The normal procedure was to clear the building and call in the bomb squad. It was *drilled* into us. Amil must have really ticked him off."

"Dead bodies mean nothing to Amil. I'm sure he's willing to die along with them."

"You're right about that," Lucy said. "We barely got away in time."

"So instead of looking for Amil, now they're looking for you?"

Lucy placed a folded newspaper on the table. "Actually, they're looking for him."

The front page of the paper contained a grainy black and white photo of Lucy wearing a man's suit and disguised in a short wig, fake nose and moustache. Katie examined it closely. Even with the poor resolution she could see a resemblance to her late brother.

"Why does he look like Chuck?"

"After we saw *Mission Impossible*, he had a life mask made. I wore it that Halloween."

Katie put her hands to her face. "I should have never agreed to this. They'll exhume his grave, arrest me and interrogate my mother. The press alone will *kill* her."

"No they won't. Chuck is dead and your mother knows *nothing*. They can't pin anything on you because you've on a cruise ship the entire time."

"The same ship as you," Katie said. "When they look into Chuck's past they'll find you and that will lead them to me."

"There is nothing tying my real name to Chuck. I would never betray you, Katie. I'll die first."

"I knew I should have turned the file over to the FBI the moment I found it."

"Do you think we had a choice? Your brother gave the file to the *President* of the *United States* and look what they did to *him*. No one is out of Spectrum's reach. They'll kill millions more if we don't stop them. This isn't about taking lives, Katie—it's about saving them."

"Tell that to the innocent victims in Dillon."

"Fifty times that number died in Hiroshima and it eventually killed my grandmother as well."

"That was war, Lucy."

"This isn't? What do you think Amil will do when he gets his hands on one of Spectrum's bombs?"

"He'll either put it in Times Square on New Year's Eve, or use it on Jerusalem."

"*Exactly.*" Lucy said. "Six million people could die, and Amil was bragging that Spectrum had already agreed to sell it to them. If you can live with what they've done; with what they're about to do, now is the time to leave."

• • •

Crosby was half asleep, as he lay on a bench on the back of a chartered yacht, an empty coffee cup in his hands.

Kelly Rankin was on his cell phone. "Yeah, he's aboard. Hey, Crosby, you awake?"

Crosby raised one finger in a less than professional manner.

Rankin laughed. "Let's just say he's not in tip-top shape yet." The boat's engines started and a deckhand untied the mooring lines. It slowly pulled away from the dock.

"You want *me* to tell him? Hey, Crosby, Marti says good morning."

Crosby repeated the gesture.

"I think he's reading the wind direction. I'll explain it later." As Rankin listened his smile vanished. "What? Are you sure?" Rankin got out his notepad. "In Egypt? What was the flight number?" He jotted on the pad. "No, it's a relief, right? Yeah, call me when you have confirmation. Oh, I can't wait to tell him. Don't forget to call." He punched the End key and added for Crosby's benefit, "Love you too, sweetheart."

Crosby opened one eye. "What?"

"Buddy, you'll never believe this. They've found Amil."

• • •

Katie sat on the beach for a long time, reviewing how she had gotten herself into this mess. Lucy's offer to let her walk away was tempting, but she knew she couldn't. That would be the worse type of betrayal and Lucy had taken great risks to hold up her end of the bargain. Now that it was her turn, she couldn't just leave her friend hanging. She was too involved already, and the punishment for accessory to murder was just as bad as committing the crime.

She pushed her bare feet through the warm sand, letting it flow between her toes. Her toenails were painted black, the same color as Lucy's—mourning toes. She recalled the first time she had seen Lucy's black toenails in a pair of open-toed pumps at the gravesite of her brother, Chuck. For years Chuck had never once mentioned a girlfriend, but Lucy Harris, along with Chuck's best friend, Ryan Papineau, had accompanied her brother's body on its final trip from Tennessee for burial in the family plot.

The graveside service was short, and afterward Katie spoke with them briefly. Ryan was nervous and secretive, saying only that he and Chuck had worked together in Chicago. Lucy was open and friendly—exactly the kind of girl Chuck had been attracted to in high school. Lucy worked for a bank in Chicago and had grown up near Denver. Chuck made frequent trips to a research facility in Batavia, thirty miles west of Chicago and at some point they had met and fallen for each other.

Katie remembered the tears streaming down Lucy's cheeks, the only time she had ever seen her cry. Lucy's hair had been black then. Her striking dark eyes had just the slightest almond shape, betraying an oriental gene somewhere in her past. They were about the same age and had both worked in the banking industry. She would have made an excellent sister-in-law if things had been different.

They exchanged e-mail addresses and phone numbers before parting, promised to keep in touch, but didn't. A little over a year later, Katie read in the *Chicago Tribune* that Ryan Papineau's car had plunged off a bridge into a frozen river. His body had floated away under the ice and was presumed dead. That very day, Katie opened the safety deposit box containing her brother's secret file, and upon reading the contents, placed a call to Lucy Harris.

"I know who killed them," was all she said.

•   •   •

The Navy diver spit into his mask, rubbed the saliva over the glass, and fell over backwards into the clear ocean water. Kelly Rankin was looking over the shoulder of a sonar technician watching the outline on a small screen. The object resting on the bottom sixty-five feet below was the length, width and height of the fishing boat in question. If it was the boat, they should have a name within thirty minutes.

Devrin Crosby was leaning on the rail watching the diver's bubbles break the surface. Rankin came up and slapped him on the shoulder. "Cheer up, Crosby. With any luck our unsubs are still inside."

"Are they *sure* it was Amil?"

"Hey, don't shoot the messenger. Marti said INTERPOL had a photo of Amil getting off a plane in Egypt two hours before the Marquesas bomb exploded. Nothing's been confirmed, but if it's true, there's no way he was aboard this boat."

"It's a plant. He wants us to believe he's in Egypt."

"Could be. But have you considered the possibility that he placed this bomb on the island *before* he did Dillon?"

Crosby rubbed his temples. "Amil left his calling card on the island."

"Somebody did. Maybe his accomplice. We do occasionally make mistakes, Crosby. I thought you had learned that."

"Go to *hell!* I'm going below. Let me know when you hear from the diver."

●　　●　　●

"What are you thinking?" Lucy stood beside Katie on the beach.

"Black toenail polish."

"That day we met at Chuck's funeral."

"Back when we were only innocent bystanders."

"You still are."

Katie shook her head. "Not anymore. Why don't we just take their money, disappear and pretend this never happened?"

"You know I can't. I loved Chuck, but it's more than that; I owe it to my grandmother. I won't stand by and let our government do this again."

"It must have been weird, you and Chuck. You never told me how you met."

Lucy sat down on the sand next to Katie. "When I first moved to Chicago, Ryan Papineau lived in the same apartment building. We met in the elevator and he had that sexy French accent. He wasn't my type, but I had him over every now and then for a late night slam."

"Only you could reduce casual sex to that level," Katie said.

"We got pretty comfortable with each other. One night when we were lying in bed, I told him about my grandmother. He was shocked and said his best friend's father had helped drop the A-bomb. After he introduced me to Chuck, I discovered that your dad wasn't with the Hiroshima crew. They dropped the bomb on Nagasaki."

"I bet it still stung."

Lucy bit her lip. "Yeah."

"How did you feel?"

"I don't know. Mostly curious. Chuck was this ordinary, wonderful guy and once I got to know him, all that hatred vanished. It wasn't his fault. It wasn't your father's fault. They both were just following orders. Unfortunately, those orders came from a government that cared more about its weapons than its people. Twenty-three hundred American citizens were in Hiroshima, but they still leveled it."

Katie nodded. Lucy had told her this many times.

"You know, if Chuck and I had never met, he wouldn't be dead; the President wouldn't be dead and we wouldn't be here, planning ways to bring about our own demise."

Katie took Lucy's hand and squeezed it. She put her face against her friend's cheek and felt the wetness from her tears. "We'll stop them, and together we'll get through this."

•   •   •

Gerald McMullen had seen all the tourist spots he ever cared to. He had snorkeled with the giant stingrays of Grand Cayman, visited a sea turtle farm, and even mailed a postcard from a post office at a volcanic outcropping named Hell. Katie Froscher had not been at any of them. His entire reason for taking the cruise was so he wouldn't have to spend his vacation alone. Yet here he was, still alone with the cruise half over. As the tour bus headed back to Georgetown, he vowed to quit wasting his time and find a real estate agent before they sailed.

•   •   •

The remote desktop program on Katie Froscher's laptop allowed her to access her office computer at First Nations Bank from anywhere in the world. She started to check her e-mail, but she was on vacation, damn it, and any real problems could be handled by Mandy. With a few keystrokes she was able to open her automated message program at the bank and place a call to Denver. A message appeared on her screen: OleWest National Bank. Please select from the following menu.

Katie clicked the Human Resources Department icon. A few

seconds later, the HR Department screen appeared, and she clicked on the Employment Confirmation icon. She typed in First Nations National Bank and the name of the employee applicant: Vanessa Lucille Harris.

A text message appeared: One moment please.

Katie held her Alt key down and pressed the F7 key. The remote micro in her keystroke capture program began recording.

•   •   •

An hour later Lucy emerged from the bathroom, a towel wrapped around her and a shower cap covering her hair. Katie was already dressed in a white blouse and tan skirt, casual enough for the islands with just a hint of professionalism. She was sitting on the edge of the bed watching a newscast on CNN. Lucy sat down beside her and dried her legs.

"Any news from the mainland?" Lucy asked.

"The Vice President had a news conference in Key West yesterday," Katie said. "I think I saw Agent Sanders in the background."

"He's the one they call Raptor."

"Chuck's file didn't have his real name, only that he was with the Secret Service and had bad acne scars on his cheeks. Sanders' face looks like a moonscape. He also fits the description of a man seen leaving Chuck's apartment the day he was murdered. He looked taller than I expected and had something covering his ears."

"What did it look like?"

"I'm not sure. Maybe bandages."

"Could be a ringing from the blast. He may have been closer than we realized." Lucy reached in her purse and removed a thirty-eight caliber pistol. "You may need this."

"I can't take that into a bank," Katie said, alarmed.

"Not here. I'm mailing it to a post office box in Charlotte. Once you arrive, you'll need to keep it near you."

Katie shook her head. "I don't—"

"Never underestimate him. If he spots you, shoot him, point blank in the head, before he can react. Understand?"

"*No*, I can't do that."

"Katie, if you don't, he *will* kill you, just like he murdered Chuck. You know *that*."

"I know, but you can't expect me to just shoot someone in cold blood."

"I expect you to defend yourself. Chances are he won't die with only a thirty-eight in him."

"I won't need it."

"The gun will be at the post office just in case."

"I'm not a murderer, Lucy."

"Then if he kills you, at least I tried. And remember, it's Gwen. We've got to keep this straight. One screw up and we're both *dead*."

"I know. I've got it."

•   •   •

At precisely 10:00 a.m. Katie Froscher, bearing the identification of Annie Kagle, walked into Grand Cayman National Bank. By the time she left, twenty-eight million dollars had been transferred to a bank two blocks away. At 10:30 a.m., Gwendolyn Fisher entered the second bank and transferred twenty-six million over to The Lords of London Grand Cayman Branch. One million was then transferred to a bank in Panama. The second million went to Bermuda. And so, the process of bouncing the money around the Caribbean began. At some point the bidders would come looking for it, but with over eight hundred fifty banks on Grand Cayman alone, tracking it would be a nightmare.

By noon, the bulk of twenty million dollars had landed in a series of foreign mutual funds with a combined growth of sixteen percent the previous year. If everything went as planned, in a week, two banks, one in Panama, the other in Bermuda, would send a surprise statement to the Internal Revenue Service stating that Norman Trexler, whose name was on both accounts, had suddenly become a millionaire. A separate statement, forwarded from a post office box in the town of Hell, Grand Cayman, would show a daily flow of interest, siphoned off the top of the mutual funds and automatically wired into numbered bank accounts in Switzerland. From there, like the morning fog in a Swiss valley, it would vanish into thin air.

CHAPTER 14

KEY WEST

"*Island Breeze*," Kelly Rankin said into his phone. "Yes, sir. The diver thinks the interior is empty. We'll know when it gets to the surface." He listened. "Yes, sir. It'll work. The Coast Guard cutter should be here within the hour. They do it all the time."

Crosby frowned.

"Yes, sir. We'll keep you posted." Rankin closed the phone. "They're checking to see if *Island Breeze* rings any bells in Key West."

"What did you mean by, 'when it gets to the surface?'" Crosby had forgotten his sunglasses and his eyes ached from squinting in the bright light. He also had a splitting headache.

"The diver said the hull looks sound. You don't want to dive down to it, do you?"

"I don't dive."

"That's why we're bringing it up."

"Kelly, it takes weeks to get a salvage team. We don't have the time."

Rankin smiled. "No, it won't. Years ago, a friend of mine was skiing behind his dad's thirty-five-footer in the ocean. They were having a party aboard and too many girls were on the upper bridge—"

"Is this going somewhere?"

"Just listen. The boat made a sharp turn, my buddy cuts his ski too hard and," Kelly snapped his fingers, "the whole boat tipped over on its side and sank."

Crosby rubbed his temples. "So, everyone drowned. What's this got to do with the *Island . . .* whatever?"

"*Island Breeze*. And no one drowned. It sank in only fifteen feet of water, so the upper bridge was sticking above the surface like an oil platform. The e-purb went off when she sank and signaled the Coast Guard. An hour later, a cutter shows up, sees them standing on the upper bridge and rescues them. My buddy thought his dad's fifty-thousand-dollar boat was a total loss."

"What's your point, Kelly?"

"Here's the thing, a couple guardsmen jumped overboard, hooked a cable to the front of the sunken boat. The cutter took off and the whole damn boat came to the surface like it was a toy. Most of the water ran right out the back from the inertia. They pumped out the remaining water, cleaned out the fuel lines and started up the engines. I swear the only things he had to replace were the mat-tresses, the radios, and a TV set."

Crosby waited to hear the punch line to a joke. "Are you serious?"

"Yes, it really happened?"

"You think it will work?"

"It did then. This one is much deeper, but one of their naval engineers told me as long as the hull is sound it's worth a shot." Rankin laughed. "Engineers love a challenge. Hey, did you hear the one about the three engineers debating who designed the human body?"

Crosby closed his eyes. There was no use in trying to ignore Kelly's jokes.

"So the first engineer said, 'The human body had to be designed by a mechanical engineer. Just look at all the skeleton's moving parts.' The second one said, 'No way. It was an electrical engineer. The human nervous system is a work of art.' Then third engineer said, 'You're both wrong. It was a civil engineer.' The other two asked how he could possibly think that. 'Well,' he said. 'Who else would put a toxic waste pipe through the middle of a recreational area?"

Despite the headache, Crosby found himself smiling. Even he had to admit that Kelly had his moments.

* * *

The line of passengers trying to catch the one o'clock tender to the Carnival *Victory* stretched around the wharf. As Katie Froscher neared the security guard post, she whispered to Lucy. "I'll go through the right line, you go to the left. The guard in the right line checked me aboard at Cozumel."

"Okay," Lucy said. "Will I need the birth certificate?"

"No, just the cardkey and your license."

"What about the card reader?"

"Make sure each of us have the same number of people in line in front of us. If one line goes faster, simply let someone go ahead. Pretend to fumble through your purse. We need to scan our cards as close to the same moment as possible. So keep an eye on me."

"Won't the scanners detect the duplicate?"

"Yes, but each guard has a portable reader, and the data isn't uploaded into the ship's computer until *after* they get aboard. It will look like I swiped it twice. Double swipes happen all the time and as long as it's within a second or two, it won't raise a red flag."

"Okay," Lucy said.

"Keep the driver's license handy, but be sure you pull out the right one."

Lucy held it up. "Gwendolyn Fisher, that's me."

"No, you'll need the Katie Froscher license, not Gwen's."

"Right. I'll show him some cleavage so he won't look too hard at my face."

"At least you're acting the part of a stripper."

The security guard was a burly Panamanian sporting a closely cropped flattop. Lucy was right; he took one look at her chest and never saw her scan the card right on cue with Katie.

Lucy cleared her throat. The guard looked up at her, smiled and waved her through. She rejoined Katie at the dock and they walked hand-in-hand aboard the tender.

"Any problems?" Katie asked.

"He wanted to squeeze my melons."

"Cool your jets, Elvira. The last thing we need is to *attract* attention."

* * *

For a brief moment Gerald McMullen thought his luck had finally changed. He was sitting aboard the tender watching it fill with passengers when he spotted Katie Froscher coming through the checkpoint queue. He laid a newspaper in the seat beside him, so it would remain empty, and available if she came his way. But when she stepped aboard, he noticed that she was holding hands with another girl. They found two seats near the back and continued to hold hands as they sat together. Then he saw Katie lean over and either whisper in the other girl's ear, or kiss her on the cheek. He couldn't tell which.

No wonder Mandy was so suspicious when I suggested that we were an item. She's gay. Gerald shook his head. It was the one thing he hadn't considered.

* * *

Robert Lynch only had two agents present for the daily briefing and held it in his temporary office. All morning Dr. Matthews and Agent James had poured over the NORAD satellite photos trying to determine how Amil Yaspar had slipped through their fingers, and a crucial set of the previous day and night infrared photos had yet to arrive. Lynch started with the latest news.

"INTERPOL is still trying to track down the man fitting Amil's description who passed through Cairo International on Monday evening," he said. "His flight originated in Mexico City, which is slightly over a thousand miles southeast of Agua Prieta, where Dills' plane crashed. If Amil has returned to the safety of his homeland then we need to determine who was aboard the *Island Breeze*, and if there are additional targets."

"In order to make the flight from Mexico City, Amil had to leave the day before the blast," Dr. Matthews said. "That's a minimum six hour flight from Key West through Miami."

"The satellite photo shows the dark haired unsub still aboard moments before the explosion," Agent James said. "Someone left the angel on the beach."

"At least one of them could have been our Dillon unsub," Matthews said. "Since the dinghy was left on the island they had no way to escape once the boat engine quit."

"Why not take the dinghy with them?"

"Maybe they thought it would slow them down. Dinghies are usually pulled behind. If I just armed a ten megaton bomb, I would want to get away as quickly as possible."

"Could a helicopter have picked them up?" Lynch said.

"Yes," Agent James said, "But both were aboard the next day working on the engine."

"Agent Crosby thinks this is a ruse," Matthews said. "He said Rankin proposed a theory that Amil planted the bomb last week then paid some fishermen to draw that symbol Saturday night."

"That's the best theory yet," Lynch said. "We're going to need earlier photos."

"Yes sir," Agent James said. "I'm expecting infrared enlargements any minute now. They'll tell us if any other boats or aircraft were near the area after nightfall."

"Good. I'm headed back to Washington this afternoon. If they recover the boat, I want it gone over with a fine toothed comb. We need answers before he strikes again."

. . .

The raising of the *Island Breeze* proved to be more challenging than Agent Rankin had first described. Given the depth, and the amount of water displaced, it was feared that the strain would either tear the cleat from the bow of the sunken vessel, or snap the cable. Therefore, with the aid of weight belts, divers placed deflated rubber rafts in the forward and rear cabins of the *Island Breeze*. Once in place and the weights removed, the divers partially inflated the rafts using the compressed air from their scuba tanks, but left enough room for the air to expand as it neared the surface. Sine the rafts couldn't be inflated enough to raise the boat, a winch cable was attached to the forward cleat to snatch the boat off the bottom. The order was given, the cable tightened, and the *Island Breeze* headed for the surface.

. . .

Lucy Harris froze when she stepped aboard the gangplank of the Carnival *Victory*. Ninety one hundred dollar bills were hidden inside her handbag, and just beyond the entrance, people were placing their pocketbooks on the conveyor of an X-ray machine. Katie had an equal amount in her bag.

"You didn't mention this," Lucy whispered.

"Just relax and act normal."

"Relax? It's an X-ray. They'll *see* the money. How can we explain that much cash?"

"Tell them you went to the bank. There's a casino aboard the ship. Trust me."

Lucy placed her handbag on the belt and held her breath. One security guard stared blankly at the screen while the other seemed focused on Lucy's cleavage. Katie's bag received the same nonchalant treatment. They retrieved their bags and set out in the direction of the elevators. Lucy let out a sigh of relief. "That guy didn't even notice," she said as the elevator doors shut.

"Same thing happened in Cozumel. Maybe the machine only detects metal and explosives."

. . .

Gerald McMullen stood against the back wall of the overcrowded elevator, pretending to read a newspaper. He had vowed not to follow, but having already invested twenty-three hundred dollars in this wild goose chase, he wanted to be sure. He would observe from a distance and perhaps locate her cabin. If the other girl joined her, he would have his answer.

· · ·

The pumps were still hard at work when Agents Crosby and Rankin stepped aboard the *Island Breeze*, or what was left of it. The upper superstructure had been splintered and melted into a mass of pointed shards that leaned at a sixty degree angle to port. Everything was black, and the smell of seawater mixed with burned polyester resin wasn't helping Crosby's headache.

"I'll take the front cabin," Crosby said. As soon as he climbed down the stairs, he stepped into several inches of water. He looked up to see Rankin's feet on the top step, enclosed in a pair of rubber boots.

"Where'd those come from?"

"Boy Scout's motto; always be prepared."

"*Wonderful!*" Crosby's leather oxfords were soaked. Rankin stepped down beside him, the tops of his boots high and dry.

"Wait a minute. You didn't have any boots when we left this morning."

"Didn't need to. The Coast Guard's got plenty aboard."

Crosby glared. "You're a *real jerk*. You know that, Kelly?"

"That's what my ex-wife used to say after I had sex."

"Why? You couldn't please her?"

"No, she said that *after* I called to let her know I'd be home in thirty minutes." He grinned. "I'll check the aft cabin. Looks deep back there."

There was a three-inch flexible pipe in the lower deck hallway, running into the lavatory. Crosby waded through the water and watched a crewman pumping water out of the shower stall. Ahead, he could see the door to the forward cabin. As soon as he released the latch, it sprang open. The entire doorway and room was filled with bright orange; the now expanded rubber raft. He turned back to the lavatory and stuck his head in the door.

"Hey, buddy. Any way to deflate those rafts in the room."

The crewman looked up. "You could stick a knife in them, but I wouldn't if I were you."

"Why not?" Rankin stood behind Crosby, looking over his shoulder. "Same problem aft."

"They may be the only thing keeping this wreck afloat," the crewman said.

Other than the hall, the kitchen and the lavatory, there was no other place to examine, so the two agents headed back upstairs. Crosby squinted in the bright sunlight and poured water out of his shoes. He noticed what appeared to be some type of melted metal frame shoved into one corner. Apparently it had once been a lounge chair. What was odd was there seemed to be a face melted into the remains of the webbing. He knelt down to examine it closer. He had read about human shadows being burned into concrete, but this was different. It was some type of plastic.

Rankin saw it too. "What the hell is that?"

"I have no idea."

• • •

When the glass elevator stopped at the lobby floor, Lucy's eyes widened on a world of marble and tropical plants. Before her stood a fourteen-story atrium crowned with a two hundred ten-foot water slide at the top and a full dance floor and bar at its base. A grand staircase climbed the far wall with a bar at each landing. It was more luxurious than most five star hotels in Europe.

"I spent three days on a smelly submarine while you had this?" Lucy said.

"You wanted something nice and we still have three days aboard. Wait until you see our room."

Cabin 9203 was on the Lido deck, one deck above the bridge. It was one of three cabins that faced out the front of the ship. The semi-private promenade outside was actually the roof of the bridge, affording them not only a panoramic view of the ocean ahead, but also a view along both sides of the ship from the bridge "wings."

"How much did this set us back?"

"Believe it or not, these cabins are the same rate as ones at the bottom of the ship. The view is supposedly obstructed by the promenade."

"You're kidding."

"No, I'm not. Best of all, nobody comes out here. You know what that means."

They both slapped their hands in a high-five. "No tan lines." they said in unison.

•   •   •

Rankin and Crosby arrived back at the temporary field office a little after three in the afternoon. Their FBI windbreakers and shirts were stained from grease, sweat and seawater, plus they were starving. Rankin stopped at a vending machine while Crosby continued to Lynch's office.

Lynch was at his desk. "You look terrible."

"I feel worse. They recovered the wreck."

"So, Rankin's idea worked?"

Crosby was in no mood to pat his partner on the back. "It's floating."

"Did you find anything?"

"Not much, just a folding lounge chair. Something was melted into the webbing. I'll ask Dr. Matthews to take a look."

"Where is it?"

"Still on the boat. The Coast Guard is towing it back. They should arrive around seven this evening."

"I'm heading back to Washington in a few minutes," Lynch said. "You and Rankin did well today. Keep at it."

"Sir, with all due respect," Crosby said with exasperation, "I believe I'd work better with—"

"Don't even ask."

"He's a selfish *jerk!*"

"Rankin thinks on his feet like a cop, and that's what *you're* missing. His idea on raising that boat was brilliant. Whatever your differences, set them aside until this case is resolved. Understood?"

"Yes, sir."

Rankin entered the room and placed a Diet Coke in front of Crosby.

"Diet? I said a Coke. Regular *Coke.*"

Rankin patted Crosby's? belly. "You need it."

Crosby scowled.

"Director Gregory wants your report when I get back to Washington, but you won't have time." Lynch handed Crosby a manila folder.

"What's up boss?" Rankin said.

"The photo tech sent this over. The *Island Breeze* originated at a pier here in Key West."

Crosby read the first page of the file.

"I'll inform the Director that your reports will have to wait," Lynch said.

"Have you got an address?" Rankin said.

"Captain Barney's Marine and Fishing, 8000 Front Street," Crosby said.

•   •   •

FROSCHER was painted in faded red letters on the mailbox, just outside of Denton, North Carolina. The dark blue sedan came to a halt beside a driveway lined by a white rail fence in bad need of repair.

"Looks like the place," FBI Agent Tom Hucks stated. In his lap was a portable GPS unit and directions from the local postmaster.

"One way to find out," Agent Mario Prichett said. He drove the sedan towards a brick ranch-style farmhouse. Tires popping on the gravel, they came to a halt, and the two agents dressed in dark suits got out. It was a quiet, peaceful setting, the house surrounded by tall loblolly pines, and an old barn sat abandoned in a field out back. Patches of puffy white clouds dotted the Carolina blue sky. Mrs. Ruth Froscher was already standing at the screen door when the agents reached the porch steps.

"Good afternoon," she said through the screen.

Agent Prichett held his FBI identification out in front of him. "Are you Mrs. Charles Froscher Sr.?"

"I'm Ruth Froscher," she said. "My husband, Charlie, is deceased."

"I'm Agent Prichett and this is Agent Hucks. We're from the Charlotte office of the FBI and we would like to ask you a few questions."

"Dorothy at the post office called and said you may be stopping by. What's this about?"

"The questions have to do with your son, Ms. Froscher." Prichett glanced at his notepad. "Charles Jr.?"

"Chuck was murdered three years ago." Sadness filled her voice.

"Yes, ma'am, we understand that. We're sorry and this won't take long," Hucks said. Unlike Agent Prichett, Hucks was a native of the area.

Ruth pushed open the screen. "I fixed a pitcher of sweet iced tea. Would you gentlemen care to come in and sit a spell?"

"Yes, ma'am," Agent Hucks said. "That'd be very kind of you."

• • •

Agent Crosby knew something was wrong the moment they turned into the drive off Front Street. Bright yellow crime scene tape surrounded Captain Barney's Marine & Fishing and an unmarked police cruiser blocked the entrance to its parking lot. Crosby parked the car on the street, and he and Rankin stepped under the tape. A few paces in, a voice cried out telling them to halt.

"You can't come in here, gentlemen," a Key West police officer said. "This is a crime scene. You need to turn around and leave."

"FBI. I'm Special Agent Crosby." He flashed his identification. "This is Agent Rankin with Homeland Security. Who's in charge?"

"Detective Dwight Chapin." He pointed toward a cinderblock building. OFFICE was painted on the door. "He's in there."

"Thank you."

The office was a wreck with papers and files strewn all over the floor. A man was on all fours gathering and examining papers. A second man, in his mid thirties with short hair, looked up at them from a file cabinet he was going through. "Who the hell are you?" he demanded.

"Are you Detective Chapin?" Crosby asked.

"Who wants to know?"

"This is Agent Rankin with the office of Homeland Security. I'm Agent Crosby with the FBI." He pulled at his windbreaker to show the logo.

Chapin huffed. "Why is the Bureau interested in a second-rate homicide?"

"Homicide?" Crosby said. "Who was the victim?"

"It's on the sign outside."

"Barney Taylor?" Rankin said.

"*Wow.* You guys can read."

"How did it happen?"

"Someone stuck a knife in his neck. Cut that major vein."

"The carotid artery?" Crosby said.

"Yeah, whatever. Some punk came up behind him and drove the knife into his neck. No signs of a struggle. Probably was looking for a way off the island. After the explosion, the whole city was in a panic."

"Where's his body?" Rankin asked.

"It's been in the morgue since Monday."

"What's the time of death?"

"Sometime that morning. Taylor was working on one of his boats when it happened."

"You're sure it wasn't earlier?" Rankin asked.

"The coroner said Monday morning."

"Why is it taking so long to process the crime scene?" Crosby asked.

"Look, there's one road in and out of this town, and we've been a little busy this week."

Rankin gestured at the floor. "What happened here?"

"They ransacked the place. The cash box was empty, and they went through the files looking for something, maybe the boat keys, money or drugs. Somebody shot two holes in this drawer." Chapin pointed to holes in the metal. "I recovered both slugs from the block wall behind it. They're on the desk. Whoever did it tried to move the file cabinet, but the late captain had it bolted to the floor."

Rankin used his handkerchief to pick up one of the slugs and examined it.

"Why bother?" Chapin said. "Not a chance of printing that and it's too mangled for decent ballistics."

"Why would somebody shoot a file cabinet?" Rankin asked.

"Maybe he missed whoever was standing in front of it," Crosby said. "Did you find any fingerprints on the drawers?"

"Hell *yeah*." Chapin said. "That's what's taking so damn long. They're all over the place."

"How many boats did Captain Taylor own?"

"Do I look like his secretary? How the hell should I know?"

"Forty caliber," Rankin handed Crosby the bullet. "Same kind we use."

Crosby cleared his throat. "We appreciate your cooperation, Detective Chapin. We'll be assisting in the investigation from here."

"The hell you *will!*" Chapin said. "This is *my* investigation!"

Rankin picked up the second slug from the desk. "Not anymore."

•   •   •

A tray containing the pitcher of sweet tea and two glasses was on the coffee table in front of Agents Hucks and Prichett. Hucks had a full glass, while Prichett's remained empty. Prichett was from New York and never understood the Southern obsession with sweetening everything.

The living room was large and comfortable. A fireplace with dusty gas logs was at one end. Centered above the white mantle was a large tinted photo of Captain Charles Froscher in his flight officer's uniform, taken during World War II. On the right side of the mantle stood an eight by ten photo of his late son, Chuck. Flanking it on the left side was a glamour photo of Chuck's little sister, Katie.

Ruth Froscher smiled at the two men as she placed a platter of Girl Scout cookies in front of them. She noticed the empty glass. "Mr. Prichard, would you prefer unsweetened tea?"

"It's Prichett, Mrs. Froscher. No, but thank you."

"How about some ice water instead?"

"I'm fine."

Ruth took a seat in a cloth-covered chair across from them. The room was spotless, but a faint smell of dust hinted at the fact that it was seldom used. She slid the platter of cookies towards them. "I hope these aren't stale. I try to help out our local scout troop, but my daughter is the only one who ever eats them. Katie doesn't get by that often anymore."

"Thank you, ma'am," Hucks said, taking a cookie and looking up at Katie's photo. "She's lovely."

"And single," Ruth said with a smile. "She lives right there in Charlotte, you know."

Agent Prichett smiled at his partner.

"Mrs. Froscher," Hucks said, "what exactly did your son do for a living?"

"Oh, he was so talented. He worked at a research facility in Oak Ridge, Tennessee. His daddy wanted him to go into the Army, but Chuck would have none of that. He was a physicist. He always wanted to become the next Einstein."

"Did he have a girlfriend?" Prichett asked.

"He had lots of girlfriends in high school and a few when he was at State. His daddy was the biggest Tar Heel fan that ever lived and it about killed him when Chuck announced that he was going to NC State. But I convinced his father that State had the best program in his field of interest. Charlie finally gave in and paid the tuition." She thought for a moment. "Chuck never mentioned having a girl in Oak Ridge."

"Did he get along with your husband?"

"He felt he was in his father's shadow; Charlie having been a war hero and all. He wasn't famous like Col. Tibbets or Tom Ferebee, but he had his part in winning the war. You know Ferebee lived right up the road apiece."

Hucks had no idea who she was talking about and moved on. "This is a difficult question, ma'am, but one I need to ask. Is it possible that your son is still alive?"

Ruth's smile vanished. "Oh my. I certainly wish he were. My daughter identified the body, and she gave me his wallet and class ring. A burglar shot him. She said there was no question about it. It was definitely Chuck."

"Did you view the body?" Prichett asked.

Ruth shook her head. "I couldn't look at my baby that way." Her eyes filled with tears. "I have a copy of the death certificate if that would help."

Hucks nodded. "Yes, ma'am. That will do just fine." He bit into one of the cookies. It tasted like cardboard. "These are real good, ma'am. Thank you."

• • •

Lucy and Katie settled into one of the two hot tubs at the very bow of the Carnival *Victory*, their towels and margaritas within reach. Members of the crew usually occupied these hot tubs during off hours, but there were no rules prohibiting their use by passengers. This afternoon, the deck was empty and that afforded them a sense of privacy.

Lucy leaned against one of the jets and stretched out her arms. Her blonde hair cascaded around her shoulders. The water was hot, which suited them fine considering the cool breeze blowing across the bow of the ship. She licked some salt from the rim of her margarita. "So how's our little worm coming?"

"I tested the routine on one of my old computers last week. My secure socket layers are not as sophisticated as Spectrum's, but with 256-bit encryption, I believe it's ready."

"It better be. We only have one shot at this." Lucy breathed in the hot steam, covering the water like a cloud. Except for the crewmen high above them in the bridge, there was no one around. Lucy unhooked the clasp to her bikini top and put it beside her drink. Katie kept hers on in case the steam cloud cleared.

"So, what's the schedule?" Lucy asked.

"The e-mail file is set to initiate at midnight a week from today. The worm is embedded within it. I'll deliver the bait the day before. The only way to break into Spectrum's secure intranet is through one of their computers and Trexler's laptop has got to be their weakest link. I figure it will take the kid about six hours to break into Trexler's user file, but I've allowed twenty-four just in case."

"Who's your hacker?"

"A kid named Jonathan. He's a freshman university student from Portland, Oregon who is already bored with college. We met six months ago in a UFO fan forum. Jonathan's into cracking the serial numbers of sci-fi and UFO games."

"He'll need all of that and more if he going to break into Spectrum's server," Lucy said. "What's the bait?"

"I told him the Vice President's laptop has a direct link into Project Bluebook's Majestic database. I'll give him Trexler's log-in address."

"That's what those numbers were for?"

"Right."

Lucy frowned. "What's Majestic?"

"Supposedly some super-secret government group formed in the late forty's to investigate UFOs. All of the UFO nuts are convinced it's real. They'll do anything to prove it."

"Sounds like Spectrum." Lucy took another sip of her margarita. "Why should he believe you?"

Katie spoke in a child's voice. "Because my very best friend in the whole wide world is Trexler's sixteen-year-old daughter, Lisa. He thinks we go to the same private school together. I told him Lisa and I got into this argument about the existence of little green men, and to prove it, she showed me the site on her daddy's computer. She even told me the code name."

"Let me guess. Spectrum."

Katie grinned and sipped her drink.

"He believes you're sixteen?"

"Seventeen," she chuckled. "I sent him a picture I lifted from a modeling agency. She's about six times a babe."

Lucy stretched out her arms to cool them on the hot tub's rim. "What makes you believe he'll run the risk of breaking in?"

"Because I told him I don't have the password, and it would be absolutely *impossible* to hack into it."

"Oh, that's *sweet*. Nothing beats telling a teenage boy he can't have something. He's probably already digging for it."

Katie shook her head. "I haven't given him the IP address yet. I told him Trexler's daughter made me *swear* not to give it to anyone. He's almost to the point of begging, but he'll get it next week along with a little undetectable worm."

"You think he'll break in?"

"Oh yeah." Katie sipped her drink. "It's the ultimate challenge. The *truth* is in there."

CHAPTER 15

THE WORM

Robert Lynch was boarding the FBI Learjet, when Crosby hurried toward him from the hangar. "Mr. Lynch," he called.

Lynch wheeled. "What is it?"

Crosby caught up to him. "I just got a call from the Key West sheriff's office. He has a missing persons report on a helicopter pilot who disappeared the night of the blast."

"Was it near the Marquesas Keys?"

"Yes. Agent James just confirmed it with the infrared photos."

"Check it out and call me. I'm late."

• • •

The sun had dipped behind the ship's superstructure and the air blowing across the bow was noticeably cooler. Katie was ready to get out, but there was still much to go over with Lucy and the hot tub afforded them absolute privacy.

"Won't Trexler's Secret Service agents recognize you?" Katie asked.

"I doubt it," Lucy said. "I only spent two or three nights with him over a two month period, and I wore a short wig and sunglasses whenever the Secret Service was around. He had a different girl every week, but Trexler may remember me. Whenever his wife was away he liked being tied to his bed."

"So, there's no way they can track you from your District of Columbia driver's license?"

"I did away with that identity a long time ago and I've never been fingerprinted under my real name. The club where I danced burned down," Lucy winked, "along with all those employment records."

"Speaking of which, I was able to purge your name from the OleWest computer records in Denver, but there's nothing I can do about the hard copies in their files."

"How did you pull that off?"

"I contacted their human resources department through our bank's computer and asked for a routine background check on Lucy Harris, who has applied for a job at our branch. Then I ran a micro to record the keystrokes as the clerk accessed the information. Last night I logged on to their server using the access code in the micro and deleted your file."

"*Cool.* Why didn't you transfer a couple of million while you were at it?"

Katie laughed. "That's a whole different level of security. If I could do that we wouldn't need Jonathan to break into Spectrum."

"What did my file say?"

"You had a satisfactory performance evaluation, but no details. Anything negative and they risk being sued." She looked Lucy in the eye. "Is there some other reason you picked the Dillon bank?"

Lucy's eyes looked down and to the right. "I told you why. If I wanted to cover up something, I would have let Amil take out Denver. Right?"

"True," Katie said, but recalled from her sociology class that the eyes looking down indicate a memory, but not necessarily a lie. She took a sip of her margarita. "You're sure Trexler's laptop is the only one in his house?"

"It's the only one I could find. He was using it once when he thought I was upstairs asleep. The cabinet where he kept it was locked, but I found a notepad containing all his passwords and user names. Trexler can't remember anything."

"Chuck's file said they communicated via the intranet and secure phones," Katie said. "If that's the computer he uses, then it's probably his primary link to Spectrum. If not, we're screwed."

"If he still has it."

"I confirmed its existence last week though our bank's Washington branch," Katie said. "Trexler keeps his checking account on it, so I ran a routine to notify me whenever he accessed that account. That's how I got his IP address. It appears to have a dedicated line. I can ping it, but I can't risk logging onto it myself."

"If this kid breaks in, what do you think he'll find?"

"Enough proof to bury them if we're lucky, but it doesn't matter. Once Jonathan is in the server, the worm is delivered. The databases are immediately downloaded back to Trexler's computer and the e-mails begin. The smoking gun is the private messages I inserted where Trexler discusses the deposits in Panama from the Dillon and

Marquesas demonstrations. The plans for those and the Monster will be more than enough to put them away forever."

"They will appear to have been leaked?"

"It's very subtle, as though Trexler hit the wrong key and sent them to Justice by mistake."

That's perfect," Lucy said. "They all think he's an idiot anyway. What if Raptor monitors his messages?"

"You said the computer is locked inside of Trexler's desk. Not even Harold Sanders can break into the Vice President's residence and start tearing the place apart. Besides, by the time he gets to it, it will be too late."

"I wouldn't underestimate him," Lucy said. "Chuck didn't believe they could stop the President's speech either."

Katie didn't respond. "It's getting cold. Are you about ready?"

"Sure," Lucy grabbed her towel, stood and wrapped it around herself.

Katie noticed her looking up at the bridge, where several crewmen were smiling down at them. One of the crew mouthed something and Lucy opened the towel for a second, allowing them a glimpse of her bare breasts.

"Oh, that's smart," Katie sneered. "Why not write your name across your forehead?"

"No harm done," Lucy said with her back to the crew.

"Unless one of them sees you coming out of our room and asks the purser for your name. Isn't it odd that he never noticed you before Grand Cayman?"

"I have a ticket."

"With *my* photo."

Lucy stepped out of the hot tub and left for the room.

Katie shook her head. Despite Lucy's bravery and intelligence, she was a compulsive flirt. She doubted that anyone would remember Lucy's face; they were too busy concentrating on her curves. Still, she needed to drive home the point. One screw up and their dream of exposing Spectrum and living out the rest of their days on a Caribbean beach would be short lived. Katie waited a few minutes for the crew to lose interest before following.

•   •   •

Gerald McMullen, standing on the balcony directly above the bridge, witnessed the scenario and was left more confused than ever. Katie and her friend had spent an hour in the hot tub, drinking from champagne glasses and in deep discussion over something. Then her friend stood up and flashed the crewmen on the deck below him. Her flirtation seemed odd for a woman to do in front of her lover. Perhaps it was a dare. Still, Katie had reprimanded her for it, and the other girl had left.

Gerald was convinced that it was time to forget her and get on with his life. He already felt like a peeping Tom, and that was something his mother would have hung him out to dry for.

•   •   •

"What have you got?" Robert Lynch said, calling from the Learjet.

"I spoke to the woman who filed the report," Crosby said. "Ms. Arturo Neavis said her husband runs a helicopter charter service. He took someone out at about ten Sunday night."

"Air traffic control had no record?"

"No, sir. He was probably below the radar. She said the chopper wasn't equipped with a navigational computer, so at night he would have flown close to the surface."

"Did she give you a description of the passenger?"

"She never got a look at him. Says her husband hurried into the house, threw five hundred dollars in cash on the table and said he would be back in an hour. He never returned."

"Are you sure they were headed out to the Marquesas Keys?"

"Well, the Coast Guard Air Rescue picked up a survivor on an island fourteen miles east of ground zero. When asked how he got there, he said he had been aboard a helicopter."

"Did you get a name?"

"Yes. It's Harold Sanders."

"*Sanders*. Are you sure?"

"I double checked. The description fits."

"What the hell was he doing out there?"

•   •   •

Dust was descending fast on the eighteenth hole and Harold Sanders was alone in his golf cart, sipping bottled water when Stalker called. The Vice President was attempting a twenty yard putt, so he kept his voice low. "What have you got?"

"The FBI found your handiwork at the boat yard." Stalker's tone was sarcastic.

"Took them long enough. They have nothing."

"No, they have a couple of slugs that were dug out of a murdered file cabinet. Tell me you weren't that stupid."

Raptor bit his lip. "I'll take care of it."

"They've also tracked down the wife of a missing helicopter pilot and they want to speak to the survivor who was rescued by the Coast Guard. Sound familiar?"

Raptor crushed the water bottle in his fist. "I'll *handle* it. You concentrate on finding the bastard who's setting off these bombs."

•   •   •

"Is this Special Agent Crosby of the all-mighty FBI?" a voice said dripping with sarcasm.

"Who is this?"

"Detective Dwight Chapin of the Key West Po-lice Department." He sounded drunk.

"How can I help you, detective?"

"We seem to be the ones helping *you*. With all the resources of the federal government, you jerks still use our little lab for your forensic tests."

"You've made your point, detective."

"My point is this: the Feds can't make a silk purse out of a sow any more than we can. Those ballistics on the slugs are a bust, and as for the fingerprints, it appears that every person in the whole freakin' islands touched those cabinets. Criminals two, Feds *zip!*"

Crosby ignored the sarcasm. "Anything on the files?"

"They haven't even started on those. Just thought I would let you know."

"Yeah. Thanks for calling, detective."

"My pleasure," Dwight sneered.

Crosby hung up. "I'm sure it was."

•   •   •

After four hours of watching Trexler play golf and then babysitting him as he fondled lap dancers at RockaCharlies, Harold Sanders was in no mood to travel. However, the Vice President was flying to Washington tonight, and the spare barrel assembly to his Glock service revolver was locked in a safe there. He needed to get it because a ballistics test on the two slugs found at Captain Barney's might link him to the crime site. His temper would cost him several hundred dollars to replace the barrel. He always kept a custom made spare engraved with matching serial numbers and now it too would have to be replaced, the original, finding a home at the bottom of the Potomac. He entered his Miami hotel suite and noted the blinking light on the phone. Accessing the hotel's voice message system, he found a nervous message from Trexler.

"Uh, this is Viper. We need to talk. I just got a message from the head of the Secret Service. Section Chief Lynch of the FBI just—uh, oh jeez, I just realized what phone I'm on. Call me ASAP."

Sanders shook his head in wonder. *How could an idiot like Trexler become Vice President?* He deleted the message and dialed the number for Air force One. "Be ready to leave in two hours."

• • •

"Hey, Crosby," Kelly Rankin said into his phone. "I'm down at the docks. The Coast Guard just removed the rubber rafts from the *Island Breeze*. We searched the entire boat. No bodies aboard."

"Why doesn't that surprise me? What about the chair webbing?"

"Marti feels it's some type of plastic that was melted by the blast, but she won't know until she gets in the lab. Did they find any rental records at Captain Barney's?"

"Detective Chapin isn't very cooperative. Agent James has a couple of agents going through the files. The *Island Breeze* file is missing."

"Another night in paradise," Rankin said. "Hey, do you know how to make holy water?"

"I'm working, Kelly."

"You boil the hell out of it."

Crosby was glad Rankin couldn't see his smile.

"Anything new on Amil?"

"They haven't found his trail since Cairo. Lynch just called. The Mexican police found a dirt landing strip near the wreckage of Troy Dills' plane. It may have crashed on take off."

"So, Amil probably had a plane waiting there," Rankin said. "You believe he had time to fly to the Keys before heading to Mexico City?"

"No. I think your scenario is much more plausible," Crosby admitted.

"Like you said, somebody left that beach message. With Amil in Egypt and our bomber aboard the *Breeze*, then that means we have a third party involved. I have a feeling they didn't go down with the ship."

"There may be more than that. Harold Sanders rented a chopper Sunday night and flew out to the Marquesas Keys."

"*No shit*. This is getting better by the minute. Maybe he's your bomber."

"No. He's over six feet, Kelly."

"Too bad."

• • •

Crosby's desk was littered with so much paper that he began to worry that critical pieces of evidence might get misplaced, or worse, go unnoticed. It was time to put everything into its proper file. Most of the clutter was lower resolution weather satellite photos, now made obsolete by the hi-res NORAD pictures. They were big and bulky and he debated whether to keep them or toss them into the trash. *Better keep them*, he reasoned. They could always be thrown away later. He began rolling several up together, binding them with rubber bands. Beneath these enlargements were earlier shots—the pre-enlargement views showing the *Island Breeze* no bigger than a thumbnail. On one, he noticed a dark blotch in the water, miles south of the boat and almost at the edge of the photo. The ocean bottom at this point had dropped off into deep water and the object appeared bluer that the surrounding ocean. It was several times the length of the *Island Breeze* and on careful inspection he could see a white plume above the blowhole and the wide flukes of its tail. "That's a whale," he concluded and rolled it with the rest.

The OleWest employee records lay under these. Leslie Pryce's photo reminded him that these were real people who had lost their lives for no apparent reason.

He returned to the file that he had started reading earlier; the Dillon branch manager, David Anthony. The photo showed a heavy-set man in his thirties with his hair combed straight back, probably to cover a balding spot. He had been with the company for seven years, serving as a manager at several Denver branches, before transferring to the Dillon branch three years earlier. He was a divorced father of four and maintained an apartment in Fresco, four miles west of Dillon. Crosby jotted down the address along with a note to ask if any of the Denver Agents had checked out the site. A Littleton address was listed as the residence of his dependent children. *They probably live with the ex-wife.* Another note reminded him to check if she had been interviewed.

He was just about to open the next file when Agent James entered the makeshift office.

"Got a minute?" James was holding yet another satellite photo.

"Sure. What's up?"

"These are infrared enlargements based on the missing helicopter report." James placed the photos on Crosby's desk. He pointed to a bright spot on the pictures. "This is the exhaust signature of that type of helicopter. He was out at the Marquesas Keys all right. He also was near the last recorded position of the *Island Breeze.* I don't know for how long. The next shot shows the chopper near the island at ground zero. He may have landed there. Check out the time." He pointed to the time stamp. "Not more than ten minutes before the explosion."

"*Jeeze!* That's cutting it close."

"Obviously he didn't know what was about to happen."

"Did he pick up any passengers?"

"I can't tell. The sand on those islands gets so warm during the day it takes a while to dissipate. It's masking any heat we may have gotten from someone on the island. How many survivors did the Coast Guard pick up?"

"Only the one." Crosby didn't offer him Sanders' name.

"You're going to interview the guy, right?"

"I hope to."

"Good. Ask him."

• • •

"Devrin, it's probably our last night in the Keys," Marti Matthews said as she entered. "Let's have one dinner on the expense report."

Crosby smiled. "Suits me. As long as it's not hot wings at a topless bar."

"Buy me oysters and I might dance on the table for you," she said with a grin.

He brightened. "Really?"

"I'm kidding."

"*Shoot!*" He snapped his fingers. "Is Kelly tagging along?"

"Nope. Just you and me . . . if that's all right?"

"That's great."

"Actually, he's having hot wings at a topless bar."

Crosby laughed. "I should have guessed."

"Do you like seafood? I hear there's a great restaurant down on Duval Street."

The expression on Crosby's face was all the answer she needed.

•   •   •

"What have you learned?" Stalker asked.

"We've recovered the boat," the informant said. He was at a pay phone outside a restaurant in Key West. "No remains aboard, but we found some interesting items attached to a lounge chair."

Stalker already knew what those were. "Anything else?"

"They know about Sanders' flight out to the Marquesas Keys. They believe he rescued the suspects from the boat."

"Good luck finding them."

"Sanders will have some explaining to do."

"He's ready when they are," Stalker said. "The chopper only had two seats and no winch. Make sure they know that beforehand."

"I understand."

"Any progress on how they escaped?"

"Not yet, but you'll be the first to know."

•   •   •

Marti Matthews was stuffed. A plate piled high with crab leg shells lay between her and Devrin Crosby. He was still eating, but was losing steam. A spot of melted butter had stained his tie and he was rubbing at it with a wet napkin.

"I have a closet full of these," Crosby complained. "Thirty dollars down the drain."

"I can get it out," Matthews said.

"It's hopeless. I've tried everything. Butter and mustard seem to be the worst on silk."

"You weren't applying a scientific solution. If we can get Teflon™ to stick to a pan, then I can certainly get rid of a butter stain. Why don't you give it to me and I'll have it clean in the morning?"

"You can do that in your hotel room?"

"I'll pick up something when I go by the lab tonight to check on the results of your chair. Speaking of which, we were able to pull a few ballistics off those slugs."

"Detective Chapin was bragging that they were too mangled."

"For a comparative ID, but not totally." She opened her notepad. "It was forty caliber, the barrel had a right, hexagonal twist and they estimate the length at four inches."

"What does that mean?"

"Hexagonal rifling indicates it may have been a Glock. The model 23 is forty caliber and has a barrel that length."

"Same thing we use. I wonder what Agent Sanders carries?"

"Standard issue is the SIG Sauer P229, chambered for the .357 SIG cartridge," Marti said, "but Kelly uses the Glock model 32 because the barrel is interchangeable with the forty caliber model 23."

"You mean his pistol can shoot either size bullet?"

"Yes, if he switches barrels."

Crosby gave a heavy sigh. "I don't know what to believe anymore. It's apparent that Amil was no where near the Keys. Our bombers on the *Island Breeze* vanished into thin air and now we're reduced to accusing the Secret Service of having a part in the crime."

"It's been over three days with no explosions," she said. "Just because we couldn't find their bodies doesn't mean they're still alive. Maybe Amil arranged for the *Breeze* to break down so he could silence his partners. While we were looking the other way, he made his escape through Mexico."

"If he's in the Middle East, what was the point of the explosions?"

"They must be a prelude to something," Matthews said.

"Every time I look at those files I get the feeling that the answer is right there. It's like I'm looking at an elephant through a micro-scope."

Matthews placed her hand on Crosby's. "Look, we've been working this non stop for almost a week. Maybe we need to take a couple of days to relax and clear our heads."

"That's easier said than done." Crosby squeezed her hand in appreciation. "I have a stack of OleWest employee records to go through."

"I know. I'm following up on the leads Dr. Gebo gave me."

"Any progress?"

"The Charlotte FBI interviewed Chuck Froscher's mother. She gave them a copy of the death certificate and we have the name of the guy who drowned in Chicago. Ryan Papin or something like that. He was a physicist and fits the description. They're digging up his past." She rubbed her forehead. "I sure would like to speak with Dr.

Gebo again. Maybe we could convince Lynch to send us back to Denver."

"*Right.* I'll let *you* ask him." Crosby rubbed his neck and grimaced. "That cot is killing me."

"You need a good back rub," she said. "After we stop at the lab, we'll go up to my room and I'll give you one."

Crosby's eyes widened.

Matthews smiled. "Don't read anything in to it. I'm just going to rub your neck and show you how to get rid of a butter stain."

"A back rub and hot butter!" he said, grinning. "Things are looking up already."

* * *

"You two back already?" Rankin said, as Crosby and Matthews entered the hangar at Boca Chica Field. Agent Michael James was with him.

"You missed out," Crosby said. "We had a decent meal for once."

Rankin grabbed Crosby's tie. "I see you used your napkin."

"That's one of the reasons we're here. She needs something from the lab."

"I'll be right back." Matthews excused herself.

"What's up with Marti?" Rankin said.

"She has a spot remover in her desk that will lift out the stain."

"Sounds like an exciting date," Agent James said.

"It's not a date," Crosby said. "We ate seafood and she's going to wash out my tie tonight. That's all."

"Maybe it's an excuse to get you back to her room," Rankin hinted. He lowered his voice. "Hey, I have some of those little blue pills if you might need one."

"Not likely."

"Yeah, guys our age are too old for Viagra®," Rankin said. "The only reason the doctor gave me these is so I wouldn't roll out of the bed at night."

Crosby found himself laughing for once. The three of them standing in the open hangar; their voices echoing around the chamber, was a shot of adrenalin to Crosby. It had been years since he felt like laughing, but tonight he did.

Matthews returned and asked what was funny.

"I was just telling Crosby what a fish says when he hits a concrete wall," Rankin said. "Dam!"

Matthews grinned and the laughter resumed. "Why are you two still here? Looks like everyone's left for the evening."

"We were discussing the case," James said. "Lynch called. He wants Crosby to head back to Washington tomorrow for a meeting with Agent Sanders."

"*Oh, great*," Crosby moaned.

"While you're at it," Rankin said, "ask him how they managed to rescue two survivors in a chopper with only two seats."

"It only held two?"

"It was an old Bell 47-B," James said. "That's what they say."

●   ●   ●

Not the children, Lucy murmured in her sleep. *Please God not me.* "Not me!"

Lucy's eyes opened wide, awakened by her own voice. She sat up, realizing she was in a strange bed, and took a deep breath. Her heart was racing and all around her was darkness. The only light was the glowing numerals of the clock-radio. It was one a.m. and she felt the gentle rolling of the ship.

The dream was vivid. She switched on the reading lamp and tried to relax. Katie turned over in the other bunk, still asleep. Lucy thought of the innocent children that had died in Dillon. She had doused them with fire and turned their tiny bodies into ash. What kind of monster would do that? She had truly become the angel of death. She had poured out her vial upon the sun and been given the power to scorch the innocent.

"Stop this," she whispered. She had to be steadfast and strong. If not, millions of children would die. Only one thing could restore her resolve. She reached for her bag, removed her grandmother's memoir and began to read.

I saw a shiny object falling from the plane, and a parachute open above it. I pulled on mother's skirt and pointed upward, "Papa-san! Papa-san!"

"Kato," Mother said, "it's Papa, not Papa-san!"

"But Mama look, Papa has jumped from the plane. He's coming to get us."

I pulled harder on Mother's skirt and implored her to look; please look. In that moment I had convinced myself that my American father was parachuting into the city. Our prayers had been answered. The war was over and Father was coming to tell us. Mother finally gave in, gazed up at the tiny object, and blocked my view for only a second.

In that moment the sun seemed to explode. It was so bright that I could see the purple outline of my mother's ribs through her dress. In the dream, Father had told me to turn away from the light. I heard Mother cry, "Kato!" and suddenly I was lying flat on my back in the garden. Mother was on top of me and I couldn't move. Her weight was intense, and my body sank into the soft earth of the garden. I called out to Mother but she didn't respond.

With my free hand I managed to dig out the dirt beside me and after what seemed hours, crawled out. The beautiful clear morning had turned as dark as a moonlit night. Black smoke poured from everywhere. The vile smell of burned hair and flesh filled the air and it hurt my lungs to breathe.

Our home had been pulverized into a million shards of wood and glass. A section of one wall covered my mother's body and this was why she had felt so heavy. I reached for her hand and to my astonishment it moved. She was alive! I tried to lift the wall, but it was far too heavy for my small body to budge. I pulled on her arm and felt her skin slip, sliding off into my hand as easily as the skin of a roasted tomato. A wet thread of viscous liquid streamed from the blistered peelings back to her blackened fingernails. I held the fragile pieces in disbelief, too stunned by the sight to utter a word.

Even in her agony, Mother thought only of me. "It's all right, Kato," she kept saying from within her tomb. "As long as you're alive, everything will be all right."

CHAPTER 16

JAMAICA

Thursday

Katie and Lucy stood on the bridge balcony of the Carnival *Victory*, watching the sun rise over the distant mountains of Ocho Rios, Jamaica. The cool morning breeze tangled their hair and the salty smell of seawater tickled their nostrils. They sipped their coffee and discussed their plan.

"The worm is almost ready," Katie said. "How is Ryan's Monster?"

"He welded all the screw heads in the air-conditioning unit from the inside, so the installers can't open it. They may start taking off panels and we can't risk that."

"How will Amil access the dummy warhead?"

"I gave him a key," Lucy said. "Ryan has assured me that the warhead looks convincing enough, even for Amil."

"Why not used a cooler like the others."

"I told Amil that it's a stolen Spectrum prototype. Ryan based the Monster on the Baghdad design, the one Chuck was working on before the Iraq invasion negated the need for it. That's the design Amil was most interested in. His people nicknamed it 'Jerusalem.'"

"That figures," Katie said. "He can't remove it?"

"No. Amil has this bomb exactly where he wants it; payback to the infidels. It's his holy war and for him to die fulfills his life's mission to Allah."

"What if Spectrum's agents arrive first?"

"They'll think Amil has cut his own deal and either kill him or seize him. Either way, it will be too late. I have a clear view of the rooftop from my apartment plus the cameras and sensors we've planted. The moment I spot Amil, I'll notify the FBI. If your little worm works as planned, the Feds will have everything they need to nail him red-handed."

"Thank God it's not real." Katie pushed her hair out of her face. "If they're late it won't take Amil long to smell the trap. What if they miss him?"

"The FBI will eventually locate the Monster and the cameras will lead them to the apartment. The video and copies of Spectrum files will be there." Lucy smiled. "Once they find that, Trexler and Spectrum's team are finished."

"What about us?"

"The next day you and I will meet in Grand Cayman, gather our investments and disappear into paradise."

Katie finished her coffee. "A lot can go wrong. Suppose Amil is arrested when he enters the country?"

"What makes you think he left?"

•   •   •

For the first time in almost a week, Crosby awoke without a stiff neck. He was on the couch in Marti's hotel room where they had fallen asleep while watching TV. At one a.m. he found Marti's head lying in his lap and moved her to the bed, which was large enough for both of them. However the morning would be less awkward if he returned to the couch. The next morning her smile convinced him that he had made the right choice.

The Learjet was waiting outside the hangar when Dr. Matthews drove Crosby there at 7:30 a.m. Luggage and boxes of equipment were stacked on the tarmac beside the jet. Evidently, he was not returning to Washington alone.

As Crosby was about to step out of her car, Marti took his hand and squeezed it. "Thanks for last night," she said.

"Dinner was your idea. Thank you."

"I meant being with you. I had a great time."

"Me too. Want to do it again?"

"Maybe after all of this is over." She leaned over to give him a kiss, but was interrupted by a tapping on her window. It was Kelly.

"Check your cell phone battery," Rankin said. "I've been trying to reach you all morning. You got your stuff with you?"

One suitcase was all she had, but it was back at the hotel. "No. What's up?"

"You're headed back to Washington. Lynch's orders. Most of the team is going back."

"What about the forensics on the *Island Breeze?*"

"They're sending the chair to Washington. I'm staying a couple more days with the rest of the team. Lynch wants us to try to locate the missing helicopter. Have you checked out of the hotel?"

"No."

"I'll send someone to help you pack. You have about forty-five minutes. *Hurry.*"

• • •

Vice President Trexler jogged past the intersection of 34th Street and Massachusetts Avenue toward the southwest corner of the block. He ran past the gates leading up to the Queen Anne style home and caught a towel, football passed to him by one of the Secret Service agents who ran with him every morning. Trexler entered the basement door to the Vice Presidential residence and took a moment to dry the sweat from his hair before bounding up the stairs to his home office. He heard the shower running upstairs and knew he would have thirty minutes to surf the web before his wife would begin yelling that it was time to get ready for the memorial service. Two hours of praying, singing with an obligatory wide-eyed message from the President, was no way to spend a morning. He, no doubt, would be asked to lead the closing prayer. All of this, so he could stand before members of the Christian Coalition and claim to be a born-again believer with a saving faith in the Almighty. *What a waste of a good tee time.*

He retrieved his desk key, hidden between a dusty copy of the *Biography of Walter Mondale* and an autographed copy of *It Takes A Village*, written by a former First Lady. He wondered if the latter title referred to the raising of a child or the sex life of her husband. The key was safe because no one in his family or office staff would ever examine these books.

The computer, a laptop perpetually on, was linked, via a T-1 connection, to Spectrum's server located in a former fallout shelter in a sub-basement of the Social Security building. With it and the other equipment hidden in his desk, he could arrange a live videoconference with the top leaders on six continents. However, this morning he was interested only in a website that featured video of a teenage female performing various sex acts with multiple male partners. The steamier scenes were shocking, but in his mind he justified these forays. How could he listen to arguments over the right to display these sites, if he knew nothing about them? In his opinion, pornography was a victimless sin, and within the hour he would be safe in a church pew, holding his wife's hand and supposedly cleansed from all of these iniquities.

Seconds later, an e-mail message popped up on his screen that had the same effect as a bucket of ice water thrown onto his lap. It was from Stalker and marked confidential.

Subject: CLASSIFIED – EYES ONLY
Time: 07:51:55 Thu
From: UNDISCLOSED
To: <022.09.016.05.018>
References: 1

EYES ONLY

The FBI is questioning Agent Sanders today about the disappearance of a helicopter pilot on the night of the Marquesas Key explosion. You will be asked to confirm the "fishing" story. Don't panic. If you need help with the details contact me via secure channel.

By the way, the material you are downloading may prove embarrassing for your future political aspirations. I suggest you consider this when logging onto an unsecured site. S

THIS MESSAGE WILL SELF-DELETE SIXTY SECONDS AFTER OPENING

Norman broke into a cold sweat. *Was there anything Stalker didn't know?*

•   •   •

The flight to Ronald Reagan Washington National Airport was un-eventful. Dr. Matthews sat in the seat beside Crosby and slept the entire way. They said their goodbyes with a hug and Crosby took a cab to the condo he leased from Gerald.

The place smelled like death the moment he opened the door. A quick check of the rooms revealed no dead bodies. He found the culprits in his refrigerator; a half-pound of ground beef and a carton of milk that had expired over a week earlier. He sealed them in several freezer bags and took the garbage out to the dumpster.

Coming back in, he passed Gerald's former office, he spotted the blinking light on his voice mail system. He played the messages while he got undressed. Most were unimportant, but the last message was from Gerald McMullen:

"Hey buddy. I wanted to let you know I'm stretched out on a white sandy beach here in Jamaica sipping mint tea and eating turtle soup. Thought about you and had to call. Listen, I'm thinking about buying a place down here and opening a dive shop. I could use a partner if you're still considering a move from the Bureau any time soon. You wouldn't believe the bikini that just walked by. In any case, I'll be up your way next week. Here's my number in case you didn't write it down. Give me a call and check to make sure I have clean sheets on the spare bed."

Crosby wrote the number on the back of a business card and put it in his wallet. He had time for a quick shower before his interview with Agent Sanders. Thank heavens it would be on his turf at the Hoover Building.

•   •   •

Harold Sanders sat in a gray government-issued chair in a small office located in the J. Edgar Hoover Building in Washington. Beside him was Daniel Whiteman, one of the in-house attorneys for the Secret Service. His job was to make sure the questions neither violated Agent Sanders' rights, nor divulged information that may be a security risk to the President. Across from them was Agent Heather Kane, an FBI attorney with the Office of the General Counsel, with a yellow legal pad propped on her lap.

Crosby arrived two minutes late and took a seat across a gray metal desk from Sanders and Whiteman. Whiteman appeared to be a real stickler for time and Crosby's tardiness was greeted with a terse, "You're late," as they shook hands.

"Sorry. I just flew in from Key West." Not technically a lie, but close. "Thank you for agreeing to see us," he began. "Can I offer you some coffee or a soft drink?"

Both men shook their heads. Even though the room was dimly lit, Agent Sanders wore aviator sunglasses. Lynch had reminded Crosby that the Secret Service was tight lipped and would resist divulging anything that wasn't already on the record. Lynch had interviewed Sanders following the assassination of President Barnett and found him to be cool under pressure. He doubted they would gather much from the interview.

"What's this about?" Whiteman asked.

"We have some questions concerning the disappearance of Artuero Neavis from Key West, Florida. He was a helicopter pilot."

"Is my client being accused of a crime?"

"No. We just want to clear up some things from that evening."

"First, I object to the taking of notes," Whiteman said, nodding at Agent Kane. "My client never agreed to give a deposition."

"This isn't a court of law, Agent Whiteman," Crosby said. "There is no one to rule on your objection."

"I'm aware of that. Nonetheless, for the record, we object to any recording of this proceeding, either by tape or transcript."

"So noted," Crosby said. "Agent Kane, we can dispense with the notes. Now, may we begin?"

Whiteman nodded his approval.

"Agent Sanders, did you fly out to the Marquesas Keys in a helicopter on the night of November 25?"

"My client cannot answer that question. It violates his oath to protect and defend the office of the Chief Executive."

"How?"

"He has taken an oath not to divulge routes, modes of transportation and security measures," Whiteman explained.

"Fine. Have you ever met a Mr. Artuero Neavis?"

Sanders whispered something into Whiteman's ear.

"Not that he recalls," the lawyer answered.

"He ran a private helicopter charter service in Key West and disappeared on Sunday, November 26, right around the time of the blast. Sound familiar?"

Whiteman and Sanders exchanged glances. "What does this have to do with my client?"

"Your client was found on a desert island, less than fourteen miles from the blast crater. He was rescued by a U.S. Coast Guard helicopter and when asked how he got there, admitted that he had been aboard a private helicopter. The FBI wants to know who owned that helicopter and what the hell happened to it."

Again, Sanders whispered in Whiteman's ear.

"My client admits he was aboard a helicopter. He never asked the pilot's name and did not witness what happened to him or the chopper."

"Does your client speak?"

"Of course."

"As of right now, he is not only considered a primary witness to a terrorist act, but also appears to have aided in the flight of known felons. Now, without his full cooperation, I'm sure we can find Agent Sanders a nice jail cell to await formal charges by a grand jury."

"You have no evidence whatsoever to hold my client."

"Try me."

Sanders and Whiteman whispered again.

"Against my advice, he will answer your questions, provided that Ms. Kane leaves the room. Also, everything he says must be *off* the record. Otherwise, this conversation has ended."

"Fine." Crosby knew it was a minor sacrifice. "Agent Kane, would you please excuse us?"

The agent rolled her eyes, gathered her things, and left.

"Also, please switch off any voice recorders, either here or in the adjoining rooms," Whiteman added.

"I have none and I'm not aware of any others," Crosby said.

"Regardless, nothing we say can leave this room or be used in a court of law. Understood?"

"I have to prepare a report for the Deputy Director. However, barring an admission of murder, I can assure you it will go no further."

They whispered again.

"Agreed," Sanders said. "You must understand, Agent Crosby, that I have taken an oath to protect not only the President and Vice President's lives, but their secrets as well."

Sanders voice was rough yet calm, not at all what Crosby expected.

"I understand." Crosby relaxed his tone. "Agent Sanders, we just want to know what happened."

Sanders cleared his throat. "On the evening of Sunday, November 26, I rented a helicopter from a local charter service. I paid the pilot five hundred dollars in cash. I didn't get his name, but he was Hispanic and probably was the pilot you mentioned."

"Artuero Neavis?"

"So I assume."

"Why did you need a helicopter?"

"The Vice President wanted to go out to the Marquesas Keys to do some fishing the following morning. He asked me to secure the area. His personal secretary can confirm that."

"You could have used a surveillance helicopter for that. Why all the secrecy?"

Sanders gave a wry expression. "It wasn't an *official* trip."

Crosby frowned. "What's the difference between *official* and *non-official?*"

"Official trips can get leaked to the press. This trip was . . . *private.*"

"Private as in the Vice President and a few agents?"

"Something like that."

Crosby was beginning to get the picture. "Anyone else?"

"Sometimes, his aides would tag along."

"I see. Are any of these aides female?"

"Yes. Sometimes it gets really *hot* out there during the middle of the day," Sanders said.

"Lots of suntan oil and bikinis?"

"There was at least suntan oil."

A small grin formed on Crosby's face.

"It's one of the more interesting aspects of Vice Presidential duty," Sanders added.

I see why. No wonder they wanted this *off* the record.

•   •   •

The island of Jamaica was a shoppers paradise, but the natives didn't seem to know the meaning of the word, no. Lucy made the mistake of looking interested in a necklace and the merchant followed her and Katie through the streets trying to offer them a better deal. Lucy finally gave the guy ten bucks just to leave them alone.

They took a cab to a popular waterfall and joined a group of tourists climbing the rocks as the warm water cascaded over them. The roar of the water allowed them to speak freely.

"You were talking in your sleep last night," Katie said. "Bad dream?"

"Yeah. The one where the golden statue is pouring molten metal onto the masses."

"So, your secret desire must be to become a hell's angel."

"It's the fourth angel of the book of Revelation, quoted in President Barnett's speech."

"That was clever. The symbolism ties the whole thing back to Barnett's assassination. That's got to be worrisome for Trexler's gang."

"I'm sure it is. If we didn't give ourselves a name, the media would. It's pretty close to what I've become after Dillon."

"It's their fault, Lucy." Katie took her hand. "Don't ever forget who started this."

They climbed hand in hand for a while taking in the beauty of the falls and the lush green vegetation. It was the most beautiful spot Lucy had ever seen.

"You could stay here," Lucy said. "You could deliver the worm from anywhere in the world."

"I have a situation at home. It shouldn't affect our schedule, but you need to be aware of it. It's about my father."

"I thought he was dead?"

"He is, but he still managed to reach out from the grave and control my life. My mother wants his body reinterned at Arlington National. I have to accompany the remains to Washington on Tuesday."

"Why?"

"The estate attorney overlooked a note in his will stating that he wanted to be buried in Arlington near his former crewmembers. Mom's upset about it."

"So they dig him up?"

"They move his vault," Katie said.

"You'll be there alone?"

"With his remains."

"That's got to be tough. Do you want me to come with you?"

"It's too risky. There's no memorial service. They just dig a hole and re-bury his remains. The paperwork takes longer than the burial."

"Paperwork?" Lucy raised her eyebrows. "That puts you near the scene right before all this goes down."

"True, but I sure as hell can't do it afterwards and if they find out who we are, it won't matter."

"You've got that right."

"I've made the arrangements at Arlington, but I have to hire a funeral home to transport the body from the airport. They want a fortune. I swear they get you coming and going."

"Katie, you have twenty million in the bank and you're worried about a couple of thousand? Just pay it."

"It's highway robbery. The only thing they have to do is take the damn casket across town."

"Let me help," Lucy said. "One of my regulars at the club works at Casket Warehouse. I bet if I blow him, he'll do it for free."

Katie rolled her eyes. "You know, on second thought, you're right. Just give me his name and I'll pay for it."

•   •   •

Crosby wasn't sure what he expected from Sanders, but his explanation thus far, made sense. It sounded like something Trexler would do. He had witnessed those exploits firsthand. The rest of the questions, however, might not be so easy to explain.

"The night you flew out to the Marquesas Keys, did you see anything unusual?"

Sanders thought for a moment. "Nothing worth reporting. We saw a couple of fishing boats, but it appeared the occupants had turned in for the night. We didn't disturb them."

"Did you land?"

"We sat down on one of the islands, just to check it out. Nothing except sand and trees, so we only stayed a minute."

"Where else?"

"The island where I was found. I believe the pilot called it, Joe Ingram Key."

"Why there?"

"I had to relieve myself, so I asked the pilot to find the closest island."

"You mean . . . ?"

"I had to *pee*," Sanders lied with a deadpan expression. "Thought I could hold it, but nature calls. Damn good thing since it saved my life. I was just getting out of the chopper when I saw the flash. I figured that diving under the water was my only chance. The floor of the chopper was covered with old plastic lunch bags, so I grabbed a handful and blew air into them as I ran into the surf. They kept me alive underwater for seven minutes. When I ran out of air, I surfaced. You know the rest."

It took Crosby a moment to absorb this. "So, while you were underwater, the pilot and his chopper were consumed by the blast?"

"When I resurfaced everything on the island was gone. You might find some wreckage of the chopper, but I doubt if you'll find the pilot."

Crosby glanced at the two remaining items on his list. "Have you ever heard of Barney Taylor, or Captain Barney's Marine and Fishing?"

"Not that I recall."

"What type of sidearm do you use?"

Sanders started to answer but Whiteman stopped him. "Why is that relevant?"

"It's just a question."

"It's not relevant to the disappearance of Mr.—"

Sanders cut him off. "I use a SIG 229 for standard duty, and a Glock 32 when guarding the Vice President."

"Don't both of those use a .357 SIG?"

"Yes, but I prefer the Glock."

"Do you have it with you?"

"No. It was immersed in salt water. The firearms department has taken it for cleaning," Sanders lied.

"I see. Well, gentlemen, that about covers it." Crosby stood and shook their hands.

"You understand, this goes no further than your report to the Director," Whitman added.

"It won't," Crosby assured. "This clears up many questions."

He walked his guests to the elevators. Whitman again repeated his concerns and Crosby promised that the Vice President's private life would remain private.

As soon as the doors closed, Crosby walked towards his office. It all made perfect sense, but he still felt that Sanders wasn't telling the whole truth. As he recalled, it was the same feeling he had gotten three years earlier when he had viewed Sanders' deposition of the President's assassination.

Crosby stopped at the media room door and knocked. Agent Heather Kane opened it. On the wall behind her was the frozen image of Harold Sanders face, displayed on the screens of a half dozen monitors. She ejected the DVD and handed it to him.

"Did you get it?"

"Every word. Just don't try to use it in court," Kane said.

"What's your opinion?"

"He's either lying or the luckiest bastard on earth."

Crosby recalled the conversation he had with Key West detective, Dwight Chapin. Even with the resources of the federal government behind them, they had zip.

•   •   •

Upon entering his office, Crosby found a cardboard box on his desk, shipped in from Denver. In it were the OleWest records of employees who had been terminated for cause. He would have to go through a sample of these to create a profile for the computer search. An expandable folder on top contained the Dillon branch records he had been going through in Key West. The rest of his luggage, along with the rolled-up satellite photos had been transferred from the Lear and occupied a corner. He sat and started going through the notes and memos that littered his desk. A bright pink sticky note was attached to his phone. "Call me ASAP. Marti." He dialed the number.

"Devrin," Matthews said, picking up the line, "Go home and pack. We're leaving for Denver at four p.m."

"Denver?"

"Actually, we're staying in Breckenridge. They've reopened the slopes and we'll have the place to ourselves. Do you like to ski?"

"I use to—"

"Great! So do I. Pack your coat and bibs. We'll rent the rest."

"But, why?"

"I told Lynch we had to go back to square one to see if we can pick up the scent. I also said we needed some down time to recharge. As long as we continue to work the files, we've got two days to relax before picking up the trail."

"How did you convince him of that?"

"The same way you get anything from a man. I made him believe it was his idea."

• • •

They had adjoining seats, Crosby on the aisle and Matthews by the window looking down on a patchwork quilt of fields from thirty-five thousand feet. Four hours in the Lear that morning and nearly four on this flight to Denver was taking a toll on both of them. Matthews had just awakened from her second long nap of the day, saying she was tired but unable to sleep any longer. Crosby was reading an in-flight magazine featuring an article on Grand Cayman. He thought about the message from Gerald McMullen and his offer to retire at a scuba diving shop in the Caribbean. A week earlier and he would have jumped at the chance. Now he was in the midst of the chase, narrowing the clues, and getting closer to the final confrontation that he knew would come. There was also Marti and the exciting promise that a new relationship held. How could he leave now?

"You never replied to my message this morning," Matthews said with a yawn.

"What message?"

"I left it on your voice mail."

"I never got it. I was running late for my interview."

"We got the lab results on the chair. It's not plastic. The molecular formula is C3H3N, a natural polymer referred to as cis-one-four-polyisoprene."

"Repeat that in English, please?"

"It's a form of latex rubber. This particular sample had a number of antioxidants added, which preserved it in seawater."

"How is latex used?"

"Primarily in balloons and rubber gloves, but this sample contained dithiocarbamates and calcium nitrate to help in the coagulation process. It doesn't break down when exposed to lubricants and semen. It's the rubber used in sex paraphernalia."

"What?"

"Sexual toys. The face printed on the surface is what gave it away. It's a blow-up sex doll, Devrin."

"You're kidding."

"An expensive one too. They're life size and, given the fibers we found, it was probably dressed in clothing and taped to the chair to keep it from blowing away."

"Why?"

"The same reason they left the message on the beach."

It took Crosby a moment to catch on. "To make us believe they were still aboard."

"Right," Matthews said. "The oil slick, the dolls, all of it was just a ruse. There was nothing wrong with the engine."

"They already knew how they were getting off the boat." Crosby mind was racing. "It wasn't a rescue."

"The helicopter?" Matthews asked.

"No. It only had two seats and the dinghy was left on the island. What's left?"

"I don't know. Swimming wouldn't help. Neither would scuba."

An image popped into Crosby's mind; the weather satellite, and in the lower right corner, a dark shape, submerged with tail flukes. "I'm an *idiot*. It wasn't a tail. It was *dive planes*."

"What?"

Crosby felt in his pockets for his cell phone, but it was packed it in his overnight bag. "I need to use your cell phone."

"The battery's dead, besides you can't use cells on commercial flights." Matthews reached for the air phone mounted on the seat in front of them. "Use this."

He punched in the number to Quantico.

"What are tail planes?" she asked as he entered his card number.

"Dispatch, please. Yes, this is Agent Devrin Crosby. Patch me through to Agent Michael James in Key West. Yes, I'll hold."

"Devrin." Matthews implored. *"Tell me."*

"You said Scuba. That's underwater, the one place we never checked. I just figured out how they got off the boat."

A voice came over the line. "Michael James."

"Michael, it's Devrin. I need you to check some of the infrared shots from NORAD."

"Just a second. I just downloaded the digital versions."

"Focus on the boat," Crosby explained, "right around sundown."

"Just a minute. Okay, got it. The time stamp indicates the images were taken in ten minute increments."

"Can you scroll through them?"

"Yes," James said. "It will take a moment for each to load. Hold on."

"Look for an object right beside the *Island Breeze.*"

"Wait a minute," James said. "Got something. It's a round heat signature about two feet across. Looks to be about six feet or so from the port side of the boat. What the hell is that?"

"It's the conning tower hatch of a submarine." Crosby said.

CHAPTER 17

HERMAN

Sunday, Second Week

The Carnival *Victory* arrived in the port of Miami at seven Sunday morning, but it took the ship almost an hour to turn around at the end of the channel and make her way back to the Carnival dock. Using her bow and stern thrusters, the captain parallel parked her nine hundred-foot hull beside her identical twin, the Carnival *Triumph,* just in from the eastern Caribbean.

On the roof of the bridge, Lucy and Katie watched in wonder. In their hands were their real passports, and drivers' licenses. The false papers that had identified them as Annie Kagle and Gwendolyn Fisher were now in a safety deposit box in Ocho Rios, Jamaica. The next hours would be the most dangerous portion of their journey. Neither had any idea how much the FBI knew, nor what Spectrum's goons might do to them if they fell into their hands. The slightest slip-up and they may find themselves locked in a federal holding cell, or worse, headed for the bottom of a swamp with chains around their feet.

• • •

Devrin Crosby awoke so sore that he could barely sit up on the bed. He had never been a great skier, but having donned skis for the first time in years, he discovered that his sense of balance had seemed to shift forward in direct proportion to his waistline. Marti Matthews, on the other hand, was a great skier and it was all Crosby could do to keep up with her.

Compounding matters was the elevation of Breckenridge; air thin enough at eleven thousand feet to cause a dull headache which never seemed to go away. After a full day of this agony, Crosby was ready to rest and eager to resume the chase.

Once again they had adjoining rooms, but this time the door between them remained open around the clock. Nothing was said about the sleeping arrangements, but Crosby, ever the gentleman, had retired to his own bed both nights.

Matthews was in the kitchen brewing coffee when Crosby emerged from the steam filled bathroom, wrapped in a white terrycloth bathrobe, his hair still damp. The table where they had worked the previous evening was piled high with files and little progress had made at reducing its size.

"Good morning," Matthews said, handing Crosby his coffee. "Cream and sugar, right?"

"Right. You're a quick study."

"I have a Ph.D. How do you feel?"

"Like I've been run over by a truck."

"You just need a few more days to get back in the groove. The snow is perfect."

"This is supposed to be a working vacation, remember?" Crosby nodded at the files. "How far did we get?"

Matthews frowned. "H."

"I suggest we finish the 'I' folders and then get some breakfast. Okay?"

"Agreed." Her robe parted as she sat, reveling two-thirds of her bare leg. Crosby had to concentrate on her face until he was seated.

"You want the folders this time or the printouts?" she asked.

"You did folders last night. I'll handle those."

Each printout had a corresponding folder. His job was to examine the information within, give a description of the accompanying photo, and read the termination report. Matthews would confirm that the information in the database was correct, flag the ones they needed to check and make notes on why the employee was fired.

Matthews picked up the printout and read the next name. "Hang Pham, Christina Fu."

Crosby opened the corresponding folder and called out the information. "Female; eighteen; Vietnamese; five foot two. She's a negative. Next."

"Harper, Cory Jake."

Crosby pulled the folder. "White male; twenty-three; five foot eight; one hundred fifty pounds; blond; no facial hair. Let's review him."

Matthews put a star by the name and began jotting notes.

"Littleton branch. Hired: April 28, 2004. Terminated: June 5,

2005. His supervisor was David Anthony."

"Since Anthony was at Dillon, should we red flag it?"

"We need to flag any who worked with Dillon employees. We'll crosscheck them by location and dates of employment to get matches."

"Good idea," Matthews said. "Why was Harper fired?"

"Failed the substance abuse test. Here's his last address and phone number. Next?"

"Harrill, Shanaka H."

"Female; twenty; five foot five; two hundred fifty pounds; African American." Crosby shook his head. "No way. Next."

Matthews read the name. "Hart, Germanie F."

He studied the folders and frowned. "Wait a minute. You skipped one."

"No, I didn't. Shanaka Harrill, Germanie Hart."

"You don't have a Vanessa Lucille Harris?"

"No." She showed him the printout. "See."

"She must have gotten in the wrong stack." He put the folder aside. "You said Hart, right?"

"Well, shouldn't we check her file?"

"If she's not in the computer, how can we run it?"

"I could add her to the database if she needs to be flagged."

Crosby shrugged and opened the folder. "Whoa! Check her out."

"Cute! Maybe we need to flag her for one of your *personal* interviews."

"She's only five foot six, and look at her cleavage. No way did she bind those up to look like a guy."

"You never know these days with wonder bras. She may look like me."

That wouldn't be bad. He closed the folder and handed it to Matthews. "No termination report. She resigned. Who's next?"

Matthews noticed that someone had crossed out Lucille with a pen and written in Lucy on the folder. She scribbled Lucy Harris in the margin of the printout as she read the next name. "Hart, Germanie F."

• • •

The two women rode the elevator to the Carnival *Victory's* main deck, exited the gangway and entered the terminal building. Their luggage was already in the terminal waiting to be claimed, the cash packed inside shoes and other bulky items that might hide it from X-rays. They had decided if the suitcases attracted any attention they would just leave them and get on the first bus to the airport.

"I'll go first," Lucy said. Remembering the Grand Cayman guard, she unbuttoned the third button on her blouse.

"I'll stay about twenty yards behind you and use the other line," Katie said.

"What if they start asking questions?"

"You have a real passport, driver's license and a mountain of paper to back up your story. I'll see you on the bus."

"Okay," Lucy said. "I'm Cheryl," she repeated as she neared the head of the line. Her confidence sank when she realized the customs agent was female. The cleavage trick wouldn't work this time.

• • •

"Hucks, Thomas S.," Matthews read just as her cell phone rang. "Yes, sir. Good morning." She mouthed *Lynch* to Crosby. "It's morning here, sir." She listened for a moment. "We're making progress, but nothing solid. He's right here."

Crosby took the phone. "Yes, sir."

"You're not wearing her out on the slopes are you?" Lynch said.

"No, sir. Just the opposite."

"Vacation's over, Crosby. When the director gets these expense reports it's going to look as if I'm running a damn travel agency. You're on the ski slopes in Colorado, Michael James is in Key West, and Rankin's in Grand Cayman."

"Why Cayman?"

"Your hunch on the sub checked out. It wasn't considered because of the depth where the *Island Breeze* sank. We thought they were still aboard because of the dummies and failed to take in account that the *Breeze* drifted back into shallow water after nightfall. You did good, Crosby."

"Thank you, sir."

"We have an infrared shot of the whole area. The sub surfaced about fifty miles southwest thirty minutes before the blast. A group came on deck and watched it go off."

"So, the sub commander was an accomplice?"

"They definitely took some people off the *Island Breeze*," Lynch said. "During the Cold War, the Navy set up an underwater sound surveillance system called SOSUS. They can track and identify subs and ships anywhere around the world. This sub sounds like a Kilo class manufactured by the Soviets in the 1970s. Some were sold to third world countries after the fall of the Soviet Union. We think this one may belong to the Argentine government."

"Didn't they have a coup several years back?"

"Yes. Their pocket dictator, Fernando Duarte, calls himself 'President for Life.' He vowed to build a nuclear arsenal within five years, but the CIA hasn't seen any evidence of that."

"Do we have a gripe with them?" Crosby asked.

"They're still pissed about our support of the British during the Falklands war. Duarte's father was killed during the war and he promised to take back their islands."

"Where is the sub now?"

"The Navy tracked it to Grand Cayman, where it sat for a half a day before surfacing Tuesday night. Infrared photos indicate someone went ashore at Seven Mile Beach in a rubber raft."

"So Kelly's in the right place."

"Right," Lynch said. "Cayman is a British protectorate, so we have no jurisdiction. But under the Terrorist Information Act, Homeland Security was able to send their people. Rankin arrived yesterday. We've agreed to split his expenses for a copy of the report. He's running the suspect's photos through Cayman airlines and customs, but nothing yet."

"I bet he hates that assignment."

"You're in no position to complain. Oh, I've got that unlisted number for the name and address you posted on the hotline. Her name is Michelle Anthony, 2255 Berry Avenue, Littleton, Colorado. Her number is 303-555-3875. I had Ms. Carver contact and confirm. She's expecting your call. I assume Ms. Anthony was the bank manager's wife?"

"Ex-wife," Crosby said. "She wasn't interviewed?"

"Not by us. Ms. Carver also said you had a call from a Gerald McMullen. Stay on the scent, Crosby. Post me if you get something solid. I'm out on a limb for you guys."

"Yes, sir." Crosby ended the call and searched through his wallet for the card with Gerald McMullen's number. "Marti, can I use your phone to make one more call?"

"Sure. Is it a girlfriend?"

"Hardly. He's the guy who wrote the exposé book on President Barnett's assassination. I was supposed to call him on Saturday, but we left so suddenly I forgot."

"Wasn't he the one who thought it was all a conspiracy?"

"One of many. He's my best friend." Crosby found Gerald's card and punched in the number.

"While you're at it," Matthews added, "ask his opinion on the Fourth Angel Speech recording."

•   •   •

Gerald McMullen stood in the line and waited his turn. Ten places ahead of him was Katie Froscher. For some reason her friend had gotten into a separate line and had already gone through. He wished he could talk with her for just a minute, but he knew it was best to just leave her alone. Besides, the trip had been worthwhile in the end. He had found a perfect cottage on a beautiful cove. All he had to do now was save enough money.

He watched her go though customs but was certain he would see her again at the baggage claim area. He had seen her luggage, and noted that it was all black.

Gerald's phone vibrated and he was surprised to see that the call was from Devrin.

"Agent Crosby," he said with a laugh. "Are you ready to move to Jamaica?"

"Not quite yet, buddy. Where are you?"

"I'm in a very long customs line in Miami."

"There's something you might be able to help us with," Crosby said. "You've heard the rumors about a recording of the late President's speech at Dillon, right?"

"Of course. Are you saying those rumors are true?"

"No comment, but since you wrote a book about President Barnett, I was wondering if you had a theory as to why the perpetrators might have used it. Theoretically."

"There was nothing in Dillon or the bank that could justify the use of that weapon," McMullen said. "So, I believe the explosion was symbolic of what Barnett's *real* speech was about."

"What real speech?"

"The one we never heard. Have you ever seen any of Barnett's original speeches?"

"No."

"William was always jotting notes in the margins, crossing out sections and adding a word here and there. He double-spaced the final drafts because he couldn't stop editing the damn things. Did you see the speech the Secret Service says he was about to read that day?"

"It's been a while," Crosby said.

"Typed, single-spaced, not a single note or correction. That wasn't the speech William wrote, and it certainly wasn't the one he intended to give. I'd bet my life on it."

"What makes you so sure?"

"Because of the quotation. William loved to quote from the Bible and he always picked a verse appropriate to the subject matter. So you tell me; what in the hell did Revelation 16:8 have to do with spending reform?"

•   •   •

"Do you have anything to declare?" The customs agent asked.

"No," Katie Froscher answered politely.

"Your identification, please."

Katie handed over her passport and driver's license. The customs agent gave the picture a cursory glance and slid it back.

"Do you have any fruits or vegetables on your person or in your baggage?"

"No."

"Your baggage is sorted by color on the first floor of the terminal. Please proceed through the double doors, down the escalator and to your right. Next."

Katie released a sigh of relief as she walked through the doors. *So far, so good.* When she reached the baggage claim, her heart skipped a beat. Lucy was staring back at her with a blank expression. "What's wrong?" Katie mouthed.

Lucy turned and pointed to a small mountain of black bags, all piled together just as the agent had said, *by color.* Hundreds of passengers stood around the heap, eroding it piece by piece at the lingering rate of snails.

Katie imagined the bags with the money at the center of the pile, or worse, already in the hands of another passenger.

"Makes you wish you had picked the lime green, don't it?" a baggage handler said, pointing to a solitary set of green luggage off to one side.

A uniformed guard came up from behind and touched Katie's shoulder, causing her to jump from her trance. "Move along please and be sure to compare your claim ticket with the luggage tags before leaving."

Katie and Lucy migrated slowly toward the laborious heap, their fears of inspection gone. On the back wall above the luggage was a sign: "Welcome to the United States of America."

•   •   •

Crosby watched Marti pull on her jeans in the other room as he continued his conversation on her phone. "Barnett's speech was about spending reform?" Crosby tried to recall details of his investigation three years earlier.

"It had absolutely nothing to do with angels and scorching men with fire," Gerald McMullen said, "and why the urgency? The White House Chief of Staff testified that William called him at eleven-thirty Sunday night to schedule the press conference. He said it was urgent that he speak during prime time the next day."

"His press conference was at noon."

"Because there was a state dinner Monday evening. Instead of waiting until Tuesday, William moved the speech up to catch the midday news. Spending reform was never that urgent on his list, so why the rush?"

"Do you know?"

"You need to read my book, Devrin. The Secret Service records show that President Barnett had a late meeting Sunday night. Something in that meeting scared him enough to schedule an urgent press conference."

"Who else was at the meeting?"

"The Chairman of the Joint Chiefs, Secretary of Defense Trexler and his Press Secretary, Tim Cook."

Crosby recalled the ashen-faced Tim Cook running into the bar the night before Barnett's assassination. All of the irregularities he had found at the scene of Tim's suicide came flooding back: the spotless house and equally spotless hard drive on his computer, the confirmation of the airline tickets and the pristine copy of *Sweetboy* magazine. And something else that had slipped his mind.

"The Chairman claims he left before the meeting began," McMullen said. "Trexler testified it was a routine budget meeting, but one of the Secret Service agents said it sounded like there was a heated debate. Trexler left looking very upset."

"Any ideas on what it was about?"

"No and the only witnesses aren't talking. Like I said, Revelation 16:8 has nothing to do with spending reform. It might be pure speculation on my part, but I think it sure as hell had something to do with a ten megaton blast."

• • •

"Any luck?" Matthews asked when she hung up the room phone.

"He thinks these explosions were what President Barnett intended to talk about at his news conference. That's why he referenced the Fourth Angel, but Gerald's just guessing."

Matthews sat on the bed. "I got in touch with Dr. Gebo and he's still in Englewood. He can meet with us on Monday night; assuming we're still in town. If you set up your meeting with Ms. Anthony around the same time, we can kill two birds with one stone and maybe squeeze in another run or two down the slopes today."

Crosby moaned. "My back can't take another day, Marti."

"Sure it can. I left you alone all night so you could rest." She grinned. "Give Ms. Anthony a call."

Crosby dialed the number and a child answered.

"Hello. Is your mommy there?"

"I'm not supposed to talk to strangers," the child said.

Crosby smiled. "Yes, that's a good rule. Could I please speak with your mother, Michelle Anthony?"

"Mom, it's one of those people again." Several kids were screaming in the background. "I don't know who," the child continued. "I *didn't* talk to him." A moment later his mother came on the line. "Look, we're not interested in whatever you're selling. Okay?"

"FBI, Ms. Anthony. I'm Special Agent Devrin Crosby."

"*Oh*. Right. Sorry about that. You know kids . . . well maybe you don't. We've had such a time with telemarketers, but I got the message that you would call."

"Is this a bad time?"

"It's always a bad time. Just make it quick."

"I need to schedule a time to go over a few questions."

"About what?"

"The circumstances surrounding your late husband's death."

"*Ex-husband.* I don't know anything about the robbery or whatever happened over there. I already told the police that although my kids lost their father—not that he ever hung around long enough for them to get to know him—we weren't real devastated. I can't see how I could help."

"It's standard procedure, ma'am. We're interviewing all of the next of kin."

"Can't we just do it over the phone?"

"We're required to conduct all interviews in person. We just want to know what your husband . . . I mean ex-husband was like."

"Where are you located?" she said.

"I'm in Breckenridge right now, but I'll be happy to meet you somewhere more convenient."

"You want to know what David was *really* like? I'll give you a firsthand dose. I have a babysitter coming this afternoon because I have to drive over to Fresco to witness the estate attorney go through his apartment. For some reason I'm supposed to be there. Why? I don't know, but here's the address."

Crosby jotted it down. "I appreciate this, ma'am. I promise I won't keep you long."

"I'll meet you there at around two p.m.," she said. "I'll be in a tan Honda."

• • •

Ryan Papineau stepped away from the Monster and admired his work. "Now, Herman," he said to the object, "it's time to receive your heart." He chuckled to himself at the Monster's moniker, nicknamed for the patriarch of a '60s TV show about a group of monsters living quiet lives in suburbia. He had followed the plans that he and his friend, Chuck Froscher, had developed before he had been brutally murdered. Using Chuck's thermos particle trap as a deuterium igniter was brilliant, but it was only ideas on paper. Herman was Ryan's baby. It was he who had brought this monster to life, and he who had found a solution for every problem.

Ryan was forty-five, a child of divorce, his father French-Canadian, his mother French. As a teenager, he moved from his native Canada to live with his mother in Grenoble, a university town of four hundred thousand in the French Alps. He received the finest education available, thanks to his father's trust fund. In 1987, he graduated top in his class from L'Institut National Polytechnique de Grenoble with a degree in Particle Accelerator Physics and was immediately offered a position at CERN, the European Laboratory for Particle Physics in Geneva, Switzerland. Then fate intervened. He wasn't sure of the exact day, nor the event that led him down this path, but he suspected it started on the day he read about plans to build a Superconducting Super Collider in a place called Texas.

•   •   •

"She drives a tan Honda and you're meeting her alone in her ex-husband's apartment?" Matthews said. "Does this not trigger any alarms?"

"No," Crosby was stuffing notepads and a throwaway digital camera into an overnight bag. "I'll be fine."

"Ex-husband. Real jerk. There's serious motive here, Devrin."

"This lady's got a houseful of kids, Marti. She couldn't pull off a trip to the grocery store alone, much less a bank robbery. Not to mention the Marquesas Keys."

"I'll have Denver send Agent Smith to meet you."

"It's Sunday and he won't get there until after three o'clock. Our meeting is at two."

"Then I'll go with you. First rule in the academy is *never* go in alone."

"I won't be alone. Her estate lawyer is taking inventory."

"You don't have backup. Lynch will go ballistic if he hears about this."

"It's just an interview, Marti. If I'm killed I'll testify you knew nothing about it."

"That's it. Where's my weapon and handbag?"

"I'm *kidding*."

Her expression turned somber. "Are you?"

"Yes."

"Kelly says you used to kid around all the time with him and the others. I guess things are getting better in that respect?"

Crosby nodded. "Yeah. I guess they are. Everything's better lately."

"So you're sure Ms. Anthony is okay?"

"I'll tell you what. If there's only one car, I'll call the locals for backup. While you, my dear, are going to enjoy an afternoon of real skiing without me slowing you down. Understood?"

She gave him a mock salute. "Yes, sir!"

Crosby grabbed the rental keys and headed toward the door. As he passed her, she grabbed him and planted a kiss squarely on his lips; their first.

"I've waited a long time for this," she whispered as their lips parted. "Please don't do anything stupid."

Crosby's heart was racing. "You can count on it."

. . .

Gerald McMullen sat in the airport terminal catching up on the latest headlines. Katie Froscher and her girlfriend were sitting on the row directly behind him, facing in the opposite direction. This was the closest he had ever gotten to her; so close that he could smell her perfume. He could also hear bits and pieces of their conversation. Most of it had been small talk having to do with funeral arrangements. Then he heard her girlfriend say something to Katie that almost floored him.

"Oh, look at him," the girlfriend said just above a whisper. "He has got the *cutest ass*. Okay boy, turn around, yes, this way. *Oh*, will you look at that?"

"That's not natural," Katie said. "It's got to be a sock."

"No girl. That's no sock. You're talking to an expert."

"I'm no amateur, you know."

"Okay, where's a bathroom?" the girlfriend said. "Time for a midday stall-slam."

. . .

The last place Marti Matthews wanted to be was on a ski lift headed to the top of the mountain if Crosby ran into trouble. She should have insisted on going with him. It was FBI policy and she could lose her job if anything went wrong. All she could do was work on the files while she waited for a call she didn't want to get. They had worked the files up to the letter O, and Matthews reasoned that this would be a good time to start entering the notes and comments into the computer database. This part of the job was easy since she only had to add comments to the ones they had flagged.

It didn't take her long to come across the page where she had scribbled Lucy Harris into the margin. She debated on continuing or checking out why Lucy was in the wrong file. *Better safe than sorry.* She used the hotel phone to call the after-hours number on the printout, not wanting to risk tying up her cell phone.

"OleWest National Bank," the recorded message said. "Please use your keypad to answer from the following menu."

Matthews waded through the layers of menus until she found Human Resources.

"Thank you for calling the Human Resources Department of

OleWest National Bank. Our offices are currently closed. Our regular hours are Monday through Friday, eight a.m. mountain time until—"

Matthews pressed the star key followed by the pound key and the line began to ring. "OleWest National," a female voice said.

"This is Dr. Marti Matthews of the FBI. I need someone to retrieve a former employee record for me. The employee's name is Vanessa Lucille Harris. My criminal access code is 62784."

"Thank you. Someone will pull the information and call you back within the hour."

Matthews gave her the number and hung up.

•   •   •

Lucy Harris watched Katie Froscher walk down the aisle of the commercial jet and stop at row 23, the same row she was on, but Katie sat in seat 23-D on the aisle, leaving an empty seat between them. "Good afternoon," Katie said, as if they were complete strangers who happened to be on the same flight. They could only hope that their luggage containing the cash had made it through security. Lucy had never seen so much security. Handbags, shoes, even belts were checked.

Lucy buried her face in the airline magazine. The flight was non-stop to Charlotte and continued on to Dulles International in Washington. Katie would depart in Charlotte, while Lucy would depart for D.C.

Lucy felt a pinch on her thigh. It was Katie nodding down the aisle and mouthing, "Trouble." Lucy saw nothing unusual and shrugged.

"The dark guy with the red shirt," Katie whispered. "I've seen him before."

Lucy didn't recognize the face, and his face was one she would've remembered. He was tall and muscular with a square jaw and sculpted cheeks. He came closer and stopped at their row. The man placed his bag in the bin beside theirs, glanced at his boarding pass and took a seat in 23-E, right between them.

Katie gave Lucy a horrified glance, closed her eyes and swallowed.

•   •   •

The tan Honda was parked in a space directly in front of Apartment 303. Various pieces of furniture covered the lawn lining the sidewalk, and a rollout dumpster, filled to the top with magazines and videotapes, sat near the curb. Crosby saw no sign of anyone in the apartment, but there were neighbors coming and going and he decided that it looked safe enough.

Someone had taped a yellow ribbon to the door, which was cracked open a couple of inches. He tapped on it before pushing it open far enough to yell inside. "Hello."

"Are you Agent Crosby?" a female voice called from upstairs.

Crosby placed his hand on the Glock inside his coat before answering, "Yes, ma'am." He held his badge inside the door.

A very attractive woman in her mid thirties came down the stairs. She was tall, about five foot eight and one hundred thirty pounds, Crosby estimated. Her hair was a medium brown with matching eyes.

"Good. I'm in no mood to get raped. Hi, I'm Michelle Anthony."

Crosby shook her hand. "Special Agent Devrin Crosby."

She raised one hand, palm up, around the room. "This is it. Welcome to the OleWest Pimp and Whorehouse."

Crosby smiled warily.

"Did you see the library outside in the dumpster? Filled to the lid with porn magazines and videos," she added. "You should see the list of links on his computer upstairs. I knew David had a problem, but I had no idea it was this bad."

"You suspected him of—"

"Oh, of course." She motioned towards a couch. "You want to sit down? I can't guarantee that it's clean, but there it is."

Crosby moved to a tan leather couch and sat. It was expensive and comfortable.

"That was mine," she said nodding at the couch beneath him. "It's what David left me in his will. How appropriate. I guess now I'll have to *burn* it."

"Ms. Anthony—"

"Please call me Michelle. I hate that name. I would've changed it, but I have kids."

Once again Crosby tried to begin. "How long have you been divorced?"

"Four years in June."

"Was he unfaithful?"

She looked as though it was obvious. "Well, look around."

"Ms. Anth—" He corrected. "Michelle. I never met your ex-husband. What seems obvious to you, might not to me. I look around and see an expensive leather couch in a moderately priced apartment, where it doesn't quite fit. I can only assume this wasn't your home, but something he acquired after the divorce. I can't determine what is normal in this picture until you paint a complete image for me."

"Yes. Sorry, I tend to get ahead of myself. No, this wasn't ours. We owned a very nice home in Littleton when we divorced. That's where the kids and I live. Of course, now that his child support payments are gone, we'll have to move."

"You weren't a beneficiary on his life insurance?"

"I wish!" she said. "The kids got a trust fund to go to college. I got alimony, child support and a cum covered couch. That's it! I may have hated him, Agent Crosby, but I certainly wasn't stupid enough to kill him."

•   •   •

She was even more beautiful now that he was sitting beside her, and Gerald felt like a school kid about to press the doorbell on his first date. The moment the gate agents arrived, he had taken a place in line right behind Katie. Her seat was probably already assigned, but with heightened security, she needed a boarding pass. Apparently, she was picking up her girlfriend's gate pass as well because she was given two. He had looked over her shoulder, caught a quick glimpse of the seat numbers and memorized them.

Surrendering his first class ticket for coach had been easy. He had complained of feeling queasy and that he preferred the middle of the plane. Did the agent happen to have anything available on say, row 23? She did, but it was a middle seat. "Perfect." And the seat was his.

It wasn't until boarding time that Katie and her girlfriend seemed to drift apart. The girlfriend stood near the head of the line and Katie near the rear. Then, on the plane, they sat on the same row. It was obvious they were together, but they kept drifting apart. Perhaps her girlfriend was trying to hook up with the guy she had lusted at in the terminal, but he was nowhere in sight.

On closer examination, he noticed there was something oriental about the friend's eyes. Perhaps some Chinese blood in her genes. Katie was concentrating on her fingernails and ignored him. Gerald smiled at the friend and fastened his seat belt.

•   •   •

"Vanessa Lucille Harris," Matthews repeated into the receiver.

"I'm sorry, but there's no one with that name in our database," the clerk at OleWest National said.

"Try Lucy Harris."

"Nope. There was a Jacob Harris, who worked here in 1986."

"Maybe we have the wrong branch. Which database are you using?"

"This is the master employee record. It covers all branches."

"Perhaps you're just missing her," Matthews said. "How far back does it go?"

"It goes back to 1909. Vanessa Harris never worked for OleWest."

"I have her employee file right in front of me," Matthews said. "I'm looking at her picture."

"I'm sorry, but there's no one by that name in the computer. You can call back Monday morning and speak with the Director of Human Resources."

"Thank you. I will." Matthews hung up the phone and scratched her head. *How in the hell could an employee record just vanish?*

· · ·

In January of 1993, Ryan Papineau was among two hundred and fifty foreign scientists to move to Ellis County, Texas, where work was advancing on the Superconducting Super Collider. Six months later, with more than fourteen miles of tunnel already excavated and nearly two billion dollars spent, Congress pulled the project's plug.

Ryan was devastated. His new home and BMW sat in the middle of what soon became a suburban ghost town. He spent another six months lobbying anyone who would listen about the importance of renewing the project, but it was too late. His former colleagues left town and snatched up the few remaining jobs in his field. Loans came due and banks foreclosed. With all hope gone and nowhere to go, Ryan was forced into bankruptcy, reduced to teaching high school science and sweeping floors at night. It took him nine years to recover, but eventually the impressive resume struck pay dirt. Fermi National Accelerator Lab called and offered to move him and his one remaining asset, the old BMW, to Batavia, Illinois, near Chicago.

· · ·

Katie's first instinct was to bolt and run, but with the aisle full of oncoming passengers, that was impossible. He probably was an agent with the FBI or worse, a goon from Spectrum. If so, they already knew she was aboard. Best to just play it cool and try not to implicate Lucy. The only thing the FBI could pin on her was wire fraud, but if he was with Spectrum, she was as good as dead.

•   •   •

"David and I met in high school," Michelle Anthony continued. "I should have known better, but he had a real knack for numbers and accounting. You just knew he would be successful, and I needed security."

"When did you marry?" Crosby asked.

"Nine years ago."

"When did it begin to fall apart?"

She interlaced her fingers. "Almost immediately. He was always wanting me to do . . ." she made quotation marks in the air, "weird things."

"Sexually?"

"At first it was minor. He was always trying to get me to dance on the coffee table and strip for him."

"But it progressed?"

"Yes." She crossed her legs a little tighter. "He would bring adult toys home and things he wanted me to dress up in. We were married, so I usually went along with it for his benefit. Then, I got pregnant with our first child. As it progressed, I became concerned for the baby's welfare. Especially the sadistic things he did. Spanking and the rest of that sick stuff."

"I see." This wasn't going anywhere, so Crosby changed the subject. "Can you tell me about his work habits?"

"He immediately got a job in banking when he graduated. He started at OleWest National about the time we got married. Promotions were frequent and we went from an apartment to a nice home in the suburbs. Once he made vice president, we could afford the house in Littleton. He got a real bargain, due in part to the massacre at Columbine. I didn't want to move there, but David always got his way."

"Did he have any problems with his fellow workers at OleWest?"

"Other than sleeping with them, no."

"Wait a minute," Crosby said. "He was having an affair with one of his employees?"

"One? From what I've heard, if you wanted to get to the top, sleeping with David was a rite of passage."

"How did you find out?"

"He kept coming home late with excuses; audits and tax forms he had to finish. One night, I parked outside the office and followed him. He went to a topless bar," she said in disgust. "I stormed in and poured a drink in his lap. To top it off, he had the gall to blame *me*. He said I never 'showed off' enough for him."

"Is that when the marriage ended?"

"No, we tried to work things out for the sake of the children. But he only got worse over time. The final straw was when I came home early one day and found him on that couch." She nodded in Crosby's direction.

"He was with someone?" Crosby said.

"He was *in* someone." She clinched her jaw. "In *my* house, on *my* couch."

"I know this is tough, Michelle, but I'll need a name or a description if you can recall," Crosby said.

"I never wanted to know her name, but she may have worked at the downtown branch."

"Can you describe her?"

"She had black pubic hair. *Okay!* I just wanted that bastard and his bitch out of my house."

"I understand. Just a couple more questions. Why did he move to Dillon?"

"The bank transferred him."

"He went from a vice president to a branch manager? Why?"

"Isn't it obvious?" she said. "Someone filed a sexual harassment suit against him."

Crosby took a moment to absorb this. "I'm sorry, Michelle, but we're going to have to confiscate everything in that outside dumpster, the computer and probably this couch as well."

"Why?"

"You've just given us a key motive for your husband's murder."

•   •   •

Ryan pulled on heavy insulated gloves and opened the lid of the helium refrigeration unit. He carefully removed the last of the tubular particle traps and examined it inch by inch. The electromagnets surrounding the unit were still functioning, and there was every reason to believe that the antihydrogen held within had remained frozen over the past three years. *Three years since the old BMW plunged off a bridge into an ice covered river; three years since his parents had watched an empty casket lowered into a cemetery plot; three years of hiding and planning the ultimate revenge.* Congress had taken away his job. The boys from Spectrum had wanted him dead. Now, he would return the favor.

During his second year at Fermilab, Ryan gained Ultra Black Secret Clearance and was allowed entrance into the top secret weapons research division, an area guarded by armed men and sealed off from the rest of the facility. There, he encountered Chuck Froscher leading a group of scientists from Oak Ridge who used the collider to conduct experiments in the production of antiparticles. Their experiments were going well, but they had the same problem as the rest of the world: How do you store antimatter long-term once it's created?

Two days later, while Ryan was pouring his morning coffee from a thermos, he'd had an idea.

•   •   •

"Where are you headed?" the man beside her asked as the jet's engines slowed their whine and the plane leveled off.

Katie took a deep breath and tried to relax. Even his voice sounded familiar. She had seen him somewhere. "I beg your pardon?" she said.

"I was just wondering where you're headed?"

Certainly, they knew where she lived. What was the point in lying? "I'm getting off at Charlotte and driving towards Raleigh."

"Were you on vacation?"

"What's makes you say that?"

"You have a suntan." He smiled.

She gave him a sideways glance.

"Sorry . . . It's none of my business."

Katie looked into his brown eyes for the first time. She was certain she had seen them before. "I've been on a cruise all week," she said.

"Really? Which one?"

You should know, you tracked me here. Maybe he wasn't FBI. "The Carnival *Victory.*"

"We were on the same cruise." He grinned.

Katie allowed herself a smile. If he was a Fed, he was doing a damn good job of hiding it.

"I started to take the eastern cruise," he continued, "but I've always dreamed of retiring someday on one of those white sandy beaches in Grand Cayman or Jamaica. I went down to see what's available."

"Did you find a place?"

"Perhaps, but I don't have the money yet. I have a friend that I'm hoping will move and help me open a dive shop."

"What's her name?"

"Whose name?"

"The friend to open the dive shop with."

"*His* name is Devrin."

"You really look familiar," Katie said.

"You too. Maybe we ran into each other onboard."

"I don't believe so. Have we met somewhere before?"

He frowned as if in thought. "It seems like we may have shared a conversation once, but I can't put my finger on it," he lied, wishing she would remember.

"Where are you from?"

"Charlotte. I worked in Washington, but moved back to Charlotte three years ago to help my elderly mother."

"Why don't we start with your name?" she said.

"I'm sorry. Early onset Alzheimer's I suppose." He extended his hand. "I'm Gerald McMullen."

She took his hand and held it for a moment. The name didn't ring any bells.

"Call me Gerry. And you are?"

She wanted to use an alias, but her real name had a paper trail to protect her. "Katie Froscher."

"Froscher? Sounds familiar. Where do you work?"

"I'm a systems analyst in a bank."

"Ever been to Washington?" McMullen tried his best to keep the conversation going. "I used to work for the *Washington Post*."

"I've never set foot in Washington. Are you a reporter?"

He huffed. "I was, but for the past three years I've been writing a book and working part-time as a features editor for Charlotte-Observer.com. I'm working my way toward retirement."

"You're way too young to retire," she said.

"I'm sure I'm older than you."

"You're not that old."

"My diploma from UNC was dated in 1992."

It took Katie a moment to do the math. "No way, you're over forty."

"You're *forty?*" Lucy chimed in from the other side.

Katie glared at Lucy. "Excuse me."

"No, I'm forty-six," McMullen continued.

"You don't look a day over *thirty*," Lucy added with an admiring smile.

"So you two know each other?"

"Well—" Lucy said.

"We just met," Katie interrupted, her teeth clinched, "Aboard the ship." She mouthed a *"shut up!"* at Lucy when Gerald was looking the other way.

"So, are your wife and kids moving to the Caribbean with you?" Lucy added.

"I've never been married."

Lucy leaned forward revealing ample cleavage. "Hi, I'm Lucille. Tell us more about this house you're planning to buy."

Katie put her head in her hand. *So much for maintaining their cover.*

•　•　•

"Marti," Crosby said. "I've stumbled onto something important with this Anthony guy."

"What's up?"

"I'll explain when I get back. In the mean time, we need to get a team out here to secure the evidence and they will need a truck. I also need the name, home number and address of the bank's president. The one we met with last Friday."

"Hold on a second." Matthews flipped through her notepad. "Foy, Harry Foy. I'll make the appointment."

"Thanks. It's important that I see him today, if possible. I can meet him at the bank."

"Are you headed to Denver?"

"Just leaving. I'm still at the apartment in Fresco."

"Come get me," she said. "I'll meet you in front of the hotel."

"I thought you were skiing?"

"I was worried about you."

"I'll be there in fifteen minutes."

•　•　•

Katie Froscher stepped off the plane and onto the ramp leading into the Charlotte International terminal. Slightly behind her was Gerald McMullen. She still didn't know what to make of him and half expected to feel the cold steel of handcuffs slapped on her wrists at any moment. When she was safely in the terminal she turned to say goodbye. "It was nice meeting you, although I feel we've met before."

"Me too. Are you hungry?" Gerald asked.

"What do you mean?"

"Would you care to have dinner?"

She glanced at her watch. It was nearly five p.m., but being on edge all day, she hadn't given food a second's thought. "You mean together?"

He laughed. "You don't go out much, do you?"

She frowned. "Like a date?"

"We don't have to call it that. We could call it a conference or a meeting if you prefer."

"No . . . I mean," she stumbled over her words. "I guess that would be fine. But you don't even know me."

"All the more reason. Look, it's just dinner, not a lifelong commitment. We can eat in the airport, if you prefer."

"I suppose that would be . . . okay. Would you excuse me for a moment while I go to the ladies room?"

"Certainly."

The moment Katie turned the corner into the restroom she stopped and sneaked a look back at Gerald. There was no cell phone at his ear reporting her position; no nods to fellow agents or suspicious whispers at hidden microphones in his collar. He looked like a normal guy, a very *nice looking* normal guy. Perhaps his assignment was to get to know her first. She was now certain she had seen him before, and this worried her.

• • •

Marti was dressed in a navy blue turtleneck, jeans and her down parka when Crosby pulled up to the hotel. It was a sharp contrast to his suit. The drive was seventy-five miles, but since it was nearly all down hill they would make good time.

"Did you get in touch with Mr. Foy?" Crosby said.

"Found him on the golf course. He's meeting us at the bank at six-thirty."

"Wouldn't you rather spend the day skiing?"

"Not really. I'd rather help you. Did the interview with Ms. Anthony go well?"

"Her husband was having an affair with several of his bank employees. He got sued, demoted and packed off to Dillon."

"That guy?"

"Pretty amazing, isn't it. His ex-wife was nice looking too. She caught him red-handed on the family couch."

"Why didn't anyone report this?"

"His next of kin was listed as his mother. Our agents contacted her."

"I had an interesting afternoon," Matthews said. "I was going through the files and came across the one we threw out. The real looker."

"Yeah."

"So, I called OleWest and they can't find her listed in their database."

"She was listed as resigned, right?"

"Yes, but they can't find *any* employee records of her."

"Is she that important to the case?" Crosby asked.

"Well, if she's missing, who else might be?"

"*Oh.* Good point."

•   •   •

In the ladies room, Katie spent a few moments adjusting her makeup while she waited for the last stall to empty. The moment she was sure she had the restroom to herself, she took out her cell phone. She debated whether it would be safe to use, then punched in Lucy's number. If the FBI was on to her, she reasoned, it would make little difference. Both her phone and Lucy's were in her own name and the phone records, if traced, would tell them little.

"Hello," Lucy replied after the third ring. She was still in her seat on the parked plane, less than fifty yards away.

"What the *hell* were you thinking?" Katie said angrily.

There was a long pause. "No harm done."

"*Like hell.* I told you I've seen this guy before and you go shooting off your mouth about us being *together.*"

"So? You said we met on the ship. People meet every day. He's just a casual acquaintance we saw on a plane."

"What if one of our pictures makes the evening news? Up until a few minutes ago you had no connection to me whatsoever. Now Mister Mysterious is a perfect witness."

"He was just so—"

"*Cute.* Right?"

"Okay. You're right. I wasn't thinking."

"Stunts like that will get us killed, Lucy. If I had any sense at all I'd get on the next plane out of here." Katie rubbed her forehead. "But I suppose at this point we're committed. You sent that package to the post office, right?"

"Yes."

"I need the box number and the address."

"Why?"

"I'm having dinner with him."

"You're what?" Lucy said.

"It's your fault. Thanks to you, I have no choice but to find out who the hell he is. I just hope I don't have to use it."

"You mean the gun?"

"*Yes.*"

· · ·

The building was empty, but the president and CEO of OleWest National still looked out of place in his windbreaker, polo shirt and tan slacks. Harry Foy exited the elevator on the executive floor and led Crosby and Matthews into his spacious office. He went straight to his desk, opened a drawer and pulled out a file.

"I believe this is what you're looking for," Foy said handing the file on David Anthony to Matthews. She began studying the pages.

"This would have been helpful a week ago." Crosby crossed his arms. "Why didn't you tell us?"

Foy rubbed his fingers through the short gray hair on his balding head. His cheeks were puffy and sunburned from an afternoon of golf. "David was an embarrassment to the firm. We never imagined that his personal affairs might be linked to what happened at Dillon."

"*Bull!* You wanted to protect your bank's reputation."

"Of course. But I saw no need in ruining the reputation of a dead man as well as the women he'd victimized. They've moved on with their lives."

"But you kept him on," Matthews held up some papers, "even after three complaints of sexual harassment."

"He was never convicted."

"Because you paid them off. You let this sexual predator move to another branch where he could victimize more women."

Foy held out his hand defensively, fingers spread. "We never had any complaints after he moved to Dillon, and I kept strict tabs on him. That's one of the reasons we put in the streaming video feed. There were also legal issues involved. He never committed these acts while on company time. We couldn't fire him."

"Don't give me that," Crosby said. "Now here's what we're going to do. You're going sit down and tell us everything you know about David Anthony; what's in the file and what isn't. And when you're through, we'll decide whether you were fully cooperative, or if we should recommend bringing charges of obstruction against you. Try that legal issue on for size."

•   •   •

Ryan Papineau held his breath as he unplugged the electromagnets and disconnected the liquid helium feed tube. He gingerly lowered the traps into Herman's containment and attached the Monster's power supply and feed tube. With a flip of a switch, Herman's heart began pumping the super-cold liquid helium into the twin traps. Ryan's cold-blooded monsters were at last armed and ready.

PART 3

CHAPTER 18

GERALD

Monday, Second Week

"So, now it's revenge?" Kelly Rankin said, his voice amplified by the car's speakers. "The guy should have known there's nothing worse than a woman *spermed.*"

Crosby let out a snicker, and Matthews grinned. They were in the rental car, headed back to Denver from Breckenridge.

"Was that a laugh?" Rankin said. "What's Marti done to get you to lighten up, Crosby?"

"Nothing." Crosby slowed for a curve. "There wasn't anything to laugh at until now."

"You're checking out Foy's leads before heading back, right?"

"Most of the addresses are around Denver, so we're moving to a hotel there," Matthews said. "The Sheraton downtown. Anything on your end?"

"We haven't found squat. I expect Lynch and the fellows upstairs will pull us out of paradise any minute now. Boy, Georgetown is one beautiful place. I wish we could come up with some hot tips to keep us down here for a few days."

"We'll post anything we find on the hotline."

"Be sure to check out the boyfriends and husbands," Rankin added. "Sometimes they get pissed off more that the actual victims."

"Good idea. See you when we get back." Matthews pressed the End key. "See, I told you he wasn't so bad."

"He's changed."

"You both have."

• • •

The crane was a rental and at $175.00 per hour it came with only one operator. Ryan Papineau gave directions with hand signals as the huge air-conditioner was lowered onto the flatbed of an eighteen-wheel tractor trailer. He signaled the distance and clinched his fist to show that the unit was safely resting on the four by four blocks. The line slackened and Ryan released the keeper straps.

The crane operator, a man weighing over three hundred pounds, climbed down, made sure the load was secure and lumbered over to Ryan. "That's an hour and fifteen minutes. Comes to $218.75, U.S. currency. I don't take Canadian."

"It only took ten minutes," Ryan said.

"That's right. Ten minutes to move it, a half hour to set up, another half hour to break it down and five minutes to explain the billing to morons. Now do you want to pay me or do I set the damn thing back on the ground?"

It was ridiculous to argue. The man owned the only crane within thirty miles. Ryan took out his wallet and paid with two hundreds and a twenty. The operator made no effort to offer change.

"Keep the change," Ryan finally said.

"Some tip. Next time I'll be a little more *careful*."

The load was secured, the DC power cable attached and within the hour Ryan would drive the truck to Windsor where he would join hundreds of other vehicles going through the border crossing into Detroit. He had all the necessary paperwork. His load was a commercial air-conditioning unit, no different in size or shape from any other. If he was lucky, it would receive only a cursory glance, and barring any accidents or road hazards, tomorrow the Monster would arrive in Washington, DC.

• • •

Katie Froscher awoke in a hotel with a stranger sleeping beside her. She almost never spent the night with a man on the first date, but the prospect of sleeping in the arms of Gerald McMullen was not only different, it was refreshing. She had never felt so swept off her feet. There had been boyfriends, and even a misguided attempt at an engagement, but none had come close to the giddiness she experienced with him.

They had changed into their evening clothes in the restroom of a hotel lobby and a bellhop had reloaded their bags into the rented Lexus as though they were valued guests. They had dined at the elegant Top of the Tower restaurant in the new First Nations Bank Building, the same building where she worked. He had taken her dancing at the Tip-Top Club and listened to jazz at Bayou's House of Blues. The evening had gone so well she was afraid of ruining it by taking him back to her apartment, where the real FBI might lay in wait. Instead, she had taken a room at the Marriott where they had stayed up talking until three in the morning. They slept arm in arm, both fully-clothed and awakened the same way. He could have made love to her at any moment and she wanted him, but never once had he tried. The prospect of eventually making love to this beautiful man was the most intriguing—

She saw the clock. "*Oh shit!*" she yelled, grabbing the clock as if her eyes were deceiving her.

Gerald sat straight up, wide eyed, and felt as if someone had just poured a bucket of ice water over his head. "What is it?"

"It's *10:02!*" as if the problem was obvious. Katie hopped around the room, one shoe on, the other in her hand, all the time saying, "It's 10:02." She grabbed her purse from under a blanket. "*Crap!* Now it's *10:07!* I'm supposed to be in Denton at *eleven!* That's an hour and a half drive. *Shit!* Where the hell is my suitcase?"

"Calm down. I put it in the closet," Gerald said.

"Calm down? You don't understand. I have to be in Denton in forty-five minutes or my mother will *kill* me."

"She's not going to kill you." Gerald was calm. "What's so important?"

"My father's grave is being exhumed at eleven a.m. If I'm not there, then my mother will have to be there, and she doesn't want to be there, and that's why I *have* to be there. Understand? I have to leave *right now.*"

"Not looking that way, you're not."

Katie glanced at the mirror. Her hair looked as if it had been ironed to one side. "Oh *crap!*" She collapsed on the bed and burst into tears. "I promised her that I would take care of it. I told her I would be there," she moaned. "*I promised.*"

Gerald gave her a tissue and wrapped her in his arms. "It's okay, Katie. I have an idea."

"It's no use." She kept shaking her head. "There's no way I can make it in time. It will be over by the time I get there."

"Maybe not. Let me make a call, while you wet your hair."

"To a priest?"

"You need a miracle, right? Just trust me." He picked up his cell.

Katie stumbled to the bathroom and was overcome with dé jà vu by something he'd said. When she looked back, he was on the phone.

"Ned McMullen, please," Gerald said. "Tell him it's his baby brother."

•   •   •

The call that Lucy anticipated finally came. A quick check of her caller ID identified it as a 734 area code. Ryan had made it across the border and more importantly through customs.

"Are we safe?" Ryan said.

"Yes. What time will you arrive?"

"Twelve hours, give or take."

"Change of plans," Lucy said. "Bring it to the old Piedmont Cargo terminal building." She gave him the address. "It's a warehouse on airport road. I'll have a key."

"Why the delay?"

"Katie may have been compromised. She's arriving tomorrow and I want to make damn sure she sends the worm before it's installed."

"It's your show."

"How is Herman?"

"It's *alive*."

"The name of the installers is Jenkins Heating and Air. Your contact is Mr. Smith. How long do we have?"

"Forty-eight hours," Ryan said. "That's an estimate, of course. The battery will last longer. Do you have the money?"

"Already in the bank."

"I'll call if I get held up. See you there."

The moment he hung up Lucy dialed a second number.

"Simpson Mortuary," the receptionist said.

"Clay Simpson please."

"One moment." The line clicked.

"This is Clay. How may I help you?"

"*Clay*," Lucy said in her sexist voice. "This is Elyn from the club."

"Well, *hello*."

"What are you doing tonight? I was hoping that maybe we could get together, if you're . . . in the mood."

"I could arrange that."

•   •   •

The road between Breckenridge and Dillon was picturesque. Crosby kept one eye on the road and the other on the mountain scenery. The list of names they had compiled from the files lay in Matthews' lap. On top of those were the names they had gleaned from Foy's records on the late David Anthony. Addresses and phone numbers were printed beside each. Matthews arranged them so they wouldn't have to zigzag all over town. Some were no longer valid would have to be checked out by phone. She also had the Lucy Harris file, so she could talk it over with the Human Resources Director at OleWest. That file had been bugging her all night.

"You know, Devrin, none of these victims were on our original list. They either resigned or moved to a different branch."

"If Mr. Foy had been upfront in the beginning we would have changed the parameters of our search."

"So, how did Vanessa Lucille Harris get into that profile?"

"Which one was she?"

"The cute one."

"Probably a mistake."

"Someone pulled those files based on termination reports, but she wasn't fired."

"They were probably searching for the file in front of it and grabbed hers as well."

"Someone still sorted them alphabetically. They should have caught it."

"If it bothers you just add her to the list. I'll check her out." He raised his eyebrows.

"No way am I letting you near her. This one's mine."

•   •   •

The security guard in his golf cart weaved between rows of cars on level one of the long-term parking deck at Salt Lake International. Following behind him was a dark blue sedan, its occupants wearing dark suits. The golf cart and sedan pulled up behind a 2006 tan Honda Accord, a thin layer of dust covering the windows.

"Here it is, gentlemen," the guard said to the agents as they got out. "This one has been here since Friday of last week. There's a code on the ticket."

One of the agents started writing on a notepad while the other called out the tag number. They repeated the procedure for the vehicle identification number on the dashboard.

"Where's the next one?" the second agent said returning to the car.

The guard got back into his cart and led them to the next tan Honda. It was a procedure they had repeated countless times already and would repeat again.

•   •   •

There was no way one could drive through Fresco without seeing the devastation at Dillon. The huge reservoir, which had once separated the two cities, had been drained over the past week and massive backhoes were on the lake floor loading the debris into trucks to haul it away. Everything had to be inspected for both human and bomb remains. The job was huge and Crosby wanted a last look at it before leaving.

Beyond the edge of the mountain that had shielded Fresco, the landscape was a gray ash dotted with workers in yellow suits and heavy equipment. Crosby and Matthews walked up to the crime scene tape, overlooking the site. The town had been completely obliterated, marked only by the huge crater. It was beyond anything Crosby had ever seen and he had to keep reminding himself that this was the smaller of the two bombs. To imagine this destruction in a place such as New York was impossible. The collapse of the World Trade Centers a hundred fold wouldn't come close.

Marti Mathews stood beside him and took his hand in hers. "What are you thinking?"

"That all of this might have been prevented, if one guy had remained faithful to his wife."

"Unbelievable, isn't it?"

"Does this seem like retaliation to you, Marti?"

"If feels more like terrorism. This type of hate wants to destroy the entire world."

"I know. I have a feeling there's more than one agenda here."

•   •   •

Katie Froscher leaned against the shoulder of Gerald McMullen and looked down on the fields surrounding her family's farm in Denton, North Carolina. The trip, which would have taken an hour and a half by car, had taken only twenty minutes by air. They sat in the rear compartment of the old Bell UH-1H "Huey" helicopter, owned by Gerald's brother and used for his aerial traffic reporting business.

There was no telling how much all of this was costing, but

whatever it was, she was willing to pay. Looking down on her farm she saw the black limo the funeral home had sent over to take her to the cemetery. Her mother, standing in the yard beside it, was looking up at them, probably wondering why a helicopter was hovering over her farm.

Ned McMullen found a spot in a field out back with no power lines and set the chopper down. Gerald ran his finger across his throat, indicating to Ned to shut it off.

"I thought you and I are heading back, little brother?" he yelled.

Gerald patted the top of his head and pointed to Katie's hair. Ned gave the thumbs up and cut the power to the engines.

Katie looked at Gerald and smiled. "I can't believe you got me here by eleven o'clock. Now that's a miracle. The last time this happened to me I was returning from my father's wake and had a blowou—" Her voice caught. The face she remembered at the window of her car was Gerald's; his soaked curly hair; and the words he had spoken: *It's a matter of faith.* "It was *you*? My God, it was *you!*" She threw her arms around Gerald and squeezed him tight. "I can't believe it." She squeezed tighter.

"Uh, Katie. I can't breath."

She pulled back, tears pouring down her cheeks. "That was *you*. No wonder you looked familiar."

Gerald's brother looked confused.

How am I ever going to explain this? Gerald thought.

"You drive a white truck, don't you?" Katie said.

"How did you know?"

"You stop and help old ladies who've dropped their keys."

"Doesn't everyone?"

"You do if you're in this family," Ned added. "Otherwise, our mother would tan our hides."

"And you stopped three years ago in the pouring rain to help a stranger with a blowout. You wouldn't take a dime for it."

"*That's* where we *met*," Gerald said faking surprise.

She hugged him again. "You have no idea how many nights I've lain awake wondering who you were, and once again you've just walked into my life. You're the knight I've waited for my entire life, and here you are pulling off another miracle."

"Your mom's waiting on you," Ned said.

Gerald knew this would be his last chance to tell her the truth. Once she talked with her mother or Mandy she would know that he had been following her. "Katie, I have to tell you something."

Katie looked at her mother standing in the field. "Tell me later. Come on, I'll introduce you." She took his hand and the two of them climbed out.

"Be back in a second, bro."

"Ned, you too," Katie said. "This time neither of you are getting away without a proper thank you."

Ten minutes later, the helicopter lifted off, leaving Katie and Ruth Froscher standing alone in the field with her luggage.

"What nice boys," Ruth said. "Such gentlemen too. I believe he likes you, honey."

"Mom," Katie said. "He doesn't know it yet, but I could fall for this guy."

• • •

The Human Resources Department at OleWest National was on the first floor and had just opened when Dr. Matthews arrived. Crosby said he was going upstairs to interview two employees who were on Foy's list and would call her when he was finished.

Mallory Reynolds, a retirement-aged department head who wore her gray hair in a bun, was at her desk, pecking on her computer when Matthews knocked. "Yes," Reynolds said without looking up.

"Ms. Reynolds, I'm Dr. Matthews of the FBI." She had her credentials already out.

The pecking immediately stopped. "I was wondering when you people would get around to calling. You found the file?"

"Yes. I had a question concerning one of them—"

"Lucille Harris," she interrupted.

"That's right. It was mixed in with the other names that had been terminated for cause."

"Lucy resigned. She wasn't terminated," Reynolds said. "You're wondering why she was included?"

"That's correct."

"That's my fault, Agent Matthews. I added her file to the folder."

"Why?"

"Because you weren't looking at the right people. If someone in your agency had bothered to ask, I could have saved you a tremendous amount of footwork. But no one did."

"You have our apologies, Ms. Reynolds and my complete attention now."

"In my opinion, Ms. Harris should never have been hired in the first place. Her resume indicated that she once worked at the Illinois State Bank in Chicago, but I couldn't find any confirmation of that. The decision to hire her came from upstairs. It wasn't mine."

"Did you feel she was unqualified for the position?"

"She performed adequately, I suppose. I'm not one to make moral judgments, you understand, but a bank has a reputation to maintain. Ms. Harris wore what I consider to be . . . inappropriate attire for her position."

"You mean short skirts?"

"Not necessarily short, as much as revealing. She managed to stay within the letter of the dress code, albeit barely. It doesn't mandate the tightness of the skirt nor is there any mention about the type, shape, or lack there of, when it comes to undergarments."

"She didn't wear a bra?"

"Or anything else that I could tell." Reynolds raised her brow. "Interesting way to attract new customers. Don't you think?"

"What was her position?"

"Horizontal, I suspect," Reynolds huffed a smile before she regained her composure. "Sorry. I couldn't resist. Ms. Harris was a commercial loan officer, thus my concern."

"That's very interesting, Ms. Reynolds, but why did you suspect her?"

"Her relationship with David Anthony, and its aftermath, of course. I believe she was also responsible in part for the breakup of his marriage, but that was none of my business."

"Was David having an affair with her?"

"You'll have to speak with Mr. Foy about that."

"We already have. He gave us the sexual harassment file."

"So, you already know about the complaint she filed against him."

"Her name was not included," Matthews said, "and there's no record of her in your database."

"Of course there is." Reynolds turned to her computer and began typing, "I pulled it up just last week. A request for a background check came in. We responded with the standard information."

"Who requested it?"

Reynolds pecked away. "I don't recall, but I can find out." She read from her screen. "File not found? She's *not* here." Reynolds tried again. "All of her records have been deleted." She looked at the ceiling and scowled. "I don't know how this happened, Agent Matthews, but I *will get* to the bottom of it."

Matthews picked up her things and stood. "Thank you for your help, Mrs. Reynolds. Here's my card. If you locate who made the request, please call my cell number."

"One more thing before you leave," Reynolds said. "I never gave this much thought until I saw the images lifted from the Dillon video on TV this week. It took me a while, but I finally found the Polaroid in one of the scrap books we keep in the smoking lounge." She opened her top drawer, and took out the photo. "We sometimes dressed up for Halloween, you see. This is what Lucy Harris wore the last time she participated."

Matthews took the photo and felt cold chills run up her spine. The photo showed a man with short blond hair and a mustache. He was wearing a green three-piece suit.

"She won the contest," Reynolds added. "No one had a clue who she was."

•   •   •

The exhumation of Captain Charles Froscher, Sr.'s remains came off without a hitch. The concrete vault containing the casket was raised onto the back of a vault truck with a special lift and driven to the funeral home. Katie's limo followed. She signed the paperwork, paid for a new casket for shipment and released the remains to Piedmont Air Cargo. That was it. She was free to return to her mother's farm where she hoped to get some much needed rest and wash two suitcases of dirty laundry.

That evening, the casket would be driven to the cargo terminal at the Greensboro airport, loaded aboard an old DC-3 prop plane and flown to Dulles International Airport overnight. All that remained was for Katie to catch a commercial flight in the morning, have a funeral company take possession of the remains at the air cargo freight building and write a check for the new vault and transportation. Lucy had promised to take care of the final burial arrangements on her end, but Katie had yet to hear from her. When she checked her cell phone she knew why. The battery was dead.

•   •   •

None of the employee's on Crosby's list were available. Instead of waiting, Crosby decided he would drop in on David Anthony's mother. The address listed the apartment as being ten blocks from downtown. After circling the block twice, he spotted the address of an old Victorian-style home.

The woman that answered the door was old and frail. She was also hard of hearing and Crosby regretted bothering her. At her age she probably knew nothing of her son's extramarital affairs or why anyone would want to kill him.

Her name was listed as Margaret Anthony, but she insisted that Crosby call her Maggie. She invited him inside out of the cold. Crosby was too polite to turn her down. They sat on a stiff sofa with needlepoint covering the worn fabric on the arms. A grandfather clock ticked away the time in the hall and an old gray Persian cat lay undisturbed on the cushion between them. Crosby realized too late that the back of his suit was probably covered in cat hair.

"Davy was such a sweet boy," Mrs. Anthony said. "He worked in a bank, you know."

"Yes ma'am." *He certainly had snowed her.* "When was the last time you saw your son?"

"Oh, I don't know. He didn't come by that often since the divorce. That no account wife of his never brings my grandchildren by to visit anymore. Can I offer you something to drink? I have some instant coffee that's not too bad with cold water."

Crosby cringed at the thought. "No, thank you. I need to go. I just wanted to stop by and offer my condolences."

"Why do you have to hurry off so soon? I don't get much company anymore." She picked up a photo off the coffee table and showed it to him. It was the image of a young man dressed in a World War II uniform. "This was my late husband, Thomas," she said.

Crosby took the photo. "This was David's father?"

"Yes. We didn't believe we could have children, but Davy was my surprise forty-fifth birthday present."

Crosby smiled and handed back the photo.

"We would go out dancing all the time. Thomas was the talk of the town in his day."

"He looked like a popular guy."

"Oh yes. He was a war hero, you know. The ball turret gunner was the most dangerous job, but he said the view was out of this world." She pointed toward the ceiling. "There's a picture of his plane on the wall behind us."

Crosby turned, but they were sitting too far below it. "Yes, ma'am. I'm sure he was. I need to be going now."

"Well, thank you for dropping by."

Crosby stood, and out of respect, he gave the photo a closer look. It was huge, over two feet across, and framed. The blowup showed a silver four engine bomber with the crew gathered beneath. Painted in black letters was the name, *Enola Gay*.

• • •

"Marti," Crosby said into his phone. He was in the yard of Margaret Anthony's home. "You won't believe what I just discovered."

"Whatever it is, it's not as important as this. Devrin, we know who she is. I have a photo of her wearing the same disguise she used in Dillon. Vanessa Lucille Harris. Lucy!"

"The looker?"

"Yes. We had her name all along and it was no accident that her file was in the folder. The Human Resources Director suspected Lucy was behind this from the beginning and added her file to the list."

"Why didn't she come forward?"

"Who knows? This place has a real don't-rock-the-boat attitude. She said she remembered Lucy dressing up in a man's suit for a Halloween party several years ago, but couldn't find the photo until this morning."

"She could have mentioned it."

"That's not all. Lucy's name rang the cherries the moment we posted it. A tan Honda was rented two days before the blast at A-1 Rentals just outside of Denver International. She paid cash, but they photocopied her driver's license. The address matches the one in the file. Denver PD is putting together the SWAT team as we speak. Do you want to take part in the raid?"

"No. She isn't stupid enough to still be there."

"We ran the rental's tag number and got a hit. The car has been sitting in the long-term parking deck at Salt Lake International since the day of the explosion. We're having it transferred to a forensics lab in Salt Lake."

"If they find Amil's prints in the car that'll seal her fate," Crosby said. "Are you still at the bank?"

"No. I caught a taxi over to headquarters. I told Lynch and we're scanning the photos now. They're going on the hotline as soon as the SWAT team finishes the raid."

"Make sure that Rankin and James get their copies ASAP," Crosby said. "We don't have anything to tie Lucy to the Marquesas bombing."

"So what was your news?" Matthews asked.

"It doesn't seem so earth shattering in light of that. I just discovered that David Anthony's father was a crewmember aboard the *Enola Gay*. That's the plane that dropped the first atomic bomb on Japan."

Matthews took a moment. "That's one hell of a coincidence."

"I know. Maybe it isn't."

CHAPTER 19

ELYN

"We have a name," Stalker said over the secure line, "and her address in Denver, but it's most likely an alias."

"Give it to me," Raptor said.

"Vanessa Lucille Harris. Goes by Lucy. Blonde; five foot seven; early thirties; supposedly well built. She's a master of disguise, so be on your toes. Worked in the banking industry in Denver and purportedly near Chicago. No other address."

"Chicago. Where exactly?"

"Elgin."

"Find Scholar. I need a list of our people who worked at Fermilab. Where's the photo?"

"I'm trying to lift it from the bank records now." Stalker took a moment to punch in the information. "File not found? That little *bitch*. She's deleted it." He pounded his fist on the table. "All right, we'll do this the hard way."

• • •

"Dr. Marti Matthews, please," Mallory Reynolds said.

"This is she," Matthews was at the FBI office in Denver trying to pull Social Security information on Lucy Harris.

"This is Mrs. Reynolds at OleWest. I have the records on Lucy's employment confirmation request. It came through our automated Internet site from First Nations Bank in Charlotte, North Carolina."

"Was there a name?"

"Only the company name is required. It's usually someone in Human Resources. Do you want me to call?"

"No, that might tip off whoever made the request. We'll send an agent."

"We also found evidence that someone accessed our employment records that same evening," Mrs. Reynolds said, "after hours."

"Did they break in?"

"That's what's strange. They used my access code and password. I believe that's how Miss Harris' records vanished. I assumed someone from upstairs had a hand in it, but our phone systems analyst says the call came from an outside line."

"Why? Did you suspect tampering from within the company?"

"It's obvious," Reynolds explained. "Ms. Harris went from being a teller to a loan officer in a matter of months. You don't believe she climbed that ladder based purely on performance evaluations, do you? She might have even climbed higher had David Anthony not been in the way."

"So you're saying that Ms. Harris slept her way to the top?"

"You will have to draw your own conclusions, Dr. Matthews."

"I'll send one of our technicians to do a phone trace. Your hunch on the picture might break this case wide open." Matthews thanked her, hung up and dialed the tech lab.

Crosby came by and placed a composite photo of Lucy's employment picture and the Halloween picture side by side. "This is what we're posting on the hotline. It's a go. The address is a total bust. Some college kids with bad credit picked up the lease and never changed the name. They know less than we do."

"I just got off the phone with Human Resources at OleWest. You need to head back over there. From what I gather, Mr. Foy is trying to hide more than one loose cannon."

• • •

The office of Alex Christensen was located on the thirty-ninth floor, the same office that had once been David Anthony's. Christensen's door was ajar and Crosby found him behind his desk sound asleep. Crosby cleared his throat and Christensen jerked awake, wide-eyed and startled by the intrusion.

"Whoa," Christensen said. "Can I help you?"

"You're Alex Christensen?"

"Who are you?"

"FBI." Crosby flashed his ID. "Agent Devrin Crosby. Mind if I sit?"

"Actually I was right in the middle of—"

"A *nap*." Crosby was in no mood for games and sat anyway. "Mr. Foy tells me that you and David Anthony were close friends when he worked here."

"Pretty good friends, I guess."

"What can you tell me about Lucy Harris?"

Christensen suddenly looked uncomfortable. "Uh, she was a loan officer . . . from what I understand."

Crosby leaned forward. "Cut the bull. You know exactly what I'm talking about, Alex. We already know she was having an affair with David. I just want to know who else?"

"I'm not the one you should be having this conversation with."

"Oh?" Crosby noted the photo of his wife and two children behind him. "Is that your family?"

"Yes." Christensen's face looked even more worried.

"Perhaps I should speak with your wife. We could all get together with Michelle Anthony and compare notes."

"I wasn't having an affair, if that's what you're *implying*. I hardly knew Lucy and I certainly wasn't in a position to further her career."

"But David Anthony was. Who else?"

Christensen didn't answer. "Why are you doing this? These are good people with families and reputations in this community. They didn't hurt anybody. She *did*."

"We're trying to catch a serial bomber. She's already murdered hundreds and while you sit back in your glass tower and worry about your reputation, she may be planting her next bomb. Now tell me what you know and I'll do my best to keep it out of the file."

Christensen seemed to resign. "I didn't know David until he transferred here from the Littleton branch. We became friends and started going out to bars after work for a drink."

"Topless bars?"

"Sometimes. There was this one place called Tattletails that was known for having . . . exceptional women. One night we went in and David recognized one of our bank tellers, moonlighting, so to speak."

"Lucy Harris?"

"Yes, but she used a stage name that I can't recall."

"I see," Crosby said. "Did David confront her or threaten to expose her?"

"No. It was much more complicated. You see, the guy on the receiving end of her lap dance was our CEO, Harry Foy."

•   •   •

Katie Froscher spent most of the afternoon washing clothes and telling her mother about her dinner and evening with Gerald McMullen. Most of it was true, except for the part about them meeting aboard the cruise ship and getting to know each other. It sounded better than, *I only met him last evening, Mom, and I'm ready to run off to a desert island with him.*

Ruth Froscher beamed. She asked all the important questions about where he worked, had he been married, and where he was from. She was delighted when Katie told her that he was a graduate of their beloved University of North Carolina.

"Your father would be thrilled," Ruth said as they dried the evening dishes.

"Except for Gerald's race."

"Your father wanted you to be happy no matter who you chose. That's all. I so wish he and your brother could be here to see how happy you seem. Oh, that reminds me, a couple of nice gentlemen stopped by this week asking about Chuck. They were from the FBI."

The plate that had slipped from Katie's hands crashed into a hundred pieces as it struck the floor. She didn't hear the sound, nor anything else for several seconds.

•   •   •

Over the course of the afternoon, Crosby spoke with several members of upper management at OleWest. All were tightlipped and seemed to be covering for each other. There was little doubt that Lucy Harris had used her body to climb to the top of the corporate heap, but no one was willing to step forward and admit it. The fact that Foy had taken part in it smelled of a conspiracy to bury as much as they could about their involvement with her.

It was nearly five p.m. by the time Crosby was able to follow up on his one solid lead, but first he needed to call Matthews.

"Marti, what time is your meeting with Dr. Gebo?"

"We were going to meet in Englewood, but his daughter decided to take them out to dinner here in Denver. He's meeting us at the lounge in the Sheraton at seven-thirty."

"Do you have anything we can offer him?"

"I e-mailed him the technical data report and the *Island Breeze* photos last Friday, but he's only interested in the physical descriptions of the bombs."

"It looks like I'm going to have to meet you there. I got a lead on a bar where Lucy Harris was working when she was hired. It's called

Tattletails. I'm going to run over and see if I can get an address or alias on her."

"You'll need backup for that," Matthews stressed.

"I'm just going to talk with the manager. I'll be fine."

"Lynch will have our hides if he finds out."

"Okay. I'll ask Agent Smith to go with me."

He ended the call and picked up the envelope containing Lucy's photo. He squeezed it and felt one of the bubbles inside pop. *A bubble envelope,* he thought. *That* was the item he had forgotten from the Tim Cook investigation. He opened his phone and dialed Gerald McMullen.

• • •

"The FBI was *here*," Katie whispered, "asking people all over town."

"About your brother, not you," Lucy said. "We knew they'd do that. Don't worry about it. Everything's fine."

Katie looked around nervously and pulled her coat on tighter. She was standing at a pay phone outside of Awfully Good Burgers in Denton, a fast-food hangout the teenagers called the Awful House. The slightest noise made her jump. "I don't want to do this anymore. I just want to pack my bags and leave."

"You can. As soon as you send the worm, get the hell out of there."

"I don't know. There's always the chance they'll trace it back to us."

"*Right!* I've seen the way you bounce calls all over the place. Just do it, Katie. We've already set the trap. All you have to do is spring it."

"I'm scared. For the first time in years I have something to live for. Now this happens."

"What?"

"Something wonderful, but I can't talk about it now. I'll tell you later."

"Katie, I've taken all the risks so far in this thing, but *I can't* do this part alone. You have to send that file. If you can't do it, bring it to me and I'll send it."

Katie didn't reply.

"Are you still coming to Washington?"

"I don't have a choice."

"Then give me your flight number. When you get off the plane we will meet in the restroom and pass it under the stall. No one will have a clue."

•   •   •

"Gerald, this is Devrin. Where are you?"

McMullen was in Washington. "I'm standing in your kitchen," he said.

"It's your kitchen too. Is everything okay?"

"Sure. What's up buddy?"

"Remember how you said Trexler was upset when he left the Sunday night meeting before President Barnett was shot?"

"That's what the Secret Service reported."

"Were Barnett, Trexler and Cook the only ones at the meeting?"

"The Chairman of the Joint Chiefs might have attended, but he says he left before it started." McMullen was wondering where this was leading.

"Did you ever learn anything about the envelope that was found in Tim Cook's garbage that following Tuesday?" Crosby asked.

"What envelope?"

"The one the Arlington police recovered."

"I don't recall an envelope. What did it look like?"

"It was described on the evidence manifest as an empty, nine by twelve, bubble padded envelope. It had three sets of fingerprints. At that time, two sets had been confirmed as Cook's and the postman, but I haven't heard if the third set has been identified."

"I never got access to the Arlington records. I got my information from your report, witnesses and research."

"It's probably nothing," Crosby said. "Do you know if Tim Cook had any relatives in Oak Ridge, Tennessee?"

"Does this have anything to do with the weapons research facility at Oak Ridge?"

"I don't know, but since you knew Tim, I thought you might know if he had any family living in the area?"

"Not that I'm aware of. He was from upstate Michigan." McMullen took a second to piece together the facts. "So you're saying that Tim Cook received a package from Oak Ridge, the day the President was shot?"

"No, I believe the postmark was from the previous week."

"That's interesting. I've never understood why the Press Secretary would have a closed meeting with the President and his Secretary of

Defense that late on a Sunday night."

"That seemed odd to me as well."

"Care to speculate?" McMullen asked. "I need to write a second edition."

"Maybe the package contained something damming about Trexler's handling of the weapons program."

"That, or his sexual antics. But why send it to Tim Cook instead of the President?"

Crosby thought for a moment. "To make certain the President saw it. You couldn't just mail something that important to the White House, could you?"

"Not without every Tom, Dick and Harry seeing it," McMullen said.

• • •

"Hey, Crosby," Rankin said. "Did you hear about the blonde who locked her keys in her car?"

"I'm pretty busy here, Kelly," Crosby said into his phone.

"She had to get a coat hanger to get her family out."

Crosby chuckled. He was weaving his way through the crowded Tattletails bar. "What's up, Kelly?"

"I got that photo you posted. Are you sure you didn't tear this out of a glamour magazine? I'm having one hell of a time taking my eyes off of her."

"Sort of makes you want to switch sides, doesn't she? You'll never guess where I am; a topless bar called Tattletails."

"Well, well, I'm finally rubbing off on you, buddy."

"No. It turns out our supermodel was moonlighting on the side."

"Sounds as if she was mooning in the rear," Rankin added with a laugh. "If she's still working there, hold up cause I'm on the way. I'll personally put the handcuffs on her."

"I talked to the manager and there definitely is a Chicago connection. Add the name Elyn Harrison to her aka list. That's E, L, Y, N. We're running both names at the Chicago clubs. What have you got?"

"It's a long shot, but I may have figured out how she got off the island undetected. I'm checking it out tomorrow and I'll keep you posted."

• • •

"Oh *damn it*," Lucy said, remembering her date with the mortician. He was supposed to meet her at the club in thirty minutes. She looked up the number for Simpson Mortuary and caught Clay Simpson as he was headed out the door.

"Clay, this is Elyn," Lucy said. "Look, I'm running a little late. Instead of the club, could you pick me up in about an hour at the DuPont Circle subway entrance? Yes, it's 1515 20th Street. Thanks."

She hung up and placed the second call to the business office of the *New York Times*.

"Classified department, please." She unfolded the slip of paper and studied the numbers she had written down years earlier. "Yes. I need to place an ad to run in Wednesday's personals section. Yes. Here's the message: 'Fat Man and Little Boy desire an exhibition at 10:15 on Thursday. Please call N385-4657, W770-2659. Must own new skis to enter race.' You got that? Yes, that's correct. There's an N and a W before each phone number. Yes, VISA." Lucy read the number from the slip of paper. "The name on the card is Norman Trexler. Right, T, R, E, X, L, E, R, spelled just like the Vice President's name. Yes, thank you."

·   ·   ·

Katie Froscher plugged a new disposable cell phone into the high-speed modem of her laptop and put on her headset. She dialed the number Lucy had given her and waited.

"Lisa here," the young lady replied. There was noisy music in the background.

"Lisa Trexler, please," Katie said in the most professional voice she had. "This is Mrs. Biggerstaff with AT&T security."

"This is Lisa."

"Miss Trexler, we just notified the Secret Service of a security breach on your cell phone. Someone tried to access the SIM card and we need to reset the security chip."

"What's a SIM card?"

"The Subscriber Identity Module. We need you to stop using that phone and bring it by one of our service centers on Friday. Someone will be happy to reset it for you."

"Stop using it? Look I *need* my phone. I can't wait till Friday."

"I'm sorry, but we're backed up and that's the earliest we can get to it. Unless . . ."

"Unless what?"

"You want to try and reset it yourself. We're not supposed to give out that information, but."

"For sure," Lisa said. "I'll do it."

"It's a very simple process. Press the pound key followed by nine and zero. Then hang up and wait one hour before using it again."

"No *problem.*"

Katie heard the dial tone change and punched in Jonathan Bowman's number in Portland, Oregon. The moment it squawked, she pressed Enter. The worm was on its way. Within moments her hacker would receive a few bits of code attached to a message from the Vice President's daughter.

•   •   •

"Good evening, Dr. Gebo," Matthews said as she approached the table. Gebo and his wife were sitting in a corner booth. The lounge was quiet with only a few elderly patrons gathered around the bar watching a football game on the set.

"Dr. Matthews." Gebo rose slightly in his seat. "Nice seeing you again."

Matthews greeted his wife who got up to leave.

"I'll let the two of you talk." His wife excused herself.

"She didn't have to leave," Matthews said.

"She's fine. It gives her a chance to go over to the bar and flirt with the old men." Gebo's voice seemed even raspier than the last time they talked.

"Did you get my package containing the case file?"

"Yes, I did." He looked her in the eyes. "I believe you have a *serious* problem. Because of that, I'm willing to forego certain parts of my oath for the *sake* of national security; provided that you agree to keep my name and this information sealed."

"Thank you, Doctor. My report will have a note stating that request. What's your chief concern?"

"This device isn't very sophisticated." He coughed. "As a matter of fact, it's crude."

"Crude, as in cheap?"

"The source material certainly isn't cheap."

"The positrons?"

"Positron weaponry is just a name attributed to this type of research. Positrons, which are mirror particles to the electron, first have to be converted into anti-molecules like antihydrogen. To get positrons, you need access to a particle collider, like CERN in Geneva, or FermiLab in Batavia, Illinois. But these particles are extremely small. A half million lined up could fit behind the width of a human hair. And these are *only* the igniter."

"What do you mean by igniter?"

"Originally we wanted to build a pure positron weapon, but we quickly discovered that was impossible. Even with drastic new improvements in production efficiency, the amount of antimatter required for the Marquesas Keys blast would take *thousands* of years to produce. We failed to find a solution until I recalled the simplicity of Dr. Oppenheimer's *Trinity*, bomb. All it had to do was split *one* atom, setting off the chain reaction."

"That was the first atomic bomb," Matthews said.

"Yes, but that concept became our solution. By injecting a tiny amount of antimatter into a subcritical mass of fuel such are deuterium and tritium, fusion of the fuel can be forced."

"Those are hydrogen isotopes," she said. "But it couldn't be nuclear, there was no fallout."

"Very little," Dr. Gebo said. "Traditionally it takes a plutonium *fission* bomb to generate enough heat to initiate *fusion* in a hydrogen bomb, so the radioactive byproducts were generated by the plutonium atom-bomb *trigger*. Positron triggers produce no radioactivity."

"So that's why it was so clean."

"Correct. Also a positron triggers requires no lead shielding, so it's small."

"Could someone have stolen the antimatter?"

"Not without a Penning particle thermos trap," Gebo explained. "You see this trap is a very simple design. It's just a battery keeping a charge on an electromagnetic coil surrounding an insulated containment bottle. Once it's immersed in liquid helium, any matter such as air molecules that remain in the trap will cling to the frozen walls, while the antihydrogen is held in place by—"

". . . the electromagnetic field," she finished.

He interlaced his fingers. "What *we* wanted to accomplish was far more complicated because of the problem of long-term storage. Weapons need to be stockpiled for years, even decades. That's why this crude cooler disturbs me," Gebo tapped his index finger on the satellite photo of the *Island Breeze* Marti had sent him. "You see the only people who had access to positrons, as well as the hydrogen isotopes, worked for the government. But this project was shut down years ago."

"Dr. Gebo, I believe you know who might be behind this. I know you took an oath, but someone is killing people with this bomb, and the only way we're going to stop them is if you tell us who they are."

"I wish I could, but the truth is the only people I knew with the capability of assembling a working device such as this are either dead or sitting in front you now."

•   •   •

Crosby was in the rental car making his way through Denver traffic, still trying to catch the meeting with Dr. Gebo. While he waited at a long traffic light, he dialed the home number of Lauren Hyatt, the former intern who now worked in his department.

"Lauren," he said when she picked up, "Sorry it's so late. I need a big favor. About three years ago I was involved in the Tim Cook suicide investigation. Could you get in touch with Arlington PD and find out where they store their evidence?"

"Sure," she said. "What do you need?"

"On the evidence manifest there was an item described as an empty, nine by twelve, bubble padded envelope, that I believe had a postmark from Tennessee. I need to know if all the fingerprints were ever matched on that envelope, and if so, to whom. Can you do that?"

"Sure. First thing in the morning."

"If they weren't, have the Arlington lab e-mail the prints to the Oak Ridge Police Department. They should compare them with the prints of a guy named Charles (Chuck) Froscher Jr., murdered there about three years ago. Dr. Matthews has already faxed his file to Lynch's office."

"What if the prints match?" Lauren asked.

"Call me. It's important."

"This might take some time."

"Tell them it's *urgent* and let me know the moment the results come back."

•   •   •

It was late when Clay Simpson dropped Lucy off outside an apartment building on DuPont Circle. She waved goodbye and waited until he was out of sight before walking the two blocks to her apartment building on Hillyer place. She rolled her eyes as she thought about his baldhead. There was something disgusting about morticians even with their clothes on, but the idea of doing it in a casket was a bit much even for Lucy. Still, she had secured all the arrangements and everything would be taken care of by the time Katie arrived. She owed her big time for this.

Lucy was just about to open her door when she got a call. She glanced at the caller ID and her mood brightened.

"Hola," she said. "¿Cómo está usted?"

• • •

Dr. Matthews and Dr. Gebo were still talking when Crosby arrived. He apologized for being late and took a seat. "Did I miss much?"

"Yes," Matthews said. I'll fill you in later. "Please continue, Doctor."

"I read a book once," Gebo said. "I believe it was written in 1916, by a guy named Morgan Robertson. His only claim to fame was the fact that he had written a book describing the sinking of the *Titanic* in great detail, but he wrote it fourteen years *before* it happened."

He's off on some tangent again, Crosby thought.

"In this particular book, Robertson described airplanes attacking the naval base at Pearl Harbor in December. The book ends with the U.S. dropping a bomb on Japan that was beyond the spectrum of the sun. Robertson called it a *Sunbomb.*"

"The atomic bomb," Crosby said.

"Or perhaps something worse," Dr. Gebo said. "Once again Robertson's fiction became fact. He wrote this book *twenty-nine years* before we built the first atomic bombs, Trinity, Little Boy and Fat Man."

"How does that relate to these bombs?" Matthews asked.

"Because, when I had to choose a name for our project, I named it after Morgan Roberston's book and called it, The Spectrum Project."

"This was the project that was killed in the early nineties?" Crosby said.

"Yes. The device was unstable and therefore not suitable for our purposes. But now my colleagues and I are just a bunch of old men, who sit around and come up with theories and conjecture. We've often wondered if it *might* have been suitable for someone else."

"What do you mean, Doctor?" Matthews said.

"It's strange how government funding never seems to go away. What if someone tried to revive this project, and kept the name, because the funds were still there? It would make sense. Run a covert operation to build a bomb no one knows about."

"But you said it was unstable?" Crosby said. "What good is that?"

"It's still a bomb," Gebo said. "Stability is only a problem if you take your time using it."

Crosby and Matthews eyed each other. "How long would it take to go off, Doctor?" Crosby asked.

"It depends on the conditions. In minute quantities it could be stored for years, but once it was compiled enough to serve as a trigger, it would be much more vulnerable. Our initial estimates were about seventy-two hours. The battery might begin to run low, or the coolant may evaporate sufficiently for the trap to heat up. Either way, the results are the same."

"Doctor, assuming there was such a weapon, how would a terrorist go about setting it off?"

Dr. Gebo crossed his arms and looked in her eyes. "I assure you that isn't the problem." He leaned forward in his chair. "The real problem is how to *keep* the damn thing from going off."

• • •

Matthews and Crosby remained in the bar long after Dr. Gebo left. Marti had a glass of white wine while she filled him in about the thermos trap. An untouched beer was in front of Crosby as he listened. Then he told her about his talk with Alex Christensen, which led him to Harry Foy's lap dance with the topless dancer. Foy and the girl had been seen together on numerous occasions and several patrons at the bar had identified the picture of Lucy Harris as that of the dancer whose stage name was Elyn Harrison.

"Looks like Foy had multiple motives to keep her out of the investigation," Crosby said.

"Are you going to confront him with the evidence?"

"Not unless Lynch decides to charge him with obstruction. We have Lucy's name, so we need to concentrate on finding her."

"Any thoughts on what Dr. Gebo said?"

"From what he's saying, it looks as if we're digging in opposite directions. Whoever built these bombs either worked for Dr. Gebo at some point, or worked for the government. Yet we're tracking a bank teller who was moonlighting as a topless dancer. I can't see any connection except Amil, and why would he choose someone like her to partner with?"

"I'm tired of thinking about it." Matthews noticed a grand piano sitting empty in a corner. "I wish I could play. I could sure use a little music right now."

Crosby took her hand and led her over to the piano where he began to play a soft melody. It was a piece she had never heard, but he played it flawlessly for four minutes. By the time he finished she had a look of total awe.

"That was beautiful." Marti stood behind him and began rubbing his shoulders. "I had no idea you could play, and so beautifully too."

"My mother was a music teacher. It was a prerequisite as long as I lived under her roof. I keep a keyboard in my bedroom and when I hear a piece I like, I'll pick it out. That was 'As For Us,' by Fernando Ortega."

"You're full of surprises," she said, "Let's go up to my room. It's your turn to give the massage."

● ● ●

Amil Yaspar looked in the mirror and hardly recognized his own face. His hair was completely gone, his scalp shaved, as were his beard and mustache. The silicon injections in his brow, chin and nose were far from perfect, but they would do. The green contact lenses gave his face a southern European look and weeks of studying had given him ample time to brush up on his Spanish.

It was nearly midnight, and for two weeks the phone in his Las Vegas hotel room had remained silent. Even though the call was expected, the sound of the ringing came as a shock. It rang several more times before he picked it up.

The woman spoke in broken Arabic.

"Speak English," Amil said. "You have much to learn."

She switched to English and spoke slowly, giving him time to copy the coordinates. "The ad reads: Fat Man and Little Boy desire an exhibition at 10:15 on Thursday," Lucy Harris said. "Please call: N385-4477 W770-2509. Must own new skis to enter race."

Amil reread the coordinates. "Thursday is a good day."

"Do you still have the key?" she said.

"Yes."

"Then good luck."

CHAPTER 20

CHERYL

Tuesday

The television in their room was on, but neither of them was watching. Crosby was sitting on the floor, his back leaning against the couch between Marti's legs. Matthews was on the couch, her bare feet wrapped around his waist and her hands massaging his shoulders while Crosby massaged her feet. Two wine glasses sat on the coffee table, one empty and one full, with a half-empty bottle beside them. Crosby laid his head back and looked up at her.

"You haven't touched your wine," she said.

"I have a confession to make, Marti," he said. "I used to be an alcoholic, but I haven't had a drink in over three years."

"Why didn't you say something?"

"It doesn't bother me anymore and you enjoy it."

"But I didn't mean to tempt you."

"Believe me, that is the least tempting thing about you," he said, "and if you keep rubbing my shoulders, I'm never going to make it back to my room."

"Maybe that's my plan." She winked. "That feels so good. There's something about a foot massage that makes me really . . . tempted." She ran her left heel up his thigh until it stopped. "Hum! Look's like Ole Buford wants to bust out of there."

He looked at her incredulously. "Ole Buford? No, no, Marti. You can't name my . . . associate, Ole Buford."

"Why not? It's better than 'Associate.'"

"Because I picture Ole Buford as a sad-eyed, long-eared, blood-hound. That's hardly how I envision myself."

"Oh, I'm not so sure. Bloodhounds are the detectives of the dog kingdom and they have the keenest sense of smell of any animal on earth." She pulled his head back and looked into his eyes. "Besides, have you ever seen a bloodhound's tongue?" She gave him a long, deep kiss. "Trust me. That's a *good* thing."

•   •   •

Jonathan Bowman opened the e-mail message box and read the name on the caller ID. Lisa Trexler. "*Awesome,*" he said to his college roommate. "I just got a message from the Vice President's daughter." He opened it and was disappointed to learn that it wasn't from her but from her best friend. He looked up at the babe's picture taped to the side of his monitor. Apparently they had used Lisa's computer to send it and now he had her IP address. He read the message:

Jon;
Lisa says hi. This probably won't do you any good, but here's the IP address for the UFO/Majestic site she showed me. Code name is SPECTRUM. She says no way in hell you'll get in. Good luck, but you better watch your back door. These people have some "serious" tracking tools.
    Get your hand out of your pants and quit doing what I know you're doing with my picture.
    TTFN;
    CalenderGirl

"What's TTFN?" his roommate asked.
"Ta Ta For Now."
"*Cool!*" They slapped their hands together. "You gonna go for it?"
"Of course. I'll use an electronic re-mailing service in France or Japan. Let's see them track that."
    Jonathan clicked on the attachment, popped his knuckles and began typing.

•   •   •

Devrin Crosby lay awake in Marti's bed, staring at the darkened ceiling, his bare chest still moist with sweat. Marti was curled on her side, facing away from him, her bare back disappearing under the covers just above her waist. She was asleep, but something Dr. Gebo had said was bothering him, and he wanted to ask her about it. "Marti?" Devrin said in a low voice.
    "Uh uh," she replied in a whisper.
    "Remember how Dr. Gebo said the bomb might have been

suitable for someone else?"

"Uh uh."

"Suitable for who?"

"Terrorists, maybe," she said softly. "They wouldn't care."

"They would if they weren't planning on using it immediately."

"Why would they wait?"

"If Saddam was alive what would he have done with a new type bomb like this?"

She rolled over towards him, but kept her eyes closed. "Probably used it on Jerusalem or New York."

"But don't you think he would be curious about how it worked?"

Marti's eyes opened slightly. "Yeah." They grew wider. "Especially if he paid millions and didn't know it was unstable." She lifted her head off the pillow, "A black market arms dealer wouldn't mention that, even if he knew."

"Saddam would have put his top scientists to work on dissecting how the damn thing was built."

"Reverse engineering," she said.

"Wouldn't he have hidden it away in his most secure weapons facility while he planned the perfect attack?" Crosby said. "Probably where they stored and developed other weapons. Dr. Gebo said that the battery would begin to run low after about seventy-two hours, and as the liquid helium evaporated it would begin to heat up."

"*My God,*" she said. "A bomb that size would have taken out their entire weapons research program, their arsenal, and probably their dictator as well."

"It's a Trojan Horse, Marti, and we would have complete deniability because it would look like an accident."

"So why Dillon?"

"It you were a black market arms dealer about to spent millions, don't you think your clients would want a *demonstration?*"

"Devrin, that's *it.* Amil wasn't the terrorist, he was the *client!* That's why he let her handle the bomb."

"Dr. Gebo said only the Government could set up a covert operation like this. What government agency is fighting a war on terrorism?"

"You've just figured out who's behind this. *Good Lord!* Kelly works for Homeland Security."

•   •   •

Katie Froscher stepped off the people mover into the concourse of the main terminal of Dulles International Airport at 7:20 a.m. She scanned the restaurant area where hundreds of people milled around, drinking coffee, eating breakfast and waiting for their flights. A bank of restrooms was on the left and she headed towards those. Halfway there, her cell phone rang.

"Any problems?" Lucy asked.

"No," Katie replied.

"Did you bring the file?"

"It's already shipped. Arrived last night."

"*Good.* My shoes are red. Meet me inside."

"Where are you?"

"About six feet in front of you on the left." The line went dead.

Katie looked around but couldn't spot Lucy anywhere. She noticed a girl in front of her, walking in the same direction, with short black hair drop her cell phone into her purse and turn left into the ladies room. Katie followed and caught a glimpse of Lucy's face in the mirror. She had done something to her eyes to accentuate their almond shape. The combination of hair, eyes and makeup made her almost look Japanese. It was an incredible transformation.

Katie spotted the red shoes and took the stall beside hers. "Is that you?" she whispered.

A note, apparently pre-written on toilet paper, appeared under the wall separating the two stalls. *Everything is arranged,* it said. *The company is Simpson Mortuary. I've arranged for them to pickup the casket at the Charter Freight Forwarding Hanger at the south end of the airport. They have a limo for you outside the baggage claim that will take you to their office where you can freshen up. Ask for Clay. He's only charging $400 for the vault. Transportation is free. He owes me one.*

Kate wrote *thank you* at the bottom and handed it back.

Another note appeared. *Are you sure that Gerald is not working for* THEM?

Absolutely. He might be coming with me.

The next note was more personal. *Leave town ASAP. It's not safe here. You're the only real friend I've ever had. I love you and if anything should go wrong, always remember that.*

Love you too, Katie wrote. *I'll see you in paradise.* She passed the note and heard the toilet flush. By the time she emerged from the stall, Lucy was gone.

•   •   •

Gerald McMullen waited at a deli across the concourse from the ladies room. The United flight was the only one that arrived from Greensboro, and he had decided to surprise Katie by meeting her at the airport. But as he waited, he thought he recognized Katie's friend, the one he had met on the plane. Lucille wore a short black wig and had done something to her eyes with makeup. He didn't want to spoil their meeting, so he stood back and watched. The moment Katie emerged from the concourse, Lucille turned and walked in the same direction several yards in front of her. It was bizarre since they also seemed to be talking to each other on their cell phones but acted like they didn't even know each other. His instincts as a reporter kicked in just as both of them disappeared into the ladies restroom.

Lucille came out of the restroom first but did not go down the stairs to the baggage claim like Katie did. She was probably just getting her car from the parking lot, but Gerald decided to follow Lucille, knowing that it would take awhile for Katie's bags to reach the carrousel.

•   •   •

"We have a photo and an alias," Stalker said. "Elyn, that's E, L, Y, N Harrison. She's worked in the topless industry in Chicago and Denver. Used the same name on her employment records."

"Have you cross checked it against Scholar's list?" Raptor said.

"Yes. One of the team remembers a girl fitting her description dating Ryan Papineau. He's the guy who died in the wreck. Rumor was she was a dancer. We're e-mailing the photo to see if he remembers her."

"I remember Ryan," Raptor said. "Didn't his car run off a bridge into a frozen river?"

"Yes."

"Did they recover the body?"

"No. The only hole was where the car went in. The driver-side window had been broken out when they found it. Even if he made it out of the car, with the current he had no chance of finding the hole. Body probably drifted for miles under the ice."

"Convenient way to disappear," Raptor said. "Everyone would assume that scenario."

"What's your opinion?"

"Smash the window, put something heavy on the gas pedal and

slip the car into gear. Guy walks away with a new identity."

"Only one problem. The heavy object on the gas pedal stays in the car."

"Not if it's a block of ice," Raptor said. "Ryan's our man. *Find him!*"

• • •

Lucy focused her binoculars on the limo pulling into the Piedmont Air Cargo hanger. Behind it followed the vault truck, a silver concrete vault on the back reflecting in the sun. *Clay Simpson was a man of his word.* She kept her binoculars pointed at the airport road, waiting several minutes to see if anyone else followed. She scanned the other roads. No cars followed. Lucy lowered the glasses and punched in Clay Simpson's cell number. "I'm running late. Be there in five minutes."

She disconnected and dialed Ryan's number.

"Are we safe?" Ryan asked.

"Yes. The HVAC installers and the crane company will meet you at the building in three hours. The address is 2185 Decatur Place, Northwest."

• • •

Kelly Rankin stood at the docks at Grand Cayman and watched as two security guards checked the sign and sail cards of cruise ship passengers boarding. He picked out two of the passengers in line and approached them.

"Excuse me, ladies. My name is Agent Rankin and I'm with the Office of Homeland Security in the States." He showed them his badge. "Don't be alarmed. We're doing a routine check of the security measures, and I was wondering if you and your friend would mind exchanging your sign and sail cards?"

"But we need them to get aboard," one lady said.

"That's right. You'll take hers, she'll use yours and if those two men up there stop you, you can simply explain that you got them mixed up, and be on your way. Understand? If he gives you any problem, I'll explain what we're doing."

"What if he doesn't stop us?" the other lady asked.

"Then go ahead and board. We'll talk with the guard, and he'll have some explaining to do."

"Okay," they said, as though they were part of a sinister plot.

Rankin stood back and watched as the two approached the head of the line. He had chosen one of the girls because her blouse was somewhat low cut, very much like the one in Lucy's composite photo.

As expected, the two walked right through the line without a word being said. They looked back at Rankin and shrugged. He smiled, gave them a wave, and walked toward the security guards.

• • •

Crosby took the wheel of the rental car and Matthews climbed into the passenger side. It was starting to snow, and he was concerned that they might end up trapped in Denver if they didn't wrap up the investigation soon. His plan was to drop her off at the Denver FBI office and ride down to Littleton and show the Lucy Harris photo around some of the local banks and clubs. His interview with Alex Christensen had left him with several questions. Alex indicated that David Anthony recognized Lucy Harris as being one of their tellers, yet he later admitted that their trip to the bar had taken place during Anthony's first week at the Denver branch. *Unless he knew her, how did he know she was a teller?* It was a question that seemed to stump Christensen as well. Perhaps David Anthony had worked with Lucy at a bank in Littleton before moving to Denver. Littleton was also where his wife caught him cheating on the couch, so it felt like a good place to start.

"Devrin, about last night," Matthews said nervously. "That probably wasn't a good idea."

"You're right. I stayed up all night worrying about it," Crosby said. "A greyhound is much more appropriate than a bloodhound."

Matthews playfully punched him in the shoulder with her fist. "That's not what I meant and you know it."

"I was a little surprised, especially since you said you wanted us to wait until after the case was over."

"Well, that was before I had a foot massage. It's a real weakness of mine."

"I'll make a note of that. I overcame my weakness because of you."

"Which weakness?"

"The drinking. After we met, I knew that I would never stand a chance with you if I didn't quit."

Matthews smiled. "I wish I had known. I wouldn't have wasted all that time trying to break Kelly of his habits. So what's up for you today?"

"I need to find Lucy's real name. The Elyn Harrison alias isn't going anywhere."

"Maybe it was only her stage name. Did you ask the Chicago Bureau?"

"They're doing the same thing we're doing, hitting the streets with the picture. They have twice as many agents and haven't found zip."

"You need a partner if you're knocking on doors, Devrin, and I can't be in two places at once."

"My partner belongs in the lab. I'll ask Agent Smith to come with me."

The car pulled to a halt. "Call me before you take any chances and please be careful." She kissed him before getting out.

•   •   •

Gerald McMullen followed Lucille to the short-term parking lot, got into his rental car and trailed her red BMW Sportster. She drove toward the General Aviation Building, pulled into the Rental Car Return parking deck and parked on the top level, overlooking the cargo terminals. Gerald parked where he could watch her. She got out with a huge pair of binoculars and seemed to be studying a cargo hanger on the far side of the airport. Minutes later, she drove out of the deck and he followed her car on the perimeter road towards the hanger, careful to stay out of sight. *This is weird.*

An old Piedmont Cargo DC-3 prop plane was parked in front of the hanger. Faded letters on the side of the building indicated it was the Charter Freight Forwarding Hanger. Gerald parked his car so he could see into the open hanger doors and spotted Lucy talking to a bald man in a suit. A few minutes later a forklift appeared bearing a casket. Several workmen loaded the casket into a silver vault on the back of a casket truck.

Gerald had seen enough. It was obvious that Katie's friend was simply helping with the transfer of her father's casket to the funeral home company. If he hurried he might still catch Katie at baggage claim.

•   •   •

Nathan Owenby walked his report up two flights of stairs to the desk Marti Matthews was using and waited for her to put down the phone. Nathan was a telecommunications specialist out of Quantico who was on temporary assignment to Denver while the Dillon investigation was ongoing. He looked anxious to speak with her, so Matthews cut her conversation short. "What have you got, Nathan?"

"This is one smart girl, Dr. Matthews. I believe she used a key capture routine to first record Mrs. Reynolds keystrokes and later logged on using Reynolds' user name and password."

"How do you know?"

"She got both of them right the first time she logged on. With that, she had complete access to the records and deleted them. I recovered the deleted file and checked the time stamp. It was 9:02 p.m. last Wednesday."

"After hours?"

"Right, but the phone record indicates the call originated at 11:02 p.m. This call came from the east coast."

"Where?"

"That's the real beauty of it. We know the call asking for Lucy's background check was made during working hours, and it came from First Nations Bank in Charlotte. However, the 11:02 call came from the front desk of the Hyatt Regency in Atlanta."

Matthews started to pick up her phone, but Nathan stopped her.

"Don't bother. She bounced the calls, probably both of them. We sometimes refer to it as the Pound-Ninety Scam. She most likely called the front desk at the Hyatt, told them she was a service technician at their local phone company and tricked them into pressing the pound key followed by the nine and zero keys. It's an old trick prisoners used when trying to get free long distance. The thing is, once they pressed those keys, she was able to transfer her call *through* their phone system. The call looks like it originated from the Hyatt front desk and they get the bill."

"So, how do you know the call wasn't made from within the hotel?"

"The hotel's switchboard. It came in from an outside line that could have been from anywhere."

"You said the call was made at eleven p.m.?"

"Yeah, at 11:02 to be exact."

"Well, how many calls would the Hyatt get that late at night?"

Nathan thought for second. "I'll have their phone company check the incoming call records. Good idea!"

• • •

The apartment building at 2185 Decatur Place had been in disrepair for years until a group of Washington attorneys bought it and began renovations. The interior was near completion and a fresh coat of stucco was being applied to its exterior. Three large commercial air-conditioning units were already mounted on top of the eight-story structure. The fourth unit swung from the end of a cable as the crane lifted it from the flatbed truck. Four men from Jenkins Heating and Air watched as the unit was gently lowered into place. Ryan Papineau, unable to see anything from the street, stood near the roof access door and watched as the men removed the one panel he had not welded shut and attached the wires and tubes.

A half-hour later, the men switched on the power and the air-conditioner hummed to life, fully functional, yet with major modifications to its interior. Satisfied with their work, they packed their tools and descended the stairs. Their foreman flipped the main HVAC breaker off, exited the building and left. As soon as the crane operator drove away, Ryan walked back inside, located the breaker and flipped it back on. The trap was set.

• • •

Nathan Owenby was back at Dr. Matthews' desk within minutes holding a computer printout.

Matthews put her call on hold. "What did you find?"

"The Hyatt received only two calls at 11:02 p.m.," Owenby said. "One came from a payphone at the airport and the other came from a customer service lounge at the Grand Cayman Hilton."

Matthews eyes widened. "Nathan, you just earned your keep."

• • •

The huge binoculars and video camera in Lucy's top floor apartment on the northwest side of DuPont Circle, were mounted on a tripod and pointed toward the rooftop air-conditioner units of the other building. Several bags containing her clothes and costumes lay on the bed awaiting Ryan's departure. The rest was already in her car, parked on the street below. In the living room was a maze of recording equipment all linked to a satellite transmitter located on the roof of her building. Whatever took place on the rooftop a quarter-mile away would be recorded and transmitted to a safe place.

She watched the video feed from 2185 Decatur Place as Ryan Papineau made his way off the roof of that building and down through its interior. Additional recorders in that building were programmed to come on when motion sensors were tripped, thus the need for Ryan to switch the main HVAC breaker back on. Within a few minutes he would be out front to pick up her things. She and Ryan had one more stop to make, then they would spend the night in the peaceful little town of Manassas, Virginia and watch things unfold from there.

•   •   •

Katie Froscher stood on a knoll in Arlington National Cemetery and watched as the vault containing her father's remains was once again lowered into the ground. The last time she had gone through this ordeal, her brother had been standing beside her. Now, there was only a baldheaded mortician in an ill-fitting suit. She looked down the hill toward the Pentagon and thought about the men inside who had been responsible for her brother's death. These men, who thought of themselves as patriots, were nothing more than cold-blooded murderers. They would soon pay. Over the hill, she could see the mast of the battleship *Maine*, the U.S. flag fluttering atop it. It might be years before she would be able to stand here again and gaze upon her father's grave. Or just as easily, she could make one mistake that would place her with him forever.

•   •   •

Michelle Anthony's home was just as she had described it over the phone. It sat in a nice neighborhood, on a knoll that overlooked the Rocky Mountains in the town of Littleton. A light dusting of snow coated the grass but the roads were clear.

Michelle was still in her bathrobe when she answered the door. She smiled warmly. "Agent Crosby, please come in?"

He stepped inside the foyer. "Thank you for seeing me on such short notice."

"I have four kids. Believe me, any adult conversation is welcome." She walked down the hall. "I just gave the kids milk and cookies. You want something?"

"No, thank you."

"I meant, something more adult, you know like a beer or Coke."

"I'll take a Coke, if it's no trouble."

"Sure," she pointed towards the den. "Have a seat."

Crosby entered the room and sat on a couch that was even nicer than the one in her ex-husband's apartment. She returned with two glasses and slid the pocket door shut behind her. "They're watching cartoons. I hope you don't mind real Coke?"

He nodded. When she leaned over to hand him his glass, he couldn't help but notice that she wasn't wearing much, if anything, underneath the robe. He wondered if she might have something else in mind besides the interview. Agent Smith had been working another case and Crosby remembered Marti's words, "Never go in alone."

She sat down across from him and crossed her legs. "So what do you want to know?"

"Did David ever talk about his father's military service?"

"Of course. He tooted that horn every chance he got. I was sick of it. Did his mother tell you?"

"Yes. She said some nice things about you too," he lied.

"I *bet!*"

"She's just an old lady who misses her grandchildren. She's all alone now."

Michelle sighed. "I suppose I should go by there. It wasn't her fault that her son was a jerk."

Crosby sat his glass on the table.

"That's the coffee table," she said nodding at it.

"Sorry." He put a coaster under his drink.

"No, I didn't mean that. It's where David wanted me to, uh . . . perform. You know, dance."

"Oh, right." This was getting a little uncomfortable and he half expected her next line to be, "Wanna see?"

"Wanna see?" Michelle got up, but didn't disrobe. Instead she walked over to the bookcase and took out a photo album. She flipped a few pages and showed Crosby a picture of her dressed in fishnet stockings and a bunny outfit. "Halloween. He loved that costume." She returned the album to the bookcase. "I saw that look, Agent Crosby. You thought I was about to get up on the table. Didn't you?"

Crosby smiled nervously.

She gave him a seductive look. "Would you enjoy that?"

Crosby looked at the floor, embarrassed. "Probably, but—"

"No need to worry. I have kids in the house and you're on duty."

"Well, to be perfectly honest, I came here today to talk about some photos."

"Oh *shit*. Don't tell me you found one of *my* videos in that dumpster?"

"No, ma'am. It's photos of our suspect." Crosby retrieved the pictures from within his coat and handed them to her.

"*Whew*." Michelle sat down and took a sip of Coke to relax. "You sound Southern with your 'ma'am.'"

"I'm originally from Charlotte, North Carolina."

"I thought so," She studied Lucy's employment photo for a moment. "She looks familiar. Who is she?"

"We only have an alias. Have you ever heard the name Lucy Harris or Elyn Harrison?"

"No. But I've seen her somewhere."

"Perhaps at your husband's bank or . . . on your couch?"

"Ex-husband, and her head was at the other end of the couch. I didn't get a good look before storming out." She examined the photo closer. "I wonder . . ." Michelle got up, went back to the bookcase and picked up a gold coin from one of the shelves. "I found this under the couch shortly after I caught David with her." She handed the coin to Crosby. "I figured it fell out of David's pocket, but he denied ever seeing it."

Michelle's fingerprints were all over it, so Crosby didn't bother being careful. He turned the coin over and looked at the date, 1932. It meant nothing, but it wouldn't hurt to have it examined.

She took a white yearbook out of the bookcase and flipped through pages. She held one page up for Crosby to see. "Here's a picture of David before he got so fat." She went back to turning pages. "Seems like I remember her, but I know she wasn't in our class. Maybe a couple of years younger?" She opened more pages and walked the perimeter of the room. "Are you married, Agent Crosby?"

"No, ma'am."

"I think you're a real gentleman." She turned the page. "Perhaps next time— Wait, *there* she is. Cheryl. That's her."

She showed the photo to Crosby. It was a picture of Lucy with black hair, in her teens. He jotted down the name. "Cheryl Nagai Caldwell. Can I borrow this and the coin? I promise I'll return it."

"Sure." She looked a little sad. "You have to go?"

"Yes, I'm sorry to rush off. You can't know how much I appreciate this."

Michelle stepped a little closer. "Call before you bring them back, okay. Maybe I'll get a babysitter."

.   .   .

The call from Kelly Rankin caused Marti Matthew to answer it with some apprehension. Even if Homeland Security was behind the Spectrum Project, she couldn't imagine Kelly being in on it. Her earlier e-mail to him contained only basic information about the Hyatt calls from Grand Cayman and a request for him to check out the hotel.

"Hey, Marti," Rankin said. "What do you get when you play a country song backwards?"

"You get your wife, your car, and all your money back, Kelly. You told me that one."

"Damn, Marti. You're not nearly as much fun as Crosby. He never knows the punch line."

"I'm glad you two seem to be getting along better. Even Lynch has noticed a change."

"I haven't changed. Was there a problem?"

"How's your tan?"

"I checked the hotel where your message originated, but Lucy is long gone. A bellhop remembered her face, but he said her hair was long and blonde. You may want to add that version to her hotline photo. If she stayed here it wasn't under these names. I'm e-mailing you a copy of the register list going back two weeks. Maybe the computer will have better luck."

"I'll give it top priority," Matthews said.

"I have an idea how she might have gotten off the island. Most of the cruise lines issue their passengers these sign and sail cards. Some have pictures, some don't. All you have to do is pick up someone's card, give it to the dock security guard who swipes it through a handheld reader and step aboard. The thing is, their reader just checks names against the passenger list, and is not even linked to a list of those who disembarked. Passports are not required, so once you're aboard the ship it's as if you never left the country. Passengers get off in Florida with nothing more than their driver's license or two other IDs."

"But she wouldn't have a cabin. Where would she sleep?"

"Come on, Marti. That girl? I guarantee you, she'd find a place to sleep in *my* cabin."

"You're right."

"One of the dock security guards seemed to recognize her face. He didn't speak much English, but he cupped both hands over his chest when he saw her picture. I think she's the one."

"Any idea which ship she was on?"

"No. Three or four come and go every day. I guess I'm headed back to Washington. I alerted our office in Miami, but if she departed on Wednesday, she would have arrived there on Sunday."

"Maybe they have a surveillance video. Thanks, Kelly."

As soon as she hung up, she got the call from Crosby.

"Marti. I have Lucy's *real* name."

•   •   •

Gerald McMullen walked into his old Washington condo perplexed and frustrated. He had hoped to spend the day showing Katie around Washington, but by the time he returned to the baggage claim area she had already left. Katie was probably at Arlington, but the place was huge and he had no luck in finding her when he drove around the cemetery.

In the mad rush to get Katie to her mother's the previous day, he had given her his cell phone number, but neglected to get hers. Now there was no way of reaching her until she called him. All of his morning plans had gone wrong and he couldn't understand the cloak and dagger disguise, or why Lucy had checked out the cargo terminal before going inside. None of it made sense.

He headed down the hall and smelled something hot when he passed his old office. He switched on the light and found the room still a wreck with papers piled in stacks on the floor, most of it research left over from writing his book. He had been meaning to order a file cabinet but with spending more and more time in Charlotte, he hadn't done so. Devrin probably thought the papers were important, so he hadn't vacuumed around the old desk.

Gerald got down on his knees and realized the hot smell was coming from his old computer underneath the desk. Devrin had asked if he could use it to print his reports and apparently it hadn't been turned off in over three years. A layer of dust covered it and the fan housing was so clogged it was a wonder it hadn't set the room on fire. He grabbed the power cord and pulled it out of the wall socket. He got to his feet and made a mental note to order a new computer, a file cabinet, and hire someone to clean and organize the room.

· · ·

Amil Yaspar folded the newspaper and placed it in his empty briefcase. His private charter flight from Las Vegas aboard the Citation II Bravo jet had been much smoother than the single engine plane he had taken from Reno to Las Vegas over a week earlier. His disguise was so well executed that he had walked past three security guards at the North Las Vegas charter aircraft terminal and not one of them bothered to ask him to open his briefcase. The five-hour flight had cost twenty-one hundred dollars per hour, but this was a one-way trip and money was of no concern.

The pilot switched on the Fasten Seat Belt sign and announced that they would be touching down at Ronald Reagan National Airport in ten minutes.

· · ·

Katie Froscher was walking through the airport terminal at Washington Dulles when she saw a small article on the back of a newspaper someone was holding. It had Lucy's photograph. She bought a copy at a newsstand and read the caption. The FBI was asking anyone who had seen Lucy to come forward. Katie quickly scanned the article for her own name, but there was no mention of her. She looked up and down the airport corridor half expecting a sea of agents to descend upon her. Ducking into the last stall of the ladies room, she read every word and checked the other pages for related stories. None. She knew if they were looking for Lucy, it was only a matter of time before they would have her picture as well.

She dialed Gerald McMullen's number.

"Gerald. This is Katie Froscher."

"I was hoping you would call," he said.

"Listen, I've got this crazy idea. I want you to think about it, but no matter how you respond, I'm going through with my part of it, okay?"

She's talked to Mandy, he thought. "What is it?"

"You said your ultimate dream was to buy a house on an island in the Caribbean, right?"

He sighed with relief. "Right."

"Why not today? Why not this very minute?"

He laughed. "Because I don't have the money, Katie."

"But I do, and I have the same dream as you. My father left me a huge sum in his will," she lied. "I could buy ten homes on ten different islands and still have enough for us to live the rest of our lives."

Gerald took a moment to answer. "That's a life changing commitment and you just met me. Are you sure you want to do this?"

"I am. I'm at Dulles International and my flight's about to leave. I might rent a condo on Grand Cayman or Jamaica. I thought maybe we could spend some time there until we're sure we want to go through with this."

"It's a big decision to make over the phone, Katie. I'm in Washington. Could you come over tonight?"

"Not tonight. But try to meet me tomorrow. I'll be in Hamilton, Bermuda all day and I'll pay for your flight. You can reach me at this number. If you can't make it, I'll understand, but I'm leaving Hamilton Thursday evening."

"What's the rush?"

"I'll explain later," she said. "Can you get away?"

"I'll try. Can I sleep on it?"

"Of course. I just wish we were leaving together."

"You sure know how to tempt a guy. I'll call you in the morning."

Katie closed her phone, checked the corridor before leaving the restroom and headed for the ticket counter. If she was lucky she might make it to Atlanta where she could disappear.

•   •   •

Devrin Crosby stood before the mirror in the hotel bathroom and stripped off his clothes. He looked older and had lost weight, a slight bulge pushing the waistband of his shorts. Still, both Marti and Michelle had found him attractive and having someone flirt with you was always a great feeling. He was ready to go home, hungry, and tired of the chase. All he wanted was to take a hot shower, call room service for an early dinner with Marti, and climb into bed. Steam was rising above the open shower door and he stepped inside.

Eyes closed, water pouring over his face, Crosby thought about the terrorist Amil. His mind drifted back to that lovely spring day four years ago in Lafayette Park. The FBI surveillance van had followed the suspect's cab until it stopped at the corner of H Street and Jackson Place. The suspect exited the cab, his hand gripping a briefcase. The man adjusted his sunglasses, looked in their direction and started walking through Lafayette Park towards the White House.

Crosby had jumped from the van screaming shouts to freeze, and training the sights of his Glock on the suspect's head. "Put the brief-case on the ground and step away," he'd said.

Three more agents, in full assault gear, poured from the van, their rifles aimed at a man they had identified as Amil Yaspar.

Across Pennsylvania Avenue, three Secret Service agents emerged from nowhere, their weapons drawn. The Iranian slowly turned, still clutching the briefcase to his side.

"Put the briefcase down and step away," he'd ordered. "*Now!*"

The Iranian never moved and Crosby kept his eyes on the hand grasping the briefcase. High explosives would have taken out half the block, but he held his ground.

The Iranian spoke in Farsi, but never released his grip on the briefcase. Amil would have understood the command. He was educated in Britain and spoke fluent English, yet this man acted as if he had no comprehension of what was unfolding.

Crosby had sensed that something was wrong. The man didn't react when he repeated the command, but by then his blood was up, pounding in his chest. Cold sweat ran down his neck, and the pressure of his finger against the Glock's trigger increased.

He should have known when the Iranian replied, "You make mistake." But then, as if nothing were amiss, the Iranian had simply reached a hand inside his coat.

"Devrin?" a voice called.

Only when the cordite smell filled his nostrils and he felt his fingers tight on the trigger, only then had he known. The crumpled body lying in the pool of blood, his briefcase spilling only papers, was not Amil. It was his future, his aspirations, and his own soul that seeped into the spring earth of Lafayette Park that day.

"*Devrin!*" The shower door flung open and Matthews repeated the cry. "*Devrin!* Are you deaf? I'm been pounding on the door for a minute. Lynch is on the phone. He says it's urgent."

"Uh, yeah. Tell him I'll be there in a second."

She threw him a towel, glanced down before turning, and smiled. "You've lost weight."

Crosby wrapped himself in the towel and followed her.

Dripping wet, he took the receiver. "Yes, sir."

"Crosby, I need you and Marti back here as soon as possible. See if you can catch a flight out tonight."

"What's wrong?"

"It's Amil," Lynch said. "He's *in* Washington."

CHAPTER 21

RYAN

Wednesday

Stalker found the name at a small college in the heart of Detroit. A search on the Internet for classes in particle physics had yielded the name of a professor, Paul Rivers. He taught a physics class at Wayne State University and was hired shortly after Ryan's car disappeared under the ice. The faculty biography page listed his degree in Particle Accelerator Physics from L'Institut National Polytechnique de Grenoble. The 1987 graduating class on the Polytechnique website listed no Paul Rivers, but it did list a Ryan Papineau who had graduated top of his class.

Stalker ordered a Spectrum operative from the Chicago office to visit Rivers' home, but no one was there. Breaking in, he found a workshop, an industrial freezer and a crude model of a particle trap. Upon leaving the house, he noticed tire tracks in the yard, indicating a large truck had been there within a few days. A call to the local U-Haul dealership confirmed that a flatbed truck had been rented under River's name and wasn't due back until Friday. So sure was Ryan that his past was completely buried that a trail of credit card receipts in Rivers' name led all the way to Washington, and oddly enough, to a tiny hotel in the town of Manassas, Virginia.

Stalker immediately called Raptor. "I have Ryan Papineau's alias and I know where he's located."

"I'm tied up at the moment," Sanders said. "I'll see if Mig is available."

• • •

Gerald McMullen awoke early. All of his bags were packed and waiting by the front door. He sat at the kitchen table and wrote a short note to Devrin:

Hey, buddy, sorry I missed seeing you this time, but I've met someone and if things work out the way I hope they will, I might be out of the country for a few days. I'll let you know when I get back to Charlotte and I'll send you some turtle soup. By the way I'm going to have someone straighten up the mess around my desk and replace that old computer, so save any files you need. Wish me luck, buddy.

    Take care;

    Gerry

•   •   •

Katie Froscher had spent the night in Atlanta because the private terminal was already closed when her flight landed. The private charter jet she had just arranged would take her to Bermuda by way of Dulles International in Washington. She was about to call Gerald and tell him where to meet the plane when she got a call from her executive assistant, Mandy Davis.

"Hey, stranger. When did you get back?"

"Yesterday, but I had to fly up to Washington to take care of some family business. I'm there now," Katie lied.

"Are you coming in tomorrow?"

"Actually, it will be a few days. Some important things have come up."

"Oh. Well, I'll keep collecting your mail. Does this trip have anything to do with your cruise?"

"No," fear gripping her. "Why should it?"

"Well, I was just wondering if you met up with your friend? He called me last Sunday from the port terminal. He wasn't sure which ship you were on."

"What friend?"

"Gerald McMullen."

Katie was too stunned to answer.

"Katie?" Mandy said after a moment. "*Oh no!* Don't tell me you didn't know this guy."

•   •   •

The building inspector with the Washington Housing Authority arrived at 7:30 a.m., entered the building at 2185 Decatur Place and walked up the stairs. The inspection was required after any new equipment, such as air-conditioning units, was installed. All of the tags and permits seemed to be in place. He signed each tag in turn, but as he signed the last tag he noticed a whirring sound coming from somewhere within the unit. A fan motor, he surmised, had been left on by mistake. He made his way down to the basement floor, located the breaker box and pulled the main HVAC breaker to off.

• • •

Lucy Harris and Ryan Papineau had just awakened inside a hotel room in Manassas, Virginia, when they noticed the video feed coming from the building at Hillyer Place had turned to static. A quick review of the surveillance videos found the cause. An inspector had entered the building and apparently switched off the main breaker, cutting all power along with their surveillance cameras. Without those, there was no way of knowing when Amil or the Spectrum goons might arrive.

"Lucy," Ryan said. "Leave it. It doesn't matter."

"All I have to do is flip the breaker back on. I'll be back in a couple of hours."

"You'll have to reset the computer in your apartment as well. It's too risky."

"Ryan, our clients have to receive the signal to make the bids. Without those, we don't get the *money*."

"We already have enough"

"It's not only that. If we don't get Amil on the tape we have no alibi. Don't worry, I'll be careful. If I can deal with Amil Yaspar, I can deal with anybody."

Lucy kissed him on the lips. "I'll pick up some pizza on the way back." She opened the door, walked to her red BMW Sportster and got in.

• • •

Across the street, a brawny Cuban named Miguel Parrado punched Raptor's speed dial number. "She's just left," Mig said. "I put the tracking device under her car. Looks like she's headed your way, boss. You want me to follow?"

"Stalker can track her signal. Bring the other one," Sanders said. "We may need him."

•   •   •

Gerald McMullen had just pulled into the Rental Car Return Deck when he got the call he had been dreading.

"Just answer me one question," Katie Froscher said coldly. "Who the hell are you?"

Gerald chose his words carefully. "I guess you spoke with Mandy?"

"Answer the *question*."

"My name is Gerald McMullen and I live in Charlotte."

"I want to know who you really are?"

"That's my real name, Katie. I haven't lied to you."

"You lied to Mandy."

"I stretched the—"

"Don't bullshit me. You told her we had made plans, when I didn't even know who the hell you *were!*"

"You're right. I told her that because I wanted to *meet* you."

"Who do you work for?"

"I told you, I'm a writer. I wrote a book and I do editorials for the Observer. That's all."

"So you were doing a story on me?"

"*No.* Why would I?"

"Were you the one who called my mother?"

"Yes, and I tried to tell you that when we were aboard Ned's chopper, but you wouldn't—"

"You've been tracking me for over two weeks. You set this whole thing up, and I don't see any reason why I should trust you now."

"Katie, please listen," he said, but the line was dead.

•   •   •

Marti and Devrin landed in Washington at 9:30 a.m. and drove Marti's car directly to FBI headquarters downtown. They had taken the red-eye flight from Denver with a long lay-over in Atlanta. Marti had slept the whole way, but Devrin had not and it showed. His suit was wrinkled, his face unshaven and his eyes bloodshot. Robert Lynch was waiting for them in the Photographic Operations and Imaging lab.

"You look like hell," Lynch said to Crosby.

"It was a long flight, and I couldn't sleep."

"Where is Amil being held?" Matthews said.

"He's not. Sit down and I'll bring you up to speed. Based on Rankin's report that Amil was using charter aircraft to move about, we started feeding video surveillance from the smaller airfields through our biometric facial recognition computer program. We began with the private aircraft terminals at Dulles and Reagan National, but the system has been backlogged.

"Play the video," Lynch said to a technician. An image of a bald man looking nothing like Amil appeared on the screen. A split image of an earlier photo of him highlighted ten identical characteristics.

"The program recognized Amil when he passed through the private terminal at Reagan National at 5:36 p.m. last evening. He took a chartered jet from North Las Vegas Airfield, and the pilot identified him as a Spanish businessman."

"He was in Las Vegas the entire time," Crosby said.

"So we missed him?" Matthews said.

"Yes," Lynch said. "The video wasn't processed until eight p.m."

"Well, he's here and he's changed his appearance," Crosby said. "That means we're the next target."

"Unless it's a diversion," Lynch said, "but probably not. We're running an enhanced image of him on every station and newspaper within a hundred miles. Crosby, I need you sharp, so go home and get a couple hours of shut-eye. I need you back here by noon. Dr. Matthews, come with me."

• • •

After an hour of trying to absorb Katie's call, Gerald McMullen still sat in his rental car on the top level of the parking deck. Everything he had worked for was gone and he had no place to go. He prayed she would call back and let him explain, but he knew it was useless. He finally put the car in gear and decided to drive back to his Washington town house. Crosby would have to return sooner or later, and at least there he had a friend to talk to.

As he drove toward the exit ramp, he glanced at the cargo hanger across the airfield where Lucy had gone the previous day. There, parked beside one of the buildings, was her red BMW Sportster.

• • •

Crosby lay in his bed but sleep was impossible, not as long as Amil was in town. He got up, wet his hair, shaved and went into the kitchen for a snack. He spotted Gerald's note on the table and realized that he needed to download his e-mail addresses off the old computer before they replaced it. He found his flash drive in the bedroom and went into the office. The monitor screen was completely black, the switch not working. He looked under the desk and saw that the power strip was unplugged.

Devrin got on his knees and grabbed the dusty power cord. When he plugged it in several dust covered letters fell from behind the desk.

"Here's your power bill from five years ago, Gerald," Crosby said to himself, pulling more letters out. One was a large manila envelope. "This one's dated three years ago."

Devrin moved to the chair and waited for the computer to boot up. He studied the envelope. It was addressed to Gerald but its return address seemed familiar, a street number in Washington. He almost set it aside before noticing the postmark was the same day the President was assassinated. Tim Cook's street address flashed into his mind. The return address was the dead Press Secretary's home. He hesitated since it wasn't his mail—and he wondered if Gerald would mind—but then he tore open the envelope anyway and pulled out a sheaf of pages, carefully holding them by the edges. The cover letter was on White House stationary, attached to several handwritten pages. In the margins were scribbled notes. The signature at the bottom of the last page took his breath away: *William Joseph Barnett, President of the United States of America.*

•　•　•

"Robert Lynch please," Crosby said into his phone, his heart racing. "Tell him it's urgent."

Lynch came on the line. "What is it Crosby?"

"I need to meet with you and Director Gregory *immediately.*"

"Why."

"I *know* who killed President Barnett."

•　•　•

The computer screen on Jonathan Bowman's PC beeped and flashed: SUCCESS. Jonathan turned away from his textbook and wheeled his chair in front of his computer. The screen was plain, blue with white text, but the message it displayed was far more exciting than any graphics he had ever seen.

"Sweet!" Jonathan said as he read it.

**** EYES ONLY ****
RESTRICTED SITE, U.S. DEPARTMENT OF JUSTICE
**** CLASSIFICATION ULTRA BLACK ****
SECURED AUTHORIZATION REQUIRED
ENTER USER NAME AND PASSWORD

Jonathan unfolded the page he had printed from Lisa Trexler's e-mail, typed in the code word SPECTRUM and hit Enter. The screen momentarily displayed an image he had not at all expected. It was the logo of the Office of Homeland Security.

Suddenly the screen flashed: DOWNLOADING, and within fifteen seconds another screen flashed—one that every hacker dreaded to see.

**** INTRUDER ALERT ****
**** INTRUDER ALERT ****
NON-AUTHORIZED SERVER DOWNLOAD
ACTIVATING TRACE
**** **** ****
SOURCE ISP LOCATED

"Whoa *shit!*" Jonathan yelled. He immediately shut down his computer, unplugged the power and disconnected the cable. He wasn't sure, but in the few seconds before he shut off the computer, he thought he recognized his own Internet service provider number flash onto the screen.

They tracked my ISP, through two re-mailing services! How in the hell is that possible?

Jonathan sat curled on his bed and pondered how long it would take him to pack his computer, a few clothes and drive to Canada.

• • •

"Agent Crosby," Bill Gregory, Director of the FBI, said, shaking his gloved hand. "You have something urgent to share?"

"Yes, sir." Crosby handed him a pair of latex gloves followed by the manila envelope.

"This was addressed to my friend Gerald McMullen, a former

reporter at the *Washington Post*. I'm currently leasing McMullen's home while he's on extended leave. It contains a copy of a speech handwritten by the late President Barnett. There is also a note signed by Tim Cook indicating that if anything were to happen to him, Gerald was to turn this over to the FBI. The note was dated the night before Barnett's assassination."

"Why didn't your friend report it?" Gregory said, while reading.

"Because he never opened it. Somehow it fell behind his desk and collected dust for three years. It's blind luck that I found it this morning."

"The Press Secretary mailed it?" Robert Lynch said as he donned gloves.

"Yes, sir. The night before he died. I saw Mr. Cook that night at Goodtime Charlie's lounge. He ran in soaking wet, holding an envelope just like this one. He was ashen-faced, nervous and asked the bartender where the nearest mailbox was."

"Was the seal unbroken?" Lynch said.

"Yes, sir. Until I opened it. I didn't know what was inside."

"Great God," Gregory commented as he read. "We need the Attorney General."

"What does it say?" Lynch said.

"Take a look yourself." Gregory handed it to Lynch. "The President will want to present this to Vice President Trexler. I'll have Justice issue an arrest warrant for Trexler when he leaves. This speech is clearly what Barnett was about to read when he was assassinated."

"Crosby, you posted something on the hotline Sunday about this Spectrum file he refers to," Lynch said. "That was before you received this?"

"Yes, sir."

"Agent Crosby," Gregory said, "please take a seat and tell us everything you've learned about this Spectrum Project."

• • •

"Counselor, we have a storm," Stalker said.

"Hold a moment." Christian Luther punched a code into his phone. "We're clear. What is it?"

"There's been a security breach on the Vice President's computer. Our database has apparently been downloaded and leaked out through his e-mail server. I've stopped it on our end, but we need to shut down all operations until further notice."

"Did any names leak?" Luther asked.

"Only code names, but operational information, schedules, client lists and passwords were leaked. I'm evaluating the damage, and it doesn't look good."

"Where was it sent?"

"We don't know yet. I can't get to Trexler's computer because it's locked in his home office."

"Where's Raptor?"

"I just talked to him. He thinks Trexler realized that he's outlived his usefulness to the project. Trexler is meeting with the President and he'll try to cut a deal. He will bury us all if he testifies."

"He'll never make it to trial." Luther gave an audible sigh. "Notify Raptor to proceed with Operation Disposal and start shredding the documents."

"What about Warrior and Scholar?"

"Them, too."

• • •

At 1600 Pennsylvania Avenue the door opened to the oval office and the President's personal secretary leaned in. "Mr. President, Vice President Trexler is waiting to see you."

"Thanks, Martha," President Beasley said. "Give me a minute and send him in. Notify the Capitol police that I *don't* want him arrested on White House grounds. Have them wait until he gets home."

"Yes, sir."

"While you're at it, have a couple of news crews meet him there. I want pictures of that son-of-a-bitch in handcuffs on the eleven o'clock news."

As soon as she shut the door, President Beasley looked down at the bandage still covering his little toe. "Payback, you bastard."

• • •

Gerald McMullen was stretched out on the couch in the condo, watching the news. There had been a major break in President Barnett's assassination case and reporters were lined up outside the home of the Vice President. Rumors of a secret document were mentioned and somehow Trexler was involved. After three years, it seemed like everyone was finally taking the facts in his book seriously. Gerald's cell phone vibrated. "Hello." No one answered. He was about to end the call when he heard a single word.

"Why?" a female voice said.

"Katie?"

"Just tell me why you followed me, Gerald."

Gerald's response was slow and careful. "I once changed a tire for a frightened young lady in a driving rainstorm. The truth is I never forgot your smile."

Katie said nothing for a long moment. "How did you get my name?"

"From your tag number. KT-GIRL wasn't hard to remember. I just wanted to meet you, Katie. I swear on my dying mother, that's the God's truth."

"Then why wait three years?"

"I tried calling once, but chickened out when you answered. What could I say that wouldn't sound like a stalker? I lost your number when I made the move from Washington. I found it under a couch cushion last week, so I took a chance and called."

"You mean you flew all the way to Florida and booked a cruise because you saw me once on the side of the road? Do you have any idea how weird that sounds?"

"It seemed like a good idea at the time. I had just canceled a cruise with my ex-girlfriend, so I was hoping we might run into each other onboard; maybe get to know each other better."

"I don't know if I believe you, Gerald."

"Katie, we shared the same curiosity that night on the Interstate. You said you always wondered who your knight in shinning armor was. Can you fault me for having those same feelings?"

"I'm still listening."

"All I wanted was to meet you. I swear, Katie, that's *all* there was to it."

There was another long pause.

"Were you coming to Bermuda?"

"I was at the airport this morning. My bags are still packed."

"If you're still interested, call me at this number when you get there. It's going to be hard for me to build trust again, Gerald."

"I understand, but you seem frightened, like you're running away. Is there something you're not telling me?"

"Just call. We'll talk then."

• • •

Gerald stepped to the head of the line at Dulles International Airport and waited for the next available agent. On the muted TV monitors he could tell something important was happening because a SWAT team had gathered in front of the Vice President's home.

"Next," the ticket agent said.

"Hi," Gerald said. "Earlier today I was booked on Flight 3014 to Bermuda, but I wasn't able to catch it. Is there another flight I could take?"

"Let's see," the ticket agent said. "You just missed the last one. I can get you on Flight 4086 that connects to Bermuda through Phila-delphia, but it doesn't leave until 7:40 tomorrow morning."

"That's all you have?"

"Yes, unless you want a thirteen hour layover in New York or Atlanta."

"Okay, how much?"

"Five hundred thirty-one dollars, sir."

Gerald shook his head and handed her his credit card. He had already turned in his rental car, and cab fare back into the city was more than a hotel room. He sent Katie a text message: *No flights available until 7:00 a.m. Looks like I'll be hanging around the airport tonight.*

• • •

The television stations had the Vice President's home surrounded. Every window was glowing with light. His wife and daughter had left under Secret Service protection, and Trexler had barricaded himself in his upstairs office. When Harold Sanders arrived, he volunteered to go upstairs and reason with Trexler. Norman allowed him to enter because Sanders was the only person he trusted.

"You've been drinking," Sanders said.

"Yeah, wouldn't you? The President said I'm finished. They found the missing speech, and they know about project Spectrum."

Sanders walked to the computer cabinet and opened his briefcase. "Give me the key."

"My wife and daughter wouldn't speak to me." Trexler stumbled to the bookcase and retrieved the key from between the two books. When he turned, Sanders was putting on latex gloves. "What are those for?"

"Fingerprints, you *idiot.*" Sanders removed a pair of sunglasses and a remote control pen from his briefcase. Three years earlier, he had used these to control the Briefing Room camera and fire the fatal shot. He opened the cabinet with the key and placed the sunglasses beside Trexler's computer. He took a document from the briefcase and handed Trexler the pen. "Sign the last page."

Trexler took the pen and glanced at the cover page. He was apparently too drunk to read it. "What's this?"

"Your resignation. Do you want the humiliation of being impeeched?"

"Beasley already fired me."

"He can't. This makes it official," Sanders said. "Sign here."

Trexler signed the document.

With Trexler's fingerprints safely on the pen, Sanders placed it beside the sunglasses. He took a .38 revolver out of his coat and laid it on the table. "They're coming up here in about five minutes to arrest you, Norman. You're going to jail for the rest of your life. If you choose to use it, this is your way out. If not, it's only a matter of time before Counselor orders it. You try and cut a deal, and he'll feed your wife and daughter through a wood chipper. You understand?"

Trexler nodded slightly and stared at the revolver.

Sanders returned the signed document to his briefcase. He put the keys to the cabinet in his pocket, leaving the Spectrum computer and remote control pen and sunglasses in plain sight. Norman's television was already on, and Sanders switched it to one of the stations broadcasting from the lawn outside. He opened the door and looked back at Trexler. "You can forget witness protection, Norman. Stalker can find anyone. Enjoy the show." Sanders closed the door behind him.

Five minutes later Sanders was standing in front of the reporters outside, every spotlight and camera focused on him. He was explaining the conversation he had just had with the Vice President and holding up the document Trexler had just signed. The camera zoomed in on Trexler's signature. Sanders had discarded the cover page and began reading from the second:

> I, Norman Trexler, resign the office Vice President of the United States. Furthermore, while serving as the former Secretary of Defense, I confess to being a member of an antiterrorist group called Spectrum. Upon learning that President William Barnett was planning to divulge details of our nation's greatest anti-terrorist weapon, I felt it was my patriotic duty to protect the defense of this nation by arranging and carrying out the assassination of President William Joseph Barnett. With the

unwitting assistance of an innocent cameraman, and by using virtual reality sunglasses and a remote control pen, I alone pulled the camera's trigger that ended the President's life—

Before Sanders finished reading the page, a shot rang out in Trexler's upstairs office.

CHAPTER 22

MONSTER

Thursday

It was after midnight by the time Harold Sanders arrived outside the old blast doors of a former Civil Defense fallout shelter located in a sub-basement of the Social Security Administration Building. It was a place that Counselor had once joked "would never be looked into." The inner steel door had a small sign taped to it. John Young, Security, knock. The door was always bolted, but Raptor had a key that he silently slipped into the lock, and entered.

John Young, aka Stalker, looked up from his terminal, his eyes wide. "How the hell did you get in?"

Sanders held up the key with a gloved hand. "Counselor wanted me to stop by to see how the shredding was going."

"Nearly finished." Stalker nodded at three huge plastic bags in the corner. "I've erased everything on the servers. You can help me carry those bags out."

Sanders noticed several boxes filled with software and various computer parts. "Going somewhere?"

"Aren't we all? Counselor ordered everything into the shredder." Stalker's voice sounded nervous as he continued to type, but his eyes followed Sanders. "By the way, I saw you on the evening news with Trexler's confession. How did you pull that off?"

"It was easier than Warrior." Sanders circled the room, opening the empty file cabinets one by one and shutting them.

"What happened to him?" Stalker's voice seemed a little higher and beads of sweat appeared on his brow.

"He's slumped over his desk at home. The morning paper and an empty bottle of pills are under him." Sanders slammed another drawer shut. "Scholar seems to have disappeared. Any idea where?"

"He has a vacation home in New Mexico."

"Not there either, as far as I can tell."

"I believe he has a daughter—" Stalker's voice cracked when he saw Sanders stop directly in front of a file box with a lid on it and squat down beside it. "*Hey!* That's my personal stuff."

Sanders removed the lid. Inside were green hanging file folders. "Well, what do we have here?"

"I can explain those."

"Let's see." Sanders lifted each file. "Here's one for Christian Luther, Norman Trexler and General Stephen Douglas. Ah yes, Warrior; our Chairman of the Joint Chiefs. We won't need those two anymore. Here's the file on Scholar. Will you look at that? Here's a file on Raptor, aka Harold Sanders." He pulled his file out. "I'll take that one off your hands. Isn't it interesting that I don't seem to see one here for John Young. I wonder why?"

"It's not what you think. I didn't want to risk shredding those."

"Did you think that Counselor was just going to let you walk out of here? You knew more than any of us." Sanders reached inside his coat and took out an old Colt 45 pistol.

"I've been loyal to Counselor from the start," Stalker pleaded. "This is only a setback. He'll need me."

"Sorry, but you're preaching to empty pews." Raptor took two steps forward and placed the barrel of the pistol against Stalker's skull, just above the left ear.

"*Wait!*" he screamed. "If I press this button, it will send details of Operation Sweep to the FBI and Justice. Both you and Counselor will be indicted for murder."

Sanders chuckled. "Go ahead. Let's see whose finger is faster."

•   •   •

Lucy Harris awoke to find herself tied to a chair; tape wrapped around her mouth and waist; nylon straps securing her hands and feet. The back of her neck felt sticky, and the room had a slight copper smell to it. Terror griped her at the sight of Raptor rifling through her pocketbook, but she had to concentrate solely on living through the night. Her last memory had been the knock at the door. She remembered being astonished to see Ryan's face when she had looked through the peephole; the door opening and a huge fist slamming into her face from nowhere. Ryan had been right. It had been a stupid, foolish move to return. Beyond Raptor a television was running her photo, and somehow the FBI had discovered her real name. Three aliases scrolled across the screen below her picture, but not Vanessa Harrison, the one alias her car outside was rented under; the only alias that might lead the FBI here and perhaps save her from the hands of Raptor.

Harold Sanders walked around the room studying each of the monitors and examining the equipment that was recording the image of a rooftop air-conditioning unit two blocks away. The time stamp indicated it was 4:50 a.m.

"Fascinating," he said and came over to Lucy. "I'll ask you once, Cheryl," calling her by her real name. "No more." He flipped open his pocketknife. "If I don't like the answers, I'll start cutting pieces off that beautiful body of yours. We understand each other?"

Lucy nodded.

Sanders ripped the tape from her mouth, and she grimaced with pain.

"Now, do you prefer Lucy or Cheryl?"

"There's none of Cheryl left in me."

"Okay Lucy. How did you gain access to the Spectrum files?"

Her throat was dry. Her cheek and nose hurt from where she had been hit. "May I please have a glass of water?"

"Wrong answer." He slid the knife down her blouse between her breasts and pulled towards him. The razor-sharp blade sliced through the bra strap and shirt with hardly a sound. "Shall we start with the left nipple?"

"*Wait!*"

"First you will answer my questions and if not—" He spun her chair around. "—you'll end up like your friend."

Lucy gasped at the sight. An empty chair covered with blood and bits of duct tape sat behind her in the middle of the room. Blood was splattered across the ceiling and walls and had soaked into the carpet with bits of flesh, fingers and toes scattered around the chair legs. Now she understood why her neck felt sticky. Her hair and back were probably covered with Ryan's blood. The sight was sickening, but she was determined that she wouldn't throw up.

"It took a little persuasion," Sanders said, "but Ryan eventually told us everything. I trust you'll be smart enough to save yourself the agony that he experienced."

•   •   •

Gerald McMullen awoke in a chair at the airport. A man was loading a bundle of newspapers in a rack across from him. Gerald got up and bought one from the man. The front page of the *Washington Post* was awash with the assassination story and the subsequent suicide of the Vice President. Agent Sanders' name was mentioned several times in a chilling account of the Vice President signing a suicide confession and purportedly admitting to taking part in the plot to kill President William Barnett.

It was Trexler? Gerald didn't think that seemed possible. The article went on to explain the use of the virtual sunglasses and remote-control pen to carry out the assassination. *Billy Ray was innocent all along.* The article continued to the back page, but the moment Gerald turned it over he saw a photograph that froze him in his tracks. There was no doubt that the face was Lucille. He looked up to see a flashing red warning banner and her picture on the muted TV screens throughout the terminal:

Cheryl N. Caldwell, aka Elyn Harrison, aka Lucy Harris.
Wanted in connection with the terrorist bombings
in Dillon and the Marquesas Keys.
Considered armed and dangerous.

Katie was with her, in the terminal. He thought of her red BMW Sportster and the casket. "She's *here*."

He pulled out his phone and dialed Crosby. There was no answer.

• • •

Crosby was asleep, stretched out across a couch in the break room. Lynch's orders. He needed him fresh for the long day that would lie ahead. Crosby's jacket was hanging on the back of a chair across the room. In an inside pocket, his cell vibrated quietly.

• • •

Why doesn't he answer? Gerald closed his phone, as the cab stopped at a gate outside the Piedmont Freight Forwarding Hanger where he had earlier spotted Lucy's red BMW. The guard shack was dark and the chain-link gate to the employee's parking lot was open. Lucy's car was gone, but the building was alight even at five a.m. with forklifts and workmen unloading trucks and loading freight into a twin engine cargo jet.

"Just let me out here," Gerald said, giving the driver a twenty.

"You want me to wait?" the driver said.

"I don't know how long this will take. Give me your number and I'll call."

Gerald entered the hanger through an unlocked side door and found a pair of coveralls and a hardhat on a hook inside and slipped them on over his clothes. Racks filled with cargo divided the space. He had no ID tag, so he used a clipboard to shield his chest and pretended to check inventory.

He walked to the rear of the building and entered a huge cold storage locker. The room was full of crates and boxes. A couple of caskets were on racks as well. *What the hell am I doing here? I don't even know what I'm looking for.*

•   •   •

Harold Sanders turned the chair containing Lucy away from the gruesome scene. As he did, she spotted a hypodermic needle and a vial on the dining room table. She must have been drugged, which explained how she managed to sleep through the butchering that had taken place only inches behind her. The gore left no doubt that Raptor wouldn't hesitate to carve her up if he suspected she was lying. It made little difference at this point if she lied or not. There was no talking her way out of this.

"Now, let's try again," Raptor said. "How did you gain access to the Spectrum files?"

"From Trexler. I lifted them from his computer."

"How did you get . . ." Recognition shown on Sanders' face. "You were the *dancer* he used to take home with him."

She nodded and tried to moisten her lips, but her tongue was dry.

"I thought you looked familiar. How did you get into the system?"

"It was easy," she lied. "Trexler left all his passwords on little sticky notes."

"What a fucking idiot," Sanders said. "You planned all of this?"

"Ryan and Chuck Froscher came up with the scheme. They were going to send the file to the President, build a working bomb and detonate it on an uninhabited island."

He lifted an eyebrow. "If they had the file, why bother?"

"You boys had a way of making files and even Presidents disappear. Even Spectrum couldn't cover up an explosion of that magnitude. Chuck wanted to show the world what your Trojan horse would do to their cities."

"You took out Dillon, Lucy, without any apparent regard for those living there."

"That was Amil's idea. At least I picked a day when most of Dillon's residents were away shopping."

"Don't play innocent with me, Lucy. I know about the years you spent in Saudi Arabia when your father was assigned there, and the connections you have with the Palestine Liberation Front. You're a terrorist."

"The real terrorists are in the Pentagon," she said. "They hire people like you to invade countries, assassinate leaders and stage terrorist bombings, all in the name of freedom. President Truman killed a hundred and fifty thousand innocent people in Hiroshima and Nagasaki. You know why Chuck sent that file to the President? Because I *convinced* him. Willie Barnett was the first decent man to sit in the White House in years, and you murdered him because he had the guts to stop it. Spectrum planned to wipe out every man, woman and child in their North Korean proposal."

"Collateral damage. That's the price of war."

Lucy thought back to her high school days; David Anthony standing on the auditorium stage, bragging about his father the war hero and how he had fried the Japs. She had repeated David's story to her grandmother the same evening. That night Grandma Kato had finally explained the burn scars that covered her body, showed her the gold coin that had branded the image of the angel into her flesh and given her the memoir, *Dawn's Last Gleaming*. That night she learned the truth about Hiroshima and how the Japanese-Americans were considered collateral damage by the Truman government. The innocent little girl that read those pages had indeed ceased to exist. The woman she had become wasn't afraid to die, but to suffer a long lingering death like Ryan was something she did not want.

• • •

Lauren Hyatt, the former intern that now worked in Crosby's department, found him in the break room drinking a cup of coffee and reading Trexler's confession in the morning paper. "Mr. Crosby, the results on that envelope found in Mr. Cook's home arrived last night. The prints were a spot on match with Chuck Froscher's."

"Have you notified anyone else?"

"I was about to post the results on the hotline."

"No. Call Lynch when he gets in and have someone deliver them directly to him. Tell him I know how President Barnett learned about the Spectrum Project."

"What's that?"

"He'll know"

Lauren smiled. "Did you lose some weight?"

"A little."

"I'll take it to him personally," she said with a wink.

"Thanks, Lauren."

• • •

Sanders picked up Lucy's folder and read: "Cheryl Nagai Caldwell. You grew up in Littleton, Colorado. An Army brat. Was your father stationed at NORAD?"

"No. He taught at the Air Force Academy in Colorado Springs."

"Your parents divorced. Did you live with your grandmother?"

"Until she died of multiple cancers, compliments of our government."

"Ah, yes. Grandma Kato, the little survivor of Hiroshima." Sanders touched the copy of *Dawn's Last Gleaming* on top of her purse. "I read Kato's memoir. Odd name for a half-breed."

Lucy burned with rage. "She was born an American and named in honor of our Japanese family. President Truman knew there were twenty-three hundred American citizens in Hiroshima, but to him Japanese-Americans were still *Japs*."

"That really pissed you off, didn't it? You seem to have a history of befriending the children of the men aboard those B-29's. We never made the connection until we discovered that Chuck Froscher's father was aboard the Nagasaki bomber. What a coincidence that David Anthony's father just happened to be aboard the *Enola Gay*. Was he worth taking out an entire town?"

"He was the worst," she said with disdain. "First I screwed his marriage, then I screwed his career, and finally I screwed him. *Permanently!*"

"All of that and you still managed to screw Spectrum as well. If you were so motivated by revenge, why didn't you go after the original crewmembers?"

"Where's the satisfaction in killing an old man who has only a few years to live? But to lose one's child or grandchild, now that's the ultimate blow at any age."

A grin formed on Sanders face. "We are much alike, you and I."

Lucy gritted her teeth. "Untie me and I'll *show* you."

"I bet you would." He walked to the kitchen sink, filled a paper cup with water and held it to her lips. "So, there were others?" he asked as she swallowed the tepid liquid.

"A few. One of my former roommates died in an apartment fire. They never linked me to the gasoline found in her basement. Some were nearly impossible to get. I almost gave up on David Anthony until Chuck showed me how convenient your little bomb fit into a briefcase."

"Yes, Froscher was brilliant, but his morals blinded him. Did you seek him out?"

"I knew Charles Froscher had a son living in Oak Ridge, but I had no idea what he did," Lucy said, "Chuck was always working out of Chicago, so I took an apartment in the building he shared with Ryan. Ryan introduced us. That's how I learned about Spectrum." *Falling in love with Chuck was accidental.*

"You discovered Amil was one of our clients on Trexler's computer?"

"Yes. Amil was the perfect diversion. I knew the FBI would focus all of their attention on him. He wanted a demonstration, and I wanted David Anthony dead. What better way to exact revenge than to fry that son-of-a-bitch along with your project."

"I think you just wanted to get rich. Ryan told us about your secret website and the deposits you've hidden in the Caribbean. I admire your ingenuity. But why all this?" He panned the room with his arm. "Why record it? That one has me stumped."

"You already know. We haven't been paid for the Monster."

Sanders paused for a second and looked at the ceiling. "A transmitter on the roof? You're sending the signal so they can watch and bid?"

She nodded. "Just like they did in Dillon. I convinced Mr. Foy to put a transmitter on the roof of the Dillon bank so he could keep an eye on David Anthony."

"Where was your transmitter in the Marquesas Keys?"

"On the Argentinean's sub. They provided it for first rights of refusal."

"So the bidding has started on the Monster?"

"Hopefully," she said. "And you and I get to experience the blast firsthand."

• • •

"Where to?" the cab driver asked as the Iranian got in.

"2185 Decatur Place. It's near DuPont Circle," Amil Yaspar said in English. "But first I need to stop at a hardware store."

"No problem, buddy."

• • •

Crosby was at his desk having a third cup of coffee when Kelly Rankin came in with a baldheaded guy. The man was thin, in his mid twenties and dressed in a very conservative black suit.

"Crosby, you awake?" Rankin said.

"Barely."

"Meet Clay Simpson. He saw Lucy's picture in the paper this morning and called us. He says he had a date with her last night."

"I thought her name was Elyn Harrison," Simpson explained. "I never imagined this."

"She's in Washington?"

"Yep," Rankin said, "and he knows the area where she lives."

Crosby picked up his phone. "Lauren, find Lynch and tell him we just got a lead on Lucy. She's in Washington and we need to alert the President. This could be the big one."

• • •

Sanders opened his knife again. "Clever girl. You were hoping I'd leave you here tied to the chair to await the end, James Bond style. But you see, I already know where the Monster is and it's not here. Poor Ryan admitted that much after some persuasion."

What agony Ryan must have endured for that lie, Lucy thought.

"You built all of this to lure us into your trap. Otherwise you wouldn't have returned to operate the cameras."

There was a knock on the door. Lucy started to scream, but remembered the man with the huge fist.

Sanders opened it. A huge man with black hair stepped in. "Mig, how's Ryan?"

"Here and there," the Cuban said in a deep voice. "The Potomac catfish are feasting tonight, boss."

"Perfect. Just as if he had gone off that bridge into the frozen river. Your fate awaits, Lucy."

She closed her eyes and vowed that no matter what they did, no matter how it hurt, she wouldn't betray Katie.

"Miguel Parrado, this is Cheryl Nagai Caldwell, also known as Lucy Harris. She's brilliant, ruthless, and by most accounts, a nymphomaniac. My kind of girl. Under different circumstances I might have run off with her to that island where she's hidden our money. But now I've gone and told her your name. A little insurance to help you fulfill your contract."

"I always do, boss," Parrado said.

The words INTRUDER ALERT started blinking on one of the monitors. Sanders studied the video showing a dark skinned man with a shaved head climbing the first set of stairs of the other building.

"It appears that Amil has fallen for the bait, Lucy. Your trap has sprung." He glanced at Parrado. "I'm finished with her."

Parrado tore a piece of duct tape off the roll and moved toward her.

"It's a hundred million and I have the passwo—" she managed to get out before the tape was secure.

Sanders filled the syringe. "Goodbye, Lucy," he said as he stuck it in her arm and depressed the plunger. "It truly was a pleasure."

Parrado slit the tapes binding Lucy to the chair and placed her headfirst into an rollout trash bin. He threw her purse in on top of her, scattering its contents everywhere. In the last few seconds before the drug took effect she heard Sanders say, "Make it quick. She's earned that much."

•   •   •

Crosby and Rankin rode up 20th Street, stopping at the Metro entrance at DuPont Circle. Clay Simpson was in the back seat giving directions.

"She walked north past Zorba's Cafe," Simpson said.

"Q Street is one way. Take a right," Rankin said. "Did you follow her?"

"Yeah, but she vanished. Look, I need to get back to work. I have a funeral this morning."

Crosby turned right then left onto Connecticut Avenue. He caught a break in the traffic so he made an illegal left onto R Street. "I'm just going to swing around the block."

"Where do you work, Clay?" Rankin asked.

"I'm a mortician. It's my father's business."

"Hey Crosby, have you heard how you can tell if your wife is dead?" Rankin said.

"I haven't a clue." He turned left onto 21st Street.

"The sex is about the same, but you can leave the toilet seat up."

"That's a good one." Clay laughed. "We don't get too many jokes in the funeral business."

"So you met Elyn where?" Rankin said.

"At a club," Clay said. "But this was the first time we went out. I was shocked when I saw her photo in the paper. She's nothing like that."

Crosby turned left onto Hillyer Place. "I used to live down here."

A panel van was parked outside an apartment building with a burly man heaving a large garbage bin into the back of it. Crosby drove past. "Thanks for coming forward, Mr. Simpson We'll drop you off at your car—"

"Devrin, pull *over*," Rankin interrupted. "Lucy drives a red BMW. There's one parked in that lot on the left."

•   •   •

The building was two blocks northwest of Lucy's apartment. The lock had been cut and Raptor entered it with his weapon drawn. He wasn't taking any chances. He put in his earpiece and switched on the set. He eased his way up the stairs until he reached the top landing and looked up the final staircase leading to the roof. The access door was open.

"This is Agent Sanders," he said softly into his microphone. "I need backup. I'm at 2185 Decatur Place, on the roof. I have a suspect believed to be Amil Yaspar cornered."

•   •   •

Crosby and Rankin had walked West Hillyer to 21st Street checking apartment mailboxes and showing Lucy's photo to pedestrians. They were just about to R Street when Rankin's cell phone rang. It was the dispatcher at Homeland Security. "Yeah."

"Kelly, we just got a call from the Secret Service. One of their agents claims to have Amil Yaspar cornered on the roof of the building at 2185 Decatur Place. That's at the corner of Florida and Decatur Place Northwest." Rankin opened his phone's GPS app. "Good *Lord!* That's only a block away."

"What?" Crosby said.

"Come on," Rankin said, running across the street. "Amil is on the roof of a building, right over *there*."

. . .

"Fat Man and Little Boy desire an exhibition at 8:15 on Thursday?" Agent Rick Griffin read aloud from his computer screen. "Please call: N385-4477 W770-2509. Must own new skis to enter race?"

"What the hell is that?" Agent Michael James asked. He was sitting next to Griffin who was working the FBI hotline. Agent James was checking the latest postings before calling them into his boss, Christian Luther, at Homeland Security. For a week, he had been feeding the information to someone called Stalker, but this morning he had been told to address them directly to Luther himself.

"It's from the *New York Times* personals. The computer flagged it as a possible terrorist threat," Griffin said. "It must have one of the keywords. It's nothing. Sounds like a skiing exhibition." He started to hit the Delete key.

"Wait a minute," James said. "What part of that could be a terrorist message?"

Dr. Marti Matthews was walking past with her morning coffee. She smiled at James. "Hi, Michael. What have you got?"

"We don't know. It's a message the computer tagged as a terrorist threat."

Matthews read the message. "Huh. That is weird. Hit shift F5 and it should tell us why it was tagged."

Griffin hit the keys. The words "Fat Man" and "Little Boy" were highlighted.

"What?" Agent James said. "Why would a fat man and a little boy ring up?"

Matthews remembered what Dr. Gebo had said. "Those were code names for the Manhattan Project. Try Control-R for research."

Griffin did so, and a definition popped up.

FAT-MAN: Name of atomic weapon dropped on Nagasaki, Japan. August 9, 1945.
REFERENCE: Weapons of mass destruction.
TYPE: Atomic, Plutonium implosion ignition.
YIELD: 21 kilotons.
STATUS: Obsolete.

"I believe Little Boy was the name of the other one," Matthews said.

Griffin highlighted it and hit the research keys again. "You're right."

LITTLE BOY: Name of first Atomic weapon dropped on
  Hiroshima, Japan, August 6, 1945.
REFERENCE: Weapons of mass destruction.
TYPE: Atomic, Uranium gun ignition.
YIELD: 15.5 kilotons.
STATUS: Obsolete.

"Both names in the same sentence?" James said. "What are the chances of that?"

"You better run it," Matthews said.

"Won't hurt anything." Agent Griffin pressed Control-A and the computer began to scrutinize the message.

ANALYZING COMPLETE MESSAGE: "Must Own New
  Skis To Enter Race."
WARNING: Possible Anagram: **M**ust **O**wn **N**ew **S**kis **T**o
  Enter **R**ace
REFERENCE: **MONSTER**: Weapon of mass destruction.
Classified Prototype: Project Spectrum 1990-1993.
TYPE: Thermonuclear, positron ignition
YIELD: Estimate, 58 megatons.
STATUS: Discontinued. Deactivated by Congress 1993.
ANALYSIS RESULTS: Threat Viable

*** **WARNING** ***
RECOMMEND INITIATING PRESIDENTIAL
EVACUATION PROCEDURE

"Oh *shit!*" Agent James said. "Is there some way we can verify this?"

"We just did," Griffin replied.

Matthews couldn't believe her eyes. *"Great God!* This is it." She grabbed the phone and punched in the number for Robert Lynch.

•   •   •

Sanders eased around the corner, his Glock pointed at Amil's head. The terrorist was on all fours facing away from him. He had opened one of the panels of the air-conditioning unit and in his hand was a pair of wire cutters.

"Having some trouble, Amil?" Sanders said.

Amil turned and squinted at Sanders. "We meet again, Raptor. But instead of deceiving our people into destroying ourselves, we've destroyed you."

"Not yet. Nice work on the eyes. I bet Lucy told you to just cut a couple of wires, right?"

Amil got to his feet, the wire snips still in his hands.

"She played you, Amil. Just like she played the rest of us. She has a bunch of cameras in that apartment over there, focused on this roof. She's got you red handed on video. Now she has me as well: the hero blowing your ass away. I already called the FBI and the DC police. You'll hear them running up the stairs any moment. Then you die."

"By then, it won't matter," Amil said. He glanced down at the red LED on the device. "Less than two minutes remain."

• • •

The computer terminal continued to blink PROCESSING as the computer analyzed the message.

"What now?" Agent James said.

"I guess we wait for it to finish," Griffin said.

Matthews was on her phone waiting to be patched through. She had no time to explain. "Mr. Lynch, this is Marti Matthews. You've got to get the President aboard Air Force One and away from the city *immediately*. Lucy is *here!* This is the big one, the MONSTER that Crosby described."

"We are already on it, Marti," Lynch said from his car. "The Secret Service has Amil cornered on a rooftop at Florida and Decatur Place. The President is aboard Air Force One and waiting for verification to issue the evacuation order. What have you got?"

"A coded message just came in over the hotline. Hold just a second." She read the screen.

WARNING: Possible Coded Message: "Please call: N385-4477 W770-2509."
No Phone Record in Database.

Possible GPS Coordinates: N38° 54.477′ W77° 02.509′.
LOCATION: 2185 Decatur Place, NW, Washington, DC.

"We just got his verification," she said. "The bomb is at 2185 Decatur Place. Hold on, there's more."

WARNING: Possible Coded Message: exhibition at **8:15** on **Thursday**
Possible Day and Time. Thursday 08:15:00 a.m.
EVALUATING THREAT: **THREAT LEVEL RED**
*** WARNING: ATTACK EMINENT ***
*** 08:15:00 a.m. TODAY! TODAY! TODAY! ***

"*Good Lord!*" Matthews looked up at the clock. "Mr. Lynch, it says the bomb will go off at 8:15 this morning. It's 8:13 right now."
"Oh no," was all Lynch said.
"Tell me this is only a drill," Agent James murmured.
"You tell me," Griffin said.
"I guess we'll find out soon enough," Matthews said, putting down her phone.

TIME REMAINING: **00:01:51**
IMPORTANT MESSAGE FROM OFFICE OF
HOMELAND SECURITY:
PRESIDENTIAL AUTHORIZATION: **CONFIRMED**
*** STARTING EMERGENCY EVACUATION
SEQUENCE***

Every siren in the entire city began going off, and all the television screens in the control room immediately displayed the blue emergency broadcast message.

• • •

The sound of the sirens made Sanders look up for only a second, but that was enough for Amil to leap at him. Sanders fired, but the bullet only nipped Amil's right ear. Amil jabbed the wire cutters into Sanders' rib cage. Sanders was knocked over backward, his Glock slipping from his hands and landing just out of his reach. Amil, on top now, had all the momentum and grabbed the pistol first. He placed the barrel against Sanders skull and closed his eyes.

• • •

"Freeze, *FBI!*" Crosby shouted, training his Glock on the suspect's head. Amil was laying flat on top of the agent. "Put your hands on the back of your head! *Now!*"

Rankin emerged around the other side of the cooling unit, his pistol aimed at Amil's head. "I have him."

Still clutching Sanders, the Iranian looked up at Crosby. He looked completely different, with his shaven head and green eyes. It was hard to believe it was Amil. "Drop your *weapon!*" Crosby yelled.

"No," Amil didn't move. His voice was barely audible over the blaring sirens.

"Do it now," Crosby yelled.

"Allah be praised," Amil moved the gun lightning fast from Sanders' head and pulled the trigger, the shot entering the air-conditioning unit directly above the LED.

Crosby and Rankin fired simultaneously, the bullets ripping apart Amil's skull. His body slumped before it rolled off of Sanders. Crosby kept his weapon trained on Sanders.

"Agent Sanders, are you clear?" Rankin yelled.

"Yes, I'm clear."

Rankin kicked the gun away from Amil and checked his lifeless body.

"Where is the bomb?" Crosby said.

Sanders sat forward, holding a bloody hand to his side. "There is no bomb. It's a ruse, designed to lure us here."

"How do you know?"

Sanders nodded towards the open panel. "Times up. There's a bullet hole in the bomb."

Crosby looked inside the open panel at the LED numerals, all reading zeros.

"Crosby, you can put your weapon down now," Rankin said. "Amil is dead."

Rankin was right. He had nothing on Sanders. Only his gut feeling that the man behind all of this was still in his sights. Crosby holstered the Glock just as the police reached the roof.

"Everybody *freeze*," the SWAT team captain yelled.

The agents all raised their hands while the police checked identifications and taped off the crime scene. In the following minutes, Lynch and the FBI arrived. They congratulated Crosby and

Rankin as Sanders was attended by paramedics. "What happened to the bomb?" Lynch asked.

"According to Sanders it wasn't real," Rankin said. "Lucy lured Amil into her trap so she could lay the blame on him."

"Where is she?"

"We don't know," Crosby said. "But she lives around here somewhere. The mortician said she walked north from DuPont Circle after their date last night."

"With all this, she had time to go on a date with a mortician?"

The siren began the long process of winding down and with them, so did Crosby's spirits. Lucy was probably long gone. Amil was dead, and Sanders would be hailed as a hero for locating him.

As they turned to leave the roof, Crosby heard one of the officers make a comment to the other.

"What's that smell?"

•   •   •

"*Fake!*" President Lawrence Beasley yelled to his security advisor. He was aboard Air Force One, flying to a secret location. "You're saying we threw nearly three million people into a panic because of a dud?"

"It wasn't even that, sir," his security advisor continued. "It was an air-conditioning unit."

"A what? Cancel the evacuation and take us back."

"The alert was creditable, sir. The terrorist Amil Yaspar was killed by a member of the Secret Service while attempting to set off the device. There just wasn't anything to set off."

"Turn this damn plane around and get me Christian Luther at Homeland Security. I want the name of who's responsible for this."

•   •   •

The bomb disposal team surrounded the air-conditioning unit, but found no evidence of either a detonator or a warhead. The only functional part of the Monster bomb appeared to be a cooling system and a simple countdown clock with an LED display. Great care was being taken to preserve any physical evidence such as fibers and fingerprints.

Dr. Marti Matthews stood aside awaiting her chance to actually look inside the device. Once the Geiger counter had been passed around it several times, she was allowed forward to witness the opening of the warhead compartment. The bullet hole had already destroyed any containment or cloud of vapor that might have been within. The last of the bolts were cut and the cone-shaped cover removed.

The last thing she expected was what they found. A human body, moldy and decayed, lay within, looking every bit the part of the old TV character, Herman Munster.

CHAPTER 23

A HOUSE ON THE BEACH

Katie Froscher stepped off the plane in Bermuda with a duplicate set of the identification papers she had used in Grand Cayman. With them she could access the account in Bermuda Bank and Trust and remove just enough to make the down payment on her new home. The rest she would get later.

She checked into the hotel as Ann Kagle, the name on her fake passport. She was still undecided if she could trust Gerald, but her own lies seemed to far exceed the ones he had told. Telling him the truth was never an option. The message he had left on her voice mail said he would arrive sometime that afternoon. She couldn't wait.

It was a beautiful day and warm enough to change into her swimsuit. She could spend the afternoon lying by the pool, sipping margaritas and anticipating the prospects that a night of making up might bring. Maybe she would start by giving Gerald a 'driving lesson.'

• • •

The body lay in the forensics lab of the J. Edgar Hoover building. The first thing that became apparent to Dr. Matthews was that it had already been embalmed. The man was in his eighties when he died and couldn't have been in the ground for more that three or four years. No autopsy had been performed. *Probably died of cancer or a stroke,* she guessed. The body had remained dry and much of the mummified soft tissue remained intact. She was certain that the latent prints expert could pull usable prints from some of the fingers.

The clothing had decayed from age, the World War II uniform coat being the only piece completely intact. There was evidence that the suit had once had medals attached. All had been removed; a common practice before burial, as these would have been treasured keepsakes.

This wasn't going to be easy and the chance that a World War II veteran's prints would even be in the database was a long shot, but it was all she had.

She carefully opened the fingers of his right hand and was surprised when a shiny gold coin fell out of the palm. She picked it up with a hemostat and examined it under a magnifier. It was a twenty dollar gold piece dated 1932, but the surface was in pristine condition. There was no sign of leaching by bodily fluids from the decayed flesh, nor any other ridge prints. She had little doubt that the coin had been placed there deliberately, probably when the body had been moved into the air-conditioning unit.

• • •

"Why are you upset?" Rankin said. "It's over. Amil's dead. Trexler's dead and we practically have Lucy, Cheryl or whoever's entire life history. She's got to show up somewhere."

"I don't buy that story Agent Sanders gave us," Crosby said. "This girl spent half her life planning this. She wipes out an entire town to get back at one guy, pulls off the most incredible disappearing act I've ever seen after the second bomb, and now she plants a dud, with a body in it. What sense does that make?"

"Marti says the body was already embalmed. Maybe it's a long lost relative."

Crosby thought about what Lynch had said earlier. *How would Lucy have time to plan all this and still go out on a date with a mortician?* "The mortician. *That's it!*"

"What?"

"She needed him to dig up a body. I am so *stupid*. What was the mortician's name?"

"Clay Simpson? What are you thinking?"

"Don't you see? She switched them. She's buried the bomb in the dead guy's casket."

Crosby patted his pockets, finally finding Clay's card and his cell phone in his coat pocket. There was a text message from Gerald McMullen.

Sorry buddy, he thought, ignoring the message and dialed Clay Simpson. *It will have to wait.*

• • •

The FBI Biometrics technician placed the fingerprint card in the scanner. The drum started spinning and almost immediately hundreds of fingerprints flashed onto the computer screen. The Automated Fingerprint Identification System would examine each ridge and layer and compare them to the existing fingerprint data.

"What's our chances of finding him?" Matthews said.

"About one in two hundred thirty million," the tech said.

"So there's two hundred thirty million records?"

"This could take a while."

• • •

"Clay Simpson, please," Crosby said. "Yes, I know he's at a funeral, but could you possibly get a message to him? No, it's not of a personal nature. This is Devrin Crosby with the FBI. Please ask him to call this number the moment he returns? Thank you."

"Struck out?" Rankin asked.

"He's at a damn funeral. They won't disturb him and they don't have a clue when he'll be back. *Think, Crosby.* "Where would she bury it?"

"It looked like he was in an old uniform to me."

Military uniform. David Anthony's father. It came to him. "This guy had something to do with the atomic bomb. I guarantee it."

"Some type of war hero?" Rankin said. "They bury those in—"

"*Arlington!* Of course. But where? The place is huge."

"She's a terrorist, Devrin. What place did they fail to completely destroy on 9-11?"

"*Good God!* Arlington is directly across the street from the Pentagon."

"I'll get the car," Rankin said. "You call Marti."

• • •

Kelly Rankin didn't make it to the car. Instead Agent Michael James stopped him as he entered the garage. James produced a Homeland Security ID. "Secretary Luther wants to have a word with you."

"What's an FBI agent doing with a Homeland Security ID?"

"Keeping tabs on you," James said. "Come on."

"Not now. We've located the bomb."

"That's precisely why Secretary Luther wants to speak with you." James took Kelly's arm. "Get in the *car.*"

*   *   *

"Devrin," Matthews said. "Did you post something on the hotline about a coin you found in Denver?"

"Yes. Michelle Anthony said she found it on her couch. I didn't know if it was important."

"We found the same type of coin in the palm of the dead guy. It's a 1932 Saint Gauden's twenty dollar gold piece. Looks like it was just put there."

"Marti, that guy had to be aboard one of the atomic bombing missions. I believe she buried the real bomb at Arlington in this guy's casket."

"Then why hasn't it gone off?"

Crosby thought about the Air-Conditioner and the LED counter. "Lucy left the timer on the AC unit. Dr. Gebo said the problem was keeping it from going off. I need you to locate Dr. Gebo and find out how we can disarm it. Also, alert Arlington that we're going to need the equipment to exhume a casket, or a vault. Don't tell them it's a bomb. Make something up."

"Gee thanks, Devrin. Any suggestions? I got news for you, they're not going to let anyone dig up a grave in Arlington without a permit and I can't think of a better emergency than a *bomb!*"

"You're right."

"We're running the print, but there's four terabytes of data it has to go through to locate the right one. It's going to take forever."

"Is there a way of narrowing it down to just World War II vets who were recently buried or exhumed at Arlington?"

"I'll check the Arlington burial records," Matthews said. "That cuts the list by about two hundred twenty-nine million."

"Great. Have you heard from Kelly? He was supposed to meet me here ten minutes ago."

"No. That's not like him."

"Did he bail out on us?"

She didn't reply.

"If he's not here in five minutes I'm going without him."

"We're not in Colorado anymore, Devrin. You go alone and you're putting your job on the line."

"It won't matter Marti, if we're dead."

*   *   *

Rankin entered the cabinet office of the Secretary of Homeland Security and was told to have a seat until Secretary Luther arrived. On the back wall was a painting of the original Homeland Security Secretary appointed by President Bush after the attacks on 9-11. Rankin had never met Christian Luther, but knew that he had once been a powerful senator before being appointed to this position.

Rankin stood when Luther entered the room. He was a tall man, dressed in a tailored suit. Secretary Luther extended his hand. "Mr. Rankin," he said. "Congratulations. That was a fine piece of detective work that led to the elimination of Amil Yaspar."

"It wasn't just me, sir," Rankin explained. "Agent Crosby and Agent Sanders deserve most of the credit."

"I agree," Luther said. "From what I understand Agent Sanders had already found Amil. Frankly, we're not so sure about Agent Crosby. That's the main reason why I've asked you to come in. The President is under the opinion that Agent Crosby has become a loose cannon, so to speak. I believe that is backed up by his record. He'll most likely go down as a result of the false alarm this morning. Have a seat and we'll discuss ways we can get you into a lifeboat before it's too late."

•   •   •

Robert Lynch was back in his office when one of the agents stuck his head in the door. "Sir, the phone company has tracked the Hilliard Place surveillance lines to an apartment in DuPont Circle. The apartment was rented under Vice President Trexler's name and the red BMW you found parked on the street is registered to a Vanessa Harrison."

"Who's she?" Lynch asked.

"The description matches our suspect Lucy. We have a SWAT team ready to break into the apartment. I thought you might want to join us."

•   •   •

Gerald McMullen tried his cell again. All of the lines were jammed; probably due to panic calls after the alarms he had heard filtering through the skin of the aircraft. He had called Devrin countless times and sent him fifteen text messages. Now he couldn't even get a dial tone.

They had sat on the tarmac for over an hour after the all-clear signal. Surely the airspace around Washington had been closed, and he was expecting the jet to return to the terminal when he realized they were accelerating down a runway. The jet's engines now seemed to be winding down as it began to level off at its cruising altitude. He needed to find a window, but the only one seemed to be a tiny porthole in the rear door just opposite from where he was hiding. Crossing the aisle might expose him to one of the men he had seen earlier. All four had been dressed in black and each was carrying an Uzi submachine gun.

• • •

The scene that greeted the SWAT team inside Lucy's apartment was right out of a horror movie. The bloody chair and pieces of flesh, the video equipment and recorders were all there. The SWAT team checked each room and with each call of "clear" it became evident that there was no girl.

Robert Lynch followed the team inside. "Don't touch or step in anything," he announced.

• • •

It was taking Crosby forever to get across town due to all the cars pouring back into the city after the all clear. The cellular lines were jammed as well. Crosby had repeatedly dialed Lynch's number with no success. Trying again, he got through. "Sir, you've got to get the President to order another evacuation. The bomb is real! I know where it is."

"There is no way he's going to do it, Crosby. We cried wolf once and he isn't biting."

"Sir, that's exactly what Lucy planned. She put the real bomb in a grave at Arlington, across the street from the Pentagon! Her motive is some type of revenge for what we did at Hiroshima."

"That seems to jive with what we just found here," Lynch said. "I'm with the CSI team at her apartment in DuPont Circle. Looks like Spectrum's goons got to her first. We don't have a body, but someone carved her up and hauled her off in a wheeled cart."

Crosby remembered the burly garbage man he had seen that morning. "Could it have been a trash dumpster?"

"Probably. There's a file here on Cheryl. She was a military brat, spent some time in Saudi Arabia and even got involved in the PLF as Vanessa Harrison, another alias. This apartment is less than two blocks from the building where you shot Amil. She had the other building bugged, and the apartment is loaded down with video recorders and transmitters. She put an ad in the *Times* and was broadcasting the bombing in order to get third world terrorists to bid on the devices."

"Just like Spectrum."

"Right. Maybe she was after the money as well. We believe the messages that went out from Trexler's computer were her doing. Looks as if she wanted to lure Trexler and Amil to the spot and catch them red handed."

"Maybe she just wanted them arrested." Crosby said. "That way they couldn't possibly escape."

"You may have something there. We found an old diary of sorts in her apartment. It's called *Dawn's Last Gleaming* and there was a twenty dollar gold coin taped to the inside cover. Her grandmother was a Japanese-American child who was stuck in Japan during the war. She lived in Hiroshima."

"So it's not just Spectrum she was after," Crosby said. "She's taking out the whole government."

"I think you're right about the bomb, Crosby. Find it! I'll see what I can do with the President."

•   •   •

"Devrin, our corpse was Colonel Charles Froscher, Sr." Matthews said. "His son was Chuck Froscher—the one that worked for Dr. Gebo in Oak Ridge."

"Wait a minute," Crosby said. "This was his father?"

"Yes! Charles Froscher was a crewmember aboard *Bockscar*, the B-29 that dropped the bomb on Nagasaki. You were right. Lucy had a much bigger agenda. The body was moved to Arlington *yesterday*. His daughter signed the transfer."

"His daughter? Does she have any ties to Lucy?"

"Not that I'm aware of," Matthews said.

"Have you heard from Dr. Gebo?"

"I haven't been able to reach him. I've already contacted the burial crew at Arlington and Lynch is trying to get permission to exhume the grave. They'll meet you at the south gate. Where are you?"

"I'm stuck in traffic on the bridge. Even if the President orders another evacuation, there's no way these people can get out of town."

"Maybe that was her plan," she said.

•   •   •

The grave was on a knoll overlooking the Pentagon. Crosby followed the Arlington police car past the mast of the battleship *Maine*, a ship that had already been through one explosion. At the grave, a backhoe had moved into position, ready to dig.

"Sign this." The Arlington administrator said, handing Crosby a release form.

Crosby scribbled his signature. "All right, dig!"

He was surprised at how shallow the grave was. The top of the vault was uncovered a little less than two feet down, its silver paint shining.

"You want us to remove the lid?" a crewman asked.

What to do? Crosby thought. Removing the lid might expose the liquid helium to the atmosphere, causing it to evaporate. But, if it was the wrong grave, they might still have time to locate the right one.

His cell phone rang. It was Gerald's number.

"Gerald, sorry I can't talk right now. We're abou—"

"Devrin, listen to *me* damn it!" Gerald yelled, "Lucy Harris put the bomb in a casket!"

"I know I'm at Arlington right now. We're about to open the vault. But—"

"It's not in the vault, Devrin. It's *here!*"

"Where?"

"I'm aboard a hijacked air cargo jet. We've been in the air about an hour, but we're still over land and seem to be heading northeast. I keep losing signal so read the details in my text messages."

"Oh *shit!*" Crosby realized his mistake. "How do you know it's in the casket?"

"I'm looking at it. The casket is completely covered with frost."

Dr. Gebo said liquid helium was -450°F. "Who are the hijackers?"

"I don't know. There are four with Uzi's. I watched one of them slit the throat of a pilot and say something in Spanish. They don't know I'm aboard."

The gravedigger walked towards Crosby. "You want the lid off or not?"

"Just make sure it's empty, and cover it back up," Crosby said.

"Cover it up? You sure?"

"On second thought, just leave it alone," Crosby said. "Gerald, I need to put you on hold for a minute so I can get some fighter jets up there to help you."

"I don't believe there's any helping me, Devrin. We both know this is a one way trip."

"Hang in there buddy." Then the line went dead.

• • •

"Devrin, you've got to get as far away from there as fast you can." Matthews said, her words racing. "Right *now!* Dr. Gebo said the Monster design had an estimated yield of sixty megatons. That's a blast crater over five miles across."

"It's not here Marti. The bomb is aboard a hijacked cargo jet that left Washington about an hour ago heading northeast. I need you to scramble fighter jets immediately."

"You're sure?"

"I'm in touch with someone aboard. Here is his number. Try to get a fix on his signal. "

"I'm doing it now," Marti said. "Anything else?"

"Tell the President to cancel the evacuation."

"He's already pissed. Lynch just got him to agree to it again. I thought I was about to lose you, Devrin."

"Me too. In case you haven't guessed, I love you, Marti."

• • •

Down the hill, just outside the Arlington perimeter fence, a NBC-6 news van had parked; its camera crew on the roof of the van filming the exhumation. Apparently the news was out.

Crosby kept trying to call Gerald back, but the lines were jammed. Going through Gerald's fifteen text messages, he began forwarding each one to Marti so she could piece together what his friend knew and how he ended up onboard a hijacked cargo jet. When it rang, Crosby immediately answered, "*Gerald.*"

"Hey Crosby," Rankin said.

"Where the hell have you been?"

"I was getting my ass chewed by my boss. Boy, did you ever piss him off. The President thinks you're to blame for throwing three million people into the streets."

"I'm the one trying to save them."

"That's what I told Christian Luther, right before U.S. Marshals slapped the handcuffs on him. You should have seen the look on his face."

"Luther was arrested?"

"Turns out he was in charge of that Spectrum operation you uncovered. We found the source of Spectrum's leaks in a sub-basement of the Social Security building. Luther's code name was Counselor. He ordered the assassination of William Barnett, and Trexler carried it out."

"Anything on Agent Sanders?"

"Not yet."

"Spectrum was Luther's ultimate counter terrorist device," Crosby said. "Until President Barnett decided to announce it to the world."

"Once they had Beasley in the White House," Rankin added, "Luther was a shoo-in for the nomination to Homeland Security. I'll explain when we get there in about three minutes."

"No way. The streets are gridlocked." Crosby began to hear the flop, flop, flop of helicopter blades.

·   ·   ·

The black HH-60 J-Hawk helicopter with SWAT stenciled on its side, sat down about fifty yards from the gravesite, whipping Crosby's coat up around his head. Kelly Rankin jumped out and pulled a bulky bag from a rear compartment and threw it to Crosby.

"It's a parachute," Rankin yelled. "Climb in."

Crosby climbed aboard and Rankin handed him a headset so they could hear each other over the sound of the rotors. "Why me?" he said into mouthpiece.

"It's your guy on the hijacked aircraft."

The crew slammed the door shut behind Crosby and the J-Hawk lifted off.

"Can this thing catch up to them?"

"Hell no. But it will get us in range of the AWACS communications aircraft. "What's your friend's name?"

"Gerald McMullen."

"Give me his cell number and we'll have AWACS call him when we're in range."

Crosby gave him his phone. He was still clutching the parachute in his lap, but none of the other crewmembers had one. "What's this for?"

"I thought I might need it to get you aboard."

Crosby sat it on the floor. "I'm fine."

"Hey, Crosby, you know why blind people don't like to skydive?" Rankin said.

"No."

"Scares the hell out of their seeing eye dogs."

The rest of the crew burst out in laughter.

"Only you could tell a joke at a time like this, Kelly."

"It dissipates the stress Crosby. The Feds never seemed to get that."

"So what have you got?"

"We've identified the hijacked flight as an Atlantic Air Cargo jet en route to London, England."

"London?"

"It's the Argentineans. Everyone assumed their dictator, Fernando Duarte, would build one, not buy it. His father was killed during the Falklands war with Great Britain."

Crosby remembered how the Argentine dictator had vowed to acquire nuclear weapons. "How do you know?"

"We broke into Lucy's bid site," Rankin said. "Someone named Carlos placed a bid from Mar del Plata, Argentina Monday night. They closed the deal with a one hundred twenty-five million dollar wire transfer."

"He was probably the guy on the *Island Breeze*. Don't they realize it's already supposed to have gone off?"

"I guess not. It's over Newfoundland now. As soon as it's over the ocean the President has authorized our fighter jets to intercept."

"Does the President know the fighter pilots will be committing suicide by shooting it down?"

"Why?"

"The last bomb was ten megatons and it blew away a helicopter *sixteen* miles from the hypocenter. Marti says this one could be sixty megatons."

"I'll call Lynch," Rankin said.

•   •   •

In Bermuda the afternoon sun had grown hot so Katie Froscher decided to head inside the hotel or take a dip in the whirlpool. Gerald would probably call at any minute. She pulled on a shirt over her swimsuit and went inside the lounge to order a cup of coffee. She had just taken the first sip when she noticed the TV set above the bar. The video showed a black SWAT helicopter hovering over a green lawn with white marble gravestones.

That's Arlington. Her alarms rising. "Could you turn that up, please?"

The bartender complied, and the newscaster's voice-over became audible. "Authorities now believe that a terrorist bomb, originally thought to be buried across the street from the Pentagon in Arlington National Cemetery, is actually aboard an air cargo jet, its destination unknown. Details are sketchy but sources indicate the flight may have originated at Washington's Dulles Airport and may have been hijacked. The President is reportedly conferring . . ."

Katie put her hand over her open mouth. *Lucy! What the hell have you done with my father?*

• • •

"The President just gave the order to have the fighters stand down," Rankin said. "He's meeting with his military advisors now on a course of action."

The pilot's voice came over the headset. "Mr. Crosby, the AWACS aircraft has a Mr. McMullen on the line for you."

"Gerald?" Crosby said into his headset.

"Hey Devrin. Where are we?"

"You just crossed over Newfoundland. How the hell did you end up on that plane?"

"I didn't mean too," McMullen said. "Most of it's in my text messages. Lucy Harris was in the adjoining seat on the flight from Miami. Yesterday, I was at Dulles to pick up a friend and saw her again, only this time she was disguised. It seemed odd, so I followed her over to the Charter Freight Hanger. Her car was there again last night, so when I saw her FBI photos in the newspaper, I went to check it out. That's when I spotted this frozen casket being loaded onboard a cargo jet. I just went aboard to get a closer look, but they closed the ramp behind me. That's when the men in black appeared from a shipping crate. I've been hiding since."

"Is one of the pilots still at the helm?"

"I don't know, but I'm guessing we're at about twenty-thousand feet and the ride has been pretty smooth, so I assume he is."

"We're trying to contact him," Crosby said. "Maybe he can dump the fuel without them knowing."

"I doubt it. Are they going to crash us into a major city?"

Crosby waited a beat. "We think it's London, but that's hours from now Gerald."

"That's what I figured. I've managed to get the casket's lid unlocked. I just need to pry it open."

"Gerald just wait. We haven't even tried to talk them down yet."

"They killed a pilot, Devrin. They're not negotiating."

"Hey buddy, you said you were going to tell me about someone you met; someone special," Crosby was trying to keep him on the line. "Was it Lucy?"

"No, not her. They met aboard the ship, but she's not involved in this. She's not like that."

"Who was she, Gerald? We need to be sure."

"You'll figure it out, Devrin. You're the smartest guy I've ever met."

•   •   •

Katie stared at the television completely numbed by what she was witnessing. A map displayed the location of the hijacked jet crossing from the coast of Newfoundland over the open ocean.

"To recap, a terrorist weapon, believed to be similar to the ones used in Colorado and the Florida Keys, is apparently aboard a hijacked cargo jet heading east across the North Atlantic," the reporter said. "We have confirmed that the FBI has been in contact with someone on board who has given them a description of the hijackers."

"Please, God, don't let it be Gerald," Katie kept whispering.

"This just in. The British Prime Minister has just ordered an evacuation of London."

Katie felt rather than heard her phone ring. The screen displayed Gerald McMullen's cell number.

Thank God. He's here.

•   •   •

"Katie." Gerald's voice was barely audible above the static.

"Gerald, where are you?"

"I'm sorry I didn't make it to Bermuda. I saw your friend's picture and you know me, curiosity killed the reporter and his cat."

"Oh God, Gerald. Please don't do this."

The signal faded then came back. "I don't have much time, Katie. Did you know what Lucille was doing?"

"I thought I did. I'm so sorry. This was never supposed to happen. They murdered my brother and they would have killed millions if we hadn't tried to stop them. Please Gerald, I can't live knowing that I did this to you." The line turned to static again.

"Katie, listen. I'm losing signal. Just do me one favor?"

"Anything."

"Buy that house on the beach, sweetheart. Live there, and when you walk on those warm sands at night, remember that some things *are* worth living for. If you will just do that, I will see you again. It's just a matter of faith. I love you and I'll carry you in my heart always."

"*Gerald!* Please don't go." Katie screamed, but the line was dead.

•   •   •

Gerald redialed the AWACS aircraft and again was put through to Crosby. "Okay Devrin, you need to have your aircraft pull back to a safe distance. I'm going to end this while I can. I've opened the casket lid and inside is a frozen cooler wired to a bank of batteries. How do I disarm it?"

The line was silent for long moment.

"Come on Devrin. One way or the other, the result is the same."

"You can't disarm it," Crosby said fighting back tears. "But you could take it with you."

Gerald spotted the red emergency escape handle beside the rear hatch and knew what to do. "That's a great idea, Devrin. You promise me to take care of yourself?"

"I . . . I will, buddy."

"Ned has my will," he said. "I've left you the condo."

Crosby couldn't respond.

"Take care, Devrin. Tell Katie I *really* loved her." Gerald spotted two of the hijackers emerge from the cockpit. He grabbed the frozen cooler, yanking it free of the ice. The hijackers started running towards him, their Uzi's bearing down. He placed his back against the hatch, grabbed the emergency release and pulled. In those fleeting moments, he saw blue skies; bodies flying past; then only peace.

•   •   •

In a flash the entire northern sky turned a blinding white. Katie Froscher felt all of her energy slip from her. Collapsing into the warm sand, she wailed in sorrow.

•   •   •

The AWACS pilot's voice came over the headset. "Agent Crosby, the President has requested a meeting with you and the FBI Director, the moment we land."

Crosby closed his eyes in resignation. He had misread Lucy's intentions; the President had accused him of starting a panic; and now his best friend was dead. He took out his badge and pistol and held them out to Kelly.

"What are you doing?" Rankin asked.

"I've had enough," he said. "They can have my resignation."

Rankin laughed. "You're a hero, Crosby. You just saved millions of lives. Don't you realize that?"

Tears streaked Crosby's cheek. "No, I didn't. Gerald was the hero."

Through the window, towards the distant northeast, a second sun appeared for a few seconds, became a brilliant white ball and faded to the last gleaming light of day.

CHAPTER 24

EPILOGUE

Ten days later

"Please state your name and occupation for the committee," the senator said into his microphone.

"Agent Harold R. Sanders. United States Secret Service, formally assigned to the Vice President and head of the White House security detail."

"Mr. Sanders, it's our understanding that you are willing to testify before this committee as to the role the late Vice President and the Director of Homeland Security played in arranging the assassination of President William Joseph Barnett?"

"That is correct, Senator."

"You have also agreed to testify that you witnessed the signing of a confession by Vice President Norman Trexler, where he admitted that he carried out the assassination?"

"That is correct."

"You further agree to testify that Senator Christian Luther, Director of Homeland Security, was a coconspirator in arranging to have a weapon, disguised as a camera, brought into the White House Briefing Room?"

"Yes."

"And in exchange for your testimony, you've been granted full and complete immunity from prosecution for your role in the Spectrum conspiracy?"

"That is the agreement, sir."

"I think we are ready to proceed," the senator said. "Swear the witness."

The bailiff stood and faced Sanders. "Place your right hand on the Bible. Do you swear to tell the truth, the whole truth, and nothing but the truth, so help you God?"

"I do," Sanders said.

• • •

Devrin Crosby was back in Washington after spending ten days in Charlotte, mourning the loss of his best friend and attending the memorial service with Ned McMullen and the rest of Gerald's family. At the closing, he had played Chopin's funeral march on the piano for his friend. Marti had spent the weekend with him, and together they decided that he was ready to return to Washington and complete their reports on the Spectrum investigation.

He was sitting in the conference room at the J. Edgar Hoover Building with Robert Lynch and Terrance Chisholm, a special prosecutor assigned to the Spectrum investigation. Chisholm was reading through an FBI file that was marked on the outside with the name, Kathryn Froscher.

"Mr. Crosby," Chisholm began, "do you have anything you want to add to this file before we make a determination to send it before a grand jury?"

"I have the testimony from the bartender at the Grand Cayman Hilton. It states that Ms. Froscher was seen sitting by the pool with our primary suspect."

"Ms. Cheryl N. Caldwell?"

"Also known as Lucy Harris. We also have the testimony of the luggage handler at the port of Miami, where they were seen together."

"Guilt by association," Chisholm said.

"Sir, may I remind you that her father's body was found in the fake device, and that she was in Washington the day prior to the explosion."

"Yes, but Mr. Clay Simpson, of Simpson's Mortuary, stated that the arrangements for picking up the body in Washington and their subsequent removal to Arlington, were arranged by Elyn Harrison, another alias of Cheryl Caldwell," Chisholm said. "He said Ms. Froscher was alone at the internment and immediately returned to airport."

"Crosby," Lynch said, "we know that Mr. Froscher's body was exhumed in North Carolina and arrived in Washington aboard a Piedmont Cargo flight. We also know that Miss Froscher did not leave North Carolina until the next morning. There is no way we can tie her to switching the caskets."

"We have Miss Caldwell's phone records which indicate a twenty minute phone call from Denton, North Carolina on the night the body was moved," Crosby said.

"Yes," Chisholm said flipping pages. "From a pay phone at Awfully Good Burgers in Denton. Not Miss Froscher's home. Look, it seems fairly obvious that these two women knew each other, but we simply can't convict Ms. Froscher based on anything we have in this file. I'm sorry."

"Do you believe this is the woman that Mr. McMullen, referred to?" Lynch said.

"Yes, sir. I think he had finally found the love of his life."

"If that's true, eventually she may come forward on her own."

Chisholm closed the file. "Thank you for coming in, Agent Crosby." He stood and shook Crosby's hand.

•   •   •

Dr. Matthews was standing outside Robert Lynch's office when he returned. In her hand was an envelope containing a file folder found in the basement office of John Young, the man called Stalker according to Spectrum's personnel files. Marti had addressed the envelope herself and marked it: Director's Eyes Only.

Robert Lynch took the folder and moved to his desk. "Lock the door. Is this the file you mentioned?"

"Yes sir." She latched it and remained standing. "Latent Prints has fingerprinted the rest of the material, but not this one."

"Do you believe we could have solved the case without his help?"

"No sir. He kept us on track."

"Would he be willing to testify against Christian Luther?"

"Perhaps, but considering his age, I wouldn't want to put him through a public display. Besides, we now have Agent Sanders' testimony before the Senate sub-committee."

Lynch put his hand and shook hers. "I'll speak with the Director and do what I can. Thanks for bringing this to my attention. You did the right thing Marti."

"Thank you, sir." She paused at the door. "He was a good, decent man, sir."

Lynch nodded and locked the door behind her. He tore open the envelope, studied its contents, and fed each page of the file labeled *Scholar* through his paper shredder. As the last page entered the unit he watched as the name, Dr. Urban L. Gebo, disappeared into confetti.

In a few years Gebo would take his secrets to the grave and only Lynch and Marti would know that while honoring his oath, he still managed to save the world from the weapons he helped create.

• • •

Twenty minutes later, Crosby and Matthews were sitting in the Quantico break room. Marti was reading a thin little book with a worn cover. On the spine, in faded gold letters, was the title: *Beyond the Spectrum.*

"Fascinating," she said. "This is the book that Dr. Gebo mentioned."

"The one about Pearl Harbor and the sun bomb?" Crosby said.

"Yes. It's incredible. Morgan Robertson wrote this in *1914.* He must have been clairvoyant, because he also wrote a book about the *Titanic, fourteen* years before it sank. Get this; he named his ship *Titan!"*

"I've got to read that." Crosby said.

Kelly Rankin came through the door. "Miami police just found a dumpster along a swampy area of Highway One with four bullet holes in it. Inside was a pocketbook with several pieces of identification belonging to a Vanessa Harrison with the Washington apartment address."

"Where's the body?" Matthews asked.

"Missing," Rankin said. "But they found her wallet, duct tape and blood spattered inside the dumpster. They haven't run any tests, but I'll bet my ass it's from Lucy and that Sanders had something to do with it."

"Your ass isn't worth it," Matthews said. "Kelly, what was that about a leak in Lucy's apartment?"

"Yeah, they found a closet right next to the bathroom with several empty canisters of helium. That evening all the pipes in the wall were leaking. The plumber said they had been frozen."

"She must have had the bomb there," Crosby said, "but then how did it get to the airport?"

Rankin shrugged. "Who knows? Did you see Sanders on television? That SOB has agreed to testify before the Senate Committee in exchange for complete immunity."

"He's testifying right now." Matthews switched on the television.

• • •

The television cameras zoomed in on Senator Alicia McAllister from North Carolina speaking into her microphone. "Mr. Sanders. I just want to clarify the last part of your written statement. You stated that the aforementioned members of this Spectrum group revived the project in order to build an *unstable* weapon of mass destruction?"

"That is correct, Senator," Sanders said.

"They wanted to *sell* this weapon on the black market to a terrorist state?"

"Yes, Senator."

"What in Heaven's name were they thinking? Were they not concerned that it might be stolen or end up in someplace like Washington?"

"Yes, but this wasn't Spectrum's weapon. Project Spectrum was brilliant. It was designed to have a built-in tracking system, so we would always know where it was, and it was far too expensive for a terrorist organization to waste it on just *any* target. We piqued their curiosity with its non-radioactive technology and by doing so, it insured that they would take it to their absolute most secure research facility; the same facilities where they were developing nuclear and chemical weapons to use *against* us. With such a prize, their top scientists would immediately attempt to reverse engineer the device to discover its design secrets."

"You stated earlier that there was no way to disarm it?"

"There wasn't. But they wouldn't know that, would they? It was the perfect anti-terrorist weapon."

The committee members looked disgusted. Senator McAllister continued. "So the bombs that exploded in Dillon and the Gulf, were they made from this positron material stolen by your weapons designer Ryan Papineau?"

"Yes, Senator. We believe he sold those to the terrorist Amil Yaspar and his accomplice, the woman referred to as Lucy Harris in the documents before you."

"Where is Mr. Papineau now?"

"Based on the massive blood loss and DNA evidence found in Ms. Harris' apartment, we believe that Amil tortured and killed Mr. Papineau, and possibly Ms. Harris as well."

"I see," the Senator said. "Just one more question. Do you believe that Mr. Papineau built any more of these bombs?"

"Since the device that exploded in the cargo jet over the Atlantic was much smaller than anticipated, it appears that Mr. Papineau had exhausted his supply of the positron antimatter."

"So, you're certain there are no others?"

Sanders maintained his deadpan expression and closed his eyes for just a second, savoring the last moments of Ryan's interrogation. *Herman's monster were twins,* Ryan had said. *One for the Argentineans and one to avenge Lucy's grandmother.* It had been right there all along. In the closet of Lucy's apartment.

"Not to my knowledge, Senator," Sanders said with great satisfaction. "Not anymore."

•   •   •

"What a sick bastard," Matthews said. "He's *proud* of the damn things!"

"I still can't believe it," Crosby said. "The man is guilty as sin and still walks."

"There's no way that idiot Trexler pulled the trigger," Rankin said. "At least Sanders is out of the Secret Service. If they prove he's lying, he can still be prosecuted."

"He'll blame it all on Luther and Trexler," Crosby said. "They'll treat him like an Oliver North hero. Then he'll write a book and make millions, while Gerald's family is left with an empty grave and a commendation from the President."

"There's talk of a memorial," Matthews said.

"I'm not holding my breath."

"At least we know that Lucy's gone. Probably in the belly of some alligator," Rankin said.

"I don't buy that either," Crosby said. "That girl was a survivor."

"Anyone hungry?" Rankin said. "Let's eat out. My treat."

"*Right!* You still owe me," Crosby said.

"I'm good for it."

"Okay. I know this great little bar with hot wings and a Rubik's Cube," Crosby said. "Here is the bet. We each get five minutes, and whoever solves the cube first gets his tab paid for a month."

"Deal," Rankin said.

Crosby smiled and took Marti's hand. "Hey, Kelly," he said. "What do you call a boomerang that won't come back?"

Rankin looked at him, surprised.

"A stick!" Crosby said with a grin.

"Well, I'll be damned," Rankin chuckled. "He's back."

• • •

The building was called the Yongbyon Nuclear Research Facility, located at Nyŏngbyŏn in the North Pyongon Province of North Korea. Thirty feet under the site of the old Magnox reactor building, three scientists were using a crowbar to remove the lid of a wooden crate which had just arrived by truck that evening.

To their surprise, the box was filled with layer upon layer of foam insulation. What lay under the last layer looked nothing like the object that they had so eagerly anticipated, and certainly not worth the millions it had taken to acquire. It was only a car battery and a blue plastic cooler, completely covered in a white frost.

As one of the scientists inserted the crowbar into the crack beneath its lid, a phone on the wall rang. Their supervisor walked to the phone, picked up the receiver, listened for a moment then looked back at the others just as they pried open the lid.

He dropped the receiver and cried, "*Wait!*"

The receiver vaporized before reaching the molten mass that had been the metal floor.

• • •

On a farm in Denton, North Carolina, Ruth Froscher opened a plain white envelope with no return address and read the letter within:

Dear Mom,
I just wanted to let you know I'm okay. I have access to so much, but I've lost nearly everyone I cared about. Someday, maybe I'll get up the courage to come home and face the consequences for what I've done. I can't right now, but until that day, please know how much I love and miss you. I carry your smile with me always. It's all I have left.
    Love you Mom,
    Katie

Ruth Froscher, with tears in her eyes, closed the letter and turned over the envelope. The postmark was from Grand Cayman. The name of the town was Hell.

THE END

AUTHOR'S NOTE

Thank you for reading *The Spectrum Conspiracy* and I hope you enjoyed the story.

This book is a work of fiction. However, there are parts of this novel that are based on real events and real science. I am not a theoretical physicist, nor do I claim to have any more than a rudimental knowledge in the subject. My only training in this area is the result of research and reading.

In 1995, scientist at the CERN collider in Switzerland were successful in bringing into existence *nine* antihydrogen atoms and storing them in a Penning trap which uses magnetic repulsion to hold the anti-matter suspended. But that is a far cry from producing enough to use in the positron weaponry I described herein. Even as recent as April 2011, scientist were able to trap 309 antihydrogen atoms, some for as long as 17 minutes, and this was longer than anti-matter had *ever* been trapped before. While 309 atoms sounds like real progress, a million of them, lined up shoulder to shoulder, could still hide behind the width of a human hair.

In addition CERN recently announced that a new facility would begin large-scale production of antiprotons, and once fully operational, that facility may be capable of producing ten million antiprotons per minute. However even at 100% conversion of antiprotons into antihydrogen, it would still take 100 billion years to produce one gram of antihydrogen. Not the "thousands of years" I postulated in the novel.

Thank goodness, because theoretically the power contained in only one gram of antimatter *could be equivalent* to the energy stored in 23 Space Shuttle fuel tanks.

Finally, I have the greatest respect for law enforcement, and for the brave men and women who serve and defend our nation in the FBI, the CIA and the Offices of Homeland Security which includes the U.S. Secret Service and other branches. The antagonists characters I described within the story were a fictitious group of extremist, who under the cloak of patriotism, came up with this unique idea of an anti-terrorist weapon. Thankfully they do not exist. The only reason I portrayed them as members of these Government branches is because that was the only way the story seemed plausible. Still, I thought the idea was pretty cool.

—Craig Faris

ABOUT THE AUTHOR

Craig Faris is sixteen-time published author in short fiction, non-fiction and plays. He has won twenty-five literary awards at regional, national and international levels, eleven of which were first place. His short story, House of Ruth won fourth place in the 80th Annual Writers Digest competition, and won first place in the 2010 Carrie McCray Literary Award before going on to be a short-list finalist in the 2010 and 2012 William Faulkner Pirates Alley International Writing Competitions.

Craig lives in South Carolina with his wife, Deena, and their two children.

Visit Craig online at www.CraigFaris.com.

CPSIA information can be obtained at www.ICGtesting.com
Printed in the USA
LVOW120747210213

321091LV00001B/58/P